THE TAKEDOWN

THE TAKEDOWN

PATRICK QUINLAN

headline
review

First published in the USA in 2007 by St. Martin's Press

First published in Great Britain in 2007
by Headline Review
An imprint of HEADLINE PUBLISHING GROUP

1

Cataloguing in Publication Data is
available from the British Library

ISBN 978 0 7553 2827 7 (hardback)
ISBN 978 0 7553 3577 0 (trade paperback)

Typeset in Fournier MT by Palimpsest Book Production Limited,
Grangemouth, Stirlingshire
Printed and bound in Great Britain by Clays Ltd, St Ives plc

Headline's policy is to use papers that are natural, renewable and
recyclable products and made from wood grown in sustainable
forests. The logging and manufacturing processes are expected
to conform to the environmental regulations of the country of origin.

HEADLINE PUBLISHING GROUP
A division of Hachette Livre UK Ltd
338 Euston Road
London NW1 3BH

www.reviewbooks.co.uk
www.hodderheadline.com

For my mom.

Life is not a spectacle or a feast; it is a predicament.

— George Santayana

AVON CALLING

The van was still there.

Dick Miller glanced through the blinds again, looking for the pizza man. No pizza, but the white Time Warner Cable TV van was parked about fifty yards away, in front of a house across the road. It had been there for at least forty-five minutes, since Dick had started looking out the window. Something about that van didn't seem right. He would be glad when it was gone.

He let the blinds drop back into place.

He was out at Fat Sam's place in Stinson Beach. The house was a tiny saltbox shack that sat, beaten by the Pacific winds, high on a bluff overlooking the ocean. Sam had ripped out the back wall of the old house, and replaced it with a huge bay window. Next to the window was a sliding glass door to a small wooden deck Sam had just built. The house was so small that Dick could stand by the front door and look out the back window. You could not beat that view. As Dick watched, a white speedboat came into sight, cutting from left to right across his field of vision. If the view wasn't enough, you could leave the deck and walk a quarter of a mile down a sandy trail to the beach.

A full hour had passed since they ordered the pizza. Nothing. No delivery. Just that cable van. In the meantime, Dick returned to the living-room couch. He had been sitting on the couch since this morning, smoking grass, counting money and drinking beer. His mind floated somewhere above the task. His stomach growled. He hadn't eaten all day.

Business was good, and getting better. It seemed like it could go on forever. They had so much goddamn pot, they couldn't keep it at Dick's place in town anymore. They had rented an extra apartment under the name of Sam's grandfather, just to have a place to store the stuff. They had a voicemail drop where their dealers (Sam called them 'associates') could place their orders for the next day, and they had another voicemail drop where their special customers – their money people – could place orders. Two weeks into January, and it looked like it was going to be their biggest year yet.

Dick had so much money, just counting it made him tired. He finished the joint he was smoking, and lit up another from the small pile on the weathered coffee table. He smoked them back to back these days, high-quality shit. Success had gone to his head. He sucked this latest one deeply.

The more grass he smoked, the more he got to thinking about the strawberry-blonde girl Sam had with him. She was a bouncy little thing, looked like she was made of hard rubber or something. That girl made him nervous. She had come in from the beach wearing a bikini a while back, but now she paraded around the place, wearing nothing but a tiny pair of white panties and a T-shirt that showed her belly button. She kept floating in and out, laughing about some damn thing or another. She was deeply tanned, that girl. She moved around the living room, shaking to the constant beat of the jungle rhythm music Sam liked so much.

Dick couldn't take his eyes off her. His eyes had a mind of their own. They followed her around like two orphaned puppies. The thing about her was her face. She was so beautiful it could make a man cry.

'Hey, Sam,' Dick shouted. 'You think we could turn down this music for a while? I'm trying to do something here.'

He'd been trying to count the money for a long time. It was hopeless. Music shrieked from the speakers, the sexy girlfriend danced around, the pizza wouldn't come, there was a suspicious van parked outside, and twenty plastic baggies of grass sat in front of him on the coffee table. Pounds and pounds of grass were bundled into white Hefty kitchen bags and piled up like a small mountain in Sam's spare bedroom. Add to all of that the joints Dick had smoked, the beer he had drunk, and the spectacular view out the bay window. He just couldn't concentrate.

There might've been nine thousand dollars in his hand. There might've been twelve thousand. Stacks of money sat across from him on a chair, waiting patiently to be counted. They were rich. He didn't know how much money he had. He didn't care.

'Sam! Turn down that fucking music!'

Fat Sam came out of his bedroom, wearing a pair of tight red nylon shorts. He must have stuffed a sock or a washcloth in there. No way was Sam sporting that bulge. He stood about five foot eight inches, and weighed well over two hundred pounds. His Buddha stomach hung out over his waist. He was covered with sweat, and he was breathing hard. He lit up a joint almost as fat as his stubby fingers. He had a hairy chest and back, like a bear.

He stood in the doorway, smiling and playing invisible drums. 'I love this music,' he said. 'It's so primal.'

'Well, turn it down, will you? It feels like somebody's banging a goddamn sledgehammer against my skull.'

Sam smiled again. He was having a good time. He turned the stereo all the way down. Now the house was silent.

'Dick, what are you upset about?'

'I'm not upset. I'm hungry. I'm tired. I want to get everything done here, call it a day and go home.' He lowered his voice. 'Let me ask you something. That girl in there? She looks like she must be fifteen years old. I mean, what are we running here, a day-care center? I tell you what. You're gonna bring a Mann Act beef down on your head when she runs home to Idaho and tells her parents all about her forty-year-old boyfriend.'

Sam cut Dick off with a calm wave of his hand. 'Hey, Dick. What are you putting me in my grave for? I'm thirty-eight.'

'You know what I mean.'

'Yeah, I know. I know how you like to save everyone – stray cats, old ladies, derelicts on street corners. But I'm here to tell you that not everyone needs saving. Chili in there? She knows what she's doing. Anyway, she's an adult. She must be, because I met her in a bar.' Sam placed his right hand over where his big fat heart must be. 'I play it strictly legal around here, partner. You know that. And I'll tell you something else,' he added, flashing that aggravating, ear-to-ear smile. 'I think she likes you. I know she does. She told me herself.'

'Yeah?'

'Oh, yeah. She says you're cute. Thinks you look like an actor.'

Dick sat back on the fluffy couch. He stroked his chin with the money in one hand, and took another sip of his beer with the other. The joint burned on between his middle and third fingers. He was like a one-man band, all the things he could do with his hands at the same time. What Fat Sam was saying could be true. The girl had smiled at him a few times already. She could want him.

'I don't know, Sammy.'

'Why not? Just go ahead. She's in there, waiting for you. It's all in fun, anyway.' Sam took a mighty toke on the joint, then held his breath, letting all that good smoke seep into whatever was left of his brain.

Dick stopped. 'You know what? Nah. I mean, are we in business here? This is a business, right?'

Sam let the breath out and laughed, a short, rasping bark. 'You're too much, bro. Too fucking much.'

Dick laid the money on the table. He'd have to start over again, the next time he got straight enough to think. The way things were going, there was no telling when that would be. He got up to use the bathroom. There was a heaviness in his bladder that hadn't been there a minute before. Chili stood in the doorway to the bedroom now. Her nipples thrust from the ends of her firm young breasts, practically poking holes through the belly shirt. She had her hands behind her back and a shy grin on her face. She was a beauty, all right.

Dick had to figure out a way to get rid of her.

'Your eyes are so blue,' she said. 'Did anyone ever tell you that you look like a movie actor?'

'James Dean,' he said. 'But bigger. That's what they usually tell me.'

She frowned. 'James Dean? I don't know . . .'

'I think he was before your time.'

He went into the bathroom and shut the door.

At that moment, the doorbell rang. It was loud, and Dick could still hear its echo for several seconds afterward. The house had become awfully quiet since Sam turned the music down.

Chili squealed on the other side of the door. 'That must be the pizza. Sammy, can you get it? I'm not decent.'

'Yeah, babe,' Sam said. His voice moved away. 'Let me just grab a beer.'

Dick stood in front of the toilet and let out a long, steady line of urine. It was good to be alone in the bathroom with the house finally quiet. He noticed the tension in his neck and shoulders. There was tightness all down his back. He and Sam had been going nonstop, ten hours, twelve hours, every day. Working too hard. Maybe he needed some time away. Hawaii. Yeah, that was what the doctor ordered.

The doorbell rang again, more insistent this time, and it occurred to Dick what bothered him about the cable van. He had gone for a walk two days ago to work some kinks out of his legs, and to get some beer at the general store about a mile down the road. On the way back he had glanced in one of the windows of that house where the van was parked. Just a glance, no more than one or two seconds, but that was enough. The house was empty. Stripped to bare wood inside. There weren't even any curtains on the windows. Nobody was living there at all.

'Sam!' he said. 'Don't open that door.'

Dick stepped out of the bathroom, and Sam bolted past him, moving fast for a big man, his eyes wide, his mouth gaping like a fish on a hook.

'What is it?'

BOOOOM! The front door blasted off its hinges, sending huge wooden splinters flying just inches from Dick's face. The door came to rest on the carpet, and he blinked at the dusty haze that remained in the air.

'AVON CALLING!' someone shouted, and half a dozen cops burst into the room. They were big guys, with short hair and bulletproof vests. Their vests were black. They carried shotguns and baseball bats, and wore baseball caps on their heads.

Dick looked back at Sam, who had managed to wedge himself halfway through the bathroom window, then got stuck there, no chance of sliding his fat ass through that tiny opening. His legs hung down, his feet dangling off the floor.

Dick glanced past the cops, through the kitchen and out the back window, catching a last look at the green and brown hills sloping gently down to the Pacific Ocean. The water was a dark, sparkling blue. The whole peaceful scene might as well have been on another planet, or in a painting. That's how far out of reach it was. Fifteen minutes before, he could have walked out there and enjoyed the view as much as he liked. He could've even strolled down to the beach and gone for a swim. Three cops stood out on the back deck now, peering through the sliding glass door.

Dick turned his back on what might have been.

He stepped into the living room. He toyed briefly with the notion that he might be invisible to these cops. The pot in his brain told him it might be so. It seemed the only explanation as to why they hadn't grabbed him yet. Already, they had pulled Sam down from his perch, and slapped the cuffs on him. Already they had put some clothes on Chili, and were leading her out. Dick alone remained free, and nobody noticed.

A young cop leveled his shotgun.

Dick looked into the cop's beady eyes, squinting down over the enormous barrel of his weapon.

'Hands on your head,' the cop said. 'Or I blow it off.'

Dick laughed, and the sound seemed natural. He felt good. Business was over. Now that it was gone, he already didn't miss it. A new chapter was starting right in front of his eyes. He put his hands on his head. The cops swarmed him, and he made no attempt at resistance. They handcuffed him, and the cold steel of the cuffs bit into his wrists. They sat him down on the couch.

At some point, a young guy – pimply, skinny, maybe in his late teens – walked through the open front door. He carried a red imitation leather pizza warmer and a sixty-four-ounce bottle of Pepsi. He navigated his way through the giant cops. He looked around in wonder.

'Anybody order a pizza?' he said.

The cops looked at him, then looked at Dick.

Dick nodded. 'Here.'

'Whaddya got?' said an older cop, a guy with a graying flat-top haircut, like a Marine.

'One large pepperoni,' said the kid, poring over the order slip like it was a final exam. By the looks of him, he was none too bright. 'And one large with onion.'

'We'll take them.'

The head cop reached over onto the coffee table and picked up one of the hundred-dollar bills lying there. A couple of the other cops guffawed and clapped each other on the back. Fucking cops. *They knew* Dick was looking at a mandatory five years for possession with intent, and that the judge would have very little leeway in sentencing. *They knew* he was going to sit for the next two days in a county lockup with nothing to eat except lukewarm baloney on stale white bread, and nothing to drink except orange-colored sugar water. The cops were all the same. They'd steal the pizza from a condemned man.

'Looks like it's your lucky day,' the cop said to the kid. 'Keep the change.'

THREE YEARS LATER . . .

1
ANGELS IN THE SNOW

Dorothy Racine's life flashed in front of her eyes. So this is what it's like when the end comes, she thought. They show you pictures.

Images appeared and disappeared in her mind, sepia-toned with age, much like the old slide photographs that her family would project on the living-room wall when she was a child. Here I am when I was small. See how happy I was? Everybody said I was a happy child. Here I am at twelve, precociously long and leggy. The high-school boys were already watching me, you bet they were. Here I am when I was Queen of the Prom. Dig that Farrah Fawcett haircut. And the King? Let's just say he didn't measure up. Look, there I am as First Runner-Up in the Miss Ohio Pageant, 1982. There's Miss Ohio. Boy, I hated that fake bitch.

Dorothy was about to die.

She knew it just by looking in her rearview mirror. The heavy snow kept falling and the strange car was still there, some kind of big SUV. It kept back about twenty yards now, its headlights shining bright, its grillework like a malevolent smile. A moment ago, it had accelerated and smashed into her rear bumper, throwing her and her boyfriend, Dick Miller, around like straw dolls.

She glanced over at Dick now. Good old Dick. He called her Dot. Sure, everybody did. Dick sat slumped in the passenger seat. Dick could handle a tough situation, but there was something not right with Dick just now. He was passed out, his head lolled to and fro, and once in a while he would come awake and start raving at her. It was like he was very drunk, but Dot had seen him handle more alcohol than he had tonight. A lot more.

Dick wasn't drunk, Dot decided. He had been poisoned. Heck, she had been poisoned herself just a few months ago, right? Back when everything started going haywire? That's what the doctor told her, and she believed it. She knew who had done it too. She couldn't prove anything, but she knew.

She recalled how sick she had been after that episode. It had lasted for days – the headache, the nausea. Oh, yeah, and the amnesia. Even now, she couldn't remember what actually happened. Just the aftermath, and that was bad enough. From the looks of things, Dick was going to be hurting tomorrow. Being poisoned was no fun. Dot could vouch for that.

The drinks she had knocked back at the office party tonight had burned off. The light, pleasant pre-Christmas buzz was gone. A headache and a churning knot in her stomach were the only party favors left. God rest ye, merry gentlemen. Mortality will do that to you.

Who was back there? It wasn't a car she recognized, but that hardly mattered. The face of the killer didn't have to be one she knew. It could be anyone. They could have hired someone.

'What?' Dick said, his head rolling, his eyes half open. 'What?'

Dot checked the rearview again. Still there. The bastard had edged closer. Why didn't he make his move? The snow came down heavier now. There was no one on these darkened streets except her and that car behind her. She glanced at the pocketbook at her side. Her gun, the little snubnose .38 that Dick had given her, poked its snout out the top of the bag.

'That's nice, Dick,' she said. 'What makes you say that?'

'Unnnh,' Dick said.

Big Dick Miller – who refused to carry a cellphone because cellphones caused brain cancer. OK, not the brightest bulb in the package, but damn good-looking. A man's man – ex-convict with less than four months out of the slammer, pride of the jail-to-work program, delivered by that program into Dot's loving arms. Now reduced to babbling incoherence in the passenger seat. She glanced at him again. They must have slipped him a whale of a dose, because he was a mess.

The heater in this big car was working overtime, and Dot felt a trickle of sweat run down the back of her neck. It was Dick's car, a Pontiac or Oldsmobile or some other goddamn prehistoric beast of Detroit steel. The snow made the car slide all over the road. Dick had some kind of patriotic mental block about cars. He had to drive an old American car with rear-wheel drive, even though front-wheel drive or, God forbid, *all-wheel drive* was better in all types of weather.

What made matters worse than the car they were driving was the fact that they were headed in the wrong direction. They should have come to the bridge over to Brooklyn by now, ten minutes ago, maybe twenty minutes ago. This was Dot's city – *her city* – and she had no idea where she was going. And this bastard behind her meant she couldn't turn around.

Well, soon the deep snow would force her to stop altogether. Then they would see what was what. The thought made her heart skip a beat.

Dot Racine, forty-two years old and still beautiful, still sexy, still ripe and randy and ready for anything, was afraid. The chickens had come home to roost. They were roosting in that car back there, the one with the sinister purpose, the one she had always known would be there some night, the one that the Dick Millers of this world were supposed to keep at bay.

Dorothy Racine: Daddy's little girl. Head Cheerleader. Prom Queen. Beauty Queen. Trophy Wife. These were the titles from the first thirty years of her life. But there had always been something missing. When all the vivacious chatter died down, when all the fabulous guests went home, boredom awaited. Melancholy lurked just below the bright white, all-American smile she flashed at the world. Beneath the sparkling surface, there was only emptiness. She knew it. She was beautiful – she wasn't dumb. She was one chesty, leggy, drop-dead bombshell of a babe who knew some things. And what she knew was her life, and the lives of those around her, meant nothing.

Country-club chatter. Investments. Charity fundraisers. To hell with all that. She wanted action. She wanted excitement. She yearned for it. She positively burned for it. When her husband, Ray, died, she decided she was going to get it.

The next dozen years were the ones where she hit her stride. Merry Widow. Adventurer. Executive. Embezzler. She had been all these things and more. But that last was the major thing, wasn't it? Chief Embezzler in Charge at Feldman Real Estate. She and her young side-kick, Lydia, had stolen quite a lot of money. The thought of it – of all that money and what they had done to get it – sent a tingle down Dot's spine. She was president of the company and Lydia was the office manager – all business and propriety on the surface, all crime all the time when no one was watching.

Tonight was much too soon for it to end.

'Dick,' she said, 'can you still fight?'

His head slumped to his chest. He hadn't heard her.

'Dick!'

His head came up, a small, sexy curl of hair hanging down onto his forehead. His eyes were bloodshot. He looked at her, uncomprehending.

'Can you run? Can you even run?'

He looked away, out the window, at the snowflakes falling.

The knot tightened in her stomach. Dick was going to be no help at all. As much as that frightened her, it also liberated her. There was no strong man to step in here, to run interference for her. That had always been her strategy – to have the man do it – but when that failed, she did have one last thing to fall back on.

Herself.

'OK,' she said. 'I'm going to end this right now.'

They were on a long, gradual down slope. To the left, across the East River, the towers and canyons of Manhattan twinkled in the snow, so many lights it was incredible. Up ahead, giant shapes loomed. They were sculptures. Yes, she knew this place. There was a park here on the water with all these industrial sculptures – monstrosities made from scrap metal, airplane parts and steel girders salvaged from the wrecked old hotels of Atlantic City.

They wanted a showdown? They wanted high noon? They were going to get it, and this alien landscape was the perfect place for it. Her formidable resolve kicked in, a thing that seemed to have a life and a mind of its own, and she realized that she didn't feel too bad at all, thank you. As a wise man once said, 'Bring 'em on.'

The hill grew steeper near the bottom, and she lost control about two-thirds of the way down. The car slid, turning sideways into the unplowed snow, moving in slow motion. At the bottom was a parking lot. There were no cars here at all. Away in the snowy distance was an old building – it might have been a factory.

The other car came slowly down, tires easily gripping the snow. Sure, it was some kind of SUV, probably with all-wheel drive. The two cars faced each other, twenty yards apart, the SUV's higher head-lights shining in Dot's eyes.

Dot pulled the gun from her bag.

It was small, and fit snugly in her small hand.

'Come on, Dick. Let's go see who's here.'

Some awareness must have still been awake in him, because he opened his door and tried to clamber out. When his feet hit the ground, he slipped in the snow and fell. He lay next to the car, his hands on the door.

Dot climbed out, holding the gun low and out of sight.

Across the way, the driver's side door of the SUV opened. The strains of the stereo greeted the cold night air. A man climbed down and slammed the door. The music died. The man was slim, probably not very much taller than Dot. He wore a sheepskin jacket buttoned tight, black driving gloves, and a bright orange ski mask over his face. His eyes lurked back inside the mask, bright and sharp. It made him look like a jack-o'-lantern.

'Nestor?' Dot said. It was a reflex to say his name. Nestor Garcia was the classic ex-boyfriend-from-hell, the one they made down at the factory, knew they could never improve upon, and so broke the mold afterwards. He was the demon that old peasant women the world over told stories about to frighten young children. Dot remembered how dangerous it had felt to be with Nestor – she had never considered how dangerous it would feel to *not* be with him.

Men were supposed to serve their purpose, then go away. But Nestor didn't see it that way. If this man – the pumpkin man – wasn't Nestor, he ought to be.

In one gloved hand the pumpkin man held a gun, much larger than Dot's, a long silencer attached to the end. The effect of it was fear-some. This person, this Halloween nightmare, came to do business. The man's eyes regarded Dot as he trod through the snow toward where Dick was slumped next to the car. This was a very small man, Dot realized. Was Nestor this small? Could be yes, could be no. Dot's fevered mind couldn't focus long enough to decide. Still watching Dot, the man placed the muzzle of the gun, that big silencer, against Dick's head. Dick mumbled something to himself. A plume of breath came from the ski mask.

Under there somewhere, the pumpkin man frowned, or seemed to.

Dot brought her gun up, pointed right into the intruder's chest. Her arms extended across the hood, the gun held in that two-handed grip Dick had always said was best, the man only a few feet away from her muzzle. She wouldn't miss, not at this distance. She was ready. She was going to blow a hole in this asshole, then four more.

'I will fucking kill you,' Dot said, her voice loud and strong. 'If you shoot him, I swear to God I will kill you.'

The eyes watched.

Slowly, the gun came away from Dick's head.

'That's right, you bastard. You understand.'

But the gun kept coming. It came up, pointing at Dot across the hood, the hood wide across like a football field from her high-school days, and she madly turning cartwheels, blonde-brunette-blonde (wasn't that the old joke?) as Andrew Jackson High ground down their opponents, one after another after another. The two guns came closer. They were inches apart now, and the maw at the end of that silencer was like a tunnel, like a cave, like the abyss itself. She had never been at the point of a gun. A lifetime, but never this experience before. She could not take her eyes off that black hole – it would swallow the entire world.

'Drop it,' she said, but her voice was smaller now.

The gun went nowhere. If anything, it inched closer, and now the two guns were so close they could almost touch. They were like two nervous lovers, coming together for their first kiss.

Patrick Quinlan

'Drop that fucking gun!' she screamed, her voice dampened by the snow.

Light flashed at the end of the tunnel. And again. The gun moved a bit, hardly at all. Dot heard a clacking sound, like that from a staple gun. She pulled her own trigger and the sound was loud in her ears, deafening. She pulled it again. And again.

Her ears rang and it was like her head was inside a helmet stuffed with cotton. The only sound was the ringing. Again she pulled the trigger but now there was no trigger or gun and she stared up at the night sky, bright with the nearby lights, snow falling around her.

She used to make snow angels when she was a girl, lying back like this, spreading her arms and legs, nice and toasty warm inside her big parka. And then she would stop and close her eyes, open her mouth and wait for a great big drop to land on her tongue.

The first thing Dick Miller knew the next day was pain.

Searing pain throughout his head, with waves of nausea – not like a hangover, not even like the morning after a concussion – but something worse. Dick had taken a concussion in high school when he played tight end for a Franklin K. Lane team that didn't know how to pass the football. The quarterback had a habit of hanging Dick out to dry by lofting the ball just beyond his fingertips. One time, while Dick was in the air, an opposing linebacker had speared him headfirst to the turf – hard enough to put Dick on Queer Street for three days. But even that didn't feel like this.

The phone rang, so loud it made Dick sit up with a start, his eyes popping open. His stomach lurched. The room spun around him and he didn't see the phone right away. The ringing got louder and he put his hands over his ears. There it was – right there next to the bed.

Good God. His skull was cracked, he was sure of it. It was

18

Christmas Eve Day, he had a fractured skull, and the phone was ringing.

He picked up the receiver. 'Hello?' With his free hand he rubbed his temples.

'Dick. I want you to know something. OK? You think you can treat me like shit because of how I am. But you can't. You can't leave me sitting by the telephone all fucking night. You can't do it, OK? You can't do it.'

Oh, shit. Desiree.

'Desiree, look—'

'No, you look.'

Desiree went on and Dick tuned out. The voice was sultry, deep, almost masculine. He pictured the person it belonged to. Desiree Milan, a transvestite, a transsexual, a tweener, Dick didn't know what Desiree called herself and didn't really care. She had a dick and thought she was a woman. She dressed like a woman, and she looked like a woman – a beautiful black woman. It was a crazy situation. She was a convict like him, but she was a mess, and he was trying to help her. That was all. He was trying to get her some skills so she could keep a job and stay out of the joint. The joint was a bad place for people like Desiree. Dick had seen it. The thought of it made him cringe. Jesus. They passed the Desirees around like candy.

He was supposed to have met Desiree for a drink the night before, a date he had meant to keep and had evidently missed.

'Desiree,' he began again.

'Fuck you, Dick.'

The phone clicked off. Desiree was gone. In a moment, that loud, annoying buzzing sound would start. He didn't think he could stand it. Somehow, he managed to get the phone back onto the hook.

He looked out the window. The snow was still falling, giant grayish flakes floating slowly past his window onto the fire escape. The window was open a crack, and from outside came the quiet of snow piling on snow. Somewhere below, a car passed by with chains on its tires. Usually there was noise, any time of day or night. He had grown used to it. The quiet was unnerving.

He closed his eyes and tried his best to melt back into the pillow. But now that he was awake, the pain would not let him rest. He needed to get up, at least to take some aspirin and drink water. A sudden spike of pain pierced his head, and with every beat of his heart the spike was driven deeper toward the base of his skull. He tried to piece together the events of last night. But nothing would come.

'Shit,' he said.

He was sprawled across the mattress, fully dressed, as if dumped there. He had one shoe on. He sat up again, more slowly this time. Then he gathered his strength and stood. When he glanced at the clock, he wasn't surprised to discover that it was already past noon. Out the window he could see the street three floors below. The gray streets were blanketed in white. It was a peaceful scene.

Everything was OK.

Slowly, he undressed, right down to the skin.

It was a thousand degrees in that room. New York heat, the kind that makes you open your windows when it's ten degrees outside. The kind of heat he didn't need, with his cottonmouth and his pounding headache and trembling hands. He dressed in sweatpants, put on a jacket, boots, and went out into the street. He was hungry. He wanted a bagel, milk and juice, and also some painkillers. Tylenol. Advil. Whatever was extra strength. He headed along his street, a street of old industrial buildings, shuffling his feet through the thick snowfall. Then he noticed his car. It was a big gold Oldsmobile from years gone by. It was parked in a tow-away zone, in front of a small factory. The front end stuck out a good four feet from the curb, and the rear end was practically on the sidewalk.

He didn't remember driving the car. He didn't remember coming home.

He walked over to it. The street was deserted in every direction, and it was a good thing that it was. The front passenger side window was smashed in. Blood stained the yellow seat.

His heart added a counterrhythm to the pounding in his head. He caught himself and leaned against the side of the car. He closed his eyes and an image came to him. He was running through deep snow in a forest, running between the trees. He tripped and fell, and then he was falling through the sky, his arms frantically pin-wheeling.

When he opened his eyes, he was sitting in the snow by the side of the car. His head rested against the quarter-panel, his hands rested on his knees. The snow had soaked through his sweatpants. That was what had awakened him. He looked around. No one. The windows of the warehouses and factories were dark. Everywhere the late afternoon shadows deepened. He was alone. Suppose the snow hadn't awakened him? It was cold out, and now he was chilled. It would be a shame to freeze to death across the street from his home.

'Better get moving.' He wasn't sure if he said it or thought it.

Very slowly, using the side of the car for balance, he stood up. He swayed, gave himself half a minute, and made sure he had his balance. He reached into the car, unlocked the door and opened it. It looked like someone had punched the window and cut their hand on the glass. He glanced uneasily at his own hands. The knuckles on his right hand were scraped raw. Now that he thought about it, his wrist was sore.

I punched the window out. I've done that before. No problem.

But it was a problem. It scared him. At that moment, everything scared him. He was badly spooked. Absently, he popped open the trunk. There was a blanket in there. Maybe he could duct-tape it over the window – at least stop the snow from coming in.

Something else was in the trunk. It was so big, he didn't even see

21

it at first. He tried lifting it out of his way, moving it, pushing it – but it was too damned heavy. Finally, he looked at it. It was wrapped in two green garbage bags, one going north, the other south. It was long and doubled over in order to fit in the car. He stared at it for a full minute. It was a body.

The thought gave him the nastiest sort of shock. Electricity thrummed through him, as though the current came up from the ground. His scalp itched; he was sure his hair was standing on end. Around the neighborhood, the buildings seemed to laugh, their darkened windows like eyes. He stood there, breath pouring from his mouth.

Maybe she isn't dead. Maybe she's just been hurt very bad, and needs a doctor.

Of course he didn't believe it. That body was wrapped up nice and tight, ready for deposit. Without looking, he knew the body was dead, just as surely as he knew who it was before he had seen anything to indicate the identity. It was a murder, and he knew too much about it when he shouldn't have known anything. His memory was a blank slate, and yet he knew.

'Dot,' he said, and his voice came out small and shaky. He heard it, and it did not sound like him.

He had to make sure. He reached for the plastic bag. It was fastened with duct tape, probably his own. It took him a few minutes to get it untied, working with numb hands in the cold. When the bag opened, blonde hair spilled out at the top. Dick glanced around one last time, assuring himself no one was around. He pulled the head out, got a look at the face, and immediately wished he hadn't.

Dot's eyes were wide open, staring. In death, she looked surprised, as if she didn't expect to see him there. In the painful days that had just passed, he had thought often about getting back at her, about hurting her somehow. In his darkest hours, he had even been angry enough to . . . what? To kill her?

Dick's mind hurtled backwards, fifteen years into the past. A small man sat in the middle of an empty warehouse, bound hand and foot to a chair. His eyes gaped in terror. He shook his head, he moaned, he cried.

'Don't do this,' he said. 'Don't do this fucking thing.'

'Gimme that fucking gun,' Dick said. He took the gun and pressed it to the man's head. No hesitation. No sound. Every line etched clean, in a circle of bright white light. He pulled the trigger and . . .

. . . stood alone on this empty street in Brooklyn, with this body stuffed inside the trunk of his car.

Holy shit, he had trouble.

Things had happened fast with Dot.

Too fast, Dick reflected now, on the couch from which, hours later, he stared out at the blinking Christmas lights of the surrounding buildings. He grimaced and didn't know he was doing it. The lights out there were supposed to give the windows – indeed, the whole neighborhood – a festive air, but somehow they made everything even more dismal. Despite his predicament, he could barely keep his eyes open. Sharp flashes of pain lit up his skull like lightning on the horizon line. He still felt like vomiting. Afternoon had given way to evening, and Dick was no closer to an answer. Dot was dead. In his car. Out in front of this very building. He had left her there. He had taped some cardboard and plastic sheeting over the broken window, but that was all he had done. That was all he could bring himself to do.

Had he killed her? Any homicide detective in any interrogation room in the country would say he had reason enough. But he couldn't remember.

All his life, since he was a teenager, strange women had taken him to bed. It wasn't that he had a way with them. He didn't dress especially nice. He didn't try to charm them. He often didn't know what to say. He just liked them – women in general – and he let them do all the talking. So it never came as a surprise when he ended up with any woman. Which meant that one question he didn't ask himself was why his boss had any interest in him.

Of course, Dick was nervous that first morning – the day the BreakOut Program had sent him to interview at Feldman Real Estate. Normally, he was a late sleeper. But that day, a Monday, he was up with the sun. Half a dozen times, he decided not to go. It was his first job interview since the time he got the supermarket job as a kid, when they didn't really interview him but sort of gave him the once-over to see if he had a pulse or not, and asked him when he could start. He knew this would be different.

He paced through his apartment, up and down and all around. Finally, he got dressed and walked through the bustling streets of Williamsburg to the office in Greenpoint. He got there on time, but she made him wait forty-five minutes in her outer office until she let him in to see her. He had bought a new tie for the occasion and it had taken him half an hour to actually tie it. Now he was sitting there on the couch with the damn thing strangling him. Again, he fought with himself. One minute, he was leaving without another word. The next minute he was staying and toughing it out. He must have looked like a yoyo, the way he kept standing up as though he would leave, then changing his mind, and making a circuit around the waiting room. He pretended he had some interest in the cheesy paintings and photographs that hung framed on the walls. At one point, he got it in his head, maybe he should steal something before he left. Only there was nothing to steal except the paintings.

Finally, a young woman poked her head into the room. 'Mr Miller?'
'Yes?'

'Ms Racine will see you now.'

The woman brought him down to the boss's office and, of course, through his fog he noticed her skirt. He noticed these sorts of things. The skirt was short and she had some fine legs. She had black hair and big dark eyes. She smiled at him, but it seemed kind of a shy smile. He enjoyed watching her walk. It took his mind off the nervousness.

'And your name?' he said as she dropped him off.

'I'm Lydia.'

He stuck out his hand for a gentle shake. 'Well, Lydia, I'm very pleased to have met you. I hope we'll be able to work together.'

The boss was behind a big desk when Dick came in. She was on the phone, but gestured to a small wooden chair in front of the desk. He sat down, and the chair was too low. He was barely at eye level with the desk itself, never mind the boss, who seemed to tower over him. This was a standard trick, and Dick knew it already. Put someone in a small chair and make them look up to you. Whatever. Dick wouldn't succumb to feeling small. He stood as she hung up the phone.

'You can sit,' she said.

'That's all right. I like to stand.'

'OK. That sounds like fun. Let's both stand.'

She came around the desk and leaned against it. She looked good. She must have been older than he, but it was hard to tell. She could have been younger. Her skirt – part of a skirt and jacket ensemble – was even shorter than the one on the woman who had let Dick in. A little higher and there was no reason to bother wearing it. She had a lot of ass packed into that skirt. Her high heels put her an inch or two over five feet. Her fingernails were long and red, and her long hair hung down in blonde curls. Her look alone probably put a lot of men on the defensive.

'I need a good typist,' she said. 'And they tell me you're about as good a typist as there is. Ninety words a minute – that's impressive. You learned to do that in prison?'

Dick shrugged. 'I was always a good typist. I just got caught up in other things.'

'Well, we're trying something new, being good corporate citizens by going with the BreakOut program. But I'll tell you what I don't need here, and that's a felon committing crimes or causing problems in my workplace.'

Dick waited a moment before responding. He gave his next words some thought. 'Have you ever smoked pot?' he said at last.

The question poked a hole through her act. She smiled. She held her thumb and forefinger about half an inch apart. 'Maybe this much.'

'Even though it's against the law?'

She raised her eyebrows. Shrugged.

'Has it harmed you in any way?' he said.

She seemed to enjoy back-pedaling from him. 'Can't say that it has.'

'Ever think about the guy who sold it to you? The risks he's taking?'

'I have to admit, I never gave it much thought.'

Dick smiled. 'I was performing a public service. Wouldn't you say?'

'You're hired,' she said. 'Call me Dot.'

A few weeks passed and then it was early October. By that time, any positive early feeling had faded. Dick was just hanging around, hoping to survive until Christmas. After that, he was going to think about getting a little something going. Jail be damned. Working nine to five, chained to a desk, was its own sort of jail, with the added detraction that once inside, it got its grip. It started looking like a life sentence. The options seemed to shrink away to nothing.

Then the funny thing happened, and Dick's plans changed.

One day, he had just typed up about twenty pages of documents. He did it fast and clean on the computer. He even spell-checked it. He went in Dot's office to hand it to her. She looked up as he came in.

'You finished those already?'

'Nothing to it.'

'How are they?'

'Done. Clean. Perfect.'

She leaned back in her chair and Dick caught a glimpse of her skirt behind the desk. She had some legs.

Dick turned to go.

'Dick?'

He stopped and looked back at her.

'Can you shut the door a minute?'

He shut the door.

She looked over the top of reading glasses at him. 'Did anyone ever tell you that you look just like James Dean?'

'Yeah,' he said, 'but bigger.'

'I have a meeting today,' she said, 'but do you want to have lunch tomorrow? It's on me.'

The next day they left the office early, eleven thirty, to beat the noontime rush. Dot drove them in her Lexus five minutes south into Williamsburg and pulled up in front of a nice-looking brownstone. There was a garage on the side and the door opened automatically.

'This is the place,' Dot said.

Inside her house, Dick took a moment to drink in the stylish luxury of the living room. The hardwood floors, the original art on the walls.

'So, Dot,' he said, 'what's on the menu?'

She was already unzipping her dress down the back.

'You are,' she said.

On the night before Christmas, some creatures *were* stirring.

'Nobody ever dies,' Nestor Garcia said.

He said it even though his antennae were twitching like crazy. He said it because death was on his mind. He said it because it just slipped

27

out. He wouldn't normally share information like this. Maybe he was preoccupied – so many things were happening these days.

The two men looked at him. The skinny one stood by the bar mixing up some drinks. The fat one sat on the couch across from Nestor. A fat one and a skinny one, Nestor thought, how lovely. Behind the two of them, a floor-to-ceiling window revealed a south-facing cityscape from forty stories up. The lights dazzled Nestor. He loved views like this. He loved a city like this – New York City – glittering like countless jewels in the darkness. Dozens of blocks away, the Empire State Building glimmered in red and green lights for the Christmas season. They could be in a helicopter up here – they owned the city. Nestor wanted a view to rival this one. He wanted *this* view. The view from his place was good, but it wasn't this . . . panorama. It seemed somehow unfair that these silly men had this view and he did not.

'Nobody ever dies?' the fat one said. 'What the fuck's that supposed to mean?'

Nestor regarded the fat man and debated not saying anything. The fat man wore a three-piece suit and a silk handkerchief in his breast pocket. The man appeared to be sweating. How could you explain something so . . . complex . . . to a man like this?

Nestor didn't trust either of these men. Instinct told him something was wrong here. 'It's just something I read about,' he said with a shrug. 'Modern science.'

'Yeah?'

'Atom theory. If you fire an atom at a wall, and you force it to choose between one way to go and another way, it doesn't choose. Instead, it simply becomes two atoms and goes both ways. We are made of these things called atoms. This makes some scientists think that perhaps no one ever dies. They think that every time a decision is made, every time an event can go one way or another way, it doesn't have to choose. Instead, it goes both ways. If I shoot you and you die, perhaps there is another place, another reality where I miss. Or where I didn't shoot you at all.'

'You planning to shoot me?'

The fat man laughed and the skinny man joined him. Complex theory was wasted on types such as these. The skinny man came from the bar with two drinks. He handed the fat man one, and then handed one to Nestor.

'Cut with the bullshit philosophy and drink up.'

Nestor could not drink the drink. It was not possible to do so. He did not know these men yet, did not know their intentions. Of course, he knew what they claimed their intentions were. They claimed to be interested in buying – at twenty thousand dollars per key – the two kilograms of cocaine he had in the small leather brief-case on the sofa with him. If the coke proved to be good, they claimed to be interested in buying more weight at a later time. These things they claimed, but Nestor had his doubts. It was too easy. It had happened too fast. And he had the bitter sting of experience to teach him what happened when things were too fast and too easy.

He gazed out the window at the falling snow as the two men upended their glasses. He placed his glass on the table in front of him. If things were as he suspected, the problem would come now.

And come it did.

'Hey, buddy, I made you a drink there. Don't you want it?'

Nestor shrugged. 'In a moment.'

'In a moment, the guy says.'

'Let's do the deal first. Then I will drink it to celebrate.'

'I'm giving the guy hospitality,' the skinny one said, 'and he blows me off. What do you think of that, Ed?'

Ed shrugged, his fleshy neck jiggling a bit. 'I think it's all right.

Guy wants to do the deal, OK? Maybe he don't drink, you ever think of that?'

The skinny one looked at Nestor. 'You don't drink, is that it? Have a problem with the sauce, so you quit drinking?'

'No. I drink.'

'Look,' Ed said. 'I'm gonna go in the bathroom over there and take a piss. Then I'm gonna come back out here, and we'll do the deal. All right? Our friend wants to stay and have a drink with us after that, great. If he wants to skip the drink and go, that's fine too.' The fat man named Ed looked at his watch. 'See the time? After midnight, right? It's officially Christmas Day now, for Chrissakes. I say, everybody be happy. Do what you want to do.'

'All right,' the skinny one said. 'Go take your piss. That all right with you, Mr Cheerful?'

Nestor shrugged again. 'Of course.'

Ed labored to move his bulk off the chair he was sitting in. He half turned to get a good grip on the chair, wheezing a bit as he did. Nestor opened the leather briefcase. He removed one bag of coke. Nestled underneath was a Glock nine semi-auto with silencer attached. He pulled it and shot Ed through the throat. Behind Ed, the window glass shattered and the bullet whined off into the night.

As Ed grabbed his throat and undulated on the chair, Nestor turned to the skinny one and fired. The glass in the skinny one's hand blew apart.

'Holy fuck,' the guy said.

Ed made gobbling noises. He clawed at his throat. There was plenty of blood, but not too, too much. Not the kind of pulsing, jetting spray of blood you expect from a catastrophic neck wound. The bullet had passed through, somehow missing the carotid artery, the jugular vein, and the spinal cord. That was a thick neck Ed had. A smaller man, the bullet would have just about chopped the head right off his body.

'Now is your chance to live,' Nestor said to the skinny one. 'Open the briefcase.'

Nestor gestured with his head at the fine leather briefcase that the two men had brought to the meeting. It rested on the glass table where Nestor had only moments ago placed his drink. Nestor's gun never wavered. He pointed it at the skinny man's heart. He felt very little, other than curiosity and a sense of time pressure. He needed to leave soon, certainly before any friends or associates of these two arrived.

'You crazy fuck,' the man said. 'What'd you do that for? We gotta call an ambulance or he's gonna die.'

'If you don't open the briefcase, you are going to die. At this moment, I am performing a favor for you. Now come here and open it.'

The skinny one came around to the table. 'Look, I don't know the combination. It's Ed's briefcase, and you just shot him. Are you listening to me? I can't open it. And you just shot the only guy who can.'

'You have three seconds,' Nestor said.

Ed rolled over onto the floor. He moaned. He gobbled.

'I can't open it.'

'Two seconds.'

'You comprende English, pal? You fucking comprende?'

'One second.' Nestor applied an infinitely small amount of pressure on the trigger. He took a deep breath.

'All right, I'll do it. All right? Don't fucking shoot me. I'll do it.'

The man played with the lock combination. It took him several seconds. His hands were shaking, and he had to start over. Nestor said nothing while he did. Then the man opened the small case. Five piles of hundred-dollar bills were arrayed across the box. In order for there to be forty thousand dollars, each pile would have to contain eighty bills. At a glance, Nestor thought the piles looked reasonable.

'See? It's only money.'

'Count it,' Nestor said.

'It's all there.'

'Then count it.'

'It's all there, I swear to you.'

'Show me before I kill you.'

The man picked up a pile of bills. Nestor saw that three or four bills down, they stopped being dollars. They were green, sure. They were probably even Crane's paper, the same paper that money came printed on. Crane's was nice paper, made to last from cotton and linen rather than cheap wood pulp. But this nice paper was blank. It was dummy money. The man made a sorry attempt to hide this fact with his fist. It did very little good. Nestor noticed that the man even looked a bit sheepish.

'Do you know,' Nestor said, 'what the white powder in these bags is?'

The man looked at him blankly, still holding the funny money in his hand. It was dumb to use fake money. Why not use the real thing? That would have lent the whole affair a feeling of authenticity that it no longer enjoyed.

'Do you know?'

The man shook his head.

'It is cocaine, perhaps eighty percent pure. I came here with the intent to sell it to you for a fair price. And you were here with the intent to . . . what? Kill me, I am thinking. Was that your intention, to kill me?'

The man said nothing. On the floor, his friend Ed had stopped moving altogether. The carpet was stained black near Ed's head. The stain looked like two wings extending from either side of Ed's neck. Ed's eyes were wide open and staring.

'You are *assassins*?'

Outside, the snow continued to fall. It had become colder in the room since the window panel had shattered.

'Speak,' he said.

The skinny man eyed him. 'You're out of time,' he said. 'They want you dead. You've fucked around too many times.'

'And you were sent to kill me? There was a gun in the bathroom that this other one was going to retrieve? Maybe it was taped behind the toilet?'

The man gave a small shrug and a smile. Nestor shot him, then shot him again. The shots made almost no sound. When the second shot hit high on his torso, the man fell backwards over the sofa behind him. Nestor stood and paced over to the man sprawled on the carpet behind the sofa. He hovered over the man, gun pointed down at his head. The man was still very much alive. He clutched his chest and stared up at Nestor, anger in his eyes. He was skinny, but he was tough in his own way. He was a hard-hearted man. As Nestor sighted down the barrel, he pictured Dick Miller in this very same position – helpless before him.

'When you want to kill someone,' Nestor said, 'the best thing is to get to it right away. Otherwise, the situation can get out of hand.'

The existence of these two men meant that Nestor had very big trouble indeed. It was the cocaine. Freelancing cocaine was against the rules and had been for some time. Nestor knew this, and yet found himself unable to comply. The last time he had died, the bad time in Miami, it had been because of the damned cocaine. You would think he would leave it alone and find some other source of money. He shook his head. He himself didn't fully understand the forces that drove him. Now they were coming for him again, coming to finish him. It was time to leave New York, with Dot or without her.

Then again, how could he leave all of Dot's money behind? Answer – he couldn't. A fortune in stolen cash had been as good as his until

Miller had come on the scene. And Nestor would stay long enough to get the money, regardless of the dangers.

'Think of it this way,' he said to the man on the floor. 'Maybe the scientists are right. Maybe nobody ever dies.'

He pulled the trigger and unloaded into the man's upturned face.

2
CHRISTMAS DAY

Andrew King lay awake in the hours before dawn. He had a lot on his mind.

In the semi-darkness, he glanced around the bedroom of his apartment – he called this place the Bat Cave. It was a basement apartment in Sunnyside, Queens. The room next door, ostensibly the living room, was wired to the gills – sound equipment, computers, digital video. He had three computers in here – three superfast dream computers he had built himself with components he pieced together. He had the receivers to the telephone listening devices – one to Dot's house and one to her friend Lydia Sante's apartment. Two-dozen wires snaked along the floor. Tiny digital video cameras – one mounted in the peephole to his front door, and one mounted on one of the windows to the alley off Bliss Street – constantly monitored the outside environment and broadcast it on a video monitor fixed to the wall. Andrew always knew if someone was outside his apartment – this was his bunker, his last stand. He had been driven underground.

He took a moment to gaze ruefully down at his left hand. The pinkie was entirely gone – cut off where it met the bones of his hand – a keepsake from the run-in he'd had with Nestor Garcia.

One day, nine-fingered Andrew hoped to return that favor and more.

Andrew wasn't a cop, or a CIA spook, or anything like it. Hell, no. He was entirely a private operator. He was part of a new breed of men, men who used technology to get what they wanted. Andrew King, high-school loser and dropout, former multiplex-movie-theater usher, could make anything happen with the equipment at his fingertips. Dot had thought she could scare him off with Nestor, but instead she only made him more determined.

In his mind, he could still hear Nestor's clipped voice, in the moment before he took the finger. 'You will no longer contact Dot. You will no longer be paid. If there is a problem with the computer, Dot will contact you and you will fix the problem free of charge. You will not call the police. Do you understand?'

'We'll see who understands,' Andrew said now to the bedroom. He had reason to feel confident.

There were three people in Andrew's crew. Himself, the ringleader, thin but ripped, and proud of his body. He wore urban commando-style clothes, pants with cargo pockets and form-fitting black shirts. He had floppy blond hair like a surfer, and sported black, thick-rimmed Calvin Klein glasses. He made six figures last year building databases and intranets for corporations. That didn't even count the tax-free stake he had taken from helping Dot set up the Feldman computer system to support her little embezzlement scam – the stake that had come to such an abrupt and painful end. He drove a BMW 540i, four-door sedan, now parked in an underground garage on Queens Boulevard. The car had black aluminum alloy-style rims, with run-flat tires just in case. There was an MP3 player in his fucking car – a thousand downloaded songs made sure he could go weeks without hearing the same song twice. He subscribed to two magazines – *Wired* and *MIT Technology*. He was hyper-caffeinated – he drank Red Bull by the case. His brain was on fast-forward. He thought fast, he talked fast, and he made his dreams into reality – revenge was the dream on order these days.

Then there was Big Henry. He was two hundred fifty pounds and growing. He ate constantly. He had a problem with his metabolism, maybe. That's what he claimed. Andrew had met Henry in the downtown club scene. For a long time now, Henry had been the man to see at the Limelight for X, K, acid, mushrooms, whatever was the hot topic. Even crank. Yes, crank. Crystal meth. If you wanted to turn your brain to cobwebs and your body into a shivering wreck, if you wanted to become a groveling toady willing to suffer any humiliation to feed the jones, Henry would put you there. Andrew had seen them, the hungry-eyed shells hovering near Henry in the crowd, getting ready to move in and ask for *the favor*. Society called them addicts. Henry called them slaves.

And finally there was Breeze – the Cool Breeze.

It could take a week to describe Breeze. Young, a tomboy, a street urchin, she was what they meant when they coined the term cyberpunk. She was small, but her presence was big. She wore tight black leggings over her muscular legs. Her hair was peroxide white and spiked. Her lips were blood red, and the mascara was black around her eyes, with their long, fake eyelashes. Her left eyebrow was pierced. Piercings ran the length of each ear. Her tongue was pierced. A teardrop tattoo dropped from her left eye. She was Henry's girl, but Andrew knew that each of her nipples was pierced, and more tattoos covered various parts of her body.

Breeze was, to put a word on it, beautiful.

Andrew smiled. He felt good. Dot's little world was caving in around her. The thought pleased him to no end. Dick Miller and

Nestor Garcia – her protectors – had been set against each other. At the same time, both of them were ready to wring Dot's neck. Meanwhile, Andrew knew Lydia, Dot's little helper, had the keys and the numbers to the safe-deposit boxes. He knew where the banks were down in Nassau. And Breeze owned a New York State driver's license in the name of Lydia Sante, and had mastered forging Lydia's signature. His smile went ear to ear. Soon he would make his move.

In the weak morning light, the phone began to ring. He got it on the second ring.

'Hello?'

'Andrew?'

'Yeah.'

'He threw me out, baby. I'm on the street.' It was Breeze. Jesus. Speak of the devil. Not this, not now. Andrew took a deep breath and sighed. OK. OK, he would handle it. What other choice did he have?

The hour had come around at last. The shit had finally hit the fan. Henry had thrown her out this morning – Christmas fucking morning.

Breeze could still see him: the fat boy, getting dressed at dawn for his long drive up to Connecticut to see his family. She sensed the anger coming off him in waves. Careful. Henry was strong. A man this big could hurt her. And he was misreading her – he was misreading the excitement, the high, the animal electricity that was humming through her body and for all she knew, sizzling from her pores. Oh, she was excited, all right. But not for the reason he thought.

'You cunt,' he said. 'I know what you've been doing.'

She had meant to stay quiet, but she couldn't. She just couldn't.

'What have I been doing? What have I done that you never made me do? You pimp me out to that evil bastard and now *you're* mad at *me*?'

He raised a hand and it sliced through the air like a knife, cutting off any further debate. 'I want you out. Now. Take all your little shitty things and get the fuck out. Anything you leave here you can find on the street when I get back.'

The eyes told her it was real. The eyes told her that waiting much longer would be a dangerous enterprise. She packed a couple of small bags with clothes, some shoes and makeup, and she hit the streets. The rest of her stuff? Fuck it. What was it anyway? A cheap combination radio and CD player. A bunch of CDs. Some paperweights she had started collecting. Things. They just weighed her down. Henry could smash that stuff to dust for all she cared.

She walked the cold morning streets of Greenwich Village, feeling lighter for having left it all behind. East Eighth Street, St Mark's Place, heading toward the river. No one was out. She walked and waited, waited and walked. It reminded her of the times when she used to walk and walk, with nowhere to go.

She held out until seven and then she made the call. When he answered, his voice was blurry. 'Hello?'

'Andrew?'

'Yeah.'

'He threw me out, baby. I'm on the street.'

'Where is he now?'

'He left for Connecticut.'

'Where are you?'

'St Mark's and First.'

'Shit.' He sighed into the phone, letting her know he didn't approve – this was too much, too soon. They made it clear, the men, what a burden she was. 'Go inside somewhere. I'll pick you up in half an hour. Maybe forty minutes.'

Breeze spent the time daydreaming over a cup of coffee. She thought of the night they played the game with Dot. Dot had been drinking alone at a neighborhood bar in Chelsea. Breeze had followed Dot for weeks, and had learned that it wasn't out of the ordinary for Dot to wander the city and drop into strange bars. That night, she had taken the subway into Manhattan, and Breeze had never been far away.

It was a Monday night, and the bar wasn't half full. A handful of guys were playing darts and laughing. Two more played pool in the back room. Now and then, a guy would saunter over, slide onto the stool next to Dot's and try to make a move on her. Dot wasn't buying what they were selling. She didn't even engage with the bartender except to order another drink from time to time. A few people sat at the bar watching a football game on the TV. The bartender, a fat middle-aged guy with unkempt red hair, seemed engrossed in it. A good sign.

Breeze slid onto the stool next to Dot and ordered a draft beer. She knew she didn't have to do anything more. Dot would approach her. It was simple. Dot was selective with men – she only picked them if she could use them for something. But she struck up conversations with attractive young women. She couldn't seem to resist.

And Breeze knew – a lifetime had taught her – just how sexy people found her. They had been finding her sexy since she was ten years old. Ralph had sure found her sexy by then. Good ol' Ralph, Mom's new hubby. Ralph was a good earner – he was a handyman by trade, and he knew his way around a toolbox. He was handy with any number of tools – a little too handy, if you asked Breeze. Ralph's face was like sandpaper, his body was muscular from weightlifting, especially his arms – the focus of much of his attention during his mammoth workout sessions in the garage – and his penis was large and uncircumcised. It was Breeze's first penis, and over time, as she came to know more of them, she learned that Ralph's was larger than most, and that it smelled funny. She thought of mentioning it to her mom, but that wouldn't fly, would it? 'Say, Mom, why does Ralph's dick always smell like that? It makes me want to gag.'

Breeze's mom often worked nights at the diner, leaving Breeze under Ralph's supervision. Who knew what Breeze's mom – Kathryn was her name, Katie they often called her – thought she and Ralph were doing all that time she was away? If Breeze ever saw her again, maybe she would ask her. But it had been a long time since she had seen either Katie or Ralph, and it would probably be a good long time before she saw them again. After two years of Ralph's sweaty ministrations, at the age of twelve, Breeze skipped town.

'Can I buy that for you?' Dot said as the beer came out. It had happened faster than Breeze had imagined it would.

Breeze shrugged. 'If you like. As long as you understand that I'm spoken for.'

'Oh, I understand that. I'm spoken for myself, in more ways than one. I'm just in it for the conversation. Although I must say you look like an interesting person.'

Breeze might have blushed just the tiniest bit. Dot had her charms. Breeze looked down at the bangles on her arms, the black T-shirt, the fishnets. She thought of her peroxide white hair – this week it was white – and the diamond nose stud. Yes, she was interesting-looking, for sure. And beautiful. They often told her that – right before they tried something. Or succeeded at something.

But she and Dot had a nice conversation. Dot was a little bit drunk already. She wanted to talk, and Breeze gave her the room to do it. She told Breeze about the Miss Ohio Pageant of 1982. So many people were sure she was going to win. And then she didn't win. She lost. She was the First Runner-Up, but it didn't matter. Losing was losing. And Jennifer Caan became Miss Ohio. What a hollow bitch. She cracked under pressure in Atlantic City and ended up out of the running. Dot remembered watching it. They didn't show much of Jennifer at all. She faded into the background with the others, all-American girls with big smiles pasted to their faces, walking ramrod straight along the stage, one state after another. All the losers. But that was OK. Being Miss Ohio was enough. Miss Ohio was a launching pad. If Dot had won Miss Ohio, maybe her entire life would be different now.

'What happened to the winner?' Breeze said.

'Jennifer? I don't know. She got married, I think, had a few puppies. Probably ended up selling real estate.'

'Is that good?' Breeze said.

Dot smiled and shrugged. 'I don't know. Some people might say it was.'

She excused herself to go to the bathroom.

And here was where Breeze made the future happen. Here was where Breeze knocked Dot's little train right off the tracks. Dot seemed OK. But how OK could she be? She had gotten that crazy bastard Nestor to cut Andrew's finger off.

It didn't matter. Breeze could like Dot. She could like Dot, or hate her. She could lust for her. She could kill her. To Breeze, it didn't much matter how she felt about a person at any given time. She could change that feeling if she wanted. Feelings were ... what? Feelings were wisps of cloud. Feelings were tissue paper. Feelings were nada, nothing.

She reached into the tiny change purse in her oversized bag. She brought up two small white pills stamped with the name Roche. The pills were two milligrams each. On the street, at the clubs, at the floating rave parties that went from squat to squat, from North Philadelphia to New Haven and everywhere in between, people called these pills by a variety of names – roofies, roachies, la rocha, ribs, roopies, and ropies. Whatever they were calling them now, everybody knew what they were – sleeping pills from Europe, ten times more powerful than Valium. In low doses, they helped you groove a little groovier than you normally would. At high doses, they obliterated your inhibitions. They made you totally passive. They gave you amnesia inside of fifteen minutes, amnesia that could last eight to twenty-four hours. They made you sick for days, while you tried to reassemble the shattered pieces of your mind and, sometimes, your life. Alcohol multiplied the effects.

Trip-n-Falls, Breeze called the pills. The date rape drug.

'Sleep tight, little Dot,' she said. She dropped the pills into Dot's half-finished beer. The beer foamed just a bit as the pills dissolved. The pills, once dissolved, had no taste. Breeze glanced around. The bartender was all the way down at the other end of the bar, entranced by watching men half his age, boys really, monstrous impossible boys, demolish each other on the football field.

Breeze brought out her cellphone and speed-dialed a number. Her call was answered on the second ring. She didn't wait for the person on the other end to speak.

'Fifteen minutes,' she said. 'From now.'

She hung up just in time. Dot was returning from the bathroom.

Dot smiled. 'Did you get a call?'

'Nope. Just checking my messages.'

She watched in silence as Dot took a long sip of her spiked beer. 'Do you want to order two more?'

'Sure,' Breeze said. 'Why not?'

Now, months later, as Breeze sat in the warmth of a coffee shop on Christmas morning, she glanced out the window and saw a sleek blue BMW pull up to the curb. *Look at me!* the car screamed. *Look at the car I drive!* It was a boy car, a car for boys trying to convince themselves they were men. Andrew, a boy – and the architect of Dot's downfall – was at the wheel.

Breeze finished her coffee and collected the bags around her. She smiled to herself. Things were just starting to get interesting.

* * *

Lydia Sante was dreaming.

In the dream, she stood in an old walled garden, a black and blighted wasteland of dead and overgrown plants. Ahead, she could see a stone path leading to a beautiful and empty white sand beach, awash in bright sunlight. But she could not make her feet follow the path. As she watched, creeper vines grew from the dense underbrush at either side of her. They stretched and reached her feet, then began to climb her legs. They clawed up and over her body, tightening their grasp, beginning to pull her down. She tried to scream but couldn't. They pulled her back into the underbrush. There were rustling noises back there. She looked up the path, the beach still beckoning. She tried to open her mouth, one last chance to scream, but her jaw was clamped shut by the power of the vines.

Her eyes opened, the scream just behind her teeth.

It was Christmas morning, and she knew Nestor Garcia was in her apartment. She hadn't heard anything – the apartment was deathly still. But Nestor had a presence about him; he changed the environment when he walked into a room. The door to her bedroom was shut, but she knew he was out there somewhere, in the kitchen probably, chain-smoking by the open window.

Nestor being here was a bad thing.

'I have calm self-assurance and confidence,' she told herself in hushed tones, 'in all situations and with all people.'

She pulled back her soft comforter and climbed out of her double bed – a gift, like many things in her well-appointed one-bedroom apartment, from Dot Racine. The items in this room, in this entire apartment, screamed money. Dot liked to spend money.

Dot had wanted her to move here to Brooklyn, to Williamsburg – she wanted Lydia right nearby. Dot wanted her out from under her father's thumb. Dot was her mentor and friend. Dot was her boss at Feldman Real Estate. Dot was her lover and her partner in crime.

Lydia sighed. Maybe she and Dot had crossed too many lines together. But Dot wanted her to be free and happy – of that Lydia had no doubt. Dot was almost – *almost* – like the mother Lydia had never had. At least that had been the story before everything started turning to dust.

'I have calm self-assurance and confidence,' Lydia began again.

She was nude, but the apartment was warm. She moved quickly and with catlike grace to the closet. As she did, she took a quick glance in the full-length mirror against the wall. Her body was firm, young and strong. She did aerobic dance, yoga, even some Pilates. She hiked in the mountains when she had time to get out of town.

'In all situations and with all people.'

She pulled on a T-shirt, hooded sweatshirt and a pair of jeans. She slipped her feet into a pair of sandals. Before going out, she looked at herself in the full-length mirror again. Her long hair was tousled and sleep was still in her dark eyes. The jeans and sweatshirt covered nearly every inch of her body. All the same, she looked good. Sexy. Not too sexy, please. Not too sexy if Nestor is here.

She took a deep breath. Just before she reached for the door, she had an urge to call her father. *Daddy, there's a man here and he's scaring me. I need you to get him out.*

She would never do it. Her father, the TV stereotype of the tough Latin, was sixty years old. Her whole life, he had been overprotective – he had stifled her through high school and two years of college. Even now, he demanded that she come over every week. If he had his way, she would come over every night, or even move back in with him until she found a man to marry. All she had ever wanted to do was get away from him and his grief and his sacrifice. Now, when maybe she really did need protection, he was an old man and it was too late.

She went out. She moved along the carpeted hall and into the kitchen.

Nestor sat at the narrow table by the open window. Outside, the snow that had fallen off and on for two days was still coming down. The flakes were big, delicate things, more like lace doilies than snow-fall. In the street, it was quiet. The normal traffic sounds of a Friday morning were not on display today. It was still pretty early, 8 a.m., and a Christmas morning after all. People were sleeping in.

The man – the intruder – in her kitchen was slim almost to the point of pain. His fingers were long and delicate, like a pianist's, and he held his cigarette between his thumb and forefinger, pointed straight up in the air. He wore rings on every finger, except his thumbs. All of his fingernails were painted blood red. He sat in a strangely effem-inate manner, his right leg in black jeans crossed tightly over his left. He wore alligator boots. His face was narrow and handsome, his hair slicked back tightly to his scalp. He wore a blue Polo sweater. He had diamond studs in both ears, and gold around his neck. His gun was placed in front of him on the table.

He looked up as she came in, surveyed her clothes. His eyes fired twin laser beams, and Lydia thought about how once you started down a certain path, it was very hard to go back the way you had come.

Nestor smirked. 'I liked you better how you were sleeping. Nude.'

'How did you get in here?' She tried to sound harsh, but came off to her own ears as peevish and scared. Everything he did was calcu-lated to throw a scare into people, even the smoking – he knew she didn't let people smoke inside the apartment.

He regarded his cigarette as if reading her mind. 'Why do you hide?' he said. 'You think, just because you get dressed, I can't take you out of those clothes?'

'Put out that cigarette.'

He smiled, no mirth in his eyes. 'Take off your clothes.'

'Nestor, I'm warning you. You don't have permission to be here. In one minute, I'm going to call the cops.'

Nestor's eyes lit up and he flashed his first real smile since she walked in the room. His face was aflame with delight. 'Good. They'll be here in an hour.' He shrugged, then slowly rotated his head around as if to stretch his neck. 'By then, it'll be too late.'

Lydia stalked to the kitchen drawer, reached in and pulled out a carving knife. She pointed it at him, keeping the sharp edge level with his eyes. Maybe acting angry could make it so. 'You get out of my apartment right now. You get the hell out.'

He took a long draw on his cigarette. He let the smoke out in a stream, not even bothering to face the window.

He stood, picking his gun up off the table as he did so. He took a step toward her.

'Come any closer, and I swear I am going to gut you like a pig. You remember pigs from the old days, right? *Puercos* eating grass by the side of the road back in Colombia? You're going to bleed like one.'

He raised the gun in one hand and sighted along the barrel at her head.

'Do you know,' he said, 'where Dot went?'

Lydia felt herself starting to tremble. Her heart pumped in her chest. Nestor was insane. It was impossible to know if he was fooling around, and it didn't matter anyway. It would take nothing at all for Nestor to kill her right now. Nothing. A mistake. A mental lapse, a spasm. Anything.

It had all been a terrible mistake. Everything with Dot, the money – all of it. It had been fun and exciting and terrifying and very lucrative. For the first time, Lydia had burned. She had burned for the money and for Dot and for the walk along the edge of a razor they were both taking. But it had all led to Nestor, and Nestor was a madman. It was as if she and Dot had been kids playing with a Ouija board, and their fooling around had conjured this . . . demon . . . up from the depths. Now they couldn't make him go away. Dot had brought Dick Miller on board thinking Dick's presence could exorcise Nestor. But it couldn't. Nothing could. Nestor was with them forever.

She shuddered. 'Nestor.'

He took another step closer, the gun pointed at her head.

The knife handle was wet from the sweat of her palm. She felt the knife slip out of her trembling hand. It clattered when it hit the kitchen floor.

'Please.'

'Tell me. Where did she go?'

'She didn't go anywhere. As far as I know, she's over at her place.'

He placed the barrel against her temple. With his free hand he reached under her sweatshirt and her T-shirt and began to rub her stomach, smoothly, sensually. Slowly, his hand moved up over her breasts and came out through her collar. The hand, manicured, so like a vampire's hand, appeared with its many colorful rings, its red nail polish like blood, then rested at her throat.

'You are shaking so much,' he said. 'Maybe you are hiding something?'

'Nestor, I swear to God. I haven't seen her since the office party two nights ago. But if she was going somewhere, she would've told me.'

He inched closer, and she could smell his cigarette breath. 'I've been to her home. She wasn't there. Not yesterday. Not last night. Not this morning. Where did she go?'

His grip tightened on her throat.

'I don't know.'

'Really?'

Lydia nodded. 'Really. She didn't tell me anything.' She braced herself for the next question, the one he couldn't fail to ask.

'Who has the keys?' he said.

'She does.'

'Who?'

'Dot. Dot has them.'

Lydia felt the fingers pressing into the flesh of her neck. Blood beat hard in her brain. Her air was being cut off. She heard a buzzing sound in her brain. It grew louder and louder. It might be pleasant to just drift off with that sound. Then the grip loosened the tiniest bit. Lydia gulped the available air as if it were water after a long crawl across the desert.

'Dot has the keys,' Nestor said. 'And Dot seems to have disappeared without mentioning it to you. Does that strike you as odd?'

'Nestor, please.'

He let go of his grip and pulled his hand back out through her shirt. He left the gun against her temple. 'I believe you. I believe you because you would never lie to me, right? You know better than to lie to me.'

He let the gun slowly drop to his side. He stood inches away from her.

'I also believe you because I searched your apartment before you arose. Mostly that. But God help you – only God *can* help you – if I find out you are lying.'

'I'm not lying.'

He leaned closer. 'I have to go now. But we'll be together again soon, my love. That I promise.' He kissed her cheek, brushing it lightly with his lips. Again, the ghastly cigarette smell was on her face. Then he was gone. She heard him close the front door as he went out.

The seconds spun out and became minutes. Ten of these things called minutes passed and she still hadn't moved off the wall. It was as if the wall had its own force of gravity that kept her pegged there.

Only after she was sure he was gone and wasn't coming back, she peeled herself away.

She went back into the bedroom and opened the closet again. Inside the closet she kept a clothes hamper, a wicker basket about four feet high. She pulled the lid off and dug through her overflowing laundry. There, at the bottom, was a small lock box. Had he really looked in here? Had he really looked? How would he know the combination to this box?

Fingers shaking, she spun the dial and opened the box.

A key chain with five keys on it sat amid cottony tissue.

She stared at the keys, her breath catching in her throat.

'Thank you,' she said, the tears coming now. 'Thank you.'

But she wasn't sure if it was a curse or a blessing that she still had the keys.

Dick Miller, awake and in bed, didn't want to think about Dot. He especially didn't want to think about her corpse, and so spent much of his morning doing exactly that. The fact that he had left Dot in the car overnight made his stomach drop – anyone could reach through the broken window and get into the car. Then they could just pop open the trunk and take a poke around.

So what to do now? Should he call the cops? And say what? Volunteer the information that he, a convicted felon, had a corpse in the trunk of his car? That sounded terrific.

Should he take her somewhere and bury her? He rejected that choice out of hand. The city had experienced a cold snap for the past two weeks. There was snow everywhere. The ground was frozen solid. Unless he planned to drive her body to South Carolina, burial was out. He pictured himself cruising down Interstate 95 in heavy traffic, Dot's body quietly rotting in the trunk. No thanks.

He could drive over to the East River and just dump her in. Should he do that? That was a possibility, but there was no telling whether she would pop up again to nail him one fine day, probably at the end of some fisherman's hook. Even if she didn't, the scuba cops routinely dove into the river and fished bodies out of there. Dumping her was just too risky, too uncertain.

He could carry Dot upstairs into the apartment. At least she wouldn't be sitting out there on the street for anybody to find her. That brought problems to mind as well. In the car, she was effectively frozen. She could sit out there like that until the next time it warmed up. If it only got warm for a day or so, or better yet, if it stayed cold until spring, she could sit there for months without attracting attention to herself. Once inside, in the warmth, in the superheated environment of an apartment during winter, it might be a matter of hours or less before she started to rot and smell and alarm the neighbors.

No, Dot needed to stay right where she was, at least for now.

Today, he felt a little better than yesterday, but not much. He was still dehydrated, still shaky and weak. He still had a nagging headache. Two nights ago – the night Dot died – remained a blank. He toyed with the idea that he might have poisoned himself somehow. Most times, with a serious hangover, with blackouts, he would begin to remember the events that took place, often with real embarrassment. This time he remembered nothing and it looked like it was going to stay that way.

He went to the window and checked on the car. Five floors below, it was still parked where he had left it and the trunk was still closed. The cardboard and plastic were still in place. Satisfied, he lit himself a joint. He sat in his easy chair, smoking it down to the nub. It was Christmas Day and he was getting high. His mind turned off and he floated serenely along. It was a pleasure to sit there and not have to think about anything. He knew there would be hard thinking in the days ahead, but for now he was content with nothing on his mind.

Somewhere in his psyche a shadow loomed. He could almost see it. His troubles were deeper than a matter of mere logistics. Dot was dead. His friend Dot. His boss. His lover. That was really Dot's body in the trunk and she really was dead. Beyond the question of what to do with the body, a black train was coming, loaded with much heavier things. Grief. Mourning. Remorse. When these kicked in, he would be unable to function the way he needed to.

He had to get rid of her before then. He pictured himself holding back the raw emotion with nothing more than the force of his will.

Time went by.

Something terrible has happened.

Lydia smiled her way through Christmas festivities at her father's modest house in Plainview, Long Island. But the thought kept returning. It was beyond her control – impossible to stop, like an onrushing train.

The house was filled with smiling aunts and cousins, nieces in pink dresses, nephews in dress pants and shirts with ties hung askew or clip-on ties gone altogether. And of course there was Uncle Ted, ninety-three years old if he was a day, in great shape, playing the piano and singing those great old songs. There he went now, and he had even gotten some of the family to go along.

'We wish you a Merry Christmas, we wish you a Merry Christmas . . .'

Lydia's father was here somewhere too. Smiling, drink in hand, a little drunk. He was close shaven, hair slicked back, looking fit and younger than his sixty years. He liked to open the house on the holidays. He liked having the family over. Normally, she did too. There were times, she remembered, when she had loved these gatherings.

These aunts were almost like mothers to her, and even as she thought it, she realized how pathetic that was, always looking for a mother and never finding one.

'. . . and a Happy New Year!'

Laughter now. Shouting.

They launched into the next verse, but she tuned it out.

Something terrible has happened.

Lydia was in the upstairs bathroom. Hiding. Thinking. Trying to make sense of what she had seen. She stared at the wallpaper – newspaper advertisements for patent medicines from the 1800s. Ryno's Hay Fever-n-Catarrh Remedy. Dr Fast's All-in-One. It was supposed to be funny, the things people bought back then. On any other day, it would be.

Earlier today, with the car packed for her dad's place, she had stopped by Dot's beautiful brownstone near McCarren Park. It hadn't rung true what Nestor said about Dot. Sure, she and Dot had had their differences of late, but Dot wouldn't just disappear without telling her. That wasn't like Dot at all. But what *was* like Dot? After nearly three years, Dot remained a mystery.

Lydia rang the bell several times. If Dot was asleep, or in there with Dick Miller or some other lover – that was OK. What they once had, that spark, was gone. Lydia didn't own Dot, Lydia didn't want to own Dot, and she was past the point of worrying about disturbing her. But no one answered. So Lydia let herself in with her own key.

The place had been ransacked.

Even now, hours later, Lydia was still overcoming the shock of it. Every room had been turned upside down. The furniture in the living room had been ripped open. All of the kitchen cabinets had been emptied. The valuable paintings in the gallery had been slashed with a razor – every one of them. The huge plasma TV in the living room was smashed. The bed had been ripped open. Dot's clothes were strewn about. The house, which had been a showpiece, had been pulled apart and reduced to a shambles. It wasn't the work of thieves – it was the work of someone angry, someone who hated.

Lydia had wanted to run away, leave before whoever had been there returned. But she steeled herself, and she went upstairs. She paced through the master bedroom to the walk-in closet. Like the rest of Dot's home, everything in the closet had been destroyed. Thousand-dollar dresses ripped to shreds. Shoes thrown everywhere. Lydia entered the closet and, hands shaking, went to a drawer at the bottom. There were eight identical drawers all along the bottom of the fixture, all of them locked with built-in combination locks. There were eight for just one reason – to throw off the scent should any problem arise. It would take a lot for someone to break open these eight drawers. Indeed, the intruder hadn't bothered to touch them. With insider's knowledge, Lydia went straight to the special drawer. It was locked with a combination Lydia knew well. She knew it so well because it was her mother's birthday.

She opened the drawer. She pulled it free. There, inside, was what she hoped she wouldn't find – absolute proof that Dot hadn't run away. Until that moment, she figured it just barely possible that Dot had gone to the Bahamas without telling her. She would even go so far as to think that Dot had betrayed her. She could almost believe that her lover and mentor had taken off for good, getting a day or two jump on her, leaving her holding the bag for everything they had done together.

But here was the evidence that it wasn't so.

In the drawer were stacks of bills, unmarked, in no sequence, and in different denominations. She counted them in a hurry, knowing before she started that there would be just over ninety-eight thousand dollars there – a little less than one-tenth of the money that was already waiting down in the Caribbean. Now the ninety-eight thousand was in the trunk of her car. On the surface, she was enjoying a Christmas party at her father's house. Everything was fine. But she had the sneaking suspicion that Dot was not fine, and soon, nothing would be fine ever again.

She opened the bathroom door and was startled to see her father standing there. Briefly, she flashed to the scene of her father pulling to the curb beside her one cold morning long ago, as she walked to school with her friends. He had a look on his face, one that she had never seen before. As an adult she would define that look, when she saw it on the faces of others, as *stricken*. Her father was about to bring her into the car and announce to her that her mother was dead.

'Everything all right, Lyd?' he said now. 'It's not like you to hide upstairs by yourself for so long.'

A wave of love passed through her for this man who had done everything for her when her mother died, had put his life on hold so that she could grow up to become the woman she was now. She wondered – if he found out what kind of woman that was, would he feel that it had been worth it?

She tried on a smile and decided it just might pass for real.

'Everything's great,' she said. 'Must have had something that didn't agree with me, that's all.'

Dick drove over to Astoria, to his parents' apartment, the plastic sheet that covered his broken window flapping in the breeze. It was loud, like the wings of a duck slapping the water at takeoff.

The day was cold and sunny. They had cleared the snow from the highway and there was hardly anyone on the road. Dick had smoked a nice pile of dope – two fat joints back to back – and had climbed neatly up and over that nasty hangover. He felt much better. The view to his left was of Manhattan. About a mile away, the massive skyscrapers towered over the rest of the city. There were millions of windows over there and they twinkled like jewels in the sun.

With the view and the nice day and the good dope, Dick felt almost like he didn't have a murdered corpse in the trunk of his car, the car he was driving right at this moment. He turned on the radio, pumped the volume way up to drown out the sound of the window, and surprised himself by singing along to a couple of the tunes. A cop pulled up alongside of him in the passing lane. The cop looked at that flapping window, then looked at Dick.

For a long time, people in the drug business had told Dick that when he saw a cop on the road, he should adopt a look of *studied nonchalance*. Fat Sam used to put it like this: 'You pull up on a cop at a stoplight. The cop is there, you're there, and you both know it. You glance over at the cop, not too fast, not too slow. The cop looks at you, you look at him and, ever so slowly, you see nothing of interest there, so you look back at the road ahead. The cop is not important to you – you have other things on your mind.'

But studied nonchalance, as a strategy, had a lot of pitfalls. For one, you couldn't look away too fast or too slow. Too fast, and you're guilty of something. You got a big neon 'GUILT' sign flashing over your head. Too slow, and now you're *staring* at the cop. Cops are like apes. In the primitive cop mind, you're challenging the cop. You don't want to challenge a cop when you're carrying a load in your trunk. Finally, studied nonchalance was a strategy that the cops had seen too many times. Cops caught on to things. They would look at you and think: People are not neutral about cops. This guy is pretending it doesn't bother him to have me here.

So Dick had evolved a better strategy. He had evolved *ownership*. The way he worked it, he would look right at the cop in his cruiser. He wouldn't act bored by the cop. Instead, he would nod to him. He'd smile. He was glad the cop was there. This cop – he worked for Dick. He was keeping Dick's kids safe, he was keeping Dick's wife safe. He was the reason Dick could sleep at night and go out and make a living in the daytime. Dick and this cop were on the same team. Dick paid the cop's salary. In a subtle way, Dick owned this cop. It was a strategy that had never failed.

So now, with a broken window, plastic flapping in the cold air, and body in his trunk, he looked at the cop, shrugged and smiled. The cop smiled back, hit the gas, and a few moments later, was a thousand yards ahead.

When the cop was gone, Dick drifted along, right at the speed limit. He began thinking about his friend Block. Kevin Blockovich, his best friend from high school, who said he was going to stop by today – drop in for a little Christmas hello. At first Dick didn't explore how Block could maybe help him with his problem, but thought about the man himself, the lines in his face and the large, powerful carriage of his body. Block chewed gum. As far as Dick knew, he always chewed gum. His massive iron jaws had been working some piece of gum or another since they were kids, possibly since Block had emerged from the womb, bent on world domination.

'So, we got this auto body parts place here and it runs twenty-four hours a day,' Block said on Dick's first day back in New York. 'During the daylight hours, we do repair jobs for regular people, mufflers, wheel alignments, whatever. It makes everything look real and it pays for itself, so what the hell? At night, I got a crew of Puerto Rican kids that go out and boost cars, bring 'em back in and pull 'em apart until dawn. Then we ship the parts to a warehouse I got up in Westchester. We distribute the parts all over the country from there. It's grown a lot over the last few years. Orders coming in over the computer, the whole works.'

They were sitting in Block's tiny office, upstairs from a garage called 'Ace Foreign Service', along Broadway in Long Island City, just over the Fifty-Ninth Street Bridge from Manhattan. Broadway was a commercial zone, with a lot of auto body shops, and small factories and warehouses. The neighborhood was densely packed with people, and Broadway itself sat underneath an elevated subway line, so everything was in shadow even in the middle of the day. Every once in a while, a subway train rumbled overhead, filling the world with the shriek of metal on metal and the heavy groans of the train itself.

The office walls were covered in dark brown paneling, making the place seem forever trapped in 1974. It was late summer and the heat was stifling. Block's huge bulk rebelled against the size of the office. If he wanted, it seemed he could rip the walls down around him and smash the cheap furniture to splinters.

'I don't really see you boosting cars, to be honest. It's mostly younger guys – kids – do that stuff for me. Late nights. Grunt work. Plus you need a lot of technical know-how. These kids, all they think about is cars. You know?'

'Sure,' Dick said. 'I understand.'

Block went on, 'But we do have some bookmaking. Also some loans. We can always use a big guy to make collections. I'm sure you could move up in that side of the business. I got an old-timer wants to retire next year and head down to Florida, and you could buy his book if you want. Runs the thing out of a coffee shop in Flushing. You get a piece of the video poker in the back room. Maybe once a month he runs a card game back there. I let him have it. I pretend I don't know about it and he pretends he doesn't know that I know.' Block smiled. 'You'll like this guy. Real old school. He actually gets up and sells coffee and bagels to the subway crowd in the morning.'

'Block,' Dick said.

'Yeah?'

'That's not what I came to you for. I'm really just looking for a good place to crash until I get on my feet.'

'A place to crash?'

'Yeah.'

Block's face creased. 'What's that mean? Crash?'

'It means just to sleep. To eat. To live. I'm planning to get a legit job this time around. You know, like in an office? I took up typing in jail.'

Block's head cranked around to look at the wall behind him. For a second, Dick thought his head might twist off his shoulders altogether. Then Block turned back and peered under the desk. He glanced at the lamp, looking for a microphone or hidden camera, no doubt.

'What?' He smiled like maybe Dick was trying to put some kind of joke over.

'Yeah. I'm good at it. I can type ninety words a minute with hardly any mistakes. I came home here to get a job and become like a normal person.'

Block's face dropped. His shoulders sagged. 'Let me get this straight. You want to get a job? You want to type?'

'That's right.'

'Dick, you're thirty-five years old. I think your chance to go straight passed a long time ago.'

'Hey, look. If you don't want to help me, that's cool too.'

Block put his hands in the air as if this was a stickup. 'No, no, no. I do want to help you. Listen. Personally, I think it's a bad idea. But if you want to play it straight, if you want to see where that gets you, I think I've got the perfect thing.'

They drove out to Brooklyn in Block's white Lincoln Town Car. They took the Brooklyn-Queens Expressway and the road was choked with bumper-to-bumper traffic. In front of them, all around them, the heat radiated off the other cars. They had the windows up and the air conditioning cranking.

'Is this not a nice car?' Block said, patting the dash. 'It's like driving a couch. You smell that? You smell that leather? Brand new. I don't care what anybody says, big American-made cars are still the way to go when you want to ride in comfort and style. Gas prices? Who gives a fuck?'

They drove to a huge old factory building. The neighborhood was ugly, low-slung and gritty with soot. Block parked the car in front of the loading dock, took out a key and they went inside. The front door opened up on a long hallway with several doors on either side.

'I bought this building for a song about four years ago,' Block said as he fumbled with his keys. 'I don't know why I bought it, I just did. Maybe I thought I was going to use it as a warehouse, move some merchandise through here. Anyway, as it turned out, a whole better scam appeared out of nowhere as soon as I got the place. I had some Jamaican guys throw up some drywall here and there, cut the place up into separate areas. Then I ran some plumbing and electricity into each one, and I rent them out as apartments.'

'Apartments? Who would want to live here?' The place was ancient, crumbling, dusty. God only knew what they used to make in there. Chemicals, probably. Glue. The atomic bomb.

'Artists, my friend,' Block went on. 'Artists want to live here. We are exactly two miles across the East River from SoHo and Greenwich Village. The rents over there are too high for these kids, so they move over here. Six blocks north of here, on the other side of Metropolitan Avenue? It's already turning into a second Greenwich Village. Three years ago, it was still like it is here. Now, forget about it. The stockbrokers are moving in and pushing the artists down here, into Bushwick, into Bed Stuy. A place like this? They'd turn it into a fucking showpiece. Meanwhile, the starving artists love my building just how it is. The apartments are big, the ceilings are high, and they can fuck the place up as much as they want. It can't get much worse than it is. They can do their oil paintings and their metallic sculptures here, use all kinds of solvents and poisons, and nobody bothers them. They don't even have to take the subway into Manhattan. Half the time, they ride their fucking bicycles over the Williamsburg Bridge. It's right there, a hundred yards from the door. It's great for them here, and it's great for me. This place is making way more money for me than it would have as a warehouse – and I can do even better. I've done the math. I can clear six figures a year here, as soon as I nail one last item into place.'

Dick looked around, the information hitting him like a poke in the ribs. Who would see the money in this place? If someone had offered to give him this building free of charge, he wouldn't have taken it. But Block had seen the potential.

'What item is that?'

'You,' Block said as he found the right key and opened the door. 'I need you to collect the rent.' They walked into an open space with a ceiling that was probably fifteen or twenty feet in the air. There was no rug on the floor, only cement floors stretching a good twenty or thirty yards away, to windows that were at least eight feet high and caked with grime. Since they were on the third floor, there could be a pretty good view of the street below. Outside the windows was a fire escape that seemed to wrap around the entire building.

'Why?' Dick said. 'Is there some kind of problem?'

Block shrugged. 'For one thing, I hate driving down here with all that traffic. For another thing, these kids are always just scraping by, you know? There's always five or six people staying in any one of these apartments. I come down here or I send a guy down here, it seems like whoever is on the lease is never home. Or if they are home, they want to give me a check from their mom for half the rent, plus a couple of hundred-dollar bills they got from somewhere, and assorted loose change they pulled out from between the pillows on the couch. All of which adds up to six hundred dollars, and they want to know if I need any work done around the house, or can they play the guitar at my kid's birthday party in exchange for the other four. You know what I mean? Nothing but headaches.'

'So you want me to come down and collect the rent?'

'Better than that. I want to make you the super. Sure, you collect the rent every month. You turn all the cash and coins and recyclable bottles and jewelry and pottery and everything else into checks, and send them to me. If somebody has a problem, you take care of it. You know, if something breaks, you fix it. You watch over my investment here.'

'And what do I get?'

'You get this vacant apartment free of charge and I'll pay you a little something on top of that. I don't know, how's a thousand a month sound? You'd be doing me a solid. Basically, for the cost of two apartments down here, I get rid of all my problems. At least in this building.'

Dick thought about it for ten seconds. There wasn't much to think about. Free rent and a thousand bucks a month, in addition to any straight job he might get.

Still, he hesitated. 'I don't know much about fixing things.'

Block nodded. 'All the better. The kids probably won't bother you too much.'

'Sold,' Dick said.

Big Kevin Blockovich made his Christmas rounds.

For a man like Block, Christmas Day was a busy one. Block gave his family all day on Christmas Eve, then the morning on Christmas Day. Diana and Kevin, Jr – Little Block – would wake at dawn and open their presents. He and Trish would preside over the spectacle. By noon, Trish was getting the kids ready to go their grandparents' house, and Block was out the door. Block had many friends and associates, and Christmas was the day when he went to see them.

He drove the Lincoln along the Van Wyck Expressway, near Jamaica Bay. The sky was clear and blue, and traffic was light. Just ahead of him, a plane came in low toward Kennedy Airport.

Block was a lucky man. Was it luck? Was it really luck? Sometimes he wondered about that. At thirty-five, he had more than eight million dollars. He had scams coming out his ears, making him more money all the time, even while he slept. He had a wife and two great kids, and a house in Oyster Bay that he never would have imagined himself in while growing up. He also had a two-bedroom condo down in Sea Bright, on the Jersey Shore, right across from the beach and just a hop, skip and a jump down the Garden State Parkway, if he caught the traffic right.

That condo was becoming his favorite place in the world. He laughed, the short bark of a pit bull. He had mentioned the condo to Dick Miller when he first set Dick up in the Williamsburg building.

'If you can't get me at the office, and you can't get me on the cell, and you really need to talk to me – I mean if the building burns down or the Arabs put anthrax in the ventilation system – you can try me at this number down in Jersey.'

Dick looked at the paper. 'Yeah? What is it?'

'It's an apartment. On the beach.'

'What do you do, run down there with the wife to get away?'

'No, I don't. As a matter of fact, if you ever talk to Trish, do me a favor and don't mention the apartment. She doesn't know anything about it.'

Dick smiled, but the smile looked pained. He poked Block with one finger. 'Hey, Block. What do you got, a little love nest down there?'

'Look, Dick, Trish and I have an understanding. OK? We have a lot of money. She has a nice life, two great kids. She don't have to work, she's very comfortable. People are starving in this world, you know what I'm saying? She could be worse off. But I'm a man and I have needs, and Trish doesn't always meet those needs, so . . .'

'So you look for it somewhere else.'

'You know what I'm saying. Trish doesn't ask a lot of questions, and I don't volunteer a lot of information. We keep it at that.'

Dick had given him a look then, a look that implied judgment. OK. Dick could judge him. It wasn't going to stop him from doing what he wanted.

Block sighed heavily. Dick fucking Miller. The cat that came back. It was too easy to just forget about the early days sometimes. The truth was, the house, the cars, the money, the little empire Block was building – in a sense, he owed the whole goddamn thing to Dick.

Dick's father was small.

The smiling man who opened the door was stooped over to begin with. But since Dick had returned to New York, gravity seemed to be pulling his old man closer to the ground with each passing month. Richard Miller the First had worked in a print shop for forty years, operating a press all that time. He almost never missed a day. It was hard manual labor and it left him bent over. His body looked like a question mark. At an early age, Dick had taken a look at this honest man – this father of his who had worked for years and played it straight the way the system demanded – and he had said, no thanks, not me.

Now, his father looked up at him. 'Hi, Dick. Nice-looking face you got there. Lose a fight with the pavement?'

Dick touched his face. He had forgotten what kind of impact it might have on his family. He had been popping painkillers more or less constantly for twenty-four hours. That and the pot had kept him numb.

'Yeah, well . . .'

'Nah. Never mind. You look great. Gives you character.'

Dick stepped inside the apartment. His father held his hand out and Dick pumped it once. The front door opened directly into the living room. Dick surveyed the scene before saying anything. There was a tall, fat Christmas tree in one corner. It was decorated garishly with multi-colored glass bulbs and yellow garlands and icicles, along with a profusion of candy canes and plastic odds and ends. There were strings of multicolored lights, all blinking at different times. Perched at the top was an angel, whose head was blinking. At the bottom of the tree was a manger scene, also with lights, and a train rumbling around a track, all strung with lights, lights, lights. The train had a white headlight, and every few moments, it whistled as it passed. There were dozens of gifts wrapped and piled under the tree.

The gifts puzzled Dick. His parents didn't know that many people.

Either way, the thing was a masterpiece. It reminded Dick of Las Vegas. He put his packages down with the others, the brightly decorated, red-ribboned ones. On a whim, he picked one up to see if he could find a name on it. Of course. It was as light as a feather. He picked up another one and found the same thing. All of the packages were empty. They were decorations. His mother had made them in her spare time. They were supposed to give the place more of a holiday air.

Dick went into the kitchen and was momentarily alarmed by the size of his mom. She was even smaller than his dad. How had these people spawned a man the size of Dick Miller? Dick hadn't seen his mom since Thanksgiving, and she had shrunk again. Both his parents were in their mid-seventies and every time he saw them they seemed to have gotten smaller and smaller. Soon they would disappear altogether.

'Hi, honey,' she started, and then stopped. 'My God, what happened to your face? Oh my God.' She raised her voice as she ran her hands along his cheekbones. 'Rich, come and take a look at this.'

'Merry Christmas,' Dick said.

'I saw it,' his father called from the other room. 'Terrific. At least he's not back in jail. At least he's still alive.'

His mother sighed. 'You've been fighting again, haven't you?'

'Well,' Dick said, 'you know how it is.' The whole face thing had slipped his mind. He had no answer planned.

'My little adventurer,' she said.

They had the typical family dinner. Dick's father was morose and picked at his food. He talked about the Democratic Party and how they had handed the country away to a bunch of right-wing maniacs and religious fanatics. The more he talked, the more morose he became. In stark contrast, Dick's mother smiled a lot and peppered Dick with questions about his job. She didn't bother to listen to the answers. Instead, she said, 'Isn't that wonderful?' She said it whenever she got the chance, and she seemed to mean it. Everything was swell.

Not for the first time, Dick wondered what meds she was taking. He looked around the table. His father stared at his plate. His mother smiled like a saint. Very little was said. They were waiting for Block to arrive. It was unspoken, but it was there. They were waiting for the life of the party, the boy from the neighborhood who had become a big success in life – the businessman, the one who had never gone to prison. An awkward silence spun out through time.

The downstairs buzzer sounded.

They all looked at each other.

'He said he was going to come,' Dick's mom said. She pointed at Dick. 'Your friend Block always keeps his word.'

Dick went to the intercom.

'Block?'

'Yeah, Dick. It's me.'

Dick buzzed the big man in.

Lydia's Christmas dinner was almost over.

Around the dinner table, the last stragglers still laughed and joked. The wine bottle went around another time, then another. Then the bottle was empty and a new one went around. Aunt Sylvia was slurring her speech. Uncle Ted smoked a cigar in the house, practically daring someone to send a man his age outside. Lydia did what she could to follow along. She ate apple pie and drank coffee. She smiled when everyone laughed. She stared at each new speaker as if she were paying attention. But she wasn't paying attention. She was thinking about money. A lot of money.

The smuggling worked exactly as Dot had said it would. They did it with a technique Dot called the Twin Bag Trick. Lydia had no idea where Dot had learned it.

'I have my ways,' Dot said when Lydia asked.

The first time, they tried it with thirty thousand in cash. The money had been diverted from the accounts of Feldman Real Estate, where Dot was the boss and Lydia was her right hand. Feldman owned more than two thousand rental apartments in the City of New York. Old Jack Feldman was so rich he would never miss thirty thousand dollars – he wrote donation checks for more than that to the Coney Island Aquarium and the Brooklyn Museum of Art.

Three hundred bills, in the denomination of one hundred dollars each, were stuffed in a long, sealed manila envelope, then folded into one of the legs of a pair of new blue jeans, size twelve. The jeans were packed in a nondescript black suitcase, fastened with stainless-steel latches, and packed with more brand-new women's clothes, all size twelve, along with some toiletry items. Dot, size six, packed that suitcase herself, wearing Playtex Living Gloves the whole time she did it. With a shoe, she rubbed a small scuff mark into the suitcase. Then she took another suitcase – an exact duplicate of the one with the money – and packed her own belongings into it, this time without the gloves. The second suitcase had her fingerprints all over it.

Dot and Lydia rode the same plane from La Guardia down to the Bahamas. Lydia sat several rows behind Dot. At Nassau Airport, Dot picked up the scuffed suitcase from the carousel. At Customs, if they asked her to open the suitcase, she would open it away from herself, with the lid blocking her view. She wouldn't be able to see what the Customs agent was doing. While the agent looked through the bag, she would fiddle around with the rest of her stuff – paying no attention to the agent at all. If the agent found the envelope and opened it, Dot, ever the actress, could still claim it wasn't hers. She had never seen the suitcase before in her life. Look at these clothes. They would never fit her. *That* must be her suitcase – the one still running around on the carousel over there. She'd picked up this bag by mistake.

If Dot made it through Customs, she would go in the first ladies' room she saw and punch in Lydia's number on her cellphone. Lydia's phone, set to vibrate, would alert her that Dot was through. Lydia, standing in the crowd by the carousel, would pick up the remaining bag, the bag with Dot's real belongings.

Beautiful, healthy, leggy Dot. Everybody's all-American. The Customs agent was too busy ogling her to look inside her bags. Lydia stood by the carousel for no more than ten minutes before her phone vibrated against her leg. It was illegal to leave the United States with more than ten thousand dollars in undeclared cash, and they had just entered the Bahamas with three times that amount.

Lydia paced through the crowded airport lobby, passing a lack-luster calypso band going through the motions for the tourists. She joined Dot in front of the airport entrance, near the cabstand. As she left the terminal, the hot wind hit her like a blast from a furnace. A dark, heavyset cab driver took their identical bags and put them in the trunk of his Toyota.

Dot, her loosened hair blowing in the breeze, her eyes hidden behind reflector sunglasses, leaned in close to Lydia. 'Next time we'll bring twice as much.'

Two hours had passed since Block had shown up at the door. It was after the wine, the dessert and coffee, after all the small talk and the catching up, and Block was getting ready to leave. He had to get back to his wife and kids, so he said. Dick's parents were cleaning in the kitchen, and Dick pulled Block aside.

'Block.'

'Yeah, Dick?' Block may have been a little drunk.

Dick hesitated to go on. 'Ah, I've got a problem.'

'Something with the building?'

'No, the building's going fine.'

Block shrugged. 'Something else, then. Anything I can help you with?'

'Yeah, I think maybe you can.'

Block winked. His eyes glinted. He grinned. Sure, he was a little bit gone on Christmas cheer. 'Dick, you know I'm ready to help you any way I can.'

Dick grinned back. 'I've got a body on my hands.'

'A stiff?'

Dick nodded. 'Uh-huh.' The smile felt pasted on now, like soon it might crack and fall sideways onto the floor.

'Did you kill it?'

'I don't know.'

'One of those, eh? Does it have anything to do with the way your face looks?'

'I think so, yeah. Probably so.'

Block waved his hands. 'OK, let's not talk about it here.' He was still smiling. Dick figured the two of them looked like a couple of guys chatting about something pretty amusing. 'Not with your mother and father around. Maybe I could come to your place? Sunday night, say? I got a busy weekend – the wife has me returning gifts tomorrow. It's a family tradition. If I break the tradition, then it looks funny, right? Situation like this, you don't want anything to look funny. Will it keep that long?'

Dick thought for just a second or two. He gestured to the frost that obscured the view from the living-room windows. 'It's on ice. I think it'll keep.'

'Sunday then.'

With that agreement made, Block went in the kitchen and said his goodbyes. Later, when it was Dick's turn to leave, his mother reached way up to kiss him on the cheek. Her body had to stretch and elongate in order to accomplish the task. It seemed to take several minutes for her lips to reach him.

'Please take care of yourself,' she said.

Nestor lay awake on the sofa in his suite, sipping a rum and Coke and smoking a cigarette. It was dark in there, his curtains were drawn aside, and he gazed out his window at the glittering neon of Times Square.

He sighed. The view would normally please him, but now he took no joy in it. Across from him, a quarter of a mile away, a music video played ten stories high – scenes flashed and jumped, nearly naked women, muscular men, sleek expensive cars racing through dark, empty streets. It made very little sense at all. As soon as it ended, Santa Claus appeared, waving and smiling and flying through the night sky behind a line of reindeer.

There was no Christmas for Nestor. Ghosts didn't get a Christmas. In a week, the famous ball would drop right outside his windows, ringing in the New Year. But ghosts didn't get a New Year either. Instead, they got to brood alone in opulent hotel suites above Times Square, remembering their own death in the high jungle. The first time Nestor had died was when he was just eighteen years old, a conscript in the army, fighting the FARC guerrillas in the eastern jungles of his homeland.

That time, it seemed he had been shot in the head. In fact, it didn't seem so. It had happened. Everyone had seen it. Everyone said so. In a skirmish, in the hot, sweaty confusion, he had lost his helmet and died. He remembered how, moments before, they had been moving slowly uphill along a steep path through the underbrush. A squad of them, the urban poor, press-ganged into service straight from the streets of Bogotá and Medellín and airlifted into the wilderness. Nine thousand feet above sea level, and the heat was incredible. The air was like the heavy sack that Nestor carried on his back. Dark clouds lowered in the sky. Lightning flashed and a moment later, thunder rolled. Nestor could feel the rumble in the air.

His comrade in arms, his *compañero* Miguel, was talking. He always talked when they went on these marches. These insane, suicidal, homicidal marches through the bush, with Miguel the cynic talking, talking, talking as if he didn't need to save his breath for yet another step, yet another kilometer.

'We are not heroes,' Miguel said. 'No. Don't fool yourselves. We are not heroes and the enemy are not heroes.'

'We are cowards, then?' someone in the group said. A few men laughed at the thought of it – teenagers who had already lived through battle after battle.

'No. Surely not cowards. We are brave, and so are our enemies. But we fight, and we die, not for any noble idea, and neither do they.

71

We fight to see who controls the narco traffic to the North Americans. If we win, the fascists control the drugs. If we lose, the communists control the drugs. I ask you – why do you care who controls the drugs? Will you see any of that money? Will you experience any happiness from it?'

Miguel half turned, looking along the line of men behind him.

An instant later, he was gone.

His voice had tipped off the guerrillas to their approach. Nestor knew this because Miguel was the first one to die. The first shot, before it even rang out, pierced his face. He didn't have time to look shocked. One second he was there, talking as always, the next second there was a crater where his smiling face had just been, and then his body was on the ground and Nestor could hear the muffled crackle of gunfire through the damping effect of the heavy air. The gunfire came from their right.

As Nestor turned, the man behind him fired his weapon. The gun blast went off a hand's width from Nestor's ear. Instantly Nestor was deaf to the sounds around him. Instead, there was only a ringing sensation, very loud. The noise of it would drive him mad. The other men were down in the mud, many of them not shooting, not even looking up. Nestor was on his knees. He knew he should get down into the mud, below the mud, he should crawl to the center of the earth. But he was moving too slow. His helmet was gone. Where was his helmet? Why was he moving so slow?

Madre de Dios, he thought. Mother of God. Help me.

Silent bullets flew by all around him. He could feel their breeze.

He felt something very gentle. A soft impact, a push. A light tap directly in the center of his forehead.

A moment later a tone sounded. It was a musical note, very clear, almost like someone had tapped a spoon on a glass bowl. The pleasing sound went on and on, reverberating but not growing any weaker.

Then Nestor hovered above his body, above the skirmish, perhaps two stories in the air. Ernesto, the medic, crawled like a worm toward Nestor's limp body. Gunfire crackled and men shouted. From this height, it seemed like a children's game. Somehow, he knew the game was nearly finished – the guerrillas were only four men, and soon they would fade back into the forest. Mission accomplished, they had killed three of the troops, not counting Nestor. Harassment, not victory, was their goal today. Nestor knew this without seeing it – much of the battle was obscured by the low jungle canopy. He simply knew.

He turned and a tunnel was there. He felt drawn to the tunnel. The battle was still below him but it no longer seemed very interesting. He entered the tunnel and moved through it. The tunnel was dark but he felt no fear. At the far end, very far, was a tiny pinpoint of light. As he moved along, the light grew larger and brighter. There was a room at the end of the tunnel and in the room was that bright light. He heard a voice – a voice from his childhood. His little grandmother – his *abuelita* – was calling to him.

At the threshold, the light was so bright that he could see nothing. Again she called. He stepped into the light. There were figures here, shapes. They seemed to be made of the light itself. They were part of the light and not part of it. Then he saw his beloved grandmother. She was not the woman he remembered, and at the same time, she was. Her appearance had changed. She was young and she stood with a young man, his grandfather, a man Nestor had never met.

'Hello, *abuelo*,' he wanted to say to this man, but there was no need to speak.

They smiled and a feeling came to Nestor, one he had never experienced. It was a feeling of calm, of understanding, of acceptance. There was no need to worry. About anything. These things that had bothered him for so long – his anger, his poverty, his feelings of powerlessness – they were of no consequence.

After a moment, it became clear to him that it was not yet his time. He was supposed to go back. Going back seemed natural and right. He moved through the tunnel, away from the light and an instant later he was above the battleground again. There was a terrible sense that he was late, that it was important he reach the body before Ernesto did. The body pulled him and as he approached, he saw it. It was a dead thing, like a dog by the side of the road. It frightened him. He didn't want to re-enter it.

With instant knowledge, he understood that re-entering would be like jumping into a pool of cold water. There was no more time. He must go now. He leaped and splashed through a barrier, like a thin crust of ice on a lake in winter.

He opened his eyes and shivered from the lingering cold, which retreated before the oppressive heat of the jungle. He was lying on the ground, looking up at the sky through the tangled canopy of the trees. The leaves dripped with moisture. Ernesto kneeled nearby, his face dirty and sweaty, his bright eyes gazing down at Nestor. Ernesto had the eyes of a deer.

Suddenly Nestor knew – in the same way he had known everything else – many things about Ernesto. He knew that Ernesto's body had not yet known a woman. He knew that Ernesto's family had come from Cuba and had named the boy for the great author Hemingway. He knew that Ernesto would survive this war, attend school and become a doctor. He knew that Ernesto would live to bounce tiny grandchildren on his knee. But this was the last message about Ernesto that Nestor received. The feeling, the knowing, had already faded.

'Am I dead?' Nestor said.

'I thought you were. I thought for sure you must be. I saw you shot in the head. But now it appears you were not.'

'Am I hurt?'

'No.'

'Where did the bullet go?'

The young medic shrugged. 'There is no bullet.'

Then Ernesto was gone. Other men were screaming and dying and Ernesto's responsibility was to those men.

Nestor had stayed on his back for a long time that day, much like he was doing now. He had stared at the sky as he now stared at the ceiling. The high jungle was the first time he had died – a young man fighting for the lies told by old men. He reflected that, all things considered, the first death was a good one. A pleasant death.

He sipped his rum and Coke.

The second death was not nearly so pleasant.

3
THE JOCK BASTARD

Dick lay in bed, somewhere between asleep and awake, somewhere between alive and dead, reliving past glory.

Back in San Francisco, Dick Miller was like the mailman – every day, rain or shine, he made his rounds. No. He was more consistent, more predictable than the mail. He was like the sun, the planets, the stars. At the same time every morning, eleven o'clock, he stopped at the same health food restaurant and ordered the same thing. Carrot juice. On an empty stomach. Dick believed that the only way to drink carrot juice was on an empty stomach. The vitamins surged to the bloodstream that way – nothing impeding them. Dick had only tried cocaine a few times, but he believed the carrot juice was a better energy rush. It certainly lasted longer.

By lunchtime, he was downtown in the Financial District when the suits came out of the brokerage houses. The district was home to the big money – Wells Fargo Bank, Charles Schwab, Barclays, the Bank of California, even the Twelfth District of the United States Federal Reserve. And Dick was the medicine man to the tribe. He was like one of the hot-dog guys, except what he was selling was better than hot dogs. He'd get there right around noon and cool his heels for a little while in the shadow of the Bank of America building, or the Transamerica Pyramid. He might pace Montgomery Street or Market Street, then sit on a bench, watching the pigeons peck their way back and forth.

The suit people would exit the buildings and come right to him. They needed something to take the edge off their day and he'd give it to them – consistently high-quality weed. It worked like this: they'd sit next to him, eating their sandwiches or whatever, never quite looking his way. A hundred dollars would suddenly appear on the bench between them and he'd pick it up. Into his pocket. Then a clear plastic bag would appear and they'd pick it up. Into their briefcase or pocket book. Hundred-dollar eighths for the high-rent crowd – sinsemilla straight off the plane from British Columbia, high THC content, mixed with a little local flavor to fill out the bag. Dick scraped ten-eighths out of each and every ounce. His customers could buy their eighths elsewhere in the city for fifty or sixty dollars, maybe less. *Probably less.* But with Dick, they knew they were getting quality, and quality was worth the price. Peace of mind was worth the price. What was a hundred-dollar bill to a twenty-seven-year-old kid who cleared half a mil last year? It was nothing compared to the embarrassment of buying a beat bag from some unwashed, half-price hippie in Haight-Ashbury. Hundred-dollar eighths? It was a fucking bargain. After each customer walked away, a few minutes would pass, and another would sit down. There was no lack of demand.

Every day, 1.30 p.m., after he finished serving the lunch crowd, Dick stopped in at Little Dan's Vegetarian for a Veggie Abdullah sandwich with feta cheese. Maybe once a week he would order the grilled portabella or falafel instead. Then there were the afternoon rounds to make. There were the mind workers to minister to – the people who worked on computers right out of their apartments or houses, or in small three- or four-person offices. Designers, architects, programmers, whatever. They were a pretty high-rent crowd too. More laid back than the bankers and brokers, for sure, but also willing and able to part with a hundred dollars for a high-quality high. Dick liked them. But Dick liked both groups. When it came right down to it, Dick liked people, especially people who had the money to pay for what he was selling. The bottom line? You couldn't be in Dick's line of work if you weren't a people person. Dick was a people person. Dick was hot shit, and people knew it. Dick was going places.

First, he was going to jail. Then, after serving exactly half of a five-year sentence, he was going home to New York. He remembered those first days out of prison, wandering San Francisco like a ghost, as nostalgia for the Big Apple grew quietly in his mind. He remembered thinking: Home is where they let you start over.

'Watch this guy Miller,' Andrew said. 'He's a real jock bastard.'

'Gotcha,' Breeze said.

They trudged south along Bedford Avenue, through the frozen streets of Williamsburg. Saturday, the day after Christmas, temperature in the teens, steam swirling out of grates in the sidewalk, and the sidewalks themselves almost empty. Andrew had lived here the past eight years, up until just a few months ago. He had seen the neighborhood – north of Metropolitan Avenue – go from down in the mouth, rundown, all the way down, the barest trickle of money coming in, to what it was becoming now – ultra-hip, ultra-trendy, cutting edge, glittering, and whatever else the magazines chose to say about it this month. Yeah, he had been here the whole time and had ridden the wave. He loved this fucking neighborhood. He fucking loved it. One day, after all these problems were over, after people like Dot were put in their place for good and people like Nestor were ... neutralized, Andrew would move back here.

And soon they would be neutralized. Andrew had it all figured out now. This was about more than just avenging the wrongs done him by Dot, by Dick Miller and by Nestor Garcia. There was money at stake here, and more than just the paltry ten percent Dot had been paying him from the beginning, or the more acceptable twenty percent he had demanded of Dot just before she cut him off. There was real money at stake. Andrew would bet there must be more than a million dollars in tax-free cash stationed off the coast of Florida, and now he wanted it. If not all, then certainly half. That was Dot's punishment for playing hardball. Andrew was going to strip away her two protectors, and when they were gone, and Dot was helpless before him, he would give her the ultimatum – cut me in or you are going away for a long time.

Funny, though. At the moment, Dot already seemed to be gone. Sixty hours and she hadn't returned home. That wasn't like her. Andrew had that sinking feeling again – and the thought came to him, not for the first time, that his plan had already worked better than he had hoped. Instead of setting her formidable protectors against one another, he was afraid he had set at least one of them on her.

He pushed that thought away.

'He's a criminal. If you let him have even the slightest chance, he'll go berserk. So here's the deal. When we get to Miller's apartment, we see if Dot is there. If she is, great. We give her the message. We're still around and we want our money – we want what's coming to us. If Miller has beaten her up, we rescue her. We get her out of there. Even better. Now she owes us one, she's pathetic, and we still want our money.'

Breeze stopped walking. She stood under the torn awning of an old Polish butcher shop, shuttered now, surely soon to reopen as something fabulous and up-to-the-minute. 'You're worried about her, aren't you?'

Andrew took three more steps, stopped and then turned back. 'Am I worried about her?'

'Yeah. You act like she's . . . important to you.'

Andrew didn't want to have this discussion here, in public on a frozen street corner. He didn't want to have this discussion anywhere. 'She is important. She's important to us.' He pointed at Breeze with one gloved finger, then back at himself. 'You and me. She's sitting on a lot of money. And we're going to make it ours.'

'I'm not sure that's it.'

'Well, I am, so would you please come on?'

Breeze hesitated. Then, momentarily mollified, she began walking again. Andrew fell in step with her. He was half afraid that before this was over, he would end up dragging her along by a rope. 'If Miller gets out of line – and I mean the slightest bit – he makes the slightest move, you just let him have it. He's a big damn guy and I don't want him getting started.'

This time Breeze smiled. 'Are you afraid of him?'

'Hell, yes. I'm afraid of him. This guy is dangerous. In a game like this – hardball, this is hardball – it's no shame to be afraid of somebody. The best thing to do is admit you're afraid, admit it to yourself, then take steps to neutralize that person. So anytime you feel like giving him a blast, it's not too soon.'

'Gotcha, boss,' Breeze said. The cold air plumed from her red, red lips. 'He'll never know what hit him.'

Dick came in the room that first day with five other cons. They sat down to a row of old IBM Selectric typewriters. The screw guarding them sneered at the very idea – typing class in a state penitentiary. The teacher told them how to turn the machine on. He gave them each a sheet of paper and explained how to put it in the machine. He started to introduce the concept of touch-typing but by then Dick was already gone.

His fingers had a mind of their own and they flew across that keyboard, haltingly at first, but then with more and more speed and confidence. It was like a love affair that had been long interrupted.

'Miller!'

His fingers danced, and he wrote things without even thinking about them. He remembered, and he disappeared into the act of typing. He didn't even look at the keys – he looked at the words as they magically appeared on the paper. They came fast. Dick was a typing machine.

'Im in jail,' he typed, 'and I want to get out of jail and just get stoned and get some sex the only good thing about being here is typing on this sheet of paper'.

'Miller!'

In his mind, it was almost twenty years before, and he was sitting in a cheerless high-school classroom. The rows of the class were filled with seated kids peering down at their typewriters and pecking at keys one finger at a time. Clop, clop, pause, clop. But Dick was different. His fingers flew along in a blur. He stared at a Mimeograph to his right, reading the purple words there. He never even looked at the machine. His brain told his fingers the words and his fingers knew where to go. He was doing well in a class – typing class. He was going to get an A. He gazed up and out the window, his fingers flying on, finishing the three sentences he had just read, which he had no conscious memory of, but nevertheless were imprinted on his mind like a great neon sign. Outside, the sky was blue. Against the back-drop of the other buildings he saw a bird flying. It looped and soared. Dick was that bird.

'MILLER!'

He opened his eyes. It was Saturday, and he knew it wasn't a hang-over anymore. He had been sick since Thursday, and Wednesday night was still a blur. It's not a hangover after three days. Then it's sickness. He began his day by stumbling into the bathroom and vomiting. He crouched in front of the toilet, hands gripping the sides of the bowl. The convulsions racked his body, each one coming like an express train, harder and faster than the last. Between each series, he caught a glimpse of himself mirrored in the toilet water. It was not a flattering picture. The mirror was marred by chunks of his Christmas dinner.

Eventually, there was nothing left to give. He stayed there a while longer, just in case. It became a peaceful time, kneeling there, his head hanging above the bowl. He was awake, but no thoughts crossed his mind. There were just sensations, like the cold of the porcelain in his hands, the steam heat blasting from the radiator behind him, the nubs of the pink bathroom mat on the floor and the feeling of his abdominal muscles, which were already becoming sore from the workout they'd just had.

Dick stood up and left the bathroom. He needed to talk. Just to sit down with someone, start talking and see what came out. Maybe if he just started talking, the answer would flow out of him, the memories would come flooding back, and he could describe to the person sitting with him just how and why he had killed Dot. There were the photos, for one thing. He would start with the photos. If the cops got a load of those photos, it would be an open-and-shut case, wouldn't it? Shit. Might as well call up the precinct house now.

Someone banged on the front door.

Cops?

Dick rushed to the window. Nothing on the street. No police cruisers. No commando team on the fire escapes. He looked around the apartment. A vast empty space, shadows climbing the concrete walls – nothing incriminating in here.

The banging came again.

He went over to the door. There was no security peephole. Whoever was out there, he was going to have to deal with them. Oh, well.

He opened the door and a small young man stood there, with black glasses and a mop of hair like a surfer dude. It took Dick a minute to place him and, although he knew better, he entertained the thought that he was one of the kids from the building, come to pay his rent a few days early. But no, it was Andrew King – Dot had pointed him out before, this weird little creep who always seemed to be somewhere nearby, shadowing Dot. One warm day in the fall, he had parked a van across the street from them while they ate lunch at a little outdoor café in SoHo. When Dick crossed the street to talk to him, Andrew had peeled rubber getting out of there. Dick had the vague sense that Andrew had been taking photos just a moment before.

He had a girl with him now, a pretty girl with the fashion sense of a raver, a girl who could have easily lived in the building. Dick had met her somewhere, and recently, but that didn't mean anything. The kids came and went, and Dick had no idea who was living in what apartment at any given time. There was something about her, this girl, something different from last time, something he couldn't put his finger on.

He shook it out of his head. Shit. Whatever. He had seen her around.

'Andrew,' he said, 'how did you get in this building?'

Dick figured anybody could have let him in. Half of Williamsburg and at least ten percent of the East Village, not to mention smaller percentages of Bushwick, East New York, Bed Stuy, and DUMBO must have had keys to the building's front door.

Andrew smiled. 'I knocked on the door until somebody let me in. There's no bell downstairs.'

'What do you want?'

'What do you think I want? I want to see Dot. I know she's here.'

Inside Dick's head, air-raid sirens howled and raged. But he shook his head slowly, with a sad grin, as if Andrew was the simplest of simpletons.

'Dot's not here. We broke up weeks ago.'

'Don't bullshit me,' Andrew said. 'I want to speak to her.'

For a moment, it was almost as if Dot wasn't dead. It was almost as if she was here, and Dick was protecting her from having to talk to this creep. But Dot wasn't here in the apartment. She was outside, in the trunk of Dick's car.

Andrew tried to squeeze past Dick and into the apartment.

He was unbearable, this kid. He moved like an eel, trying to squirm his way into the middle of Dick's grief. Dick grabbed him. 'Look, you fucking gnat. You know everything about Dot. You're the one who follows her around everywhere. I'm sure you already know she's not here, so why don't you go look for her someplace else?'

Dick shoved him, and Andrew stumbled back a few steps. It gave Dick a feeling of great strength just doing that. Andrew was as light as air. He was one of those types who begged to be abused.

'Don't you dare push me.'

'Too late, I already did. And if you don't get the fuck out of my building right now, I'll take you in my apartment and throw you out the window.'

Dick grabbed him again. He got a good grip on the front of Andrew's jacket, and lifted him a couple inches off the floor. It was just that easy. Dick could pick this weasel right off the ground and hold him in the air.

Suddenly the girl was there. She hadn't said a word. She had faded into the background. Now she produced a small black canister from her oversized coat. It took Dick one precious second to realize what it was, one second too long. Mace. He released Andrew, but it was too late. Before he could turn his head, before his hands were free, she blasted him in the eyes. She got him good.

'Fuck you, Miller!' Andrew shouted. It was a roar of triumph, and it echoed through the corridor. 'Fuck you!'

The juice stung Dick's eyes and he stumbled back against the wall. He was blind. He sank to the ground, hands to his face. He had the urge to use his fingers as claws and tear his own eyes right out of his skull.

'Dot?' Andrew called. From the sound of it, he had gone into Dick's apartment. Dick didn't care right now. He crawled on the floor, panting like a dog. He couldn't breathe. The shit had gotten into his lungs. He gasped and gasped, and each breath came shallower than the last. His throat seemed to have swelled up. Nothing was passing through his windpipe.

A hand grasped him by the hair and pulled his head back. There was nothing Dick could do. He opened his eyes an eighth of an inch – he couldn't have opened them any more if he wanted to. He could just see a fuzzy outline of Andrew, crouching there. Andrew spit in Dick's face. Dick closed his eyes again. There was no fight in him at all. The mace worked like magic.

'People who fuck with me pay the penalty, OK? That's what you're learning here today. I'll consider this the down payment.'

Dick opened his eyes again and the girl was there, still silent, looking down at Dick like a scientist might look down at a lab rat. She smiled, and it was a pretty smile. More than anything, she looked innocent. Then she blasted him with the mace again, all over his face.

'Oh, wow. I really got him that time.' It was the first thing she had said.

Dick grunted. He groaned. He rolled around on the floor like a dog. He sucked in air, but didn't get any oxygen. This went on for a moment and then he must have passed out. When he came back, he felt a little better. Andrew and the girl were still there. Their feet and the bottoms of their legs were right in front of Dick's face.

Dick gasped. The words came slowly. He worked hard for each one. 'I'm going to get you for this.'

Andrew laughed, then gave Dick a kick in the mid-section. It didn't hurt at all. 'Look at you,' he said. 'You're not going to get anybody.'

Andrew started to walk away. Dick could hear him open the door to the stairwell. 'Hey,' he called just before he and the girl went down. 'Tell Dot I'm looking for her.'

Dick started inching toward the door to his apartment.

It was amazing the things you could do.

Night had come again, and Breeze lay awake far past midnight, Andrew sleeping beside her. She was celebrating, in a sense, the way they had put Dick Miller down today. She was nude, and light from the street outside cut across her body. The bars on the window made it look like she had stripes, like a tiger. It was the only light in the room, besides the red glowing digital numbers on the clock. It was toasty warm in Andrew's apartment, even with the window open a crack, and she liked the way that made her feel languid and relaxed. She had a Scotch on the rocks on the bed table beside her, the ice slowly melting. The drink helped give her that relaxed, sexy, liquid feeling.

She stretched out to her full height. She felt like a cat. If she ever changed her name again, she would change it to Cat. Or maybe Kat. That's what she was – an alley Kat. And this nice person had brought her in from the cold. But he'd better watch out, because he might get scratched.

She reached onto the table and picked up her lighter and her pack of cigarettes. The smokes were Lucky Strikes, nothing exciting there. The lighter was a gun. Somebody had given it to her a while back. Some junkie? Some freak? She couldn't remember and it didn't matter. She liked that lighter. She remembered how this forgotten person had told her how the gun was made to look like a two-shot derringer. Everything about it was the gun – the same size, everything. Except pull the trigger and it didn't shoot, it just had a flame that came out of the top of the barrel all the way at the end. It was neat. She pulled the trigger now and sparked a light for the Lucky.

Then she pointed the gun at Andrew's sleeping head.

She enjoyed the way she had power over him. Andrew was thin, but he worked out a lot and he had a good body. Better than Henry, for sure. Andrew was gentler than Henry. And Andrew wasn't quite as much of an asshole as Henry. Funny to think of it this way, but it was almost like being with a woman, being with Andrew. But you know? Andrew was hardly a prince. He had let Henry smack her a couple of times, had *witnessed it*, and said nothing. He also had a double standard about Dot. He wanted revenge on Dot, or so he claimed. But he didn't really want to hurt Dot. At the same time, he was happy to have ol' Breeze go up to the bedroom with Nestor to get a few pictures. She shivered at the thought of looking into Nestor's eyes that night. Something was there in those eyes, all right. Something bad.

Of course, that was back when Breeze was Henry's girl. And Henry could degrade his girls any way he liked. Drug them up, pimp them out. Big Henry had the drugs, and that was what every girl wanted. So Henry could make them do things, and if they wouldn't do it, somebody else would, and what did Andrew care? Maybe he cared, but if he did, he sure didn't say anything about it.

Andrew was weak – that was the thing. And weak people got hurt. For instance, right now, she could get up, go to her travel bag, and pull the hunting knife out of there. Then she could creep back here and slice poor weak Andrew's throat. He probably wouldn't even wake up until it was too late. His eyes would probably open wide in sudden terror as the life force flowed out of him and onto the sheets. For a few seconds, he might even buck and thrash, like some kind of electricity was going through him. Then he would gradually begin to subside, and subside a little more. Then he would die. She had seen it happen.

The thing about men was they liked to fall asleep after sex, especially if they had knocked back a few drinks beforehand. It happened so often she didn't even wonder about it anymore. It just was. Grown men would fall right to sleep like babies, even when they had just fucked a little girl they had gotten from some street pimp, a little girl maybe thirteen or fourteen years old, one that hadn't eaten since yesterday, one that could use a little more meat on her bones. One they should have known better than to fuck.

Yeah, that was probably the first one. Age fourteen, the distant past. So long ago, it was almost lost in the mists of history. An over-weight guy – fat, the guy was fat, middle-aged, gold wedding band. Weak. He was probably trembling inside when he talked with Chief to set up the date. And the girl with the knife, already more savvy than most people would ever be or need to be, crouched in the corner of the room. She watched him flop and bleed like a big-eyed fish, and then watched him subside. He hardly made a sound, and that was good because the walls were like cardboard. And when he was gone, she went through his wallet and took the cash – two hundreds, a few twenties, and some singles. Her hands didn't shake at all. She felt like a doctor performing surgery. But she didn't take the wedding ring. Hard to get rid of, a thing like that. She knew a couple of fences, but nobody she could trust – they were all friends with Chief, and she was going to be avoiding Chief from now on, wasn't she? She'd end up taking the damn thing to a pawn shop somewhere, just about the first place the cops would check when they found this married guy without his precious ring. Pennies on the dollar, and oh yeah, it was a kid, a girl that brought it in. I don't know, about five foot five, black hair, skinny. Street kid, you know what I mean?

She left the fat man's nice ring right where it was, thank you. She left the fat man for the cleaning crew, and for the newspapers. *New Jersey Businessman Slain in Brooklyn Hot-Sheet Motel*. No leads, no witnesses, nobody saw anything.

Front desk clerk: 'I don't know, maybe a little girl, but little girls don't go around slicing people like that. Guy must've had enemies, you know what I mean? If there was a girl in the room, you'll probably find her in the river.'

And Chief?

You mean Chief the pimp? Yeah, the pimp. If he knew anything, he wasn't saying. She smiled. He was a bad, bad man, but he had style. She could imagine him wearing one of those wife-beater T-shirts he liked so much, reading the *New York Post* on the porch of his ramshackle house as the cops rolled up. A lazy flex of his muscular shoulders, a slug of the Old English 800, and a hit of the home-rolled. The hat with the feather tilted at the perfect angle, the cops looking square – feeling square – next to this man. 'It's tobacco, *officer*. In any case, yeah, had a girl looked like that once, used to call her Button. On account of she was cute like one, you know? Nah, ain't seen her in some time. Ran off, probably in college now. Dead guy? Read about it. Sorry, can't help you there.'

And the Cool Breeze was born. The Cool Breeze was different from what had come before, Button or whoever or whatever. The Cool Breeze watched and waited. She was smart, she was slick, she was still when it was time to be still, and she moved when it was time to move. She let them think they were winning. She let them think whatever they wanted to think. Then she struck, and a moment later, she was gone.

The Cool Breeze was a hunter.

4
THE PACKAGE

The next day, Sunday, football was on – the last game of the regular season. Dick watched the TV in sullen silence, waiting for four o'clock to come, when he would go meet Block for an early meal.

On the screen, the New York Jets offense drove the New England Patriots defense backwards on play after play. Dick stared at it, barely seeing it, the action a dreary rehash of the Nazi blitzkrieg rolling over Poland. 'Jesus,' he said absently, as the quarterback completed yet another pass, the tall receiver reaching one long, languorous arm in the air and pulling down a ball that could have easily gone into the stands. The Jets were his favorite team from childhood, but nowadays Dick didn't even know the names of the players. He was back after so many years away, and suddenly the hapless Jets and their long-suffering fans looked like they were rolling toward the Super Bowl. It must mean something – like an omen, or a good-luck charm.

Dick needed some good luck right about now – needed to turn the momentum his way. Things had been going good for a while. But now? Shit. He remembered the moment that everything had fallen apart. One day – just a few weeks ago, but it seemed like a year – a package arrived in the mail. It came in a big manila envelope, with 'Photographs: DO NOT BEND' stenciled along the side. The envelope was folded up and stuffed into Dick's post-office box. He didn't know anyone who would send him photographs, and he brought them home with that giddy rush of excitement he was prone to when something unexpected came in the mail. He took his time opening the envelope because he wanted that feeling to last.

There was no return address. The mystery of it was killing him. The desire to know, the pain of not knowing, was exquisite. He sat impaled by these two warring emotions, like a bug on a pin. Finally, he sat down with the envelope and sliced it open with a steak knife. He peeked in the top. There were indeed photos in there. He upended the envelope and let the photos slide out onto the table.

For a long time, he did not take a breath. It seemed that shadows moved in from every direction and would soon engulf him. They were black-and-white glossy 5 x 7s, exceptionally well done. In fact, every one looked like a work of art, as though the photographer had lavished attention on them, had labored over each one until it was just right. All the same, it took him a long moment to fully appreciate what they meant.

Each photo was a shot of Dot in various sexual positions. In some cases, a man was in the photograph with her. As Dick looked longer, he noticed that each photo was taken at Dot's apartment, mostly in the bedroom, but a couple in the bathroom. There were a few of two silhouettes behind the frosted glass door of the shower. If he believed what he was seeing, and there was no way not to, it seemed impossible to take these photos without the cooperation of the subjects. It appeared likely that they had been using a remote-controlled camera, or worse, had someone taking the photos for them. The photos were date-stamped, and the date was forever after etched in Dick's mind – 5 December, just a week before the photos themselves came in the mail. On 5 December, Dick and Dot were in the throes of an ongoing relationship.

The man in the photos was Nestor. The evil bastard had engineered this somehow, had these photos taken, and then sent them on to Dick. But what about Dot? True, they had never signed any sort of agreement, made any pact that they would be true to one another. But this? He had before him no less than ten photographs of her with another man. When did she find the time to cheat on him? The answer hit him like a fist on the nose: *anytime you weren't around.*

Several days passed after that and each morning found Dick in the same funk. He had been on a cloud for a short period and now he was sinking to the bottom of the sea.

He called in sick every morning. On the fourth day, Lydia was worried.

'Dick, what's the problem?'

'There's no problem, Lyd. I'm just not feeling too good.'

'Are you mad about something?'

Dick looked at the phone. He couldn't tell Lydia about Nestor. Not yet, anyway. Perhaps after he kicked Nestor's ass. 'No, of course not,' he said.

'Then what is it?'

'Lydia, I'm sick!'

'OK. Do you want to talk to Dot?'

'No. Just tell her I'm sick. I'm not coming in.' He tried to make his voice sound as though he was really sick. He didn't have to try that hard. He felt like he had no energy even to rise from bed.

On the other end of the line, Lydia paused. 'Uh, Dick?'

'Yeah?'

'Don't you think you should talk to her? You're out four days in a row, you know, you've got to talk to her, even if she is your girlfriend. She's also the boss.'

'Just tell her I'm sick,' he said again, hung up, and pulled the phone out of the wall. The next day, he stopped calling in sick.

This was his state for a couple more days. He did not get dressed. He did not shower. He ate the little bit of food in the refrigerator and smoked the last of his dope. Mostly, he stayed in bed and brooded. Sometime during that week, however, he began to come back. He had been struck a blow but he would recover. One day, he got up and went out of the apartment. He rode the subway into Manhattan. He wandered the streets for a while, feeling good just being outside. Then he stopped in a bar and had a few drinks by the window, watching people outside move to and fro. He stayed out until late at night. When he came home, he half-expected her to be there, waiting outside for him. She wasn't. He plugged the phone back in, but she didn't call. It seemed she was willing to let him drop off the face of the earth. Then it was Wednesday, two days before Christmas – the night of the office party. He wondered what would happen if he showed up. Would she talk to him? Would there be a scene? Would he get drunk and try to . . . do something . . . to her?

Alone in his vast apartment that day, he had a few drinks to steel his nerves. As he did so, he came to notice a set of Dot's keys hanging on a peg in the open kitchen area. House keys, car keys – the keys to Dot's life on a metal ring. He had never returned them. He could give them back tonight, if he wanted. But something told him that maybe he didn't want to, not just yet.

He left the keys right where they were.

There was an afternoon party in the building, so Dick went there first. A lot of the kids were going back to wherever they came from for the holidays. He was invited to the party, so he went. The apartment was on the floor below his. Two guys were on the lease, but his thoughts were that about eight people lived there. The place was a warren of tunnels and walls and wooden lofts – you could get lost in there, like in the old funhouses they had when Dick was a kid. The entire place pulsed with the beat of trance music. As he walked through the crowds a black light blinked on and off, making it seem like everyone moved in slow motion.

Even in the middle of the day, these kids were going wild. There was a lot of booze there and the smell of grass hung heavy in the air. Young girls paraded around in tight clothes, showing skin.

Artists.

Dick had been invited to a few of these parties but, so far, he had never showed. He was glad to be there. The music was thumping and the girls were cute. He would put a head on, then sail up to Greenpoint to see Dot for the final showdown, whatever that might amount to. In the meantime, he drank a few beers, took a few tokes of a joint that went around – shit, it was really shit – and made small talk.

A skinny kid came up to Dick, handed him a beer. The kid was probably twenty years old. He had long hair, tied into a ponytail. He wore a ripped, paint-splattered T-shirt. He might have been one of the kids on the lease. He might have been anybody.

'Thanks.'

'No problem, Mr Miller. We're glad you could make it.'

'What do you do here?' he asked the kid.

'Do?'

'Yeah. I mean, like, for a living? Or whatever. How do you pass the time?'

The kid thought about it for a moment. 'I paint dolphins,' he said finally.

'You paint dolphins?'

'Yes.'

'Like dolphins,' Dick said. 'The fish?'

The kid smiled, a simpering half-smirk. He knew he was smarter than Dick now. 'Well, actually,' he said, 'they're mammals.'

'Yeah, mammals. That's right.'

'Some people think the dolphins are actually more intelligent than we are.'

'That's interesting.'

They stood and stared at one another. There wasn't much to say. Dick didn't believe for one minute that this kid painted dolphins for a living.

'What color do you paint them?'

'Well, it's not like that. I'm painting murals with dolphins in them. I'm just getting started with it. I painted one in my apartment across the hall. Have you ever heard of Wyland? It's kind of like what he's doing.'

'Wyland?' Dick heard himself say.

'Yeah, Wyland. Just Wyland. No first name, no last name. Wyland. He paints murals of whales. His murals are massive. I mean, fucking gigantic.' The kid spread his arms apart all the way, the full wingspan, just to give Dick the gist. 'He's very famous for these whales that he paints.'

'So he paints whales, and you, uh, paint . . .'

'That's right.'

' . . . dolphins.'

'Yes.'

Dick checked his watch. It was already six thirty.

'Listen, I gotta go,' he said to the kid.

He left the building, feeling good, and drove up to the Feldman party. It was already snowing out. The place was a bar down the street from the office. All the employees and contract workers were there and so the room was crowded with a lot of men – rental agents, custodians, handymen, electricians – anybody who had done ten minutes of work for the company in the past year. For a long time, Dick couldn't even see Dot. Then he spotted her in a corner, talking with old man Feldman. Feldman was old – lined and fragile and ancient, like he was already dead. Dick didn't ever want to get that old.

A young woman, blonde, foxy, bumped into him on her way to the bathroom. He sort of saw her coming, winding her way through the drinkers, but didn't think she would hit him. Then she was there and their bodies made contact.

'Whoops,' she said. She put her small hands on his. For a second, he thought she was going to try to take his drink away. 'Sorry about that.' She kept going, swaying the tiniest bit. Drunk. Must have been somebody's date. Dick had never seen her before. There was something about her – about her face – that was unusual, but he couldn't put his finger on it. Then she was gone and he let it go.

He mixed and mingled a little with the few people he knew. He saw Lydia there, across the room. She waved, but didn't come over right away. Dick put his elbow on the bar. Dot was still mingling and, since she was the boss, she had a lot of people to talk to. It wasn't clear when he was going to talk to her.

He already had a strong buzz going, which was getting stronger by the minute. Shadows danced in the corners of his eyes.

There was nothing to be done, Dick decided. There was really no reason to be here. Maybe he would just leave without ever speaking to Dot again. In that moment, he realized he could do it. Forgive and forget, all of it. Move on. There was no shame in leaving, after all.

It was time to go home. And on the heels of that came another thought – maybe it was too late to go home. He was getting dizzy. All of a sudden, the room moved sideways in a sudden lurch.

'Hey, sailor,' Dot said. She had crossed the party and now stood right in front of him. She seemed to glow under the dim lights of the bar. 'Want to buy a girl a drink?' The memories ended there, abruptly, like a videotape that someone had half-erased.

Dick shook it all away as, on the TV screen in front of him, the

Jets scored yet another touchdown. The commentator went into ecstasies. The stadium crowd roared. As Dick sat slumped on the couch, he knew that somewhere in the distant past, the Dick Miller of his childhood was leaping to his feet, arms in the air. It was a big season for the green and white. Go Jets. The commentator babbled on while in the background, the crowd launched into the team's famous cheer: 'J-E-T-S – Jets! Jets! Jets! Jets! Jets!'

Dick stared and stared.

Should she call Dick Miller or not?

Desiree Milan gazed at the phone, trying to decide.

It was a green GPX Slimline. It had big buttons that lit up when she held the handset. Touch-tone compatible, it would have been cutting edge back when people still had rotary dial. It was cheap, about nine dollars, and had no features – no digital read out, no built-in answering machine, no nothing. She had stolen the phone from a midtown electronics store – she removed the plastic antitheft tag with one deft snap of her strong wrists and hands, slipped the box under her coat and she was gone. It was self-destructive to take that phone, she realized that – the kind of thing people did when they were trying to go back to the joint. The stealing – that was a problem. But now she had a phone and it was better than nothing.

Anyway, everything was a problem right now. Just being Desiree was a problem. The problems, the problems, the problems. Her mind went in circles, dealing with all the problems. Or not dealing with them – just going around and around, touching on them, running off to something else, then coming right back around again. The rent was a problem, the little bit of rent for this pathetic one room – she couldn't even call it an apartment – in a sleazy hotel on the west side of Manhattan. Her mother in the Bronx had disowned her forever, so there was no going that way.

There was one more week left before the new month started, and there was no money. She could go out on the street and get some money if she had to, but she didn't want to face that. She had done it before, of course, but that didn't make it right. The men on the street – there was something wrong with them. It was a spin of the roulette wheel what you were going to get once you were out there. You could find some Mr Nice Guy who worked in an office and had soft hands and three kids, and who worried out loud about their future and about the bills he constantly had to pay. That was OK. What was bad was an angry man who was looking for a punching bag to soak up his rage. Or worse, some friendly, smiling psycho with a butcher knife in the glove compartment or a box cutter in his jacket pocket – a Hefty bag waiting in the trunk and a whole series of safe dumpsters scoped out ahead of time.

Life was a roll of the dice when you were Desiree. But she had survived. She had *survived*. Twenty-three years old. She had lived on the streets. She had been in the joint. They had fucked her and beaten her and threatened her and spit on her. There were times she thought they would beat her to death. There were times when she was sure she had the Virus. But each time, no. By the grace of some God who chose to remain absent and unavailable most of the time, the answer was no. Desiree was Negative. Desiree was going to live.

There was a reason why Desiree was alive. Something this absent God wanted from her. Else she'd be dead by now. It was that simple.

She glanced around the bare apartment – the Waiting Room, she called it. She was waiting here for something good to happen. One room, a closet of a bathroom, and a tiny kitchen crawling with cock-roaches. She had some food and that was good – Christmas stuff from a church food pantry. She had arrived there late and all the frozen turkeys were already gone. But she had some canned turkey meat, canned pork, and canned vegetables. Canned cranberry sauce.

Government surplus peanut butter. Government cheese. The cheese was a weird orange color – so orange it almost seemed to glow. Well, she wasn't going hungry. Not yet.

The phone still worked. The lights were still on. But neither would last much longer. There was a Christmas tree in the corner of the room. Fifteen dollars, plastic, bright green, it came with the lights and everything already on it. Piece of shit. She had bought it in the hope it would give this barren hole a more festive air. If anything, it made the place seem even more depressing. Anyway, she wouldn't be trapped here much longer. Unless she did something, she would be out of here soon.

She had options, but not good ones. She figured she needed to get at least five hundred dollars. Four hundred would keep her in the apartment another month. Twenty-five would keep the lights on. Another fifty would go for sundries – food, makeup, and maybe something nice for herself. The phone service was optional – it could go and she wouldn't miss it. There weren't very many people to call.

The last twenty-five would go for her Premarin. It was a non-negotiable expense. She would lose the apartment before she lost her estrogen pills. Premarin was the concentrated urine from pregnant mares that gave Desiree her titties, and more important than that, made her feel like a woman. She had been on the drug for two years, and it had changed her life. She couldn't explain it, but before Premarin, she had often thought about killing herself. Since Premarin, almost never. A kind-hearted pharmacy worker near Columbus Circle sold it under the table, and twenty-five dollars bought Desiree a packet that would last her twenty-eight days. The pills were supposed to be for ladies in menopause, but they also worked miracles for women like Desiree. It was fucked up for the horses, who had to get pregnant over and over again, and were forced to stand in stalls getting their piss milked out of them like cows. But you know what? There was a lot about this world that was fucked up, and none of it was under Desiree's control. If somebody was going to make the pills anyway, then she was going to buy them.

Desiree could get the five hundred. She knew she could get it. Out in the street. Out in the cold. Eight times. She would have to get in a car at least eight times, probably more. She would have to eat out while she was working, and that would cost money. She would be out there long hours, and she couldn't exactly carry a can of government pork with her. Two nights, or a long night through the next morning. She would definitely need food.

Eight times, maybe ten. Each time would be a spin of the wheel, tempting fate, begging for that square to come up, the one that said 'LOSER'. And in between, during the wait, the vultures circling, looking for a chance to rob her and take it all, setting her dial back to zero. Pimps hovering too, ready to 'protect' her, beat her down, and make her a slave. It would be a long walk across a narrow ledge, all just to keep her in this tiny hole for yet another month.

There had to be another way.

At least they didn't try to kill him.

This was Nestor's thought as he checked into the Following Seas Hotel in Mystic, Connecticut. Earlier in the day, he had driven from New York to the North End of Hartford – the slums of Hartford – where he was able to unload the two kilos to some gangbangers, remains of the once powerful Los Solidos gang. The Solid Ones – it made Nestor want to laugh. Most of the gang leaders had gone inside on federal RICO beefs, or had gone underground to avoid the charges. The ones that remained were either too young for the G-men to grab, or too dumb for the G-men to care about.

This is what Nestor was reduced to – meeting with four skinny teenagers in the kitchen of an apartment in some low-rise welfare housing. The children, all of them, wore necklaces with red and blue beads around their necks. Did they *want* to join their friends in prison? Or did they think the police were unaware of what constituted a gang symbol? Nestor sighed. The linoleum floor of the kitchen was scuffed and peeling up in places, and he spotted a cockroach on the wall. An old woman watched a huge wide-screen television just through the doorway in the living room. The teenagers all wore baseball caps and jerseys from various sports teams, with player numbers on the back. They were so unconnected that they didn't know Nestor was tainted. Nestor imagined they'd all be dead or in jail in six months.

The negotiated amount was nineteen thousand per key. When Nestor arrived, after a three-hour drive, they decided they wanted to renegotiate. Fifteen thousand.

'Fifteen thousand?'

One of them, a New York Yankee with number 42, pulled a gun and placed it on the kitchen table. As a dramatic gesture, it lacked something. Nestor stared at him, soaking in his features. The boy had pimples on his face, the result of too much pizza, and too many Ring Dings. Nestor could kill all four of them and the grandmother before the boy ever picked up the gun again.

And then what? Run away and try to find someone else to buy his product? Drive further north until he found someone as clueless as these kids? Boston? New Hampshire? Canada? Coke was a wasting asset. If he held these kilos much longer . . . he didn't want to think about it. He had to unload them now.

Shit. It had been a long day. Everything was long now. The smallest baby step seemed like running under water.

'Eighteen,' he said.

They all just stared. Nestor shrugged and picked up his case.

'Nice meeting you.'

'Seventeen,' the kid said.

'Seventeen five.'

The kid gestured and one of the others – a Chicago Cub, number 21 – brought out a satchel. He put stacks of currency on the kitchen table. In the other room, the old woman guffawed at something on the television.

Nestor counted the money. It was all there: thirty-five thousand dollars. He started putting the bundles in his case. What the hell else was he going to do? Money was money, and although his honor cried out for vengeance, there was no need to worry. They would pay for their arrogance sooner or later. Not everyone wanted to avoid a blood-bath. Not everyone needed to unload immediately. Not everyone was so forgiving. These young boys would start watching each other die in the months ahead.

Now, in his hotel room, Nestor gazed through his window, surveying the light snow falling on the bay. He had some money – a stake, yet another new beginning. He was safely away from New York. He didn't have to go back. There were people there who wanted to kill him. That should be enough to keep him gone. But there were also a million dollars back there, practically for the taking. Dick Miller stood in the way, perhaps, but Nestor knew Dick was not the man he pretended to be. He did not match up. He was larger than Nestor, certainly, but did he have the gifts Nestor had? Nestor removed his shirt and looked at his thin, pockmarked upper body. Bullet holes. His fingers traced the marks like punctures. Here, he shot me. And here. And here. And here, two shots just an inch apart.

Miami.

Well, not exactly Miami. Hollywood, just north of the city. It was all one big city to him – Miami, Miami Beach, Hollywood, Lauderdale. He was a different man from the young boy who had fought in the jungle. After his discharge, he had put his military skills to work. He killed for money – dangerous, low-paying work on the streets of

Bogotá. In those grim days, Nestor's great dream was to come to the United States, and to receive the promise of America. Indeed, he had received that promise. His life had changed almost from the moment he had stepped off the merchant ship in Port Everglades. For the first time, he made the money he deserved.

He lived in a thirty-fourth-floor condominium high above Route A1A in Hollywood Beach. He shared the place with two women – his girlfriends. The apartment had bay windows facing south, giving a spectacular view of the skyscrapers of Miami Beach, and a roof garden facing east toward the ocean, which was just a hundred feet from the door of this place. An old Japanese made the rounds and tended to Nestor's plants. At Nestor's request, he did the garden up like a Zen sanctuary. Throughout all the months the old man tended that garden, Nestor met him just three times. But Nestor paid cash, he never forgot to leave the envelope, and the Japanese was diligent and careful in his work.

Downstairs, the building had a garage under the street, and Nestor kept two parking spaces in the garage. Parked in one space was an almost new Toyota Camry. In the other was an immaculate fifteen-year-old Porsche 911T.

He operated under the fiction that he was importing Colombian roses – the very best in the world. In fact, it was true. He did indeed import the roses, and he did indeed sell them. They were very expensive, and the cocaine was a small gift that came bundled with each purchase of beautiful flowers. His flower business grew larger and larger. He leased a small, refrigerated warehouse to hold all the pretty flowers. The florist business seemed a fiction that his competitors, the police and the government all believed.

Until the night he learned that someone didn't believe.

That night, in the early hours, he sat in the driver's seat of a rental car, along Dania Boulevard. Across the wide, busy street sat a run-down strip club. The bar didn't seem to have a name. It was just a big wooden door next to two blacked-out windows. People knew what was in there, that's all. People just knew.

Nestor was supposed to meet a man named Wasco at the strip bar. Wasco was a little fat man, who talked big and walked with a stately waddle like an emperor penguin. He was balding, and had the kind of fat stomach that seemed to continue below his belt-line for several inches. Wasco owned a plumbing supply company. He had five stores in Metro Dade County. He seemed to locate his facilities based on their nearness to strip bars. He seemed to have a fondness for leaving his wife at home and taking blonde strippers to motels. Blonde strippers seemed to have a fondness for Wasco's money.

Plumbing supplies were not the only things he distributed through his facilities. In fact, if an auditor were to get his hands on an honest accounting of Mr Wasco's revenues, the auditor might find that the least portion of Wasco's business was in any way related to plumbing.

That was all Nestor knew about Wasco, and all he needed to know. Nestor had gotten greedy. He knew that about himself, and it made him nervous. There was a boat tied up at a dock in Marathon Key. The bottom was loaded with cocaine – uncut, pure, a million dollars wholesale. Street value? A lot. Nestor owned that boat. They had given him credit. Now all he had to do was unload the stuff. Wasco was the prospect.

One big move.

A million dollars? It was nothing in Miami. No money at all. They brought billions through here. But they frowned on freelancers. They made examples out of freelancers. So it had to be quiet.

Nestor went into the club. He ordered a rum and Coke at the bar and took it to a table in the back that was partially obscured by palm fronds. It was dark in that place. And it was a rinky-dink sort of club, with just the one stage, a 1967-vintage lighting show going on, and a troop of girls grinding it out on the bottom rung. Wasco seemed to like the girls with a little extra meat on their bones.

A waitress came around dressed in a miniskirt and bra. Nestor ordered two more drinks, one for himself and one for an imaginary friend.

He watched Wasco eat dinner from the happy-hour buffet. Little hot dogs, chicken wings with blue cheese dressing, and French fries. Portly Wasco went to town. A girl passed and he grabbed her ass with his greasy hands. She didn't seem to mind. She even smiled at some comment he made.

Nestor drank more. Time passed and the place filled up. The crowd had been sparse when he came in, but now it was getting thicker. It was Wednesday night, a good night to watch the boobs bounce and the cellulite jiggle. Nestor ordered another. He settled in deep behind that palm frond. He became the palm frond.

He watched Wasco get up from his table and move toward the bathroom. He wound his way through the crowd and slipped into the bathroom. He glanced Nestor's way, stared two seconds longer than necessary, and kept going. That was it – the signal. Then the door closed and he disappeared.

Nestor got up and moved toward the bathroom. It took a long minute to get there through the crowd. As he reached the door, it opened, and a tall slim guy came strutting out. Nestor went on in. It wasn't as he expected. The bathroom was small. It could barely hold more than two people. There was one urinal and one toilet, plus a sink with a mirror. He should have checked it out beforehand, but they had just called him with the meeting place today. When the door slid shut, Wasco was there, standing at the urinal letting it flow. His back was to the door and Nestor. He was a little round man practically standing in the urinal, holding his dick with both hands.

There was somebody else in there. The door to the toilet stall was closed. Nestor looked in the mirror, caught a glimpse of himself and smiled.

'Some night out there, huh?' Wasco said.

'Yes,' Nestor said to Wasco's back and to the empty chrome circle at the top of his head. 'Nice girls.'

'You said it.'

The door silenced almost all the noise from the club. The only sound in here was the steady drip of the leaky faucet and the whoosh of Wasco's stream as it weakened and ended. Wasco finished shaking the weasel and turned slowly around. Nestor waited.

Then he saw the gun in Wasco's hand.

Wasco's forehead creased.

'Greetings from some friends,' he said.

Nestor felt someone pushing the stall door open. He wheeled around. A man stood there, a tall black guy in some kind of uniform. Nestor tried to place it but couldn't. Traffic cop? No. State trooper? No. The uniform was brown, and for the love of Jesus, this guy had a gun too. The silencer at the end of it was long and sinister.

The black guy fired, the first one blasting into Nestor's gut. Nestor didn't even grunt. He stepped back and leaned against the wall. The guy fired again. Five times, six times. Then he slumped over sideways and collapsed to the wet tiled floor of the men's room.

They stood over him, haloed by the weak overhead lights.

'What did you think was gonna happen?' Wasco said. 'Stupid fuck.'

Then they were gone. Nestor stood in the bathroom, gazing down at the body on the floor, the blood spreading out in a pool around it. The dingy bathroom walls faded away, revealing a dark landscape all around him, a barren land in flames, the flames taking shape like human figures writhing in agony. The sky itself was on fire.

He passed out of time and wandered that landscape, plodding, up to his knees in muck and gore, people around him now, bony, starving, grasping at him, their fingers like ice, their skin flayed and bleeding, their eyes hollow, pleading, begging him to . . . what? Then the ground trembled and there was a presence coming, beyond the horizon, something blacker than night itself. And somehow, Nestor knew that it was coming to see him.

'Do you know where you are?' somebody said.

Nestor gazed up at the ceiling. But the ceiling had changed. The light in the room was brighter. But he was Nestor. He knew that much. And he guessed from the room that he was alive. Beyond that, he knew nothing.

'No.' It hurt to speak. It hurt his throat, it hurt his stomach, it hurt everything.

Two men stood over him now. They both wore long white coats. He didn't recognize them.

'You're an amazing man, Mr Garcia. You get shot full of holes. A medical team works on you around the clock and you linger near death for a week. Now here you are, two weeks later, vital signs good, looking at something like a full recovery. And you don't remember a thing. You're lucky, not only to be alive, but also to not remember anything. Your body has been through hell.'

'Thank you for saving me,' Nestor said. These men, modern doctors, could not know what they had saved him from.

Now, safe in a hotel room in Connecticut, he was set to risk all that again. Death, and what lay beyond. He paced the room, window to the door, and back again. He turned on the television, scrolled through the channels, then turned it off. He lay down on the bed – king size, very nice. He watched the snow fall outside the window.

It was Dot – Dot was pulling him back to New York. True enough, she had left him and betrayed him. But he sensed her, in a way he would not try to describe to anyone, he sensed her calling to him.

She haunted his dreams. It was impossible – *impossible* – that she no longer wanted him.

A memory flashed through his mind. He and Dot were at an art opening in Williamsburg. She wore a black sleeveless dress, her long blonde hair falling down over her shoulders in waves. Diamonds sparkled in the light. Diamonds in her ears. Diamonds around her neck. Rocks, she called them. They were tasteful – accents rather than the main event. Dot herself was the main event. She held a glass of red wine in one hand, and on the other arm was Nestor Garcia, late of South Florida. She was older than he, but looked younger.

As they walked the gleaming hardwood floors of the very new art gallery, mingling with the crowds, Nestor barely saw the paintings, massive canvases painted in bright colors. Instead, he sensed the eyes upon them. The eyes of the gallery owner, hoping Dot would remove her checkbook from her purse. Dot was known as a collector. The eyes of the men, attached and unattached, lusting after her. The eyes of the women, envying her. Together, they walked a red carpet that only he could see. Anything was possible for them. Dot was big time, and the big time was where Nestor belonged. With this woman on his arm, he knew that he had arrived at last.

He would go back to New York, Nestor decided. And he would claim the million dollars. But the real reason he would go back was Dot.

'So tell me,' Block said. 'What happened?'

They sat in a small restaurant not far from Dick's apartment. It was late afternoon, and the place hadn't filled up yet. The lighting was dim. Only a few of the tables had patrons. Up in front, near a tiny bandstand, a small man in a tuxedo tuned an instrument – some sort of large upright harp or member of the guitar family. Dick had never seen one before, whatever it was. The strings the man plucked were low – deep in the bass range. Occasionally, he would let loose with a burst of song, a passionate, manly sort of shouting. Evidently, this helped him tune, because afterward, he went back to manipulating the tuning pegs on his instrument.

Block looked through the menu. Each vibration of the strings, each powerful vocalization, seemed to send a shiver through him. Block was large enough, it was like watching the start of an earthquake. 'Guinea pig,' he said. 'They offer guinea pig meat. What is this place, Mexican?'

'I think it's Peruvian.'

'Peruvian, yeah? I guess they have their own kind of food down there. Like guinea pig. They're fucking crazy if they think I'm gonna eat a guinea pig. Look, you can have half a guinea pig, or you can have a whole one. A whole fucking guinea pig, can you imagine? You think that comes with the head and everything?'

'I don't know,' Dick said. 'Somebody said the food was good here. That's why I picked this place.' He shrugged, looking at the other items on the menu. It hardly mattered to him what they ate – he wasn't sure if he could choke down much of anything. 'If you don't like guinea pig, don't eat it.'

'It's not that I don't like it. I never had it, so how would I know? It's that the very idea of it makes me nauseated. You know what I mean?'

Up at the front, the little man burst into another loud torrent of song. Dick didn't speak a word of Spanish, but he imagined it to be a song of death and tragedy and broken hearts.

Block waved the waiter over.

'Yes, sir? Are you ready to order?'

'No, we're going to be another minute. But I'm wondering. Is this guy up there going to sing like that while we're eating? And play that guitar thing?'

The waiter glanced over at the musician. Then he cast a sidelong glance at Dick. Then he looked back at Block. 'Yes, he is.'

Block reached into his pocket and pulled out a new hundred-dollar bill. 'I'll tell you what. Do me a favor, OK? Give this to the guy, tell him he's got a family emergency right now, he's gotta rush right out. Come back in a couple of hours, all right?' He gestured with his big hand at Dick, then gestured to encompass the table where they sat. 'We like his music, but we got important business to talk about. We can't have it too loud around here. You know what I mean?'

The waiter, probably seeing the kind of tip he could think about, smiled and came to attention. 'Yes, sir. Of course.'

The waiter went straight to the bandstand, whispered to the man in the tuxedo, and handed him something, a bill, maybe even a hundred. Maybe not. A moment later, the man in the tuxedo was gone.

Block went back to his menu. 'I don't know, man. They have llama. That sounds better somehow than guinea pig.'

He glanced up from the menu.

'So tell me what you got.'

And Dick told him. He told Block almost everything.

Funny.

It was the second or third time with Dot that Lydia remembered most vividly – not the first. She had still lived with her father at that time. One weekend nearly a year ago, they took a car trip north to Cold Spring. They were already stealing. Had been for months. They had done at least two successful trips to the Bahamas. They were together by then, Lydia was sure of that. Her father didn't seem to mind that she would run off on weekends with Dot. He liked Dot and said so. He seemed glad that Lydia had found a mentor who could help her in the business world.

Cold Spring was Lydia's idea. She had loved the quaint Hudson

River town since she had first discovered it a few years before. They sped up from the city early that Saturday morning, Dot's Lexus racing along the curves of the narrow Taconic State Parkway, the sunroof open despite the lingering April chill. Upon their arrival in town, Lydia took Dot along a two-lane road just north to Breakneck Ridge, a hiking trail that was the reason she had first started coming to Cold Spring.

Garbed in pricey outdoor gear by LL Bean and Eddie Bauer and Patagonia – Dot insisted on buying new clothes for this little adventure – they parked the car in the dirt by the side of road and began the ascent. The initial climb at Breakneck Ridge was steep, nearly straight up in some places, and secretly Lydia worried that Dot wouldn't be up to the task. But she wanted to share this special place with Dot. So she set a slow pace.

They inched up the near-vertical trail, as behind them, the view of the river and Storm King Mountain on the other side grew higher and more dramatic. This early in the year, most of the trees were bare, and they could see up and down the river for miles. In forty minutes, they reached the first plateau, and sat on a rocky outcropping, eating granola and drinking water. A hawk circled in empty space at eye level with them. Two hundred feet below, a sleek passenger train passed along the railroad tracks. If they had wings, they would have needed only to step out into nothingness and soar like the hawk.

The morning sun had come out from behind some clouds, and now beamed directly on the rock they shared. Combined with the effort of reaching this point, it made them both hot and sweaty. Dot removed her vest, leaving her in a white sleeveless T-shirt and khaki shorts.

Dot looked at Lydia. There was no one around. They had this high, rocky place and this astonishing view all to themselves. In the sky thousands of feet above them, a small airplane passed overhead.

Lydia noticed how Dot's nipples had come erect against the fabric of her shirt. She noticed how Dot's hands, and her own, were dirty from pulling themselves up the rock faces as they climbed. She noticed how Dot had streaked some of that dirt across her cheek as she wiped sweat away from her face. She noticed too how their clothes were streaked with dirt and dust.

And she noticed how Dot was staring intently at her.

'You look sexy today,' Dot said, and Lydia realized it was the first time either of them had spoken in half an hour or more.

Dot moved closer. Her hands found Lydia and gently roamed her body. They came together in a long, deep kiss. Their bodies pressed closer and closer, until they were almost the same body. Time moved in a different rhythm now, slower, undulating, like waves crossing a vast ocean. Lydia felt her shorts, then her shirt, come off. She lay back on the flat rock, her head supported by the knapsack she had carried up the trail, Dot's blonde hair below her, above her the sky a pale blue, like a lagoon, the sun hot now on her body, the only sounds her own sharp breaths and Dot's voice murmuring like a breeze in the tree tops.

Afterward, they lay pressed close on the rock. Dot was speaking and her face shone from their exertions together and from her beauty. They had shared many similar moments after that one, and many adventurous moments. They had stolen a lot of money together, and had spent a lot of money together. But never again did Dot look that beautiful, that at peace. If only time could have stopped then. If only they could have settled for less and lived there, in that instant, forever.

Later, Lydia may have grown tired of Dot. She may have considered their relationship nothing more than a youthful experiment – hey, lots of girls tried it. She may even have wanted to escape from Dot. But in that moment on the mountain, Dot was the most beautiful person – man or woman – that she had ever seen.

* * *

Desiree rode the subway, on her way to Brooklyn. She sat quietly, swaying with the motion of the train, studying the floor, avoiding the eyes of the other riders.

The day at the BreakOut Program had decided her. It was weeks ago now. It had been the worst day of her life, one of many worst days. They should call that place the BreakDown Program. Every time she went there, that's what it felt like she was having. It didn't help that they made her travel way out to Brooklyn for her appointments.

'Mr Coleman,' the bitch at the desk had said. The black bitch, hair pulled back to her scalp, tight bitch, exploiting her own people and getting paid for it – looking at Desiree like Desiree was some kind of creature beamed down from another planet. 'You've failed in every placement we've obtained for you. You refuse to go to half your job assignments, and you refuse to dress appropriately for the ones you do go to. I'm not sure there's anything more we can do for you here.'

Desiree could feel herself coming apart, getting ready to scream. It was the worst thing she could do. There were people here, other cons, a whole row of them waiting right on the other side of that partition. It didn't matter anymore. The fluorescent overheads were making her dizzy, burning their light into her brain. Her whole body started to tremble. 'You know what you can do for me?' she said. 'You know what you can do? You can try calling me by my right fucking name. Why don't you try that?'

The bitch's face was stone. 'Mr Coleman—'

'It ain't Mr Coleman, bitch. It's Desiree. Desiree Milan. OK?' She shook her head, the tears flowing now. 'You fucking people. Can't you even try?'

The bitch's voice lowered. 'I don't care what you think your name is. I don't care what you call yourself at night or when you're at home. The State of New York says that you are Julius Coleman, ex-offender, ex-inmate in the men's state prison system. You got to accept that. You can't go to job sites and pretend you're a woman. You're a man and you got to act like a man.' The bitch paused and her face softened the tiniest fraction. She lowered her voice. 'Listen. You're smart, one of the highest scorers we have on our intelligence test. If you would just stop all this Desiree shit you could probably keep a job and maybe even move up the ladder.'

'But I can't do these fucking jobs you send me on.' She indicated the minidress she wore, her hair, her black leggings, her fingernails. 'Look at me. I can't work at a warehouse. I can't lift shit all day long. They laugh at me, don't you know that? Why do you keep sending me on these bullshit jobs?' The tears kept coming and she didn't do anything to try to stop them.

The bitch looked down at the paper in front of her. 'Because, Mr Coleman, you have no other skills. You might – and I emphasize might – be able to work as a receptionist, but I haven't found an employer yet who is willing to have an ex-offender transvestite at the front desk, greeting visitors.' She looked up and straight into Desiree's eyes. 'Do you see what I mean?'

Later, in the bathroom – the men's room – Desiree put herself back together again for the trip home. Her body still shook, but only a little. Her mascara was all streaked from tears. There were dark bags under her eyes. The face in the mirror didn't even look like her.

A man came out of the stall. He was a tall white man, handsome, like an actor. He began to wash his hands at the other sink. They watched each other in the mirror. The guy dried his hands with a paper towel.

'You know, I saw what happened out there.'

'Motherfuckers.'

The guy nodded. 'I could probably help you, if you want.'

Desiree raised an eyebrow. She'd heard that sort of noise before, but this man wasn't looking at her that way. 'Yeah? With what?'

The big man shrugged. 'Office skills. People skills. I don't know. Planning. Maybe all you need is a plan.'

'You got a plan?' Desiree said.

The man smiled. 'You kidding? I'm the star here. I type ninety words a minute. I got a permanent gig in a real estate office. The only reason I ever come back is because the rules say I have to spend a morning here once a month. That way they can look at me. Ask me how I'm feeling, am I gonna hit anybody.'

There was a pause between them.

'Listen, maybe all you need is to learn how to type. Look at it this way. If you could type, some company could put you in a closet somewhere, where you won't bother anybody. You could sit in there and type up paperwork all day long, and nobody would have to look at you and get offended.'

Desiree had laughed at that one.

Dick Miller. He was supposed to help her, but he hadn't come through. She hadn't learned to type. She hadn't learned anything. She was hard to help – she would grant him that much – but he didn't have to leave her hanging the other night. If they had gone out, she would have told him what she had so much trouble saying over the phone: she had reached the crisis point. Soon, she would be back on the street, or in the shelters, or in jail.

She had to see him. He said he wanted to help her. She would simply show up at his apartment and throw herself on his mercy. He would have to do something, if only to get rid of her.

She looked up and saw the train had reached Bedford Avenue.

One more stop to go.

'Dick Miller,' she said. 'Here I come.'

* * *

'Did anybody bump into you?' Block said. He was a hulk in his leather jacket. 'At the bar that night?'

They stood inside the cavernous space of Dick's apartment. They had opened a bottle of Dewar's Scotch and each held a glass of the liquid in his hand. After their meal, they had driven his car to a warehouse Block owned and pulled inside. Dick had shown Block the frozen body. Block wasn't fazed by it – he treated the fact of Dot's death as just another business problem to be solved. In fact, Block's steadiness in the face of the corpse had done wonders for Dick's outlook. He felt stronger just having Block around – he felt he could borrow from Block's strength, as much as needed. They had rolled the body into a large rug that Block had at the warehouse. Now, as the last light of day faded, the car was parked in front of the building. When night came, they would bring the body upstairs.

Dick shrugged. 'You're in a bar. People bump into you.'

'Well, you say you think somebody slipped you a Mickey Finn. OK. That's how they do it sometimes. They bump into you, drop it in your drink.'

'That would take fast hands.'

Now Block shrugged. He didn't say anything.

'Do you think I killed her?' Dick said.

'Does it matter what I think?'

'Yeah, it does.'

'Well, I think either way, your position is no good. Look at it this way – say you didn't kill her. So what do you do, bring the body to the cops? Oh, by the way, here I am, a con just out after a two-year pop, and I just happen to have my ex-girlfriend's body here. I don't know what happened to her. But don't worry, guys, I didn't kill her. I had nothing to do with it.' Block paused and gave Dick a long look. 'Who's going to buy that story?'

As if to punctuate Block's question, a sharp rapping came at the door. Dick looked at Block. Dick wasn't sure how many more nasty surprises he could take.

'Don't matter,' Block whispered. 'No evidence in this apartment. Open it, but be ready for anything.' They both crept to the door. Block stood behind it, Dick stood in front of it.

The knocking came again.

'Who is it?' Dick said.

No one answered.

Dick looked at Block. You ready? Block nodded.

Dick yanked the door open and jumped to the left.

A black girl stood there, bundled against the cold. As soon as the door opened, she barged right in. She wore a fake fur coat, a short skirt and high heels. It was not an ideal outfit, considering the weather outside.

'Hi, Dick,' she said.

'Desiree,' Dick said. 'How nice to see you.'

She smirked. 'Real nice, the way you keep blowing me off.'

Dick shook his head. 'All right, look. I'm sorry about that. But I'm in the middle of something right now, OK? We'll talk another time.'

She glanced over at Block.

'No,' she said. 'We'll talk right now.'

'Desiree.'

She took off her coat and held it out to Block. 'What you gonna do, big man? What you hiding there for? You gonna jump out and attack me when I come walking in here?'

Block took the coat. 'Well, Dick,' he said. 'Here's a friend you never mentioned.'

For an instant, Dick saw Desiree as Block would. He didn't like what he saw. A woman – a very sexy woman. 'Desiree, this is Kevin Blockovich. Kevin, this is Desiree. Desiree, I'm not sure if I know your last name.'

'Milan. Desiree Milan.'

'Like the cookies?' Block said.

'Like the city, honey. Milan. The fashion capital of the world? In Italy. You've heard of Italy, right?'

She stopped, looked around at Dick's none-too-impressive digs. 'Can I have a drink? It's cold outside, you know.' She glanced at Block. 'I damn near froze my cookies off walking over here from the subway.'

'You have nice cookies,' Block said. 'Wouldn't want you to freeze them off.' He poured her a shot of Dick's Scotch and she downed half of it.

'Thank you,' she said, gasping just a bit.

Block raised his eyebrow at Dick.

'Look, Desiree, I'm sorry you came all this way out here. I'm sorry I didn't call you back. If you want me to call you tomorrow to talk this over, I will. But tonight I got important business to take care of, so . . .'

She stood with hands on hips. 'So?'

'So you should have called, you know?'

'Dick, you want me to step outside for a minute?' Block said. 'Take a walk around the block or something?'

'Not necessary, Block.'

'What are you saying, Dick? That all my unreturned phone calls to you weren't enough? That I came all the way out here to see you so you could tell me to turn around and go home? So you could tell me that you got no time for me, once again?'

'Desiree, you have no idea what's going on here right now. I promise you that you don't want to be part of it.'

Desiree put her hands in the air. A few tears streamed down her face. Dick reflected that this was Desiree's strategy – put people in an awkward position, then start crying to make it even worse. 'OK,

Dick. You're right, you're right. I shouldn't have come banging your door down. It's just that you said you were going to help me, and you haven't. I got nobody helping me. I'm behind on the rent. They're gonna throw me out of there, and then I'm gonna be out on the street. It's fucking cold outside, Dick. I don't know if you noticed.'

'Desiree, come on. I'm trying to help you. It's just that this is a bad time.'

The tears started flowing now. Dick looked at Block, shook his head.

Desiree put her head on the kitchen counter. She covered her head in her hands. Her voice sounded like it was coming out of a tunnel. 'It's a bad time for me too. I don't know if you can imagine how bad it is.'

Her body began to shake with quiet sobs. Dick glanced at Block again. Block stared at Desiree. Dick turned back and also stared. They watched her for what seemed like a long time.

'Desiree . . .'

'Shit. I'm so ashamed right now. You're right, Dick. I am gonna go. I'm just gonna go home.'

'Can I call you a cab?'

She lifted her head off the counter. Her eyes were red from the tears. 'No, Dick. You've done enough already. I'll just take the subway back.'

She snatched her coat out of Block's hand and then walked out the door.

'I'll call you,' Dick said to her back as she walked toward the stairs.

'Yeah, Dick. Great.' She disappeared into the stairwell.

Dick closed the solid wood door to the apartment and locked it. He felt bad about her sudden about-face, sure he did. All the same, it was a relief to have her out of the apartment.

Block and Dick stood in the living room sipping their drinks. Time spun out in uncomfortable silence.

'Well, there goes another one,' Block said.

'Block, I don't know what you're thinking right now, but I can explain all that.'

'Dick, what am I thinking? You said you were going to help this woman and either you haven't, or it hasn't worked out. OK. I'll leave it at that. Now let's go do what we're here to do. You ready?'

'As ready as I'll ever be.'

'Then let's do it.'

Dick reached onto the kitchen counter for his car keys. They weren't there. He glanced around the large open room, looking to spot the keys. They weren't on the coffee table either. 'That's funny,' he said, 'I don't know where my keys are. We just walked in a minute ago, and I always put them there on the table or the counter.'

'Hmm. Did you go in the bathroom?'

Dick ducked into the bathroom. He glanced around. Industrial sink. Toilet bowl. Plastic bathtub and shower stall. No keys. He ducked back out.

'Nah. I left them right there on the counter.'

Block and he stared at each other for a second. A light dawned in Block's eyes.

Dick read his mind. 'Desiree.'

'Desiree,' Block agreed.

'Shit! She just stole my car.'

Desiree was bad.

She settled behind the wheel of Dick's big-man car. That's what it was, right? It was a statement, this whale of a car, Dick telling the world he was a big man with a big dick. Well, he was a big man, all right, and a good-looking man, but he should fix that window, all broken in and covered over by cardboard and duct tape. That was no way to have a car. It took too long to warm this car up anyway, and now all the heat was going out that broken window.

Shit, Dick. He was something for a big man. Most big men Desiree knew would want their car new and clean and smooth, with not a scratch on it. But not Dick. He drove this broken-down old jalopy.

Desiree checked her look in the rearview mirror, giving Dick some time to realize what had happened and maybe come out here before things went too far. If he didn't figure it out in another few seconds, then she would be gone and he would just have to come and get her. She sighed as she primped her hair the tiniest bit.

Did Desiree look cunty? Yes, Desiree looked very cunty in a skirt and sweater ensemble she had mopped from a discount store in Herald Square. Honey, you didn't have to pay a lot to look fine – to look *fierce* – you didn't have to pay anything at all. When she walked in there tonight, she could tell that big man with Dick was smelling her. He wanted some, right? Yes, he wanted some. Sigh. They all did.

She smiled at herself. She was bad. Stealing was bad. She had stolen the clothes because she wanted to look good, on point, like she was making it. And that was no good because it could put Desiree back inside with the animals. What was it that Pepper had said? 'You mop, you get locked.' And now she was stealing Dick's car.

Because why?

Because he said he wanted to help, and he wasn't helping, and now time was getting short. She was about to be out on the street, Mr Dick Miller, and she wasn't going out on the street. He had to make some-thing happen, like he said he would. This was Desiree's cry for help.

And here came Dick now – he and his big friend running out of the building. Time to go. Desiree put the car in gear and got it rolling down the street toward the on-ramp of the Williamsburg Bridge. By the time she passed the two men, she had it going pretty good. Desiree could drive. Yes, she could. She wasn't the best driver, but she could get it moving and keep it moving.

She waved as she passed them, then goosed the gas a little bit. 'Yoo hoo! Goodbye, Dick. Goodbye, Dick's big-man friend.'

'You can have her, all right?' Big Henry said. 'But I promise you something. You're going to be sorry. OK? You're going to be very fucking sorry. She's trouble. My opinion? Don't get too attached. Use her to get your jollies, you know? She's good for that. But don't think she's your girlfriend or anything. Because she's not. She's not anybody's girlfriend.'

'Are you pissed?' Andrew said. 'You sound pissed.'

Breeze watched the Roosevelt Island tram move slowly, high above the East River. She sat in the back seat of Andrew's BMW, listening to the two boys up front talk about her like she was a slab of beef. They were cruising north on the FDR Drive. Henry had come back from Connecticut earlier, and now they were deciding her future between them. It was a commodity exchange, a trafficking in human flesh. It was the story of her life. In the background, low, Andrew's stereo MP3 pumped ambient music. It was good stuff, a low groove. She settled back into it and imagined the feel of dancing for hours, the drugs keeping her awake, keeping her high, keeping her alive.

'Pissed? Nah, I'm not pissed. It's just that you could have been a little smoother, you know? I go home for Christmas, I come back here and now it's like, she's your girl. That's all right, I'll get another one. I've always got plenty. But still, you could have been smoother, you know?'

'You locked her out of your apartment. You threw all her shit in the hallway.'

'I sure did. You will too. Trust me.'

'We'll see.'

'Look,' Henry said. 'It's cool, all right? Word to the wise, that's all. You can't trust her. Just keep that in mind. That's the kind of girl she is. Ready to go at all times. You're going to love it for a little while, and then you're going to want to kill her.'

Breeze noticed that Henry stopped just short of calling her a slut in front of Andrew. It was a man thing. If she was Andrew's girl now, it would be an insult to Andrew to call her a slut. Henry never tired of calling her a slut when they were alone.

'Remember what happened with Nestor.'

Of course. This is what it came down to. Nestor. This is why Henry had thrown her out. Not for whatever reason he might tell himself, or tell Andrew, but because of Nestor. And it had been Henry's idea – just another way to try and humiliate her. The fact that it fit in with the job was just icing on the cake.

'She liked it, you know what I mean?'

The cardinal sin – liking it. You can't humiliate someone if they actually like it. But did she like it? She wasn't quite sure of that herself.

There was a midtown bar that Nestor frequented, just a few blocks from the hotel where he lived. She had been sent there a month ago with a mission. To do what she did best – seduce a man. And in this case, get some photos of him in his pristine state. She went armed with a new cellphone – the kind that could snap digital photographs. In a pinch, in case of disaster, she could also use it to call for rescue. Sure, send Breeze. She's expendable.

'Just do it,' Henry had said. What did Henry care? He fucked around all he wanted. Henry wasn't into monogamy – Breeze just happened to be the girl that lived with him. Rent free, as he never tired of reminding her.

'Look at it this way. Even if it's not fun, Andrew's paying you three hundred bucks. It's good money.'

'You ever think that maybe that's not how I want to make my money?'

'Tough break, kid.' That was Henry's standard line – tough break, kid. Any time he gave someone bad news, he accompanied it with that line. Breeze had heard him give the line to lots of people — jonesing drug addicts, girls he was dumping or passing on to someone else, even herself. Hell, he'd probably used that line on her a hundred times by now. 'You gotta play the cards you're dealt,' he went on. 'This happens to be something you're good at.'

So she went. She didn't have to go. She could do something else, but what else was there? She could leave Henry. Move on to the next stop — a stop probably no better than the one she was at now. Maybe worse. She wasn't ready to chance that yet. Anyway, things were good here, better than they had been in a lot of other places. Things were taking shape. They might well become very good before too much longer. So she did it. Not for Henry. Not for Andrew. For herself.

She decided to play it like a spy, a spy sent deep into enemy territory. And the spy game held up for a while.

She entered the dimly lit pub and sat down at the bar, two stools away from Nestor. It was just after Thanksgiving. It had been two months since Nestor had cut off Andrew's finger, and six weeks since Dick Miller had suddenly appeared on the scene. Dot had dropped Nestor, and Nestor was alone now. Nestor was sulking. Nestor was drinking. They had been watching him from afar. Nestor was a big part of Andrew's master plan, and Nestor was ripe for the picking.

It wasn't ten minutes before he approached her, as she knew he would. They always did. She signaled them with her body — she wasn't even sure herself what the signals were — and they came. She saw he was just a little bit drunk. She had a roofie for him, if the opportunity presented itself, but a man like Nestor wasn't about to let people go around slipping things into his drink. She noticed that his cruel face was handsome in its own way. He spoke to her, bar talk, but she wasn't listening. Half an hour of bullshit and they went back to his hotel room.

Her heart skipped a beat as he opened the door. It wasn't a room after all – it was a suite. There was a bedroom, a small kitchenette with a bar, a large bathroom with a full tub, and a living room. The living room had windows with a view of Times Square. It also opened to a small patio with the same views.

'Holy shit,' she said, despite herself. 'You live here?'

'Indeed.'

'Incredible.'

'I have a motto,' he said as he rooted around behind the bar. He came up with two wine glasses. He poured them each a big one. 'The best is good enough for me. I recommend this motto as a personal saying for any person.'

She took a gulp of the wine. 'It must cost a fortune here,' she said.

He shrugged. 'Nine thousand a month. I work hard to enjoy fine things.'

The spy game was wearing off. When he brought her to bed, it wore off for good. As he disrobed, she was already on the bed. She snapped photos of him with the cellphone camera. When his shirt came off, she gasped at the bullet scars, but kept snapping. Soon, he was standing naked before her.

'What are you doing?'

'I just got this cellphone. See? It takes pictures.'

He came closer. 'Why are you taking pictures of me?'

She took another one as he climbed on the bed. 'Come on. You have a beautiful body. Why can't I have a few pictures?'

He put his hand on her throat. Gently at first, but then with increasing pressure. She gasped again. 'Did someone send you here?' he said.

'No. No one sent me.'

Her eyes met his. Had she not looked into his eyes in the bar? No, not really. There was something there, simmering in those eyes, something she had only seen as a young girl, something she hadn't even remembered until this moment. Back then, she had prayed for escape, she had prayed for Ralph to die, and she had prayed for God to give her a sign – any sign at all. Then the thing had come to her in the night, the thing that whispered promises to her, the thing that would make her safe, the thing with the eyes, the glowing eyes like these. All this time had passed, and now the thing was here. It had returned. It was real.

Or was it? Maybe it was just the four drinks she'd had at the bar, the one drink she'd had here in Nestor's suite, all of it mixed with the half-dose of Valium she had dropped before she had gone out.

'Is it you?' she said to the thing.

'Yes. It is me.'

'All this time later. Do you remember me?'

He smiled. 'Of course I remember.'

When he entered her, she wanted to scream, not in pain but in fear. His hand still gripped her throat and it stayed there the whole time. And his eyes gripped hers. The eyes. The eyes. They moved together, staring at one another, and his eyes were the eyes of a demon. The eyes of the devil.

Much later, he slept. He slept like any man would sleep after sex.

She was awake, sober now, and it was time to leave. The curtains were drawn, but she knew the sun would rise soon. She crept from the bed, watching his sleeping form. Imagine approaching this bed, knife in hand. The idea made the flesh stand out on her skin, and he grunted, as if he had heard her very thought. No. She wouldn't even try to plant the listening device in the telephone, as Andrew had hoped. She got the photos and that was enough. She picked up her clothes, her bag, her cellphone, and moved nude to the bedroom door. Her first impulse was to leave the suite this way – she could get dressed in the hallway, or down in the lobby.

'Perhaps we'll meet again,' came his voice, half buried by the pillow. Gooseflesh broke out across her body. Again. 'Perhaps we will.'

'Please make sure the front door is locked as you leave.'

'OK.'

'Thank you.'

The voice emboldened her, just the tiniest bit. It was sodden and thick, the voice of a man in as deep a restful state as he ever allows himself. As she hurriedly dressed in the living room, she spotted his keys on top of the bar. Old-style keys – not the new-fangled security card. She moved to the door, eyes on the bedroom. When she reached the bar, she swept the keys into her hand.

In her pocketbook were pieces of something called the Fast-Rite Key-Duplication System. It was a two-step process for making duplicate keys on the sly. The first step was making the mold. The second step was casting the key out of a metal alloy. Andrew had bought the kit, and would take care of the second step. He had made her practice the first part twenty times before sending her on this little adventure.

She took the items out of her bag. She couldn't believe she was going through with it. It was crazy. It was suicide. Hands shaking, she took out the plastic molding tube, the syringe with plastic copying substance number one (yellow), the syringe with plastic copying substance number two (white), the syringe with the plastic fixing substance (green), the small scalpel and the stirring rod. Jesus.

She arrayed them all on the bar, then mixed substance number one and number two in the molding tube. She added the fixing substance, then dunked the first key into the mold. A minute later, the mold had hardened and she slowly cut it open with the scalpel. Then she repeated the process for the next key, and the next. There were five keys on the ring – three that could be house keys and two that were obviously car keys. She did the three house keys and ignored the car keys. The whole process took ten minutes. Each time she finished pressing a key, she glanced up, expecting him to appear in the doorway to the bedroom, watching her. Each time, he wasn't there.

She was out on the street and five blocks away before her heart started beating normally again.

Now, on the FDR Drive, Breeze realized how much better than Andrew and Henry she was. Tougher, more daring, more capable. Neither one of these men could survive the night she spent with Nestor – Big Henry could barely survive the thought of it. As Andrew took formal possession of her, she knew – she *knew* – it would be a short-lived arrangement.

The Lincoln Town Car had juice.

With Block's heavy foot on the accelerator, they were soon on the narrow span of the bridge. The Town Car wove from one lane to another, passing cars on either side. The digital speed display showed 50. Then 60.

Now 70.

The lights of Manhattan approached.

'Don't worry,' Block said. 'We'll get her.'

Sure enough, there was the car, up ahead. The Town Car zipped right up to its rear bumper. Block charged up to within a foot, but didn't ram it. Instead, he pulled hard to the left and cruised right up alongside. The two cars were inches apart.

Dick powered his window down.

'Desiree! Pull over.'

Desiree turned and saw Dick. Instead of pulling over, she stomped on the gas. Dick watched as his car surged ahead. It zoomed off, changed lanes, passed a car and whipped back into the right lane again.

'Jesus!' Block said. 'She drives like a man.'

'She is a man.'

Block looked at him. Dick shrugged. 'What can I tell you?'

Block hit the gas. He passed the same car – a green Mercedes with an old couple in the front – and changed lanes. He sped up and caught her, got right on Desiree's bumper. Dick watched the buildings approach across the water, looming, getting larger. They reached the Manhattan side going fast. The road humped at the bottom, and as they came down off the span they nearly caught air. The bridge emptied into a busy city street. Stores lined the strip. Even in the cold, people stood on the corners. They whizzed by, faces, colors blurring.

Desiree made a screaming right-hand turn down a side street. Block followed. It was a two-way street. He crossed the double yellow line and pulled out into the oncoming traffic lane. Nothing was coming.

'Block, there could be cops. We get busted and—'

'I know. I know.'

The two cars raced along the street, side by side.

Then Block sidewiped her.

Hard.

Dick's car veered off, slicing into parked cars along the sidewalk. It skidded, sparks flying, then spun around. Desiree disappeared from sight.

'Shit!' Block said. 'I didn't want to do that.'

He jammed the brakes and they slid to a stop. They looked back. The Oldsmobile was crumpled and jammed in between two parked cars. Block opened the driver's side door of the Town Car and got out. He walked around to Dick's side.

'Shit! See? That's why I didn't want to hit her. Now I have a dent in my car.'

Dick climbed out.

'We have exactly no time,' Dick said.

'I know.'

They jogged back to Dick's car. For a moment, the sight of it took his breath away. When Dick was a kid, his mom and dad had taken him on vacation somewhere in Pennsylvania. It was in the mountains and there was nothing to do except go swimming in a lake filled with snapping turtles. The high point of the trip had been when they went to some rinky-dink country fair. There was an old Volkswagen Bug there, and for a quarter you could take a swing at it with a sledge-hammer. A gang of drunken hillbillies were stationed at the car, beating on the damned thing. Halfway through the night, that Bug looked like they had dropped a bomb on it.

That's what Dick's car looked like now.

Two windows were shattered. The passenger side had been twisted into a shapeless wreck by the parked cars. Desiree was still behind the wheel. Her forehead was bleeding.

'Fuck,' Dick said. 'Would you look at my fucking car?'

'Yeah,' Block said. 'It's worse than mine.'

'Worse than yours? Block, your car has a fucking dent in it. This thing is demolished.'

'No, you're right, Dick. Your car is fucked.'

Dick put his hands on his hips and surveyed the wreckage.

'Hey, Desiree,' Block said.

She sat, staring straight ahead.

'DESIREE!'

She looked at him. Her face was blank.

'What?'

'That's better.' He pointed at the Town Car. 'Get out of that car, and get into my car. We're in a hurry here.' He looked at Dick. 'Come on,' he said. 'Let's go get that package out of the trunk.'

'Make and model?' the tiny woman cop said from behind the big wooden front desk. The desk was so high that Dick had to stretch just a bit to put his elbows on it. The cop was perched up there on

what looked like a barstool. To Dick's right there were three steps
that climbed up to a locked gate.

'Oldsmobile. Ninety-eight.'

'Year?'

'Uh, I don't know. 'Ninety-three, 'ninety-four. Something in there.'

The cop looked up from her paperwork. 'You don't know what
year?'

Dick shrugged.

It was Block's idea to report the car stolen. Dick felt totally
composed, in shock really, and the woman on desk duty didn't take
much interest in him. She looked sleepy. She took his information like
a robot. Just another stolen car in a city full of stolen cars.

'We'll let you know if we find anything,' she said.

When Dick got in the Lincoln, Desiree was still sprawled in the
back. She let out a low moan as he climbed in. She had seen them
carry Dot's body from the Olds over to this car. She had recognized
that it was a body right away – the carpet it was wrapped in didn't
fool her for one second.

'Dick, did you kill somebody?' she had said.

'Desiree, I warned you that you wanted no part of this, right? But
you didn't listen. And then you stole my fucking car. So I need you
to shut up.'

Now she was silent, except for occasional noises.

'You think she's all right?' Dick said.

Block put the car in gear and they headed back out onto the street.
He turned his head to look, taking his eyes off the road for a second.
He nodded. 'She'll be fine.'

When they reached Dick's place, they left Desiree in the car until
they could get the body inside. They carried it upstairs, just a couple
of guys bringing a carpet – a heavy carpet – in from the car. They
didn't see anyone on the stairs or in the hallway. Dick didn't know

if anyone saw them, but he imagined eyes peering through the cracks of every door. Once in the apartment, they put the body in the bathtub. They just let the carpet unroll and the body flopped on in there, still wrapped in green plastic. Dick winced at the thud it made as it landed in the tub.

They went back into the big open studio space.

'You know what's the best thing you could do?' Block said. 'Go to the store and get some ice.'

'Ice?'

'We're gonna have that body on hand for a little while. If we don't want it to start smelling up the joint, then we're gonna have to keep it frozen.'

Dick looked at Block with alarm. 'You mean we're going to keep that thing around here?'

'What would you prefer we do with it?'

'Get rid of it.'

Block smiled. 'Trust me. I got it all worked out already. I'll get Desiree upstairs, you take the car and get about a hundred pounds of ice, and when you get back, we'll see what we're looking at here.'

Dick drove Block's car around until he found an open deli and bought the ice. It came in seven-pound bags, so he got one hundred and five pounds of it, or fifteen bags.

'Having a party?' the old guy behind the counter said.

'Am I ever.'

He loaded the ice into the car and headed back to the building. Along the way, he remembered what the ice was for and he pulled over. His whole body started shaking, and his breath caught in his throat. He felt his face flush, and his eyes welled up with tears. Holy Christ, was he going to cry? He fumbled for the radio and found some jazz improvisation shrieking out of the speaker, some sax with a bass and drums and a piano, and none of it sounded like they were playing the same song. They were all going their own way at the same time.

He took a bag of dope from his pocket and he rolled a biggie by the light of the dashboard. He was five minutes from the apartment and he knew there would be dark work ahead. He needed to put a little space between himself and the problem at hand. He lit up the joint and inhaled deeply. The music had slowed and he took a look at his surroundings. Quiet neighborhood. Modest homes. No one would bother him here. He leaned back and closed his eyes.

He remembered the first time he had seen Dot's butterfly. Dot and he were at her place, soon after they had first gotten together. They were lying in bed. The windows were all open, bringing in a slight nighttime chill. They were naked under the covers. On a table across from the bed, Dot had an enormous terrarium. It must have been five feet high and at least as long. She had decorated it with lush foliage – it was thick with greenery and colorful flowers. It looked like a jungle in there. As Dick looked at it, he saw something he hadn't noticed before. A butterfly was trapped inside, making short flights from one plant to the next.

'You know you have a butterfly in with your plants?' he said.

Dot smiled. She played with the hair on Dick's chest. 'I know. She's a Monarch, and her name is Dot.'

'She's named after you. That's nice.'

'In a way, she is me. The me I used to be. Back when I was married. Oh, it's not what you're thinking. My husband was a good man. I had everything I could possibly want. Everything except my freedom. Our life together was all about him. His work, his money, his friends, his kids. I was the showpiece. I was like that butterfly, you know? A beautiful winged creature, trapped in a beautiful place, with no way to fly. And butterflies were made to fly, don't you think? So I keep her there to remind me. As long as she's with me, I'll never go back to that kind of life again.'

'What if she dies?' Dick said.

'She has died before. When that happens, I go get another one.'

Dick chewed on that for a minute. 'Dot,' he said finally, 'don't you think it's kind of cruel keeping that thing caged up in there? I mean, I've been locked up before, and I'll tell you what, it's no picnic.'

Dot looked at Dick solemnly. Their faces were six inches apart. Her eyes sparkled. She was beautiful, no makeup, no lipstick, hair come undone, the whole nine yards. It didn't matter. She was beautiful enough. She could talk about herself like a butterfly and still get away with it.

'That's what you need to know about me, hon,' she said. 'I can be cruel with the best of them.'

'Not cruel enough,' he said now.

He looked at the time. He had already been out for forty-five minutes. He put the car in gear and drove home. Back at the building, he carried the first five bags up the stairs to the apartment. He figured he'd get Block to help with the rest of the bags, then they could make just one more trip out into the cold. But upstairs, it wasn't immediately obvious where Block was.

'Block!' he called as he came in.

There was no answer. Dick carried the ice into the bathroom. The body was there, lying in the tub. Tufts of hair poked out the top of the garbage bag. Block must have ripped the top open, to get a look at the head.

Dick noticed blood streaked in the hair and a lot of blood had coagulated inside the bag. He dropped the bags of ice, and stared down at Dot. He kneeled next to the body and pulled the bag down off her head. For the first time, he got a really good look at her. Her eyes were wide open and staring at nothing.

A wave of dizziness rolled over him. He looked up at the ceiling, then back into the tub. Jesus! His body jerked involuntarily.

'Are you alive?' he said.

No answer.

He shook her, but she was solid, like a big rubber Barbie doll. Of course she was. He'd had her in his possession now for more than three days. There was no way she was alive. He stood up and walked out of the bathroom again, out into the big empty space that was his apartment. A thought occurred to him. What if he found Block and Desiree dead? What if he was killing these people, and he didn't even realize it? Was he a maniac? Was he a guy who had forty-seven different personalities living in the same body, none of which knew the others?

Something was caught in his throat, blocking him from swallowing. It didn't seem like he was in control of his own legs. He floated toward the heavy black curtain that marked off his bedroom. There was no sound anywhere in the apartment.

Then the phone began to ring.

By Sunday night, Lydia knew she had only one choice.

She had gone to a payphone yesterday morning and tried calling Dot, but there was no answer. The machine wasn't even picking up. So Lydia had decided – hey, what the heck? She had some clothes out here at her father's that she could wear, why not stay an extra day or two? She hadn't really spent time with her father in a while. Monday morning, she could drive back to the city early and go straight to the office.

And when people at work wondered where Dot was, what would Lydia say? That Dot had gone . . . home? To Ohio? Dot hadn't called Ohio home in twenty years. And what about the computer program, the one that every day transferred nearly two percent of all the daily income transactions into an account controlled by Dot and Lydia? There was no way to stop the computer. It would go on and on, automatically transferring money, with no regard as to how she, apprentice to an absent sorcerer, felt about it.

Lydia had puzzled out her options over the past two days. She could turn herself in to the police, explain the situation to them, and throw herself on the mercy of the justice system. She could tell her dad, and see what his advice was. Until only recently, this would have been the most likely answer. Or she could talk to Dick Miller.

The first option was the easiest to eliminate. She couldn't go to the police, not unless she wanted to go to prison for embezzlement.

The second option, her dad, was still on the table until yesterday.

Yesterday, while they sat together in the living room, Lydia glanced at her father. She caught a flash, a psychic whiff of another time. It was Christmas, that first year after her mother was gone. The tree, green, full and beautiful, was up in the corner of the living room. The room smelled of pine. Lydia and her dad laughed while they hung the bulbs and the garland. The stereo was on – they still had a record player then. He wouldn't hear of getting rid of it. Compact discs were a fad. They'd be gone in another year. Anyway, he still had all these great old record albums.

At that moment, 'Silent Night' was playing. Lydia was OK until then. But when they reached the part about the mother and child, something seemed to block her throat. She looked away. Out the window, a car passed by on the street. Her mother had been ripped from her, and now there was no one. Her father sensed something, came to her then, and hugged her. He was a hero during those years, and he believed that he had raised in Lydia a hard-working, honest daughter. She could never let him think otherwise. She knew that she could never burden him with this problem, this onrushing disaster.

That left the third option, Dick Miller. She smiled inwardly. The hardened ex-con – he was more like a great big puppy dog. At work, Lydia was technically his supervisor and she had become friendly with him. They used to have lunch at a nearby pizza joint a couple of times a week. Did it bother her, Dot being with Dick? No, not really. Nestor – that had bothered her. It had shown her a side of Dot that she didn't know, and didn't want to know. But Dick? Good Lord, Lydia was glad when Dot got together with Dick. It showed the woman was coming to her senses.

Then Dick had stopped coming to work. Hard to believe, punctual Dick, Dick who hadn't missed a single day since he started, clockwork Dick, as he sometimes called himself, had quit. At first he'd called in sick. Later he wouldn't even answer his telephone.

'Well, yeah,' the guy from the agency had said. 'I'm sorry to hear that. Seemed like he was gonna make it. You know, what can I say? These guys, two out of every five last six months. You gotta realize that what we're doing here, we're just giving them a chance. It's not always going to work. That's the business I'm in. So whaddya say? You wanna give it another whirl? I've got three good guys right now, and all of them have some office skills. One of them has a lot.'

'I'll have to let you know,' Lydia said.

Then, just as suddenly as he disappeared, he materialized. Lydia saw him at the Christmas party, smiling, having a drink, chatting with Dot. Lydia had planned to talk with him, but one thing led to another, a few drinks, a few laughs, and when she looked up, both Dot and Dick were gone. A cop might think that Dick had something to do with Dot's disappearance, but Lydia rejected that idea out of hand. Dick wouldn't harm a fly.

Would he?

Well, she would take her chances. She stood in the kitchen of her father's house, wall phone in hand. Her father had gone upstairs to bed. All the same, in the small Levitt-style house, she didn't want to speak too loudly. She waited as the phone rang in Brooklyn.

'Hello?' came the voice, somewhat deep. He sounded distracted, or afraid. She pictured the body that went with the voice – tall, broad shoulders and chest, face, as many women had remarked, like a movie star.

'Dick?'

'Yeah. Lydia? How are you doing?'

'I'm fine. Did you have a nice Christmas?'

She felt silly. *How's your vacation? Oh, fine. How's yours?* This while everything was on the line. But she didn't know how to start the real conversation, the one about all the money she and Dot had stolen, about Nestor, about how she was afraid that Dot was dead.

'It was . . . good. Real good. Yours?'

'Good.'

'OK, well . . . Listen, what's up?'

'I was hoping I could meet you for breakfast tomorrow. I think there's something we need to talk about.'

'Is it about Dot?'

'It is.'

'Isn't that funny?' he said. 'You're the second person who's wanted to talk about Dot in the past two days. You don't carry mace, do you?'

As Dick hung up, Block appeared from behind the curtain, wearing nothing but a pair of boxer shorts with little red hearts all over them. He was solidly built. All muscle, like an old-time laborer from black-and-white photos. At least he was alive.

This is great dope, Dick thought. I'm really flying here.

'I tell you what,' Block said. He didn't look at Dick. In fact, his eyes searched the ground. 'I gotta run.'

'Block,' Dick said.

Block put a thick hand up, palm outward, like a crossing guard motioning STOP. 'You told me you still have a set of Dot's keys, right? You never gave them back? Tomorrow night, after dark, I want you and Desiree to go over and get Dot's car. OK? We're going to need it when we get rid of the body. I've got some other things that I need to pick up.'

'Block.'

Block shook his head. 'I'm already late, man. I was supposed to tuck my kids in tonight. Trish is gonna have a fit.' His clothes were strewn about the living-room furniture. He picked up his pants and began to put them on. 'We'll take care of everything tomorrow night, OK?'

'Block?'

Block stopped and glanced up. Their eyes met and locked.

'Dick, there's things about me that you don't know.'

5
BODY PARTS

Dick stood in the offices of Feldman Real Estate, his former employer. It was eight thirty in the morning, half an hour before opening time, and Lydia was already at her desk, as always. He could see the fear in her eyes. She looked at him deeply. 'Have you spoken to Dot?'

'No. I talked to her for a little while before I left the Christmas party and that was it. I think she and I are through. What's going on?'

'It's a long story,' she said, 'and I don't even know where to begin.'

'Well, start with what's bothering you right now.'

Her eyes were wild, like animals trapped in a cage. She shook her head, then scanned the office. 'We shouldn't talk here. Let's go down to the street and buy a bagel.'

They walked through the office, then down to the street. She was walking out as her co-workers were coming in. Dick knew that normally it would bother her if people thought she was shirking her responsibilities. Now, she didn't seem to notice. They walked along the busy sidewalk, picking their way through the crush of faces on their way to another grinding day. It was cold out and despite everything he knew, Dick was becoming annoyed by this show of secrecy. He was about to tell her so.

Then Lydia spoke. 'Dot and I have stolen more than a million dollars from the company. Nestor knows about it and he wants the money. I think he either killed Dot or Dot ran off to the Bahamas and left me here to hold the bag. Either way, Dot is gone. I'm so afraid I don't want to go back to work anymore. I keep thinking the police are going to show up there, asking questions.'

'Maybe we should go to a diner,' Dick said.

Ten minutes later, they sat in a plush leather booth at a nearby diner. The place was filled with mirrors. They were laid out in such a way, however, that regardless of where Dick looked in the restaurant, he could not see himself. It was almost like he was a vampire, or he had ceased to exist. When the waitress came, Lydia ordered a vodka and orange juice.

'Breakfast of champions,' she said.

'Tell me,' Dick said.

Lydia hesitated for just a moment. She sipped her drink through a straw. Her hand shook as she held the glass. Dick was struck by how young she looked. When she finally launched into her story, it was with the abandon of a woman who had been dying of thirst, diving into a pool of clear water. It was like she had been holding a flood back. The dam broke and the story surged out.

'I've been working for Dot for over three years now,' she said. 'We became good friends. You know, I lost my mother when I was young. My father raised me. And Dot was like, I don't want to say a mother, more like she was an older sister to me, or a cousin. I felt like she was teaching me things, how to get along in the business world as a woman.'

Dick nodded for her to go on. He knew the story. Dot had told him.

'So we started going out together and became more like friends than a boss and her employee. We talked about men, went shopping together, got drunk together, traveled together, whatever. More than that, even. We were very close friends. Then one day, she told me she had a dream. In the dream came an idea about how to get a lot of money.'

'What was the idea?'

'Do you understand anything about billing systems?'

Dick smiled. 'Until this job, everything was strictly cash.'

'OK, then I'll keep it as simple as I can. As you do know, the company tracks all its receivables by computer. All the rents that come in. We receive the money through checks, every month, checks that get processed manually. You've done some of that, remember? OK. Some payments, the ones that come from companies mostly, are wireless transfers that come straight into our bank accounts. Either way, there's a formula in the computer that routes money to different accounts, depending on the purpose of the money and the needs of the company. Do you follow me so far?'

'So far, so good.'

'OK, Dot's idea was to set up a new bank account, in the company name, but which only she and I would have access to. Also, she wanted to set up the computer in such a way that every week, a certain amount of money would get routed automatically to that account, but would never show up on the computer-generated banking reports.'

'How much?'

'About one percent of the gross income, maybe forty thousand dollars a month. A little less than that, usually. Dot calls it the skim.'

'Jesus, that much?' It sounded like an impossible score, just too good to be true. 'Wouldn't somebody, the old man, one of the workers – *somebody* – notice that much money being drained off?'

She smiled at the beauty of their plan. Dick could see she had been happy to be part of it, whatever the fallout might be now.

'Don't you see?' she said. 'Office workers like you input the checks. You don't know where the money goes and you don't really care. I oversee the finances for the most part and Dot oversees me. Feldman is eighty-one years old. His wife died two years ago, and he hasn't been the same since. He's alone. He drinks too much. He may be a little bit senile. His kids live in Florida and California and they don't care. They're just waiting to get their hands on the inheritance. Feldman has a hundred million dollars, probably more. He owns two other companies, and he leaves the running of this one to Dot. Dot's husband was Feldman's broker. Feldman trusts her and doesn't watch her too closely. Anyway, he'd have to be watching *very* closely to catch her at this.'

'Why's that?'

'First, the company generates so much money that forty thousand dollars just isn't that noticeable. Second, the computer is programmed to send money to our account automatically. It's a real account. We empty it regularly. We use it as a sort of checking account, the money comes in, and we take it out. Paper bank statements reflect this. But we intercept the bank statements and replace them with fake ones that show the amount that should be in there. That way, we always know how much we've taken.'

Dick held up a hand. 'But the bank statements are also reconciled electronically. Touch-of-a-button banking, remember? That was one of the first things you told me when I came here.'

'It's an old system. We changed it so that when you do an electronic reconcile on our account, what shows up is the amount that should be there, not what's actually there. At any given time, there's hardly anything in that account at all.'

'That would take some computer know-how,' Dick said. 'You know that much about computers?'

She shook her head. 'Do you know Andrew King? That's where

he came in. We had him set it up that way – it always seems like the right amount is there, and it just isn't. Also, Dot and I are the only ones who can write checks on that account, and are the only ones who can access that account. Feldman doesn't even have access. I don't think he knows it exists. We cash the money out of the account and carry it to the Bahamas, where we stash it in safe-deposit boxes around Nassau. Dot doesn't want the money traced, and she doesn't trust the anonymous banks down there, so she won't actually deposit the money. The money is safely stowed, out of reach, and we can get it any time we want.'

'But what happens when somebody finds out the account is empty?'

'How would they do that?'

'I don't know. What if Feldman dies, they sell the company, and the new people go through everything?'

'By then, we'd be in the Caribbean with more money than we needed.'

Dick whistled. 'That's one hell of a plan.'

'Dot is one smart cookie. It was perfect. No one could figure out that it happened, unless someone involved were to spill the beans. Or unless someone were to suddenly get greedy.'

'Greedy?'

'It's a long story,' she said.

Dick motioned to the waitress for another cup of coffee. 'I have time,' he said.

Nestor took an early lunch in his room – baked stuffed sole, French fries, and a green salad on the side. Hot apple pie. A bottle of wine. He stared at the water through his bay window as he ate the meal. He hadn't felt this calm in some time. He was so relaxed that he could think of the past without pain, and without fear. He closed his eyes and let the memories of Florida wash over him.

'Do you never learn, Nestor?' Marisa had said, one evening several months after the shooting. They were sitting in his roof garden, at the table, enjoying a light meal and a glass of wine. The view of the ocean was like a fantasy. The sun was beginning to set to the west. Nestor would miss this place. It had taken him too long to get back on his feet. He was months behind on the rent. The gardener had already left, and the garden was going to seed all around him. He had sold the Porsche, and had fallen back on the Toyota. Indeed, although loyal, grounded Marisa was still here, inconstant, flighty Angelique had already left. It was a symptom of how far Nestor had fallen that a woman thought she could just up and leave him without retribution.

'Perhaps not,' he said.

'They will kill you this time for sure.'

'Why will they kill me? Because I am selling roses?'

'No. Because you are stupid.'

He slapped her then, and regretted it immediately. He had let his temper get the best of him. But she should not have called him stupid. Couldn't she see that if he was selling roses again, it was for the both of them? How could they keep their lifestyle, the things that they loved, if he didn't do what he knew how to do? He had no skills to use in the workplace, and there was no chance – no chance – that at the age of thirty he would consider a job flipping burgers.

Her hand to her face, she said. 'Just remember that I tried to protect you.'

'What does that mean?'

She stood and downed the last of her drink.

'It means that you and I are finished. It means that two men grabbed me today in the parking lot at the Publix supermarket. They drove me around, and they said that if you are still here on Saturday, you will be dead. It means that I will not stay here and die for your stubbornness.'

Nestor sipped his drink and gazed out at all that deep blue ocean. The ocean didn't care about the problems faced by pitiful humans – their constant setbacks and failures. No, the ocean didn't care. Vast and eternal, it flowed with energy, with life, and each individual life was no more important than each passing moment, than any particular wave crashing against the sand.

Nestor had been thinking for some time about moving to New York. He knew things were over for him in South Florida. He was finished. He could simply pack a bag, get in the car tomorrow, and drive north. Despite himself, he sighed. Such a lovely place, such a lovely life he had enjoyed here. Well, it would be a new start.

Marisa's voice shook now. There would be other Marisas, he supposed, other Angeliques. 'They showed me a gun,' she said. 'They meant it. Today is Thursday, Nestor. You have two more days to live.'

Nestor opened his eyes. The hotel room in Connecticut reappeared. He wondered why all the places seemed unreal, like stage sets. Colombia, Florida, Connecticut, New York, all unreal, all fantasy, as if workmen were behind the scenes, putting up the walls then tearing them back down again.

In New York, he had rebuilt everything. For a short while, life had become beautiful again. Now, it was growing darker and more ugly by the day.

He considered how Dot had betrayed him. Was it even betrayal if she never meant it in the first place? But how could that be? How could it be that Dot had merely used him, had merely acted as if she were in love with him? Then, when he had served his purpose, moved on to another? Nestor never behaved in this way. He was a sincere person. When he was angry, he was angry. When he was in love, he was in love. He was not capable of acting out false emotions.

When he learned of their relationship, he decided he would kill them both – Dot and Miller. He followed them to Sea, the Asian restaurant on North Sixth Street in Brooklyn he had enjoyed with Dot several times. It was their place – *their* place. Now Miller was there with her. Nestor walked in and hovered by the swings hanging down near the entrance. The place was crowded and the light was low, but he spotted them right away. They were seated on the edge of the indoor pond, looking through their menus. Would he walk up and shoot them right there in the restaurant? Would he dare?

At that moment, Miller looked up from his menu, saw Nestor and tapped Dot. She craned her neck around to look, saw him, and nodded. She turned back to Miller. Miller said something to her and then laughed. They both did.

They laughed at Nestor.

Nestor ran out of the restaurant before he did something that would send him to prison the rest of his life.

Now he sat in his room, far away from that time and place, gazing out at the sea as the rage coursed through him. The very thought of their laughter made his body shake. Soon, they would have much to answer for.

Dick spent the entire morning and part of the early afternoon in that Greenpoint diner. When noon came around, they ordered lunch.

'What about Andrew?' he said to Lydia.

'What about him?'

'He did all this without being paid?'

'No,' she said. 'We paid him, and gave him a stake in the profits. Ten percent.'

'Ten percent?'

She shrugged. 'He wanted more, but Dot, she was persuasive. Anyway, ten percent was good money.'

'He's a worm,' Dick said. 'I don't like that guy.'

'Believe me, he wasn't a problem. Not until later.'

'Who was a problem? Nestor?'

'Dot. Dot was the original problem. She couldn't leave well enough alone. Dot was a spender. Did you know her husband left her two million dollars? OK, he left the bulk of his estate to his kids, and that upset her. But two million dollars? You know what I mean? It was set up in a trust that she couldn't access, municipal bonds, conservative investments that return a little less than five percent per year. The trust paid her an income of between eighty and ninety thousand a year, depending on what the return had been in the past year. Also, she had a house in Westchester that she sold to move to Brooklyn, and she realized a tidy profit on that. But she wanted more. Feldman gave her the job, and he paid her well, another hundred and twenty. She still wanted more – *needed* more. For Dot, enough was never going to be enough. She told me she felt trapped. She was full of pity for herself.'

'So what happened?'

'Seven months ago, Dot doubled the amount we were taking.'

'Jesus.'

'Yeah.'

'Then?'

'Andrew didn't want her to do it – he didn't want to change the skim to two percent. He was afraid. He said we were going to get caught. He didn't want his ten percent anymore. He wanted a buyout. Two hundred thousand dollars. For that, he would make the change, then walk away and forget about the whole thing.'

'And Dot didn't go for it?'

Lydia shook her head. 'I wish that was what happened. On the contrary, she did go for it. Andrew made the change, the money started coming in like you wouldn't believe, then Dot refused to pay him. She said she wanted to keep the ten percent agreement. Told him he should be happy with that. But Andrew wasn't happy. He started making noise about going to the cops himself – not that he would, because he'd be implicated just as much as we would. And Dot had met Nestor around that time – he was selling cocaine at parties in Williamsburg.'

Dick raised his eyebrows. 'She never mentioned that's how she met Nestor.'

'Dick, don't be like that. You know how Dot is. She would do anything for a rush. Maybe you never saw it, but on rare occasions, that rush has been coke. The mistake she made wasn't buying coke from Nestor – it was dating him.' Lydia shook her head again. 'Dot has some questionable taste in men.'

Dick stared at her.

She smiled. 'Present company excepted, of course.'

'Dot told Nestor about this scam?'

'No. She said she didn't. I believe her. I don't think Dot would do anything that stupid. Then again, she might have – she thought she could handle Nestor. Either way, she told him Andrew was bothering her. Could he throw a scare into the guy? I don't know if you know Nestor, but asking him to scare somebody is like throwing raw meat to a crocodile. He put a pretty good scare into Andrew, I can tell you that. The poor guy disappeared for months.'

'What did Nestor do to Andrew?'

She hesitated. 'He cut Andrew's finger off.'

As soon as she said it, tears began to stream quietly down her face. For a few seconds, it looked like she was going to keep it together, that the tears would stop, but then she broke down completely. She wept and Dick let her go. He held her hands across the table. The waitress stayed away from them. It scared Dick that a nice girl like Lydia was mixed up in a plot to steal over a million dollars. She didn't seem to have the stomach for it. If Andrew's finger was enough to send her off the edge, then she had some long days ahead of her. After a while, the crying subsided.

'You must think I'm awful. And Dot...'

Lydia trailed off and Dick didn't say anything. He paused for a moment, digesting it all.

'So Nestor is after the money?' he said. 'And Dot is in Nassau?'

Her eyes were red. 'No. I don't believe Dot went to Nassau. The thing is we took another ninety-eight thousand out of the account, just in the past month. And the way we do it, we need two people to smuggle the money. She can't do it alone.'

She stopped.

'And?' Dick said. But he saw the entire picture coming together in his mind. It snapped to with a nearly audible sound.

Lydia sighed. 'If Dot ran away to Nassau, she left without taking nearly a hundred thousand dollars. There's no way she would leave that kind of money behind. She just wouldn't do it. But the money is still here.'

'Where is it?'

'I've been carrying it around with me since Friday. It's in the trunk of my car right now. Nestor showed up at my apartment that morning. He said he was looking for Dot and looking for the safe-deposit-box keys. After he left, I went to Dot's apartment and the whole place was wrecked. But the money was hidden. It was still there. I have the money and the keys.'

'Looks like you're a rich woman,' Dick said.

'Dick, don't you hear me? I think Dot is dead.'

Hours later, at night, Andrew watched and waited.

He melted back into the bucket seat of his BMW. The car was at the curb, along the edge of the dirt track that circled McKinney Park. He was parked under a tree, which gave him shade from the streetlights above. The car was not on. He sat wreathed in shadow, bundled in his winter clothes. He didn't want to give Nestor an idea that there was someone in this car – exhaust from an idling engine would be too much.

He kept down, below the dashboard. From this angle, he could just see the entrance to Dot's house a block away. He had a small telescope, similar to the kind a ship's captain might have used in the days of sailing and whaling. It brought the house so close that he could almost reach out and touch it.

He had gone in Dot's house today. It was something out of a nightmare. Every room in the house was trashed. Computer equipment demolished. The huge flat-screen TV smashed. Furniture punctured and ripped apart. Andrew had floated through the place like a man in a dream. In the kitchen, on the floor beneath the counter, garbage strewn everywhere, he had found the final image from the dream – a small revolver. He had pinched the barrel between two fingers and placed it in a plastic bag. Before he did, he smelled it. It had been fired. Now it was in the glove compartment. Andrew could feel it there, sending out pulses of energy to him. That gun had answers.

As Andrew scanned the street, Dick Miller appeared, walking along Bedford Avenue. Was it Dick? Yes, clearly that was Dick. He was with someone. A smaller person walked alongside of him. Andrew drew a bead on this person and focused. It was a woman, but not Lydia and not Dot. A black woman in a skirt and a long fur coat – no one he recognized. Kind of cold for that skirt, wasn't it? She was attractive – a lot of hair, a very nice body. Miller went up the steps to Dot's front door, leaving the woman at the bottom, on the street.

Nobody home, asshole.

Dick opened the door and went in. Of course. Dick had a key to the place. Andrew watched and waited. So did the woman. She stood on the street in front of the house and smoked a cigarette. Andrew watched the red ember glow brightly at the tip of her cigarette every time she inhaled.

Five minutes passed before Dot's garage door opened and her Lexus pulled out of the tiny driveway. Andrew zoomed in, as close as he could get.

It was Miller. Miller was taking Dot's car. The woman climbed in and the car pulled out into the street and disappeared down the block. In a moment its taillights were lost in the glow of light from the stores, the streetlights, and the general buzz of activity down the avenue.

Andrew sat for a moment, just thinking, letting it wash over him. Miller knew where Dot was after all. He must know. Would he take off with her car if he didn't?

Andrew put down his telescope and picked up his cellphone.

'You're a slut, you know that? I mean, you really are.'

'I know.'

Henry lay back on his bed, smoking a cigarette, talking to the Cool Breeze. People had given him different names over the years – Oh Henry, Henry the Head, sometimes just Head. But he thought of himself as Big Henry, and had for a long time now. Big Henry, larger than life. Twice as large.

Henry had come down to New York eight years before. Ever since high school – before high school – he had known he was destined for bigger things than small-town Connecticut had to offer. He had been dealing ounces of pot, and whatever pills he could get his hands on back then. When he came down here and started making the club scene, he switched strictly to pills. Ecstasy. Special K. Tranks. Whatever the kids wanted. When crystal meth came in, he broke his 'strictly pills' rule. The money was too good, and as it turned out, the money was the least of it.

He worked in a record store for three years just to cover his ass – the W2 from the store showed the government where his income came from. After that, he bought the record store and left the management of it to the kid who used to be his boss. Henry stopped in there once or twice a week and gave the place the once-over. Mostly he stuck with the drugs, hardly working at all, just enjoying the scene, enjoying the girls, his pick of the litter.

He was like a medieval king – he could have anybody he wanted. He'd stopped counting the times some meth junkie had come up to him, some prospective slave low on cash, but with a little piece of tail he called his girlfriend trailing along behind him. And Henry would say to the slave, 'I have what you need, but you gotta give me what I need.' He'd gesture at the girlfriend, then look back at the slave. And after a moment's hesitation, they would do it. They would make the trade. God, that was power. He loved it. He loved his little slaves on their knees. And he loved how, as he grew more comfortable with his power, he became ever more demented and deranged. Absolute power corrupts absolutely – that's what people said, and he believed it was true. Only just recently, he had made a new guy – a new slave – watch what he did to the girl. The girl had cried, the guy had literally shaken with anger, or humiliation, or some other emotion, but in the end they did exactly what they were told.

Awesome.

Who would believe it, a fat kid like himself, all grown up now? Of course, just like the slaves, the girls also wanted what he had – he understood that. It wasn't that they liked him or anything. But wanting what he had worked in more ways than one. They didn't call him Big Henry for nothing.

So Breeze was with him. Of course she was. It didn't surprise him. Like all the rest, she came to him almost by divine right. She was stretched out next to him, nude, also smoking a cigarette. She had a good body. Others had better. He liked her because she was an animal. She would do it all. She wanted it all. You could do things to Breeze, if you did them to some other girl, the girl would cry. Breeze liked it.

The best thing about the new arrangement was that he could still have Breeze, but he didn't have to have her living here with him.

'Yeah, you know. You like being a slut.'

The thought of it began to heighten him again.

'I can't help myself,' she said. She touched him and he was ready.

'You gonna tell Andrew? Now that you're living with him?'

'I don't see why.'

Henry smiled. An idea popped in his head all at once. Ideas were good. And this one was better than good. 'Maybe I should tell him.'

She half laughed. 'Henry, don't.'

Playfully, he began to push her head down. 'I won't tell him, but from now on you gotta do whatever I say. No more arguments. Anything I say, anytime I want.'

She went down. Now she was down there, working on him.

His cellphone rang. 'Shit.'

She kept working.

He picked it up. Speak of the devil.

'Henry,' Andrew said. 'I got a job for you. I need you to go in and search Dot's place again. I went in there today and you won't believe it. The place is wrecked. I found a gun in there. I'm going to run the prints on it, but I need you to go and bust open the drawers in Dot's bedroom closet, see if she left any money behind.'

Henry could barely focus on what Andrew was saying. 'Sounds good. I'll need backup.'

'You OK working with Breeze on this?'

Henry looked down at his hand resting on Breeze's head. She was really working down there. She was going for it.

'I don't think that'll be a problem at all,' he said.

Dot was dead, that much was certain.

Her body was on ice in the bathroom. Dick hovered near the door. Block was in there, looking over the mess. After a time, he came out, his big hands covered in blood.

'Come on,' he said. 'I want to show you something.'

They went into the bathroom and there was Dot again, floating in a tub half full of pink water and ice. Dick had a moment of longing for her, a moment of terrible loneliness, but he crushed that swiftly. There would be time for longing and loneliness at a later date.

'See the gunshot wounds?' Block said. He pointed at four holes on her torso. There was also one on her left shoulder. The force of the shot had more or less ripped the shoulder apart. 'Those are the entries. The exit wounds are in back. You don't want to look at those. But it looks like she got shot from close range by a decent size weapon. You don't even own a gun, do you?'

'No. But I gave Dot a thirty-eight. She said she was afraid at night sometimes.'

'Where is it?'

Dick put up his hands. 'I don't know.'

Block's wide brow creased as he thought that one over. 'Well, in a few hours, it's not going to matter. In a perfect world, the gun might have led to the identity of the killer. But this ain't a perfect world. And all the evidence is about to go away.'

'So we're never going to know who did it?'

Block shook his head, just slightly. 'Nobody will. Except...you know, the killer will, if it's not you.'

'That doesn't seem fair, does it?'

'Nothing's fair, man.'

Block had a pair of welder's goggles perched on top of his head. While Dick and Desiree were at Dot's house taking the Lexus, Block had gone to the hardware store. He slipped the goggles down over his eyes. He looked at Dick. The goggles made him look like a maniac. His eyes were like fish swimming in twin bowls. He lowered his voice.

'Say Dick, about Desiree . . .'

Dick shrugged. 'What about her? You already told me. You do what you want. Trish deals with it. Desiree knows about . . .' Dick made a gesture at Dot, then vaguely, at the rest of the bathroom, at the whole apartment, 'about all this. If she can keep her mouth shut, then I say fine. She's an ex-con, like me. I just stole Dot's car with her, and it was no sweat.'

'That's not what I mean. I mean *about* Desiree . . .'

Dick stifled an urge to clamp his hands over his ears, then close his eyes, and drown out whatever Block might say next. 'Hey, Block, I lived in California for fifteen years, you know? Things that seem weird to people back here are like an everyday thing out there. I mean, they routinely elect movie stars into public office. Grown men watch Japanese cartoons all day long. In California, this thing with Desiree . . . it's par for the course.' He waved the whole thing off. 'Anyway, it's none of my business.'

Block nodded. 'I'm glad you said that. We got a lot of work to do over the next couple of days. We're going to want all the help we can get, and I'd hate for any prejudices to get in the way of that. Desiree is gonna be a big help to us. And I'd hate for any, you know, rumors to go around.'

'Block, remember the guy in the warehouse? A long time ago?'

'Yeah. Like it was yesterday.'

Dick put his right fist over his heart. 'I'm a tomb. I never told a soul.'

Block turned solemn at the mention of the warehouse. 'OK, then. Let's get started.'

He produced an electric saw from a box on the floor. He plugged it into the slot above the sink, just like he would a hair dryer or an electric razor. The saw was black and made mostly of hard plastic. It was shaped like a gun, with a red button located exactly where the trigger on a gun would be. Depress the red button and electricity was fed into the saw. The blade was a long band of metal teeth that came down from the barrel of the gun when the power came on. The teeth moved back and forth like lightning, so fast Dick couldn't even see them moving. They were as sharp as tiny razor blades. On top of the barrel was a hand rest to guide the action of the saw. It was quite a machine. Just like on a gun, there was even a safety switch. Click it on and you couldn't accidentally feed the thing juice.

'We have to be careful not to let the wire fall into the water,' Block said.

He pressed the red button and held it up. The teeth moved back and forth, ready to bite and tear. The machine made a high, loud whine that would not be out of place in this building where there were forever people banging with hammers and grinding with drills and sawing things apart. Many of the starving artists built what they called 'installations', and that meant carpentry. This could be one of the few buildings in America, Dick decided, where you could do this grisly cutting for hours on end, and no one would ever notice. Even if they did, they would think nothing of it.

'I'm gonna take the hands first,' Block said.

And then, in an instant, it was real, too real. Dot's eyes, open and staring, looked straight into Dick's mind. It was like someone threw a switch, and suddenly he was standing there watching something that couldn't be happening. Something from a nightmare. This was Dot, and Block was about to chop her up like hamburger. *Dot. Holy shit. Dot. It can't be.* The walls were too close. The light was too bright. Dot's body was too . . . real. She stared at him, imploring him, begging him to stop this from happening. But Dot was dead. She couldn't implore him. What did it mean to be dead? Where did a dead person go? Dick's throat was tight, like someone's fist was caught in there. He could hear his own breaths coming in sharp, pointed rasps.

Block stared at him. The goggles came off and now Block's eyes, no longer like fish, hovered there. His face was stern, but his voice sounded far away, like it came from the other end of a long tube. 'Dick, are you all right?'

'Block, I . . .'

Block led him out of the bathroom, through the living room and into the bedroom. Desiree lay on Dick's bed, reading a copy of *Vogue*. Then Dick was on the bed next to her, staring up at the concrete ceiling two stories above his head. He realized he was crying. Fucking Dot. Dead. He looked down and saw Desiree's dark hand in his. Desiree was holding his hand. It felt good. It felt better than nothing. A moment later, the buzz of the electric saw began in the bathroom, Block going back to work. Desiree hugged him now. He pressed himself against her and the weeping came harder, welling up from the bottom, and he let it come, let it drown out the evil sound of the saw.

Nestor liked to move at night.

Like a vampire. Indeed, people had made that connection before. Be that as it may, there was something about the night that appealed to him. In the day, everything was too bright. He rarely went anywhere without sunglasses, even on the most overcast days. The sun fell heavily on him. There seemed to be a haze around everyone and everything. Even his mind was in a fog. Simple arithmetic eluded him. People would speak and he wouldn't pay attention. He tried to leave the simplest tasks for the daytime. Errands. Busy work.

At night, he came alive. The lights of the city glowed radiantly. Images became sharper, more defined. His mind made instant leaps of logic and imagination – he could finish complex math problems in his head, and work out intricate schemes. Even now, as he drove south on Interstate 95 back toward the city, passing the steel and glass corporate towers of Stamford, Connecticut, the taillights of the cars ahead of him flowed like lava, so many cars on the highway so late at night, the road filled with vampires, and he saw how he could paint such a scene in fast brushstrokes, suggesting the flow and the stark towers, rather than working out the details. He could take up painting, he decided, and should. He would probably excel at it.

He was keyed up by the prospect of returning to New York after his brief absence. The trip hadn't gone too badly, he decided. He had some money in his pocket, he had enjoyed a short respite from the stresses that had been bothering him, and he had gotten a good night's sleep in the hotel. He had eaten well, and strolled the harbor in the brisk cold without concern of being shot from behind. He had worked his problems out in his head – unwound them, so to speak. It had been good to get away.

Refreshed, that was the word. He felt refreshed. And ready to exact a cheerful revenge.

His cellphone rang.

The dashboard clock read 2.55. A little late for someone to call, wasn't it?

He reached for the phone and checked the readout. It was a blocked number. He fitted the earpiece and answered.

'Good evening,' he said.

'Good evening,' came the reply, a female voice doing an impression of Alfred Hitchcock. There was interference on the line, and a tinny quality to the call. 'Do you know who this is?'

'I wish that I did, for you sound very lovely. But alas, no.'

'Well, I know who you are.'

Nestor smiled. 'Yes, it would seem so, as you have called me on my personal line very late at night.'

'You're a night owl, aren't you?'

'Indeed.'

'So I guess I know all about you, then. I even know what you're looking for.'

'How interesting.'

'If you want to find what you're looking for, I know how you can do it. Go to Dot's house at five in the afternoon, today. Make that five fifteen. It'll already be dark. Let yourself in. But do it quietly, OK? Like a mouse. Creep upstairs to the bedroom, and I guarantee you'll find something in the closet that'll make everything a whole lot clearer to you.'

Nestor frowned. Of course it sounded like a trap. And the voice – he knew it from somewhere.

'Why should I trust you?'

'Five fifteen, this afternoon. You won't be sorry.'

He said nothing. Static hissed on the line. The cars in front of him slowed, hundreds of brake lights coming on, one after the next, like dominoes.

'And, Nestor? I'd come armed, if I were you.'

Dick woke up on the couch.

Daytime had come around again. Tuesday, and it was already twelve noon. At some point in the night, Block had come into the bedroom and Dick had moved to the living room. Now he stood up and stumbled into the kitchen. He needed to eat something, but there was nothing. Nothing except cold pizza. So he ate some of that. He also cracked open a beer.

He sat in the easy chair with his breakfast. Today he would begin disposing of Dot's body. After that – tomorrow, the next day, maybe next week – he would leave town. He didn't know yet where he would go. Anywhere was good, anywhere far away from New York City. This place was poisoned for him. He should never have come back. Perhaps he would head down to the Bahamas himself, along with Lydia. She had invited him, hadn't she? Why else would she tell him everything? It was an invitation. They could live like royalty for a while on the money she and Dot had stolen.

Of course, that thought brought Dot back to him again. Dot, dead in a bathtub. Dot, carved into pieces. Jesus.

Dick had told Lydia to spend the next few days acting normally, as if nothing had happened, and see if Dot turned up again. That would give him time enough to dispose of the body. After that, they were home free. One day, maybe in the Bahamas, maybe somewhere else, he would break the news to her that Dot was definitely dead.

'How are you feeling?' Block said as he came out of the bedroom.

'OK,' Dick said. 'I feel OK.'

'Good man. You're really showing me something, Dick. I know how hard this is for you. Today or tomorrow, we'll be done.'

'Think so?'

'Dick, I know so.'

Block sat down. He had finished most of the cutting and, as agreed, Dick would drive Dot's car and dump the pieces in any out-of-the-way places he could find. He would take no identification because Block and Desiree would stay in his place while he was out. He was to call home every hour or two. If he got picked up by the cops, he would have no identification, and it would take them a while to figure out who he was and where he lived. If Block and Desiree didn't hear from him, they would leave the apartment. If Dick was arrested, Block would deny any knowledge of what was going on. In the meantime, Block would finish cutting up the body. When he finished cutting, Desiree would sweep, mop, dust and disinfect everything.

'What did you tell Trish last night?' Dick said.

Block seemed puzzled. 'About what? Trish is in Florida with the kids. They went down the day after Christmas.'

'Block. Didn't you tell me the other night, when you left here, that you had to go home and tuck in your kids?'

Block half smiled. He put his hands in the air like a man surrendering. 'Yeah. That. Well, I lied about that. You know, you walked in, I was in the bedroom . . . I was feeling a little uncomfortable.'

'That makes sense.'

They sat for a few minutes longer. Dick settled into the chair. The pizza and beer made him feel heavy. He felt like he could sit there all day and ignore that trouble in the bathroom. It was a good feeling.

Then Block clapped his hands. 'I guess we should get to work,' he said. 'Are you up for it?'

Dick lied. 'I'm up for it.'

He followed Block into the bathroom. Next to the tub was a pile of packages wrapped in green garbage bags. That was OK. It was almost like a pile of winter firewood piled next to a house in Vermont. The tub was worse. All of the ice had melted and now a handful of Dot's body parts floated around. The worst thing was the head, which was floating face up, hair fanned out around it, eyes still open. Dick stared and stared. The feeling from the night before began to come back, the dizziness, the unreality.

'Don't look at it too long,' Block said. 'Just pack up and go.'

'Yeah. Good idea.'

Block looked on as Dick loaded up his big duffel bag with carefully wrapped packages. Dick found that if he didn't look in the tub, and focused only on the packages, he could almost make himself believe they were something else. Large cuts of meat, maybe, or those Vermont chunks of wood. He played a sort of game, seeing how many ideas he could come up with for what these packages might be other than human remains. When the duffel was loaded, Dick had managed to stuff about three-quarters of what they had in there. It looked like it would take one more trip to get the job done. He had no plan in mind, except to start dumping the parts off as soon as places became apparent.

'Do you think it's a good idea to do this in the daylight?' he said. 'I mean, somebody might see me.'

'Dick, we're on the clock here. We have to make this happen today. When I signed on to help you, I didn't sign on for a month or even a week. I want this project finished and so do you. The cops could come crawling in those windows at any time.'

There was no arguing with that. Dick finished his beer, put his jacket on and left.

He walked out to the car. A couple of the tenants milled around outside in the brightness of the cold day. They waved to him. He waved back. He felt them watching him, a man out carrying a big duffel bag and climbing into a strange car – the victim's Lexus. He hoped that it wouldn't come back to haunt him.

He started off. He kept the bag beside him on the passenger seat, thinking that it was better to have the parts closer to him for easier drop-off. He imagined himself as the local paperboy, cruising slowly through a suburban neighborhood in Long Island, hurling tightly wrapped body parts out the window and onto people's lawns.

He drove.

Street traffic was heavy. The snow had been plowed to the sides, making the streets seem like canyons between white mountains. Barely any of it had melted. He bumped along with the traffic, stopping and going until he reached the entrance ramp for the BQE. The Lexus had excellent climate control and as he cruised up the ramp the car was already toasty warm. Then, in a moment of clarity, he remembered what he had with him and turned on the air conditioning instead.

Dick drifted, driving north toward Queens, doing exactly the speed limit. Time passed as he rolled along, not really paying attention to where he was going. He checked his watch. It was one thirty, he'd been on the road almost an hour and hadn't dropped off a single piece. He also had to find a payphone to call Block. They had considered having him make calls on Block's cell, but then decided it was too risky – cops could snatch cellphone chatter out of the air. It was just as well – Dick didn't want to carry the fucking thing. Why add brain cancer to his list of problems?

He looked at the next sign coming up. He was on the Grand Central Parkway, about to pass Flushing Meadows Park and the old World's Fair grounds. He glanced over at his co-pilot, a gym bag filled with body parts.

Abruptly, he began to cry. Again.

He hit his indicator signal and got off the highway at the next exit.

Just in time, he pulled into an empty parking lot. The floodgates opened and he sat there, weeping like a child. Once or twice, he punched the dashboard and cursed. He let it come, whatever was inside him. There was nothing else to do. He was a bedrock crazy, parked in a deserted lot in the middle of winter, crying his eyes out, with his dead lover next to him, chopped into pieces and wrapped in plastic. If they found him now, there would be newspaper headlines everywhere.

Sometime later, when he got a hold on himself, he left the car. After all that crying, he did feel a little better. He carried the bag, and he crunched across the old brittle snow toward a payphone. This was the neglected section of the World's Fair grounds. It had been left to rot and slowly sink back into the garbage dump and the swamp that it was built on. Up ahead loomed the old Tent of Tomorrow, a huge oval-shaped building supported by sixteen concrete columns. The place had been trashed since Dick was a kid. He remembered there used to be a giant map of New York State painted on the floor there, and people used to rip up pieces of it and take them home as souvenirs. Then the city would fill in the missing pieces with white cement. Terrific. Nearby, the rusting observation towers stood together against the sky.

Dick recalled how the movie *Men in Black* had pretended the viewing decks of those towers were alien spaceships, and how, while watching the movie in California, he had felt a momentary bout of homesickness. Shit. That feeling was gone. All around him, the frozen grounds were stark, empty and lifeless. From where he stood, it seemed as if the world itself had ended right after the Fair did.

He reached the phone. Surprise. It worked. He dialed the number.

No answer. He got the machine instead.

'Block. It's Dick. Everything's under control. If you're there, pick up.'

Pause. Nothing.

'Block! Are you there?'

The phone squealed feedback and Block picked up. He was out of breath, as though he had just run to the phone. As though Dick had interrupted him.

'Yeah, Dick. I'm here, I'm here.'

'What are you doing?'

'Uh, I'm working here, Dick. Getting everything ready. What do you think I'm doing?'

'Where's Desiree?'

Pause. 'Ah, she's here. Everything's good over here. How's it out there?'

'It's fine. No problems.'

'Well, all right. We'll see you later then, huh?' Block hung up.

Dick slammed the phone down.

'Shit.'

He was out here in the cold and Block was back there, in his bed, with Desiree. Dick shook his head, his breath coming in plumes. He stared out at the nearest of the observation towers. Below it and to the left sat a large green garbage dumpster. Probably, the sanitation workers wouldn't come and empty it until all of this white stuff melted, and maybe not even then. He crunched off towards it across the snow.

The Cool Breeze entered the coffee shop across the street and a little way down from Dot's house. She slid into a booth next to a window and watched the street. Even dressed as she was – heavy overcoat, corduroy pants, blonde wig with a wool hat pulled down tight – she decided she didn't want to be out there when Nestor arrived. She didn't mind taunting him over the phone – it was fun, actually. It gave her a little thrill, a shimmer of almost sexual excitement. But one thing was for sure – she never wanted to see him face to face again. These guys were crazy thinking they could play grown-up games with Nestor.

Nestor was evil.

Even sitting here in the warmth, she was afraid that he would somehow read her mind, that he would see her there in the window, and that he would cross the street, enter the coffee shop, and slide into her booth. Even though she looked very different from how she did during their last encounter, he would know her. He would thrum his red nails on the table and smile.

'I'm happy to see you again,' he might say.

The waiter came over, a slim guy, dark hair. Jet-black, swooped backwards over his head. He was good-looking. At any other time, he might interest her. She might even consider taking him somewhere to kill some time. But not today.

'You want to order?' he said.

'Coffee.'

She gazed out the large window, watching the Manhattan commuters rush home through the cold after getting off the subway. The streets were crowded – lots more fabulous types, stockbrokers, businesspeople, than just a few years ago. She remembered how she used to come out here to see lousy rock bands play at a little club called the South Paris. It was gone now. The owner was an old guy, and he used to do a light show for the bands by flicking the wall lights on and off. He had multi-colored bulbs in the lights. It was ridiculous, but there was no cover most nights, and the beer was cheap. She had been dating someone then, living with him, some thin guy with spiky black hair. Brent, that was it. Brent was really into bands.

She checked the time. It was a little bit after five. Five ten, to be exact. Henry had gone in just fifteen minutes ago. It would take him a while, she imagined, to break open those locked drawers in Dot's bedroom. And, God knew, Henry would probably mess around for a while first, dig around in other parts of the house, maybe go through Dot's underwear drawer. That was Henry's thing. He liked to take his time and get his chubby fingers in all the little nooks and crannies.

Breeze recalled that night, months ago – the night Breeze slipped Dot the roofies. Dot lay on the bed in her snazzy bedroom, nude, half-awake, eyes blank, as Andrew photographed her with the digital camera. They all wore white surgical gloves, all except Dot, and Andrew's hands were shaking as he tried to take the pictures. His whole body was trembling, with fear, with desire, maybe with terror – Breeze just didn't know.

Breeze herself felt calm. She licked her lips as her eyes roamed Dot's white meat. Dot was truly an all-American – she had a lot of body. She had a big, sweet, spankable bottom. She had full, suckable titties. She had a round stomach with a deep navel. She had a tuft of golden hair between her legs.

'Smile, Dot,' Breeze said, and Dot hesitated. 'Come on, smile, have fun.' Dot's eyes lit up and she gave a warm smile. The roach was an amazing drug. Dot would never remember any of this, even when they used the photos to blackmail her, or worse. The end use of the photos was still up in the air.

'Can you, can you put her, I don't know, on all fours?' Andrew said.

'Sure.' Breeze went over and ran her hands over Dot's torso. 'Come on, baby, let's get you on all fours, like an animal.' She turned Dot over, and got her just so. She gave Dot's ass a playful smack and gripped the meat on one of Dot's haunches. 'That's dinner,' she said.

Andrew moved in with the camera. 'Henry!' he shouted. 'What the fuck are you doing, man? You're supposed to be in here helping.' Breeze had never seen Andrew so agitated. It was kind of cute.

Henry's voice echoed from somewhere in the house. 'I'm coming.'

'We don't have all night.'

To Breeze: 'Put her head down on the pillow. Yeah, ass in the air.'

He snapped more photos, dozens of them, hundreds of them, his body shaking, his finger just click, click, clicking, stopping only to swap out memory cards when the first one filled up.

Henry strolled in. Big fat Henry, eating a yogurt cup he took from Dot's refrigerator. 'Man, you should see the stuff this bitch has. Incredible. She's got a fifty-two-inch plasma HDTV. Awesome. There's stereo surround-sound built in everywhere. She's got that whole extra room downstairs set up like an art gallery – there's lighting embedded in the ceiling, and you can work it to cast a spotlight on each individual painting, or change the mood throughout the room, or whatever you want. She's got the basement finished, wall-to-wall carpeting, fully stocked bar, with an eight-foot pool table down there.' He glanced down at Dot's new position on the bed, flat on her stomach, legs spread, looking back at the camera. 'I'll bet she never even plays.'

As Henry talked, Breeze felt something well up inside her. It had been there – the feeling – when they came in the house, but now it was stronger. All the things Henry salivated over, they bothered her. Dot had so much stuff, expensive consumer shit. Breeze had walked past it all with a sort of tunnel vision. But now, involuntarily, her mind scanned back to her own house – *Katie's house* – the house where Breeze grew up. Four small rooms, barren of anything but some cheap scarred-up furniture from the Salvation Army. Canned soup in the cupboard, and one old beater car after another sitting dead in the front yard. And of course, good old Ralph doing the babysitting.

Breeze wanted to smash Dot's shit, one thing at a time, and make Henry watch.

'You shouldn't eat her food,' Andrew said.

Henry shrugged. 'She won't remember. She'll think she ate it.'

'All the same,' Andrew said, 'you shouldn't do it.' He began to unbutton his shirt. 'I need someone else to take the pictures now.' His shirt came off and now he unbuttoned his pants.

'Why are you taking your clothes off?' Henry said.

'It's the last thing,' Andrew said. 'If we want to superimpose somebody's face into these pictures, we're going to need a body to superimpose them onto, aren't we? In case we don't get what we need from Nestor, we can use my body. He and I have similar bodies.'

'You probably don't have all the bullet holes he supposedly has,' Henry said.

'True, but if we have to, we could probably Photoshop them in there.'

Breeze watched as Andrew stripped naked. He had a nice body, trembling though it was. Gently, carefully, he touched Dot and moved her through various poses as he simulated sexual positions with her. Oh, yeah. Henry snapped the photos. Breeze just watched. She watched Andrew, concentrating so hard, trying not to become aroused. And succeeding.

When Andrew was dressed again, it was almost time to leave.

'So,' Henry said, 'I think we should do her.' His voice was casual, even nonchalant. Dot was still sprawled on the top cover, breathing shallowly, doing something like sleeping. The three of them stood around, staring down at her.

'Do her?' Andrew said, as if he didn't understand. Breeze glanced at him. He understood well enough.

'Yeah, do her. You know, do her. Fuck her. You practically did already. That's what the drug is for, man. She won't remember a thing.'

Breeze shrugged. 'Sure.' She found, for reasons she didn't quite understand, that she wanted them to do it.

Andrew looked at them both. He made an exaggerated look of disgust with his face. But his eyes said something else. He wanted Dot, Breeze could see that much.

OK. So take her.

'No, we shouldn't fuck her. Are you crazy? That's not what we're here for. We're here to take the pictures and get out.'

Henry frowned. 'OK, but you're wasting an opportunity. You want revenge on her? Well, here it is.'

'Man, I want financial revenge,' Andrew said. 'This is all a big game, remember? It's like Monopoly, played in real life. It's just a fucking game. I want to win, but I don't want to rape anybody.'

Henry gestured at Andrew's hand. 'You have nine fingers. That sounds like more than a game to me.'

Andrew shook his head. 'There are limits to what I'm willing to do to people.' He gestured at Dot. 'I can win without sinking to their level. OK? And while I'm paying, we do it my way. OK?'

Breeze would remember this, a few weeks later, when Andrew had taken Henry's advice and thrown her to Nestor without a qualm. Precious little Dot was one thing. Breeze was another. That's OK – throw Breeze out with the trash. Put Dot on a pedestal. That's what everybody did.

But things had changed since then, hadn't they?

Now, as Breeze watched from the coffee shop, a slim man climbed the front steps to Dot's brownstone. He glanced around, so quickly that it was barely even a glance, as he opened the door and disappeared inside. He moved like a shadow.

She counted thirty seconds. Then she counted thirty again. OK. Time to call Henry. She downed her coffee, stood, and walked outside into the cold, already whipping out her cellphone and pressing the speed dial.

'What a bitch.'

Big Henry kneeled in front of the drawers with the power drill. It was a Sears drill, with a battery pack attached so that it didn't need to be plugged in. He wore kneepads over his jeans, thick leather gloves on his hands, goggles to protect his eyes, and a paper mask to avoid breathing in the metal dust. He was going to have to drill out the lock on each one of these fucking things, and if the first one was any indication, it was going to take a while. Well, with a little luck, maybe there'd be a big payday inside one of them.

What he'd really like to do, he'd like to take another look around this place, see what other kind of buried treasure Dot had here. From the looks of things, somebody had already gotten that idea, but who knew? Maybe they missed something. Then again, there was no time, and he knew it. He didn't like hanging around this place, especially the way it looked now, and the sooner he could break these drawers open, the sooner he could get on out of here.

Maybe he'd give it to Breeze again in the car before he dropped her off at Andrew's. That would be nice, worth hurrying for, and nothing more than what Andrew deserved. The guy was becoming a real pain in the ass. He doubted, once this job was over, that he'd be seeing much of Andrew again for a while.

Henry sighed. Money was money, and that's what this whole scam was about. Whether they ever got their hands on Dot's cool million, five hundred bucks cash seemed pretty fair for a quick breaking-and-entering job like this one. Actually, there wasn't even any breaking involved, since he had keys to the place. It was almost too easy.

He began drilling again. The bit dug in, and the metal dust began flying. He pushed, putting some weight behind it. BANG. The drill went all the way in, right through the lock and into the drawer. That one went quick. He stopped, pulled the drill out, and tried to open the drawer. Still locked.

'Shit.'

The lock was half-demolished, the drill went all the way through, and the damn thing still wouldn't open. These were good locks. Custom cabinetry at its best.

Just then, his phone rang. It made no sound – instead, he felt it vibrating against his thigh. He had it on vibrating mode in case he didn't hear it while drilling. It was a good thing these brownstones had solid walls, what with all the noise he was making. He checked the screen.

It was Breeze. Shit. His heart skipped.

He flipped open the phone.

OK. Be calm. It might be nothing.

'Yeah?'

Her voice was a hiss. 'Get out. Get out. He's coming in.'

'Nestor?'

'Oh my God, Henry, get out of there right now.' Her voice was shaking, frantic. In a flash of insight, Henry saw how poorly conceived this whole lookout idea was. He was all the way upstairs. How was he going to get downstairs and out the back door before Nestor saw him?

A window. There had to be a window. Or somewhere to hide.

A shadow appeared at the closet door. He looked up and Nestor was already there. He leaned against the doorframe. In one hand he held a large gun, with a long silencer protruding from the end of the barrel. In the other hand he held a pair of metal handcuffs. He tossed the handcuffs and they landed on the floor next to where Henry was kneeling.

Nestor gestured at the cuffs with his chin.

'Put them on.'

Henry had the drill in one hand. He still held the phone to his ear. He didn't know – maybe there was a way out, something he could do with the drill. Or maybe . . . maybe he could offer Nestor some kind of deal.

Nestor raised the gun until it was pointing at Henry's head.

'Henry?' came the voice in Henry's ear. It was Breeze, still on the line.

'Yeah?' His own voice seemed distant, no longer attached to the rest of him. With his free hand he placed the drill on the floor and picked up the handcuffs.

'He's standing right there, isn't he?'

'Yeah.' Dimly, a recognition began to come to him. He couldn't put it into words yet. It was something about Breeze. He should have paid closer attention to something about Breeze.

He could feel her smile over the telephone. It had never occurred to him before that you could actually feel someone smile without seeing it. A lot of things had never occurred to him.

'Tough break, kid,' Breeze said. Then the line went dead.

Nestor smiled as Henry dropped the phone.

'Now we have a chance to talk, all right?'

6
BAD TASTE IN MEN

Meat sizzled on the burner.

Dick smelled it as he entered the apartment. He was tired. No, he was spent, completely and utterly exhausted. He came in, sat down and saw Block in his boxer shorts, frying up some hamburgers in the kitchen. He was drinking a beer, smoking a cigar and dabbing the ashes onto the floor.

'Do you ever wear clothes anymore?' Dick said.

Block smiled. 'I don't know. The cold air, there's something about it. It feels good on my skin.' He gestured at the stove. 'Want a burger?'

'Sure. How did it go here today?'

'It's all done, just about. Desiree went to the store to get more beer. I already bagged most of the last parts. After dinner, you can finish getting rid of them. Then we clean the place and we're done. It never happened.'

'That's great,' Dick said. 'Man, I could use a drink.'

Block came over. He had a big cheeseburger on a plate. It was smothered in onions, with ketchup and mustard.

Block sat down. 'All right,' he said. 'How'd it go out there?'

Dick ran his hand through his hair. 'It was just a rough day, you know? Driving around, stashing limbs in garbage cans. At one place, I don't even know where I was, a guard came over and told me I was trespassing. He was like an old Russian guy or something. Looked like he was wearing a uniform from World War One. I could hardly understand a word he was saying.'

'What did you say?'

'I told him I just wanted to throw something in the dumpster. He said he would take it and throw it out. So he wants me to give it to him, the thing that I want thrown out. He tried to grab the bag out of my hands. Well, naturally, I'm not going to let him do that. I practically had to fight this fucking lunatic to keep control of the bag.'

Block laughed. He went into the kitchen and brought out two cans of beer. 'You're all right,' he said. He clapped Dick on the back. 'Have a beer. These are the last ones until Desiree gets back.'

Dick took the beer, opened it and poured back a long swallow. It was ice cold and hit the spot. 'That's good.'

Block gestured at the bathroom. 'I'm gonna go in and see what's left to do.'

'I'll go with you,' Dick said.

'You sure?'

'I'm sure.'

In the bathroom, there were just a few pieces of Dot still in the tub, most notably her head. The rest of her was wrapped in green plastic, and piled up like cordwood next to the toilet. Dick found that Dot didn't have the same impact on him anymore. He had spent the day throwing pieces of her away. He had cried his eyes out over her twice already. He was numb to her now. At this point, the worst of it was the smell, which wasn't that noticeable. Someone had covered it with a heavy spray of Lysol.

'Almost done,' he said. He took a sip of his beer. He thought of construction workers looking over a job. They stood in the bathroom another moment, nursing their beers. Judging by what was left, Dick guessed he had another three hours of body dumping to look forward to.

'You know,' Block said, 'I forgot to pull those teeth. Lemme get some pliers and I'll take care of that right now.'

'Why?'

Block shrugged. 'They find a head without teeth, it'll delay the identification.'

He went back out into the apartment, leaving Dick with Dot. Numb or not, Dick did not like being there. Dot looked up at him from the tub. Her face had turned a light shade of purple. Dick sipped his beer as he looked down at her. It seemed as if she would speak, but a second later Block walked in with the pliers, and Dot said nothing.

Block picked up the head and leaned against the sink with it, cradling it in his lap. Excess water ran down his thick, naked thighs. He reached in her mouth with the pliers for the first tooth.

'This is gonna be tough.'

Inwardly, Dick winced, but outwardly he showed no sign. He forced himself to watch. It was OK. After all, this wasn't Dot. Dot was gone.

One by one, Block began to remove Dot's teeth. 'The girl had good hygiene,' he said. 'Her teeth are rooted in there nice and strong.'

Andrew sat in his car, slumped down again, watching everything. Behind him, cars roared by onto the Williamsburg Bridge and over to Manhattan. He was across from Miller's building, an old warehouse, dilapidated, the kind of place that if it were ten blocks north would have been renovated already. There was an old advertisement painted on the side of the building – right onto the brickwork. It had faded and peeled so much that it was now impossible to tell what it was once for.

It made Andrew's skin crawl that people lived in that place. When he had gone in there on Saturday, the whole thing had shocked him – the layers of ancient dust, the paint peeling off of every surface, the concrete floors – whoever owned that building was renting out living spaces to humans and had barely done a thing to the place. It wouldn't surprise Andrew if it had been a factory at one time. The people who lived there should get themselves checked for heavy metals in their bloodstreams.

Jesus.

North of Metropolitan, and creeping south a little more all the time, these old buildings were being cleaned up and completely refurbished. In some cases, the absolute worst cases, they were being gutted or torn down altogether, then replaced with new buildings that just *looked* like old factories. Andrew had been in some of the lofts that resulted from the renovations. Imitation hardwood floors, huge open living spaces, twenty-foot ceilings, floor-to-ceiling windows with views of the Manhattan skyline – some of those apartments were going for a million dollars, and they might actually be worth the money. This place where Miller lived? It should be condemned. There were probably rats scuttling around in the hallways.

Andrew came alert as he spotted the figure moving along the sidewalk toward the lonely building. He trained his telescope on her. OK, it was the black woman. He had seen her go out maybe half an hour ago, just before Miller went in. Now was Andrew's chance to make a move.

He took a deep breath. Was he ready? He was. He had the gun and, if need be, he was ready to use it. He didn't like to go in alone, especially not against Miller, but Breeze and Henry were busy checking out Dot's place and Andrew was afraid they were running out of time.

'You're the boss,' he said to himself. 'You're the boss. Now do it.'
He climbed out of the car.

Desiree turned the key and opened the door to the building. She had
the bag with the groceries cradled in one arm and the door open with
the other.

All these thoughts swirled in her head. She thought of the woman
who was dead. In life, she had been pretty. Desiree could tell. She
shook her head to clear the image. It wasn't her first body – the street
had shown Desiree many things she would have preferred not to see
– but still it was hard. And it was hard to think of Block chopping
the body up, erasing it.

Block was good. He was immensely strong, and Desiree felt safe
in his arms. He was gentle, and a little bit rough at the right times.
He always smelled good. He wore expensive clothes. He had given
her some money, not a lot, but some. A few hundred, whatever he
had in his wallet. 'There's more where that came from,' he had
said. She had played it like she was offended, but she needed that
money.

A man came running up the block, one of these artist kids that
lived in the building here.

'Hey! Hold the door! I forgot my key.'

Desiree held the door open for him. He was young guy, thin, with
longish hair and black-framed Calvin Klein glasses. He wore a blue
naval pea coat over some kind of black jumpsuit. Poor thing – he had
his look kind of all wrong. He was one who could use one of those
televised makeovers. Nice glasses, though.

'Thanks,' he said, out of breath. 'I forgot my key.'

Desiree smiled. 'You said that already.'

The metal door clanged shut and they moved along the hallway,
the white boy following just behind her. Desiree's heels clacked

on the concrete floor. Concrete floors, concrete walls, this place was unbelievable. It reminded Desiree of an airplane hangar, or one of those old sweatshops they used to show pictures of. She could imagine Dick's apartment filled with row after row of sewing machines, teenaged girls stationed at each one. When she found out that Block owned this building, it had gotten Desiree's wheels spinning. Maybe Block would just give her an apartment – she could do a lot more with one of these places than Dick had. But she didn't want to live here. Might as well live in a General Motors factory.

They reached the heavy metal door to the stairwell. It was almost as if the boy had been reading Desiree's thoughts.

'Do you live here?' he said. 'I don't think I've seen you around before.'

'Honey, I'd rather live in the subway.'

He laughed, and opened the door for her. It was three flights up to Dick's apartment. She started up the metal grid staircase. They climbed half a floor, the boy still just behind her.

'Who are you visiting? Dick Miller?'

It was odd, the way the boy said it. There was almost a . . . heaviness . . . to how he said Dick's name. That couldn't be good. Desiree stopped climbing. Behind her, the boy stopped. It was quiet in the stairwell, just the two of them, breathing a little bit from the stairs. Somewhere in the building, a door slammed shut.

'Do you know Dick?' Desiree said, and slowly she turned.

The boy pointed a gun right in her face, inches away. 'Say one word, or scream, or try anything at all, and I'll blow your fucking head off. OK?'

Desiree nodded.

'Good. Now move.'

*　　*　　*

Dick – crouched on his haunches – watched Block wrestle on with the teeth. After a little while, they heard the front door to the apartment open and someone come in.

'About time she got back,' Block said. 'Wonder what took her so long.'

'Hello?' Desiree called from out in the main room. 'Anybody here?' Her voice sounded funny, kind of high-pitched.

'In the bathroom. Say, would you bring us a couple more beers?'

She didn't answer. Block glanced at Dick. Dick shrugged.

'Oh my God!'

It was a strange voice. Dick looked up and there was Andrew, holding a small revolver on Desiree. Andrew gaped at the item Block was holding in his hands. Dick could see it happen: Andrew's shoulders sagged, his mouth dropped, his skin itself seemed to come loose from his body. The sight of that head made Andrew go slack.

In an instant, Dick knew what to do. From his low crouch, he launched himself into the air. Time stood still as he flew toward Andrew. Too slow. In midair, he saw Andrew's eyes come alive. The gun swung away from Desiree and Desiree dove into the bathroom.

Andrew sighted at Dick.

Desiree screamed, a long howl that sounded like an air-raid siren.

Andrew pulled the trigger. BOOM. Deafening noise echoed in the tiny bathroom.

Dick bulled Andrew back out the door, into the living room.

'I'm shot,' Desiree screamed. 'I'm shot!'

Dick used his size and weight against Andrew. They tumbled to the hard floor. Andrew's head banged against the cement and the gun slid out of his hand. Dick pinned his arms. His legs flattened Andrew's legs. They pressed together, like two lovers.

'No! No, no, no.'

Andrew squirmed, he lashed his head to and fro, but all the fight had gone out of him. Dick knew how he must feel. That ruined head. Those wide, staring eyes. Dick headbutted him and Andrew's own eyes rolled back and showed white. That would keep him quiet a while.

Block came out and grabbed the gun.

Desiree howled and cried in the next room.

'Is she OK?' Dick said.

Block nodded. 'It's just a scrape.'

'OK, then we need her to quiet down somehow.'

'OK. OK, got you covered.'

Dick pressed all his weight down onto Andrew. Block disappeared into the bathroom, and a moment later, Desiree quieted down. Dick could just barely hear her now. She was in there, whimpering. Block came back out. His feet were next to Dick's head. He squatted down and pointed at Andrew with the gun.

'That was quick thinking, Dick.'

'Thanks.'

'Do you know this guy?'

'Yeah. This is Andrew. I mentioned him to you. Can you get me some electrical tape? We need to tie him up. He looks like he's gonna scream here in a minute.'

Block disappeared again.

Dick was left with Andrew, body to body, toe to toe. They waited together and a long minute passed. There was only one reason why Andrew could have come to his apartment packing heat. He had come looking for Dot, and he was pretty sure he would find her here. If he had known that, then who else knew?

Andrew's head started to whip from side to side again, the only part of him that could move. The shock was wearing off. Dick prepared to give him another headbutt. He didn't want to do it. His head just wasn't that hard.

'Block! Hurry up with that tape, will you?'

Block came back at a trot, carrying a small roll of duct tape.

Dick looked at the meager roll. 'Is that all I have?'

'That's it. All of it. I also brought a sock. I'm gonna stick it in his mouth, then tape over it.'

Andrew's eyes widened as Block stuck the sock in his mouth. It was an old sweat sock. Once it had been white. Now it was gray. He tried to spit it out, but to no avail. Block stuffed it in there with a firm hand, then taped Andrew's lips together. The sock pushed his mouth out, distended it, made it into a horse mouth.

Dick laughed.

Block was still crouched there. 'What's so funny?'

'I don't know. Andrew's mouth, I guess.'

Block laughed too. 'Yeah. It reminds me of a picture I saw one time. *Ripley's Believe It or Not!*, *Guinness World Records*, one of those. It was the man with the world's biggest mouth. He was a black guy, and he had a golf ball, a softball and, I don't know, a cantaloupe stuffed in there all at the same time. That guy had a big damn mouth.'

'Like Andrew here,' Dick said.

They both broke up at that one. Dick's whole day came back on him. For a few seconds, he laughed hard enough that tears came to his eyes.

After a moment, the fun subsided.

Dick turned Andrew on his side. Somewhere behind him, Desiree was still mewling like a cat. 'She's gotta be quiet,' Dick said. 'If you just finish Andrew's hands, I can get his legs.'

Block tied Andrew's wrists together smartly with the duct tape. Dick winced. The bind was tight. Andrew was going to feel some pain when they took the tape off. Dick climbed off Andrew, and Block went back into the bathroom. Andrew squirmed on the floor, legs kicking. Dick towered over him. Andrew was a pathetic creature down there, totally helpless.

Dick's thoughts took a dark turn. Could they ever take the tape off of Andrew? Dot was dead. He had seen the head and some of the parts. If Dick was going to get off the hook, if they were all going to get off the hook, Andrew was going to have to un-see what he'd seen. That wasn't going to happen. The plain cold truth of it hit Dick like a steel wedge. He wanted to be free of this mess. He wanted Desiree and Block free of it too. Andrew couldn't know what he already knew and go on living.

Cold-blooded murder.

If Dick had killed Dot – and that was a big if – it was an accident of sorts. This was different. He stood there deciding how to kill Andrew, logically thinking it through. He grabbed Andrew's legs roughly. He wrapped the heavy tape around his ankles. Dick no longer winced. Andrew was probably a dead man – might as well treat him like one.

He finished tying him and dropped his legs. He felt like a rodeo cowboy who had just subdued a prize steer. Now that it was too late, now that he was doomed, Andrew's energy kicked in. He writhed and bucked on the ground. He looked like a crazy person down there. Dick lined him up and gave him a kick to the stomach. All of Andrew's wind whooshed out through his nose. He curled up in a ball and stopped moving. That got his attention.

Dick squatted down next to him.

'Andrew, do you hear me?'

Andrew nodded.

'You have to calm down, OK? If you don't calm down, I'm going to kick you again. Do you understand?'

Andrew nodded crazily. Oh, he understood, all right. Dick yanked him up by his shirt and dragged him over to the chair. He sat Andrew down with a plop. He went into the kitchen and got himself a beer. He started to pace, waiting for a knock on the door from his neighbors.

After a few minutes, when none came, he began to rest a little easier. At least they weren't going to have any more visitors.

He turned his attention back to Andrew. He pulled up a wooden stool up and studied him. He'd probably been out in the street for a while, casing the place. He stuck that gun in Desiree's back to get in here, so he had known that Desiree was coming in and out of this apartment. He was like a private eye, the things he knew.

Jesus, what a mess.

'Well, Andrew. Looks like we have a crisis on our hands.' He took a deep breath. 'You saw what we have in the bathroom, right?'

Andrew nodded. He was starting to cry. The horse-mouth thing didn't seem that funny anymore.

'You know that it's Dot?'

Andrew squeezed his eyes shut, and his body started to shake and tremble.

'Andrew, if you keep acting like this . . .' Dick let the thought go. 'Let's put it this way: I'm trying to decide what to do with you and you're not helping your own case any. You have to be tough right now, do you understand?'

Andrew nodded again.

Block and Desiree came out of the bathroom. Desiree's leg was taped up with white surgical pads. Block was still wearing only boxer shorts. They were arm in arm.

'Motherfucker grabbed me by my hair out in the hallway,' Desiree said. 'Stuck his gun in my face, said he'd blow my head off.'

'Dick,' Block said, 'when you're done with this guy, I'm gonna rip his limbs off.' He took a long pull of his beer, hesitated for a second, then downed the whole thing like an animal. He held Andrew's gun in his other hand.

Something about it caught Dick's eye and he looked at it closely. That gun was pretty damned familiar. .38 snubnose, as a matter of fact.

'Wait a minute,' he said. 'Maybe Andrew can help us. For one thing, I think that's my gun he brought in. The one I gave to Dot.'

Block looked at the gun in his own hand, as if he had forgotten it was there. The snubby looked like a toy in Block's huge hand. 'How'd he get it?'

'That's what we're about to find out.' Dick spoke gently to Andrew. 'Andrew, I'm going to take the tape off your mouth now. I want you to answer some questions. If you start to scream and yell, I'll put the tape right back on. Then this gorilla behind me will tear your arms off. So whatever you do, don't scream and yell.'

Dick grabbed either side of the tape and in one swift motion, pulled it off Andrew's face. It made a loud ripping sound and Andrew squinted in pain.

'Give me the sock,' Dick said, holding his hand out. Andrew spit it into his hand and Dick put it on the table.

'Are you ready to answer some questions?'

Andrew nodded.

'I need you to speak, buddy. You're skating on thin ice here. I think you know that.'

'I'm ready,' he said. He moved his jaw around to get some feeling back in it. 'Why did you kill her?'

'Well,' Dick said. 'I don't know that I did. In fact, I'm leaning toward thinking that someone else killed her.'

'You don't know?'

'That's right.'

'Then how did you end up with her head?'

Dick slapped Andrew across the face. Hard.

'Good,' Desiree said. 'Hit him again.'

'Let me talk, OK?' Dick said. 'I'm asking the questions here.'

Andrew glared at Dick and said nothing. Dick slapped him again.

'OK?'

Andrew nodded, eyes on fire.

'OK. Where did you get the gun?'

'I got it at Dot's house.'

'How did you get in there?'

He shrugged, tied up as he was. 'I've had a key to her place for a long time. I used to check on the place while she was away. Back when we were friends.'

'Why did you go there?'

'I had been following her, but I hadn't seen her in days and I was worried. When I went to her place, the whole house was trashed, and I found this gun in the kitchen. It had recently been fired. I brought it home with me and checked the prints. Yours and hers. No one else. Was she shot? Is that how she died?'

Dick ignored the question. 'How did you check the prints?'

'I just have people's prints. I've dusted them from their cars, their office spaces, their apartments. Yours, Dot's, a bunch of people. Surveillance is a hobby of mine.'

Dick flashed to the photographs of Nestor and Dot that came to him in the mail. Andrew was a bright boy. Andrew was a computer genius. Andrew had the gun that had probably killed Dot, Dick's gun, with Dick's prints on it.

'Do you have Nestor's prints on file?'

Andrew hesitated.

Dick raised his fist and reared back. 'Andrew, I am going to punch your face back through your head. Do you have Nestor's prints?'

'Sure, of course.'

'But they weren't on the gun?'

'No.'

An icy calm washed over Dick. The gun had been fired. It seemed pretty clear that he was the one who fired it. He had done her in, then went into her house for some reason. Or maybe he had done her at the house. Either way, he was falling deeper and deeper. There seemed to be no way out.

'Andrew, you set up camera equipment in Dot's apartment, and photographed her without her knowing about it, right? Through some kind of remote control?'

Andrew couldn't look at him. A wave of crimson flooded his face.

'I was trying to protect her.'

Dick hit Andrew so hard that the chair rocked backward and flipped over. Andrew was sprawled on the other side of the chair now, crying again.

'Hey, Dick . . .' Block said. His big hand touched Dick's arm.

'By sending me those photos?' Dick said. 'How was that protecting her? You killed her, Andrew. You dirty fuck. I may have pulled the trigger, but you killed her. You and your photographs.'

'Dick, are you OK?'

Dick turned to Block. 'Thanks for your help, but everything's just gotten a whole lot deeper all of a sudden. I think you and Desiree should scram out of this, starting now. It's going to get bad.'

'I can still help you,' Block said. 'I owe you.'

'Block, believe me. It's all in the past.'

'Dick—'

'Block, you don't owe me anything. All right? You never owed me anything. This ship is going down. You don't want to be on it when it does. Not you. Not Desiree. I won't have it go that way.'

'Dick—'

'Block, I mean it. Get lost. Both of you.'

Block stopped. A long moment passed while he appeared to think it over. Finally, he nodded. 'All right, Dick. We'll go. But call me tonight, OK? The Jersey number.' He gestured at Andrew on the floor. 'When you're done with him. If there's anything left to do at that point, we can work it out. All right?'

Dick said nothing.

'Dick? All right?'

'All right,' Dick said, but he couldn't imagine calling Block again. Dick had more dirty work to perform and Block couldn't help him anymore. It was too much to ask of anyone. Andrew would have to go, at least, and when Dick was done with him, then he had to worry about Nestor. It was too much. Five minutes passed as Block got dressed and Desiree gathered her things. Just before Block went out the door, he turned back to Dick.

Dick nodded. He didn't speak.

Block nodded, then was gone.

Breeze walked fast.

She was on the pedestrian sidewalk in the dark, crossing the bridge into Queens, headed toward Andrew's apartment. There was no one on the bridge, and a biting wind whipped around her. It brought tears to her eyes. She should have taken a taxi, but she had gone into a panic right after speaking with Henry. She wanted to get away before Nestor came onto the street looking for her.

Andrew wasn't answering his phone.

She shouldn't have said what she said to Henry. She had given it away. He would know now – if he turned up alive, he would know that she had set him up. That could be bad. Henry had a bad temper. He would tell Andrew everything. He would do worse than that. Maybe it was time for the Cool Breeze to blow out of town.

Her cellphone rang. On the windy bridge, the ring tone sounded far away. She took it out of her bag and checked the caller. Shit. Henry calling. A sense of doomed fascination washed over her, as if she were a person sitting on the terrace of an oceanfront apartment, watching a monster tidal wave approach.

OK, it was OK. He couldn't touch her right now. He didn't know where she was.

She picked up. 'Henry?'

'You're a naughty girl, aren't you?' The calm, mocking voice was Nestor's.

'Is Henry there?'

'In a sense, yes.'

'Put him on, please.'

'Well,' Nestor said. 'I can't do that. We've had a long discussion, and I don't think he'll be talking to anyone else anymore.'

Breeze hesitated. Relief and horror were at war inside her. She did not want to be on this phone with this man. 'Can I help you?'

'I hope you can, yes. It's seems only fair, since I gather I've helped you dispose of something you no longer wanted. Isn't that correct?'

'I don't know what you mean.'

'Hmm. A pity. Well, before he went, he told me everything that you've done. Everything, do you understand? The photographs. Everything. Sort of mean-spirited, slipping drugs into people's drinks, isn't it? I can tell you I'm not pleased. I am pleased, however, to know you are the young lady whose company I've enjoyed the pleasure of once before. But we'll deal with that later. About the business at hand – your friend also helped me break open the drawers where the money was. The money is gone. Dot is gone. Tell me, if you don't mind, where is Dot right this minute?'

Breeze had a tingling feeling down her back. 'Dot is dead.'

'I see. I was afraid of that. Who killed her?'

'You did.'

'Darling, I'm not playing with you. Now tell me who did it.'

Grasping now, for straws, for anything. 'Dick Miller, I guess.'

'You guess?'

'Dick Miller did it. He must have.'

'And the keys? Who has them?'

'Lydia.'

'Does Lydia also have the money?'

'I think she must have it. If nobody else does.'

Nestor grunted. 'OK. Where are you now? I hear traffic, so I imagine you are out walking, yes? Are you headed to Andrew's underground apartment in Queens? If so, I can meet you there in a little while.'

Breeze stopped in her tracks.

'No. I'm not walking. I'm in a car. I'm driving somewhere.'

The line went dead. Holy shit. That was bad.

She rang Andrew again.

It was convenient, how close together Dot and Lydia lived. Nestor could walk the distance in perhaps ten minutes. He was wearing a long cashmere coat this evening, but the night was so cold that the coat did little good.

He kept to the back streets, away from the main boulevard. As he walked along through the empty streets, he gazed at the stars. The few that were visible above the lights of the city twinkled brightly. Nestor wondered – seemingly from a place outside of himself – whether he had gone insane.

The fat man Henry had told him everything, more than he even wanted to hear. Henry had cried during the recital, not, Nestor supposed, because he felt remorse for his deeds, but more likely because he knew what fate they implied for him. They had drugged Dot – *my Dot* – and stripped her naked and photographed her. They had sent the young woman to seduce Nestor and take his photograph. All so they could superimpose the photos together using computer software, and send them to Dick Miller to suggest the affair between Nestor and Dot was continuing. All of this to take revenge for

Andrew's missing finger. And now they believed that Miller might have killed her. They worried that things had gone too far. Well, things had gone too far, certainly they had. But that didn't stop this Henry from entering Dot's apartment and trying to steal the money.

Henry was an arrogant sort. Prideful. When Nestor had first walked in, the fat man thought that it might become a bargaining session. 'I can get you girls,' Henry said. 'I have money. I can get you drugs. Anything you want. The clubs downtown? I'm like the king. Anything you want. You just say the word.'

This kind of talk only compounded Nestor's annoyance.

'Anything?'

'Anything at all.'

Nestor pressed the gun against Henry's temple. 'I want you to tell me what you people have been doing. I want you to omit nothing.'

Nestor had listened carefully during Henry's little speech. He had quietly seethed, the anger building inside him, all the while holding the gun to Henry's head. Henry had wept bitterly at times, as Nestor's anger mounted. Henry had tried to blame the whole problem on Andrew. Andrew wouldn't give up. Andrew wanted to sink everyone. That incessant blaming had weighed on Nestor, increasing his rage. In the midst of it, an idea came to him. He covered Henry's mouth with the duct tape that Henry himself had brought. Then he drilled a hole into Henry's brain with the power drill. It was slower than the gun, more painful, and more satisfying.

Henry was alive up until the moment when the drill bit punched through bone and bit into soft brain matter. He may have been alive for several seconds after that. Nestor didn't know, but it seemed that way. He had drilled several holes into Henry's skull – perhaps a dozen, perhaps more – after that first one. He had lost track of time as he drilled the holes, one after another after another. The forensics lab would say the level of violence suggested a crime of passion.

194

Nestor would plead insanity, he would plead rage, he would plead total madness, if that time ever came. The idiots had killed Dot by mistake. By mistake! Until tonight, he had kept some vague dream alive – he and Dot walking the red carpet, the multitudes coveting them, desiring them, envying their place in the spotlight – but he was convinced now that Dot was indeed dead. Dot was dead and Henry was dead. Tit for tat. But tit for tat didn't cover the bill that was due.

Now Nestor would see Lydia. He realized as he walked that his breathing had not calmed. He also realized the heaviness in the pockets of his long coat. In one pocket sat his gun, loaded, silenced, ready to kill. In the other pocket sat the bloodied power drill. Lydia had better not have any argument for him. He would hurt her if she did. He might hurt her anyway, just because he could. He would hurt anyone who stood in his way. He had grown weary of this entire silly game. All he wanted now was the money and the keys. Once in Nassau, he could hire a new Lydia if he needed.

He turned a corner and walked along a tree-lined street. Lydia's building was just up ahead. He stopped, lit a cigarette with shaking fingers, and inhaled deeply.

All right. It was better to be calm. Go in, secure the money and the keys. Perhaps – depending upon the way she received him – invite Lydia to Nassau with him. Not necessary, but easier and more pleasurable than finding a new Lydia.

The cigarette did him good. Perhaps he could enjoy Lydia's pleasures tonight, and the two of them could leave the country together. Not tomorrow, but very soon. It was not out of the question. Of course, leaving the country should wait until after he had taken his revenge on Dick Miller and the rest of the sordid little group of embezzlers and blackmailers. Miller. Andrew. The girl called Breeze.

Well. Let's go up and see what Lydia had to say then. Yes?

Nestor walked on.

It was only fifty more yards to her door.

Andrew's phone rang again. Dick was growing tired of it.

'Do you always carry that fucking thing with you?'

Andrew didn't answer. He just lay sprawled there and stared at his feet. That only increased Dick's anger. The anger was good. Dick was trying to get his blood boiling, boiling so hard that he could do what was necessary here.

He picked up the cellphone and checked its readout window. 'It says Breeze again. Who is Breeze?'

Andrew's voice was small. 'She's the girl that came here with me the other day. She sprayed you with mace. She's a friend of mine. She knows I came here tonight.'

Shit.

Dick lifted Andrew's chin with his toe. Andrew's mouth was bleeding where Dick had punched him. 'You bullshitting me?'

There were no lies in Andrew's eyes. Andrew had been stripped bare by the sight of Dot's disembodied head. If he lived, he might never get over this night.

'No, I'm not lying. Both she and my friend Henry know I'm here.'

It hadn't occurred to Dick that people would know where Andrew was. One extra person was bad enough, but two complicated matters infinitely.

He sighed. What was he going to do? Kill them all?

He answered Andrew's telephone, holding it away from his face. Fucking cellphones.

'Grand Central Station,' he said.

'Andrew?' A young woman's voice. Sure, Breeze.

'Uh, Andrew is indisposed at the moment.'

'I need to talk to Andrew.' Agitated, shaky, maybe ready to scream.

'He can't come to the phone right now.'

'What did you do to him?'

'Nothing, he's fine.'

'Put him on. I need to speak to him right now.'

Dick covered the tiny mouthpiece. He looked at Andrew. More crazy bullshit. 'If you tell her anything about what's going on here, I promise I will kill you and take my chances at the Mexican border. You killed Dot. You did it with your dirty pictures. Remember that. OK?'

Andrew nodded.

'Speak!'

'OK. OK, OK, OK. All right? Is that good enough? I did it. I killed her. OK?'

Dick punched up the volume on the phone so he could hear both sides of the conversation. He held the phone six inches from Andrew's head.

'Breeze?' Andrew said. 'I'm right here.'

'Andrew,' came the tinny voice. 'Andrew, listen. Henry is dead. He's fucking dead. Nestor came and killed him. I tried to warn him, but he didn't get out fast enough, and Nestor killed him. All right?'

'Breeze, calm down.'

'Nestor just called me on Henry's phone. He knows everything. He killed Henry, but not before Henry told him everything. He knows where you live now. He knows everything we did. I told him Dot is dead and now he's coming for me. I'm on the street and he's coming for me.'

'You told him Dot is dead. How do you know that?'

Breeze paused for a half beat, then went on. 'I don't know anything. I just told him that. I don't know why. He's the fucking devil, man. He got me on the phone and I just started telling him things. I told him Lydia has the keys. The safe-deposit-box keys. He's probably going over there to kill her right now.'

Holy fucking shit! What? Dick's heart skipped. He looked around his crazy funhouse of an apartment. What to do? What to do? He ran to his own phone, Andrew's cell still in his hand. He picked up the phone and in a fever, he dialed Lydia's number.

'I'm on the street,' he could hear Breeze say. 'He's gonna kill me too. I can't go to the apartment. He knows where you live. He opened the drawers. He said the money's gone. It's all gone. Now he wants to kill everybody, man. Andrew, he's gonna kill everybody. Andrew, do you hear me? Andrew?'

In Dick's other hand, the phone rang at Lydia's apartment.

'Andrew?'

And rang. And rang.

'Andrew!'

An eternity passed. 'Hello?' Lydia said.

Dick's voice raged inside the cordless telephone.

'Lydia! You've got to get out of there!'

'What? Dick? Is this you?'

Lydia had been sitting inside the apartment, more or less thinking of getting out of there anyway. She didn't want to go to work in the morning. She didn't want to spend another night here. The money was still in the trunk of her car. A terrible place for it, she knew. Her car was parked on the street and anyone could break into it at any time – a drug addict looking for a few items to sell – and find the windfall of a lifetime. Actually she would almost welcome it, to walk down the street and find the car broken open and the money gone. She wished the whole thing would go away.

The deposit-box keys were in the pocket of her coat, stashed there for a quick getaway. She was wearing sweatpants and a T-shirt, OK, but she could change quickly and simply leave. Drive out to her father's house, walk in the door, and say that she was afraid. Her father would let her stay – he would love to have her. But eventually, maybe in the morning, she would have to tell him something, explain why she was there. That was what stopped her.

So an alternative plan had come to mind. Get in her car and drive the ten short blocks over to Dick Miller's place. Walk into that creepy post-industrial madhouse, throw herself into Dick's arms, and ask him to protect her. Forever. They could take the money she had, and the keys, and run away. Run away from the money piling up in the account, every day more money. Run away from New York. Run away from whatever had happened to Dot. Put it all in the past. Find a small island in the Caribbean where a million dollars would last a long, long time.

His voice reminded her of that plan, but it wasn't the voice of calm, of escape, of a tropical climate where no one knew them and no one could hurt them. It was a voice of emergency, like clarions pealing, like an air-raid siren. She caught the urgency but the words flowed by in a torrent, like a river surging over a cliff. She tuned in to what Dick was saying, she focused hard, and then it came clear.

'Lydia, get out of the apartment. Nestor's coming there. Get out now.'

Oh, shit. That got her moving. Out of the kitchen, down the short hall and into the bedroom. 'OK. I have to get changed.'

'No,' Dick said. 'No time for that. Whatever you're wearing is good. He's on his way. He's going to be there any minute.'

'What's going on?' she heard herself say.

'Lydia, no time. Just put your coat on and get out.'

She shrugged into her overcoat and rushed back down the hall to the kitchen. The keys were there, in the coat pocket, comforting somehow, the thought of all that money waiting. She glanced out the window, but couldn't see anyone or anything in the alley below. The fire escape led down there. But Nestor could be down there, waiting.

'Oh, shit. I'm wearing slippers.'

'Lydia, get out!'

Her sneakers were in the hall, by the door. It would take three extra minutes to put them on, three minutes that could save her life in a footrace over sidewalks and streets and packed snow and ice. She turned back toward the hall and Nestor stood there in the doorway. He wore a long overcoat down to his knees. His face was dark red from the cold outside. He didn't smile.

'Going somewhere?'

Lydia gaped at him. Words failed her as lightning fired along her spine.

'Hang up the telephone, please.'

'Dick?' she said. 'Dick, he's here.'

'Lydia,' Dick said. 'Listen to me. Put him on the phone.'

Nestor held a cordless power drill. He looked at it with something like surprise, then pointed it at her like a gun. The drill itself was white. Its drill bit and its body were streaked with red. He pressed the button and the drill bit began to turn, making a high whine as it did so.

'He says he wants to talk to you,' Lydia told Nestor.

Nestor shook his head. 'I'll call him back later.'

He walked toward her, brandishing the drill.

'If you'd like to make a call,' the voice told him, 'please hang up and try again.'

Dick stared at the phone.

He looked at Andrew.

'We have to get over there.'

He dropped the phone and untied Andrew's hands. His heart raced as he cut the tape off Andrew's ankles. It was already taking too long.

'There isn't enough time,' Andrew said. 'We should call the cops.'

'Nine-one-one? She'll be dead by the time they get there. It's just a few blocks from here. Come on.' Andrew climbed to his feet, and Dick realized only then that he was giving Andrew more than his freedom. He was giving Andrew a weapon. Andrew could put Dick away now. For good.

There was no time to worry about it. There was no time to worry about what would happen after this night. He needed Andrew. Two were better than one, and if Dick had to go back to prison because of that, so be it. He was going to save Lydia or die trying.

Andrew rubbed the sore areas on his wrists. He looked at Dick. 'Maybe you didn't kill Dot,' he said. 'I could see it in your eyes while I was sitting here. I don't think you have it in you. If you were going to kill me, you would have done it already.'

Dick gestured at the door. 'Then let's go.'

Nestor was six feet away with the drill and moving closer. He took another step and Lydia threw the phone at him.

He ducked into a crouch. The phone sailed over his head, hit the wall and dropped to the floor. It crunched as it hit the tiles. Nestor's head reappeared. His eyes were alive with mirth. His mouth hung slightly open.

'No more phone.'

She recoiled as he came for her. His face contorted into something Lydia couldn't describe, even to herself. It was anger, yes, but it was more than that. It was horror. His eyes were aflame – it was like he was on fire from the inside. He pulled her hair with one hand and held the drill an inch from the side of her head, the bit spinning, spinning, making that drilling sound – not a dentist's drill – deeper, a growl.

'Lydia, do you know what it sounds like when the drill bores through your skull and eats into your brain? Do you know what that sounds like?'

Lydia stared. What was he saying? Had he gone completely insane?

'Do you?' The drill bit was a whisper from her skin now. She could feel the heat of its motion.

'N-no.'

'It's silent. It hardly makes a sound at all. That's how easy it is. That's how close to death you are this very second.'

He pulled the drill away, just a few inches. He eased his finger off the button, and the drill slowed to a stop. He took a deep breath and seemed to steel himself. 'But I don't want to kill you. I just want you to cooperate with me. Give me the money. Give me the keys. I'll let you live. And I'll take you with me. We'll have a suite of rooms that open on a turquoise bay. We'll eat only the finest food, fresh from the sea. Can you see the white curtains billowing in the breeze, the golden sand, the cool, inviting water, shimmering out into the distance, as far as the eye can see? Can you see it, Lydia?'

She was in a kitchen in Brooklyn. It was winter. She didn't know where he was.

He pressed the drill to her head. Hard. All he need do was press the button.

'Can you see it?'

'Yes. I can see it.'

Abruptly, he let her go. 'Good. I knew you could. Now where are the keys?' He held out his hand, as if she would simply put them in his palm. She had an urge to do exactly that, reach into the pocket of her coat, pull out the keys, and hand them to him. If she did that, it seemed, maybe all this would be over.

No. This would never be over.

'They're in the bedroom. Top drawer of the dresser. I was about to grab them when you came in.'

The deranged light in his eyes mocked her. 'I don't think I need to tell you what will happen if you're lying to me. Do I?'

'No.'

'Good.' He stroked her chin with one red fingernail. 'Because I like you, Lydia. And I want to be able to trust you. So I'm going to go get those keys, and you're going to wait right here. And when I come back, we'll talk about where the money is and how we're going to get it. And if you move from this spot at all, I'll kill you. And if you lied to me, I'll kill you. OK?'

'OK.'

'Before I go, is there anything you want to tell me?'

'No.'

'Are the keys going to be where you said they are?'

'Yes.'

'Last chance to stay alive.'

'They're there. In the drawer.'

'Good. I'll be just a moment.'

Nestor turned and paced out of the kitchen. What was she thinking? He was going to kill her now. If she ran for the door, surely he would be standing there. Frantic, she surveyed the kitchen. The seconds passed. A long knife sat on the counter. A knife. Last time he had taken her knife away like it was a toy. But it was her only chance. There was hope in a knife. She picked it up. Then a better idea came – the fire escape. She glanced at the window, open a crack.

Knife in hand, she yanked it open.

'Lydia!'

Jesus. Help me, Jesus.

And out she went, onto the snowy grates.

Her hands plunged into the snow, the crystals so cold they almost burned. She gripped the metal slats with one hand and pulled herself out. She was on her stomach in the snow. She thought of how the snow would soak through her T-shirt and sweats. No time to worry about it.

'Where are you going?'

Nestor was there at the window, laughing now. He had regained his sense of humor, at least. He had dropped the drill somewhere and his hands were empty. He reached and grabbed her left wrist, the wrist of her free hand. His hand – strong, merciless – clamped around her wrist. She looked back at him. Their eyes met. His were as cold and lifeless now as a far planet.

She brought the carving knife around. It seemed to come in slow motion. The blade reached the back of his hand, and they both watched as it bit into his skin and she raked it backward, leaving a clean red line. An instant later, the line swelled with his blood. He yanked the hand back like he had touched a hot stove.

'Bitch!'

His other hand moved quickly, like a snake strike, and slapped the knife from Lydia's hand. It fell and nestled lightly on top of the snow, inches from the window.

Fall, she thought, fall through the grate.

But it didn't. Instead, it sat there, glimmering. Nestor reached down from the window and picked it up. He examined the blood along its edge. Lydia pulled herself up with the handrail, and now he was below her. She inched away toward the stairs, her slippers settling deep into the snow with each step, the snow pouring in like sand on top of her bare feet. She reached the top of the stairs, her eyes still glued to Nestor.

He held up the knife for her inspection. 'I should gut you with this.'

In one fluid motion, he pulled himself out the window and onto the fire escape.

It was a game to him.

Until she cut him with the knife, it had all been a game. He had destroyed – *destroyed* – a man tonight. Compared to that, she would be no struggle at all. He had dealt with Lydia before, and watched her melt like butter before him. She was not a worthy adversary. She had made him laugh, with her ridiculous lies and her attempt to escape. He would take from her whatever he wanted, and then he would move on to Dick Miller and the rest.

Then she cut him and everything changed. Now he was annoyed with her. He was . . . exasperated. That was the word. And his irritation was growing worse by the moment, watching her slip and slide down the fire-escape stairs. One story below was the second floor. There, the ladder to the alley was folded up. It was a security measure, he knew. People escaping the building in a fire could undo the latch and let the ladder fall to the street. Meanwhile, in normal circumstances, criminals on the street could not reach up and climb the ladder, thus gaining entry to people's windows. Would Lydia be able to unfold the ladder and drop it to the alley, then climb onto it before he reached her? He doubted it. Still, there was some risk here. He had to bring her back into the apartment quietly. All around them were buildings, lights on in almost every window, people watching television, reading, dreaming, eating, staying inside and warm during this cold winter night. In many places, he could see blinking Christmas lights. These good people shouldn't be disturbed. It didn't surprise him, of course, that with all this life nearby, she hadn't yet thought to scream. Often, quite often, desperate people forgot to scream until it was too late. Often – and in Lydia's case he believed this would prove to be true – they didn't even forget. They were merely being polite.

He pictured how he would corner her, slap her hard across the face, grab her roughly by the hair, then put the blade to her throat.

'Say one word and I will kill you right here,' he would say. Then he would calmly walk her back up the stairs and through the window. Perhaps he would march her straight into the bedroom, yes? Then he would fuck her. He would punish her. Yes, the idea appealed to him. She deserved no less, the way she was behaving.

He paced down the iron stairs.

There she was, puzzling herself with the process of how to unlock the ladder and drop it to the street. Her small hands moved from place to place, trying and failing to undo the frozen latch that held the ladder in place, trying and failing to move the ladder anyway, trying everything and failing. Tiny gasps of fear and exertion escaped from her, exhalations that reminded him somewhat of a woman in the throes of a growing ecstasy. She glanced up and saw him there, not ten feet away. Would she surrender now, and give herself to the inevitable?

'Lydia.'

'No.' She breathed the word, husky, deep, a growl from somewhere in her belly. Then she leaped over the railing and fell to the ground ten feet below. She made a sound when she landed – still not a scream. It was more of a bark, or a yap, the sound of a small dog in pain. She sprawled in the snow among some trashcans.

Nestor stared down at her. She might have broken her ankle, falling that far. All the same, all the same, she was down there and he was up here. He snapped alert, and in doing so, realized how fogbound he had been until this moment. She was getting away, and he was watching her, analyzing the situation like some detached commentator on the television. It was time to put a stop to this nonsense.

Lydia struggled to her feet and limped off down the alley.

Nestor would not risk the jump and hurting himself the way she had done. He opened the metal latch and released the ladder. It slid to the street almost of its own accord. He climbed down quickly. As soon as his shoes touched the ground, he began a brisk trot, his mind searching for options. He needed to bring Lydia back to a secluded place. His right hand retreated into his coat sleeve, bringing the carving knife with it. No sense in allowing any citizens out and about to view the knife.

He turned onto the street. There was little to worry about. The mercury had dropped below zero. Everyone was indoors. The sidewalks were empty. Lydia limped on ahead of him, running through the snow in her slippers. Nestor hung back the slightest bit. A car moved along, coming towards them. Lydia raced out into the street. The car slowed, until Lydia began to bang on the driver's window. Then the car sped away. Nestor caught a glimpse of a young woman at the steering wheel, her eyes round and startled. He read her mind: *Crazy people are out tonight.*

Lydia limped on toward the green subway entrance ahead. He began to run but she was already descending the stairs. Nestor sighed. He might have to save Lydia for later. Well, he would pursue and see. If there were police down there, he would fade away. They would most likely calm her down, then take her home. If there were no police, there still might be a chance to take her.

She was just ahead. She rushed past the token booth and vaulted the turnstile, entering the subway without paying. There was a man in the token booth, a transit worker, a thin man with thick glasses. He saw her go and leaned over a microphone.

'Ma'am?' he said over the public address system. 'Ma'am, you can't do that.'

Nestor walked up to the token booth. He slipped a ten-dollar bill through the slot.

'She's my wife,' he said. 'It's Christmastime, she stopped taking her medication, her mother is in a home, everything is crazy right now. You know what I mean?'

Behind the fish-eye lenses of the glasses, the man's eyes softened. 'Oh, yeah. I know. It gets everybody.' He slid a Metrocard through the slot.

Nestor picked up the card. 'Keep the change.'

He passed through the turnstile. She was up ahead, limping along the white tiled hallway. The overhead lights cast a harsh yellow glare on her. A rush of air came, warm air, with the squeal of metal on metal. Somewhere a train was pulling into the station. Nestor noticed Lydia improve her pace. He did the same. She descended another flight of stairs and he began to run, a full-tilt run. No one would blame him – he was running to catch a train. He took the stairs three at a time. She was just ahead. A few people exited the train and immediately started up the stairs. He slalomed through them. They didn't notice Lydia and her slippers – they were people pursuing their own lives and their own errands, eight million of them in this city nestled in their own protective cocoons, and if Lydia had ripped all her clothes off and began shrieking, they might take notice and they might not.

There was a case, a famous case . . . It came to him. A young woman was being murdered in the street on a warm summer night – stabbed to death. It was a crowded neighborhood in Queens. She screamed and screamed, and more than forty people looked out their windows and did nothing. They didn't even call the police. Incredible on the face of it, but in New York, not so incredible.

Lydia made no attempt to stop anyone. She simply entered the train.

Nestor reached the platform, which was emptying fast. The bell sounded that marked the closing of the doors. Nestor ran on, another ten yards, moving toward the front of the train, moving ahead of Lydia. At the very last second, he dashed to the left, caught the closing doors, and squeezed through the gap in the middle.

The lights were bright inside the train. The train itself was almost empty. A small knot of Asian teenagers were in one corner, joking about something, and two red-faced men who appeared to be drunk slumped in the middle of the car. The train pulled away from the station, moving deeper into Brooklyn. Nestor could force her backward now, from car to car, toward the rear of the train. He strode to

208

the door between cars. There she was, moving backwards, just as he had hoped.

He opened the door and passed between cars. There was that moment, between cars, on the train and not really on the train, the shriek of the wheels on the track, the wind blowing by, stale air trapped down there for generations, darkness all around, and nothing between him and the abyss except some flimsy chains that wouldn't keep a dog out of the kitchen. The cars moved independently of one another, side to side, accelerating, daring him to misstep. Somewhere, in another realm, hands reached for him. They were waiting, and not with patience.

He entered the next car. Even fewer people here and Lydia was up ahead, already opening the door to the next car. Nestor walked toward her, passing the silent riders. No one seemed to notice him. The next car would be the last. Who would be there? With a little luck, no one.

He reached the door, slid between the gap again, and came out the other side. There was no one here. Well, almost no one. An old black woman slept near the door. She wore hospital scrubs under her heavy coat, and had a Macy's shopping bag at her feet. A small handbag was on her lap. Old woman, sleeping off a long day at work, sleeping off long years of work.

Lydia moved away from him, still limping, her face contorted by fear and pain. She was headed toward the very end of the train. He saw the window there and nothing but blackness beyond it.

Libby Jenkins heard the door open between subway cars. A moment later, she felt, rather than saw, two shadows go past her. Now, through eyes as narrow as slits, she watched the man and woman move toward the end of the car.

Until a minute ago, she had dozed with her arms folded in front of her, thinking of what was in the refrigerator. Leftover pork chops and macaroni with cheese, unless Frank had polished that off when he got home. If so, there were some frozen crab cakes she could thaw, maybe put them on a bed of rice. There'd be something.

The movements of the train soothed her and rocked her, almost, but not quite, to sleep. Sixty-one years old, she was doing what she normally did this time of night – riding the L train home to Brooklyn from her job as a 'med-surg' nurse at Beth Israel Medical Center in Manhattan. Thirty years she had been making this exact same commute, at this exact same time.

She had seen a lot in all that time. In the seventies and the eighties, the city had been a different place. The trains were filthy and blighted with graffiti. In the seventies, the kids were in gangs and on heroin. In the eighties, the kids were on crack and the gangs turned deadly, shooting each other up with machine guns. New York was a dark netherworld of death and derangement in those days, from the time of the Son of Sam killer to the time of Bernie Goetz and beyond, the time when young boys killed each other for their sneakers.

In 1981, Libby started carrying the gun. Frank had given it to her because she always insisted on riding in the last car of the train. Dear Frank. The last car was closest to the exit where Libby went upstairs to the street, just a block to the house when she hit the open air, and she'd be dipped in shit before she let some teenage boys scare her from the way she chose to live. The gun was a .38 caliber six-shooter, like the police used to carry. In more than twenty years, she had kept it clean and well-oiled, and pulled it only twice in all that time. Say it loud and say it proud – Libby Jenkins did not fuck around. If these kids wanted to degrade themselves with drugs and crime, they were welcome to it. But they would not do it at her expense.

Libby sighed. Ten years had passed since she last pulled her gun in anger. She watched now as the young lady backed up slowly toward the end of the train. The man moved toward her, something bright and shiny in one hand. Sure, he had a kitchen knife. He was menacing her, probably his girlfriend, with a carving knife. Libby looked again. For the first time, she noticed that the young lady was wearing bedroom slippers.

Lydia could not find her voice.

She wanted to scream, but she could not do it. There was no one here except an old black woman, asleep. She was a nurse, or an aide, some kind of hospital worker, asleep here all alone in the last car. What could she do, an old woman? Maybe she could get help. That was all. Maybe she could run and get help. Or maybe, if Lydia woke her up, then Nestor would kill her – kill her just for waking up.

Lydia backed away from Nestor now, just backing up, nowhere to run. The final door of the train was just behind her. Through the window she could see the track disappearing into the darkness, lights zipping by then growing distant, then winking out, all in the space of seconds. The train bucked and rolled, side to side, moving like a snake. That door would be locked, she knew. There was no way to open it, and no way to break through the window.

She had no weapon, no way to defend herself. Nestor moved slowly toward her. She remembered how he used to smile at her, a mocking smile for sure, but better than this sinister glare. There was no humor left in him, no mirth, no humanity. He was going to kill her here, right here on the subway, and then he was going to walk away.

'Lydia, where are you going?'

There was nowhere to go. If there were anywhere, she would be going there. Nestor moved closer, just a few glinting inches of the knife showing at the bottom of his sleeve.

'All this running around, for what? So you can catch your death of cold?'

Lydia spotted the emergency brake, hanging against the wall, behind a small metal door. The emergency brake! Thoughts flashed through her head. What would happen if she pulled it? The train would stop, of course. It would come to a screeching, sudden halt. Then she would be trapped here with Nestor. She was trapped here anyway. They would both be thrown to the floor. That might be OK – he could be knocked unconscious. In a few moments, help would come – maybe even the police. Nestor might already have killed her by then.

She had to go for it. There was no other possible way out. She stared at the brake door and read the words printed there. *Emergency Brake. Open this cover. Alarm will sound. Pull handle down.* That sounded like a lot. What if the door didn't open? She gazed up at it. Claw at it with your nails. Bite it. Do anything. Try anything!

Too late. Nestor was on her. With his free hand he grabbed her by the hair. With his body weight, he forced her backwards against the door. The train bucked and rolled, bucked and rolled. His breath was hot on her neck.

'Not a good idea to pull the emergency brake,' he said. 'It's only for use in emergencies.'

He tilted her head back, exposing her throat. The knife came out. She saw it glinting there, above her, between her neck and the lights of the ceiling. Nestor's eyes were there. And his teeth. The blade, his eyes, his teeth. They were all she could see.

'Lydia, darling. Tell me where you put the money. And then tell me where you put the keys.' She thought of the keys again, in her pocket, just bare inches from his hands, the hands that were now about to kill her.

'If you tell, I'll bring you with me, and we can be lovers, and you can be a rich lady. If you don't tell, I promise I will slice you open, then I will go to your home and find those keys anyway. It's your choice, and now is your time to make it.'

Now he did smile, a hideous approximation of a real person's smile.

'Son,' a voice said, 'you better drop that knife or I'm gonna drop your balls.'

Nestor stopped. He squinted in irritation.

'Son, you hear me OK?' The voice – a woman's voice – was louder now.

He glanced back the way they had just come. Lydia, her head pulled back for the sacrifice, could just see that way too. The old woman was there, ten feet away, her coat off, just in the hospital scrubs now, the gun held in both hands in front of her, a shooter's crouch Lydia had seen in movies.

'Madam, I assure you this is none of your concern.'

'Talk that fancy shit at me and I'll put one in your gut for good measure. Now drop that fucking knife and ease up off that young lady's hair. You hear? I'm running out of patience.'

Nestor stared at the woman. He must have seen something in her eyes, because Lydia thought she saw it too. It was called resolve. She would shoot him if she had to.

Nestor looked at the emergency brake now.

'Go for that brake. I'll shoot you before you get two feet.'

Nestor sighed. There was a moment when he had to decide. Kill Lydia here and let the old woman shoot him dead. Or drop the knife and live for another day. It was a real decision for him. Lydia could see it. Nestor was at the end of his tether.

'That's it.' The woman said. 'I'm done. I'm not waiting another second.'

Nestor dropped the knife. It clattered as it hit the floor of the car. Slowly, he opened his fingers and let go of Lydia's hair. Lydia's scalp had gone numb. Phantom fingers still seemed to hold her in their grip.

The train slowed down. It was coming into a station. The train glided to a stop on an empty platform. The doors slid open.

'You're welcome to leave,' the old woman said. She kept the gun trained on Nestor's mid-section. 'You step out onto that platform and you stand right there where I can see you until the doors shut again. Understood?'

Nestor stepped off the car and stood trapped in the sights of the gun. He seemed bored, like a man waiting for a bus on a slow afternoon. The doors slid shut and the train began to move. Nestor didn't budge. He just watched them slide away.

The old woman looked at Lydia. Her face wrinkled in disapproval. 'Missy,' she said, 'you need to rethink your taste in men.'

7
DARKNESS ALL AROUND

'All right,' Dick said into the payphone. 'I'll see you tomorrow.'

The phone was across the parking lot from the motel room. It was cold tonight – *cold*. He paced across the lot and took the outside stairs to the second floor. He had just spent fifteen minutes on the phone with Block. The whole conversation had happened in a vague, meandering sort of code – Block was paranoid about wiretaps on his phones. Even now, Dick wondered if Block had understood him.

He came into the room, the cold still clinging to him. Lydia sat on the double bed. Her eyes were watchful, like those of a grazing animal that spends its life running from meat-eating predators. 'Dick, what are we going to do?'

It was two in the morning. Until this moment, Lydia had hardly said a word. Dick locked the door and peeked through the curtain down at the parking lot. Dot's Lexus waited just below the room – he had parked it where he could see it from the window. They were in Island Park, New York, forty-five minutes outside the city. Downstairs, the motel office was closed. They had had to ring the bell when they came, wake the guy up.

In the summer, if he rented this room, he could sit just outside the door in the white plastic chairs on the walkway, and he could look out across the parking lot, and watch the traffic out on the road roar past the bank and the KFC and the McDonald's and the strip malls, and onto the causeway toward Long Beach.

They were safe here for now. But if they were so safe, why did he keep pacing back and forth, across the room, then back to the window, to peek again behind the curtain at the nearly empty parking lot? Why didn't he take his coat off?

'I don't know,' Dick said, trying to put some cheer in his voice. 'Maybe we could order a bucket of chicken or some pizza. You think there's a place open this late?'

'That's not what I mean, Dick. I'm afraid.'

He turned to Lydia. Of course she was afraid. The fear wrote lines on her face. She still had her coat on, and she hugged herself, although the room was plenty warm enough. Under her coat, she wore gray corduroy pants, a yellow sweater, and an old pair of tennis shoes, gifts from the old black woman who had saved her from Nestor on the subway. Dick had picked her up at the woman's home. The woman had frowned when Dick showed up at her door. Apparently, she had wanted Lydia to sleep there, in the guest bedroom.

Dick nodded. 'I know. When we got to your place, and there was nobody there, I mean, forget about it. I just about stroked and died.'

'You were afraid?'

'I don't know. I just . . .'

'Why can't you say it?'

'Say what?'

'That you were afraid.'

Dick moved the heavy curtain an inch and peeked out the window again. Nobody there. The Lexus was still there, parked just below the window. The same near-silent road, empty streets leading away from it, the same barren parking lot, the same dirty snow humped and piled on the edges.

'I was afraid,' he said. 'I thought for sure you were dead.'

'Like Dot?'

'Like Dot, like Andrew's friend Henry, like maybe anybody who crosses paths with that guy.'

Lydia's body started to shake, then tears formed at the corners of her eyes, and she buried her face in her hands. 'He tried to . . . he was going to . . . he had a drill. A power drill.'

Dick came to her then, and crouched in front of her. Gently he pulled her hands away from her face. Her eyes were bloodshot, the skin around them turning red and puffy. Tears flowed down her cheeks. He held her hands in his.

'Hey. It's going to be OK. You're safe now, OK? I promise that you're safe. He doesn't know where we are, and even if he did, he wouldn't come here. You know why? Because I'm here.'

'I want to run away,' she said. 'I want to get away and go some-place safe. We have a million dollars. We can just leave.' Her eyes widened as a thought occurred to her. 'Can you even leave the country? Do you have a passport?'

He nodded. 'Yeah. It says my name is Steve Zimmer. I have a driver's license like that too. Got it renewed just before I left California. You never know.'

'OK, then. So let's go. First thing in the morning.'

'We will go,' he said. 'Very soon, but not first thing in the morning. There are loose ends I have to tie up.' He saw the haunted look on her face, and he plunged on with the story he had prepared. 'Andrew, for one thing. He knows about the money, he knows where we're going, and his friend has just been killed. He has reason to be upset, and we might have to buy him off to keep him quiet.'

Right now, Andrew was the very definition of a loose end. His friend had been more than killed. By the sound of it, he had been folded, spindled, and mutilated. The weight of that landed on Dick full force.

The tears began to flow down Lydia's face again, as if she were feeling that same weight.

'Lydia, you have to trust me. We're going to get out of here, just not tomorrow. OK?' He wished he could explain the rest of it to her, that Dot's remains were in his apartment, and that he wasn't about to just leave Block to clean up his mess. But he couldn't explain it. Not yet. Maybe not ever.

Dick sighed. It was going to be another long day tomorrow. More body parts to dump. More madness and horror to deal with. Plenty more of everything.

She stared at him. Her face had gone slack. From shock or exhaustion, he didn't know which.

'Will you please hold me?' she said.

Andrew might never sleep again.

They were in a hotel in downtown White Plains, about thirty miles north of midtown Manhattan. Andrew had the vague notion that it was an expensive hotel. There was valet parking, and he had given the guy the car. The room had a king-sized bed and gold doorknobs. The bathroom was enormous – it echoed in there. When they entered the room, Andrew had poured them each a glass of Scotch from the mini-bar. Breeze had downed hers in a gulp, then sprawled out on the bed fully dressed. Now she was either asleep or doing a good job of pretending.

Breeze was toast. She was barely speaking. Andrew had found her at a bar in Greenpoint, half drunk and listening closely to a white-haired long-haul trucker from Tennessee. She was probably ready to leave town should the old man suggest it. Later, at Dot's house, Andrew had tried to leave Breeze with the car, but she refused.

'No way, man. I'm not waiting here for him to find me. Don't worry. If you come back alive, then I'll show up.'

She stalked off down the street, head swiveling, looking everywhere at once. When Andrew returned to the car half an hour later, she appeared like smoke from the mouth of an alley. She stared at him as he beeped open the doors to the BMW, a question in her eyes. Her arms hung limp at her sides.

'Yeah,' Andrew said. 'Henry's in there.'

Her hands came up to her eyes and covered them, like the hands of a child watching a scary movie. He opened the door for her and she climbed in, hands still covering her face. She didn't speak. She didn't say a fucking word. But look at it this way: at least she hadn't seen what was left of him. Andrew didn't think Breeze was ready to see Henry.

Now, in the hotel room, Andrew lay on the bed near her, his head resting on several pillows, sipping his Scotch. He didn't even know the name of this hotel, and didn't remember how he had found it. It seemed that he was driving along a dark, winding parkway, then he was driving through city streets, then here was this hotel and he pulled into the front circle. Now they were upstairs, on the eighth floor, and the door was triple-locked. With a little bit of luck, they were safe. Nestor couldn't know they were here. He would have to call every hotel in the New York metropolitan area, and there were hundreds. No. For tonight, they were OK. It was probably even safe enough here to sleep for a while. Not that Andrew could manage that.

Seeing Dot's dismembered head was bad enough. Being tied to a chair and believing Miller and his friend were going to kill him was bad enough. Going to Dot's house and finding Henry in the upstairs closet had broken the camel's back. There was so much blood it was impossible to believe. The carpet in the closet was stained black. Henry sat on the floor, his back to the cabinets, his hands cuffed behind him. His clothes were soaked in blood. And there were holes – *holes* – at least a dozen of them drilled into his skull. Much of his face had been obliterated with some kind of power tool. His eyes . . . they were enough to make a person jump out a hotel window. His eyes were gone. Nestor had drilled Henry's eyes into mulch.

Andrew had left the body there. He remembered walking down the street in a kind of daze. If Nestor had come then, Andrew would have been defenseless. He wouldn't even have run. He probably would have submitted, without a word, to whatever torture Nestor had in mind.

Andrew finished his drink. Breeze's back was to him, and it rose and fell with her heavy breathing. He could understand why she wasn't speaking. Henry was dead, sure. Dot was dead. Nestor was on the loose and would kill them both if he found them. But it was deeper than that. It was him – Andrew. He had brought this upon them. He had brought Henry and Breeze into this game.

That was how he had thought of it – as a game. It had rules. He didn't want to rape Dot because that was going too far. He just wanted to beat her out of the money. Ruin her relationship with Miller. Defeat her at the game.

But Nestor wasn't playing a game. And now, only after it was too late, did Andrew understand this.

Andrew could see his life spreading out before him, a long, endless string of days. Each and every day, the awareness would come back to him that through his stupidity he had gotten two people killed who didn't have to die. Every day, the image of Henry's eye sockets would return. Maybe the feeling Andrew had now, the sickness he felt in the pit of his stomach, would fade over time. Maybe it wouldn't.

But he knew one thing. Before this was over he would kill yet another person – Nestor – or he would die trying. Nestor deserved the most painful kind of slow death. Of course, Andrew knew that taking vengeance wouldn't undo what had happened. It could hardly set things right. But it might, just might, make life worth living again.

It just happened, as she had known that it would.

He held her in his arms and she laid her head against his broad chest. She cried for what seemed like an hour. Then she looked up at him and found that he was looking down at her, and it just . . . happened. It was awkward at first, like they were teenagers, just learning how to do it, and part of that awkwardness was that they were wearing so many clothes.

But Dick had an awkwardness to him, and she realized, somewhere in the back of her mind, that this was what made him so endearing. He was big. He was tough – he had spent two and a half years in a California prison. He was A-list handsome, or nearly so. And he was so tender, so gentle, that he seemed just like a shy little boy.

She let her hands roam his body. It was hot in that room, and as the clothes came off it grew hotter. She pulled his solid bulk on top of her and she held him close. He moved against her, and she felt the heat rising within her. It had been months – long months – since she and Dot were together, and she had been with no one in that time. The pressure had built inside her, and the more she had denied that pressure, the more it had built. When Dick touched her, she could deny it no more. In a flood, it released, then released again. There was so much inside of her, and finally it poured forth.

Hours later, she opened her eyes in a darkened room. Dick entered from the outside, removed his clothes and crawled in bed next to her.

'Where did you go?'

He was propped on an elbow, his eyes half-closed. 'I heard a noise. Went outside to check it out.'

His head hit the pillow, he draped an arm over her, and then he was asleep so hard it was like he'd never been awake in the first place. But Lydia could not get back to sleep. She stared at the ceiling, Dick's heavy arm holding her, wondering about what would come in the morning. Would they even be alive, and together, twenty-four hours from now?

After a long time, she noticed light was coming into the room from outside. It was day and she was not refreshed.

'What did you do with the body?' Dick said.

He and Andrew sat in a booth at the Quaker Diner. The place was packed with customers, as it was any time of the day or night, despite the mediocre food – greasy eggs, pancakes like plaster, tragically over-cooked pasta. Twenty-four hours a day the Quaker slung it out, and twenty-four hours a day they had takers. From his window, Dick could watch the street. On busy Metropolitan Avenue, heavy trucks – cement mixers, eighteen-wheelers, fire engines – rumbled by beneath the overpass for the Brooklyn-Queens Expressway. On the side street, three police cruisers were parked, the cops inside here somewhere, enjoying a free meal.

Behind the third cop car, Lydia's Honda was parked. She and Breeze were in the car, both wearing blonde wigs purchased this morning by Breeze at a hair salon in White Plains, both wearing sunglasses, waiting for Andrew and Dick to finish their meeting. They were like spies out there – easy-to-spot Hollywood spies in a film that was supposed to be funny. The money was still in Lydia's trunk, and that gave Dick a nervous feeling, the money being there, ten feet away from those cop cars.

Andrew shook his head. 'What did I do with it? You didn't see this body. You couldn't do anything with it. I just left it there.'

'Jesus.'

Andrew forked a chunk of pancake into his mouth and followed it with a slurp of coffee. Dark rings had formed under his eyes. His skin was pale. Every few seconds, the corner of his mouth made a funny vibration. He looked like a man dangling at the end of his rope – like a man who hadn't slept in a long time. 'Dot has a house,' he said, his mouth full of food. 'That's about the only good news here. It'll be a while before the neighbors start to smell that thing.'

Dick had barely touched his food. Just looking at it turned his stomach. 'So what are you going to do?'

Andrew shook his head. 'That's not the question. The question is what are we going to do?'

'You and Breeze?'

'No. You and me.' His pointer finger shot back and forth, first indicating Dick, then indicating himself. 'What are *we* going to do?'

Dick shrugged. 'There is no you and me. I did you a favor last night. I let you live. Now we're splitsies.'

'Bullshit,' Andrew said. 'The way I see it, you think you're about to walk out of here with Lydia and more than a million dollars between you. I don't have to let that happen. Whether you killed her or not, Dot – oh, excuse me, chunks of Dot – are still in your apartment. All I have to do is call the cops and let them know. Even if you leave the country right now, right this minute, you think they wouldn't bother to pick you up in the Bahamas? On a murder case? Shit.'

'So you're a blackmailer now? Good. You can add that to your resumé. Eavesdropper. Pornographer. Embezzler.'

Andrew didn't smile. 'Call it whatever you like.'

'What do you want? If you tell me you want me to help you get rid of that body, I will laugh you out of this diner.'

'I want two things.' Andrew held up two fingers to illustrate the number. 'And neither of them have to do with Henry. If we move

223

fast enough, we can be out of here before anybody finds him. Number one, I want some of the money.'

Dick shrugged. 'Possible. How much?'

'One-third. I think that's fair. I have some money of my own, so I'm not going to try to stick you up. I just want enough so that Breeze and I can get the fuck out of here for a while. Live it up somewhere. Pretend all this never happened.'

Dick let out a small laugh. He had hoped to bargain Andrew down to a third. But he forced himself to stay serious. 'Twenty-five percent, and we keep the cash,' he said. 'The hundred grand that Lydia has right now. It's not part of the split.'

Andrew waved it away like it was a wisp of fog. 'Dick, that's fine. Whatever. I'm not going to argue about every penny. I don't really care about the money anymore. A quarter million and change is fine.'

'OK. So what do you care about?'

Andrew drew a circle of syrup on his plate with his fork. 'That's number two. Nestor. He has to die. I want to be the one to do it.'

Dick raised his hands as if Andrew had pulled a gun. 'That's not my problem. Listen, we'll do the money split, but if you want to go off on a vendetta, you want to try to kill somebody else, that's your problem.'

Andrew's face flushed. 'He killed Dot. I would think you'd care about that.'

'Do we know that?'

'I'm convinced of it.'

Dick shook his head. 'I'm sorry about Dot. She was a good woman, in her own way. She lied to me, she used me, and even knowing all that, I still like her. But revenge is a sucker move. You want to hang Dot's murder on Nestor? Call the cops when you get to Nassau.'

Andrew went on as if Dick hadn't spoken. 'He tortured and killed my friend.'

'If he was really your friend, I'm not sure you would have left him to rot.' He gestured at Andrew's empty plate. 'You have a pretty good appetite for somebody who just lost a friend.'

'My associate, then.'

'*Your* associate. I never met the guy.'

'Look,' Andrew said, and he talked slowly, as if Dick was a semi-bright child in need of remedial instruction, 'we need to finish him before we go. We'll never have a better opportunity than we have right now. I know where he lives, and I have the keys to his place. We can get in there before he even knows what's happening.'

'How did you get his keys?'

'Breeze got them. She went to bed with him and made a cast of his keys.' Andrew said it matter-of-factly, without the slightest sign of embarrassment or hesitation. Dick didn't respond. He saw that Andrew was all the way out there now – on the edge, ready for the nuthouse.

'Anyway, we have to do it now. Nestor knows where we're going. If we leave him behind, we'll just have to deal with him down there. He'll stalk us. He'll pick us off one by one.'

Dick saw the logic in that. But he conjured the episode from the night before, those moments when he considered killing Andrew in cold blood. He had tried to summon the anger that would make him commit that murder, and he couldn't do it.

'If he comes down there, I'll get him then,' Dick said.

'You won't see him until it's too late.'

'I'm willing to take that chance. Listen, Andrew, you want a quarter of the money? Then let's go get it. You want to hang around and kill Nestor? Fine, we'll wait for you in the Bahamas.'

'How can I trust you to wait?'

Dick smiled. 'You can't.'

* * *

A little swelling, a little pain, but nothing she couldn't handle.

Lydia's right foot was sore as she drove the gothic girl, the one they called Breeze, out to Long Island. She felt it every time she eased off the gas or stepped on the brake. It was a nasty jump from that fire escape, and she was lucky she didn't break her ankle. Then again, if she had broken it, she'd probably be dead now.

That was nothing to think about.

She glanced over at the girl. Breeze was pretty, for sure. It was possible she was even beautiful, the beauty marred only somewhat by the black eyeliner, the many bracelets on her wrists and arms, the ring through her eyebrow and her tongue, and the tattoos, including the teardrop tattoo in the corner of one eye.

'Did any of that hurt?' Lydia asked the girl.

'Did any of what hurt?'

Lydia shrugged. 'The tattoos, the piercings. I don't know.'

'No. It felt good.'

As Dick instructed, they got off the highway every ten minutes and waited a few moments to see if anyone followed them off. No one did. They obeyed the rules of the road – the last thing they needed was to get pulled over and have some nosy traffic cop find nearly a hundred thousand dollars in cash in the trunk.

Dick had taken Lydia aside for a few moments before cutting them loose. He had told her the plan – that she and Breeze would go back to the motel and hide out, while he and Andrew would take care of some business there in town. Within a day, they would all leave the country for the Bahamas. When he told her all this, it gave her a sinking feeling. The part about the 'business' was what bothered her.

'Are you going to try to kill Nestor?' she had said.

He looked her in the eye. 'It's nothing like that.'

Lydia thought she saw a lie floating there. 'Dick, are you?'

'Lydia, trust me. Please? I'm not going to kill Nestor. Andrew thinks he might know where Dot is. OK? I'm not going to say any more than that right now. You'll know when I know. So just lay low, be careful, check in once in a while, and take care of Breeze. She's been through a lot.'

Lydia sighed. 'We've all been through a lot.'

Now, in the car, she wondered how she could reach this girl – a girl who seemed like a teenager but Dick said was not much younger than herself. Her boyfriend had been murdered yesterday – or her ex-boyfriend. Lydia was under the impression that Andrew was her boyfriend. Anyway, it wasn't part of Dick's plan, but Lydia had an idea that might cheer them both up, at least a little. As long as Nestor wasn't creeping up behind them – and as far as she could tell, Nestor was nowhere around – it was probably safe enough.

'I'm from Long Island,' she said to the girl. 'I know a pretty good mall out this way. It's probably not too crowded on a weekday like today. Want to go? Just for a little while? I don't feel like being cooped up in the motel room. Maybe we can catch a movie. And anyway, I'm buying.'

Did the girl's eyes light up? Maybe the slightest bit.

'OK,' Lydia said. 'Let's go to the mall.'

Desiree was back on top.

Well, as far on top as things ever got for Desiree – riding the subway out to Brooklyn to scrub the blood of a dead woman out of the bathtub and off the floor in Dick Miller's apartment. But things *were* looking up. No doubt about that.

After leaving Dick's last night, she and Block had driven out of the city. They spent the night in an apartment down on the Jersey shore. It was the nicest apartment Desiree had ever been in. She had seen better ones in magazines – but in real life, never. It had snow-white wall-to-wall carpeting, a stone fireplace, and a floor-to-ceiling view of the Atlantic Ocean. While Block lit the fire, Desiree went out on the deck and stood there, despite the cold, just staring out at all that sea and sky. Just looking at it. When she came inside, Block was fretting. He had too much on his mind: Dick, the dead woman in Dick's apartment, the boy that came in with the gun, the cops, the businesses Block owned, his evil wife, his kids that he loved. It was all jumbled up in there. But Desiree knew how to calm him down. And she did. She went to work on him. She calmed him just right.

Later, as they lay together on the carpet in front of the fire, it was the perfect moment. She had never had one before, but she did now. One perfect moment, and she wanted it to stay that way forever.

Then the phone rang. Dick Miller, calling Block's sanctuary. Block put it on speakerphone, showing Desiree he had no secrets from her. Dick was in Long Island. Out near Long Beach. Some motel. Ocean Breeze, maybe, or Ocean View. Ocean Breeze, that was it. It sounded like a dump compared to this apartment. Dick had let the young boy go. He was confident now that the young boy wouldn't tell anyone about the bathtub.

Well, that was sort of a relief, actually. Desiree had felt bad about being an accessory to murder. She could see that Block felt better about it too.

'Don't say too much,' Block said. 'You never know who's listening.'

Dick didn't say much more. Something had happened, and they were hiding out now. There was still work to do. There were still things to talk over.

'OK, I'll tell you what,' Block said. 'I'll have Desiree swing by the place tomorrow and help clean up. You finish the dropping off. Then I'll come by tomorrow night and we'll talk. We'll get everything straight.'

They had slept on a huge king-size bed, the mattress as soft as the clouds in a summer sky. In the morning, before she opened her eyes,

Desiree was awakened by the call of the seagulls outside the window. They showered and dressed and Block gave her twenty-five hundred dollars, just before they left the apartment.

'I'm not a whore, Block. I told you that. I don't do it for money.'

'I know that. But you got bills, right? So pay some bills. It's a gift. OK?'

She took the money. Of course she took it. What else was she going to do? 'OK. But is this the end? I mean, after we drive up to the city, will I see you again?'

He shrugged. 'Tonight. You're going to Dick's apartment, right? So hang around until I get there.'

The train pulled into the Lorimer station. It was a five-minute walk to Dick's apartment from here. Block had told her to be careful and make sure this creep Nestor wasn't hanging around anywhere before she went into the apartment. How she was supposed to recognize him – that Block didn't explain. It didn't matter anyway.

'Honey,' Desiree had said, 'do you have any idea of the people that lived in my neighborhood when I was growing up? I see this Nestor person, I'll give him a slap and send him home to his momma.'

Block opened a drawer in the kitchen and pulled out a small gun. 'Better yet, you see him, you give him one of these. OK?'

Now, with the gun in her handbag, Desiree felt plenty safe. All the same, she did keep her eyes peeled for creeps. The only problem? The streets were loaded with them. She smiled. She figured she was looking at two hours of cleaning up blood. If she did a good job, Block would be pleased.

Then maybe they would go back to New Jersey tonight.

Nestor paced the wide confines of Dick's apartment.

It was a dreary place. It reminded him of photographs he had seen of closed-down auto factories in Detroit. Dust motes hung in the air, dancing in the weak winter light that fought its way through the decades of grime caked on the giant windows. It would cost, Nestor thought, a hundred thousand dollars to make just this one apartment livable, and here was a whole building like this.

He thought a little more about the apartment, and how he would redesign it. Yes, he could see how it would work – my God, a home with twenty-foot ceilings – and how, with the right work done, it could become a compelling place to live. Blast the grime off those windows to allow the light to enter. Since you were Dick Miller, and you didn't seem concerned about personal comfort in any meaningful way, do that first. Build a loft, ten feet high, against the windows, and have curtains custom made to run along the windows both upstairs and downstairs. Track lighting rather than these fluorescents left over from the industrial age. Put flooring down, something blond to lighten the place up, like a synthetic American Beech. Leave the middle of the space open – a huge living space with couches and chairs and throw rugs. Perhaps add something funky, something a little unexpected, like a hammock built for two. Art on the walls – massive, abstract, colorful, modern paintings, the kind that use forceful lines to merely suggest the subject, the kind Nestor would paint were he a painter, the kind you could have for a song here in Williamsburg at this moment in history. Rip out the kitchen area entirely and start from new. A new dining area. An entirely new bedroom. And the bathroom . . .

Well, that was the point of this whole exercise, wasn't it? To take his mind away from the bathroom. The bathroom was where Dot had been, of course. The tub was stained in a ring, and it didn't take much imagination to see that it was her blood. The floor was splattered with small pieces of flesh and gore. There was a small power handsaw in there, sitting on the toilet seat, its teeth caked with blood and meat. There were two bloodstained knives and an open box of

Hefty garbage bags. Miller had indeed killed Dot, he had cut her into pieces, and then he had wrapped her in the garbage bags. Then, Nestor imagined, he had thrown her out with the trash.

He thought of Dot for a moment, her smile, her hair, her body, the way she moved against him in the bed. He had thought of how she always left half-consumed objects behind her – half-smoked cigarettes and half-empty glasses of wine, each with the ruby-red circle of her lipstick on the edge. He thought of how he had given her a ring one night, a tasteful two-karat diamond in a gold setting.

She had turned crimson and . . . did a tear come to her eye?

'Nestor, this is so thoughtful. But you know, I could never marry you. I was married once before, and I think I'm not the marrying kind.'

'I know,' he had said. 'You are free and I would never try to cage you. But I wanted to give you something to match your beauty, and to express something to you.'

'To express?'

'Love,' he said now, his breath catching in his throat, shadows growing long in the stark confines of Dick Miller's bleak apartment. His voice echoed off the walls. 'I wanted to express love.' Again that image came, the red carpet, the crowds. Now there was a limousine and flashbulbs popping. It seemed to Nestor that he was slowly perfecting the image, creating the ideal. A hopeful thought came to him. Perhaps the dream was still possible. Perhaps there could be another Dot, somewhere else, sometime in the future.

He looked around again at the gloom, darkening now as the afternoon faded. Where was that ring now? Dot had often worn it on the ring finger of her right hand. Was she wearing it the night she died? What had Miller done with it? Kept it? Sold it? Thrown it in the trash with the rest of her?

In the hallway outside, a pair of high heels clacked toward the door. A key turned in the lock. Dot? Was Dot alive and coming here? Nestor shrank back, into the kitchen. He crouched there, watching the door. It opened, and a black woman walked in.

'Dick?' she called as she stood at the door. When no one answered, she closed and locked the door behind her. She walked into the middle of the room. She was an attractive woman, and had a sexy way about her. She moved like a dancer.

Nestor pulled his gun. The woman went into the bathroom, and he walked up quietly behind her. She stared down at the bloodstained tub, hands on her hips. She shook her head at the sight of it, and muttered something under her breath. But she wasn't *shocked* by it. That much was clear. She had seen this tub before. She knew what was going on.

She turned around and Nestor pointed the gun into her pretty face. She tried to reach into her purse, but he grabbed her wrist and squeezed it hard between his fingers.

'If you scream I will kill you.'

Instinct. She went on animal instinct alone. The things she did – a logical person would say they didn't make sense. But the Cool Breeze wasn't a logical person. She worked from impressions the environment gave her. She thought outside the box. On TV, people always claimed they wanted to think outside the box, but it wasn't true. They didn't actually want to. It would take them down roads they didn't want to travel. Breeze traveled on those roads. She knew no others.

She glanced around the room. It was an OK room.

The television was on. Breeze kept an eye and an ear on it because maybe they would show something about Henry. So far, nothing. Andrew was probably right. It would be a couple of days before they found the body.

Behind the closed bathroom door, Breeze could hear the water running from Lydia's shower. It had just started, less than a minute ago. Lydia probably hadn't even stepped into it yet.

Last night – that was bad. When Nestor had called her on the telephone, Breeze had gone into some kind of shock. She really had been in the grip of terror. He was a monster, calling her like that. She had dealt with monsters before, but this monster had knocked her loose from her moorings. It was his eyes. He was more than a monster – she didn't have a word for what he was.

When she realized what was happening, she had gone with it, like an actor going with a raw emotion. It was good to be in shock. Andrew found it perfectly normal and convincing. Then again, he was probably in shock himself. After all, he had seen what was left of Henry.

Breeze was feeling a little better now. They had gone shopping today, just the girls. In and out of two dozen stores, laughing, trying things on, not really buying anything. They had eaten a whale of a meal in the food court. And it all felt so *normal*. It was incredible, actually. She hadn't been to a mall since she was a child. To be with Lydia at the mall – it was like Breeze was nine years old again, before she got her growth spurt and things changed. Before she caught Ralph's eye, and became a woman too soon. They had gone to the movies – a cartoon about a fish that gets lost and has to travel far from home. A fish like Breeze. In the dark, in the movie theatre, she and Lydia had held hands, and there was no way – no way – Nestor could ever find them there. Breeze wished, just for that moment, that they could stay in the movie theatre forever, watching silly movies, eating popcorn with that nasty yellow butter on it and slurping huge cups of syrupy soda.

She sighed, and did not notice herself sighing. It wasn't to be. She was not a child, and hadn't been one for a long time. Events were moving along on their own track, and they couldn't be called back to the beginning. Too much had happened already. She imagined herself covered in steel like a super hero, impervious, with twin red lasers for eyes. It would be nice if she and Lydia could simply run away without the other two. They had the money, and they had the safe-deposit-box keys. They seemed to get along. They could be rich together. And down in Nassau, they would see. If Breeze decided she wanted to keep Lydia around, OK. If she decided she wanted to get rid of her . . . that would be OK, too. She didn't need Lydia. She had Lydia driver's license, she could do the Lydia signature – she could *become* Lydia if need be. In the meantime, Breeze had done the girl-girl thing before. With the right person, it could be fun. And Lydia was a very good-looking girl.

> Breeze and Lydia, sittin' in a tree . . .
> K-I-S-S-I-N-G.

If only there were some way for Dick and Andrew to meet with an accident, or some other unfortunate end. Breeze would have to think on that one.

The rifle's scope put items a hundred yards away into the palm of Nestor's hand.

He had gone insane. He knew that now. If it hadn't been clear before . . . what he had done to the *maricón* had made it clear. That faggot. Dressed as a woman. With breasts like a woman. So convincing that after Nestor had gotten some information – that it was definitely Dot who had been in the bathtub, and the name of a certain motel in Long Island that he quickly confirmed by telephone – Nestor had undressed her. He had planned to fuck her and fuck her and leave her alive for Miller to find. But when he stripped her down and saw what was there, he . . .

. . . he wasn't ready. *Madre de Dios.* It had been a nightmare.

234

As the dark settled in, he crouched on the roof across the parking lot from Miller's apartment. His breath came in plumes, the air so cold that it almost burned his throat. The setting was nearly ideal. His fevered mind knew that much. He was almost invisible up here. In the darkness no one would spot him without searchlights. Miller's huge windows were directly across from and perhaps ten feet below him. Nestor had a black sniper rifle, bolt action, with a Cyclone silencer, and a Hensoldt tactical scope. He had grown fond of such toys while in the military. The rifle would take Miller's head apart from this distance. When Miller came in and turned on the light in that apartment, Nestor would erase him from this world with one shot, a shot that would hardly make a sound.

He had considered waiting for Miller in the apartment, perhaps in the bathroom. When Miller arrived, Nestor could simply walk out of the bathroom and kill him then. It had the added benefit that he would be able to speak to Miller before he died, make him suffer somewhat, and see the look in his eyes. But what if Miller weren't alone? Then Nestor would have to kill two. And what if they were armed? Then Nestor would have to win a shootout, probably a noisy one. These factors had almost decided him, but what really sent him out of the apartment was the fact that he could not stand to wait in the apartment where Dot had died and was chopped up like a cow. Where the faggot was now, waiting for Miller to find him.

So Nestor had come to this place instead. The only problem? It was cold on this roof – very cold. There was no respite from the biting wind. He was dressed in his cashmere coat, but the wind blew through it. He wore heavy gloves. When the time came to kill, he would have to remove both coat and gloves to get a decent shot.

That was OK. That was fine. When the time came, he would do what was necessary. That didn't really worry him. Nestor's biggest concern – and his fondest hope – was that before the kill shot split Miller's head in two, Miller would see the *maricón*.

'That's a cannon right there,' the guy said. 'That's a fucking cannon. You want that? You can take somebody's head off with that thing. You could take an elephant's head off, if you want. A rhinoceros? You could blow its fucking head off.' The guy was small and stout, bald, with a patch of hair on his chin – a beard about the same size and shape as Hitler's mustache.

It had taken all day for Andrew to put this meeting together. Dick Miller had taken the .38 back, and Andrew was going to need something. If Miller wasn't going to help him kill Nestor, Andrew was going to do it himself.

He and the gun salesman were in a small, mostly empty apartment in the East Village. Alphabet City, they used to call the neighborhood, but the real estate people had given it a new name. Alphabet City made people think of junkies dropping dead in the toilet stalls of public bathrooms. The East Village – now, that could be the tony West Village, only on the other side. But this place – this apartment, this indoor weapons bazaar on Avenue C – this was Alphabet City. Andrew hefted the .44 Magnum the guy was talking about – it was huge – and glanced away from the guns arrayed on the stained mattress, through the window and down at the few people milling on the cold nighttime streets three stories below.

'Whaddya say, kid? Is that what you're looking for? The cannon? I can give you that for a very good price.'

'Too big,' Andrew said. 'I gotta carry the thing, you know?'

The salesman raised his eyebrows and smiled. 'Oh, yeah, I know. I'll tell you what I use, OK? You can't go wrong. Twenty-five caliber, small, compact, easy to hide. I carry the thing in the pocket of my coat, that's what I'm saying. It's not a cannon, for sure, but you know what? How much stopping power do you really need? You don't want to go to jail, right? So the trick is *not* to use the gun. And that twenty-five will scare just about anybody. You pull that twenty-five and it don't scare them, then, buddy, you got real trouble.'

Andrew thought of that night months ago. Nestor had asked Andrew to come out for a few drinks. Andrew said sure. Sure, sure. Skinny Nestor was going to take Andrew out for a few drinks, tell Andrew that Dot's offer was more than generous, he better think about taking it. Sure, I'll think about it. Then Andrew would go back to what he was doing. Andrew didn't know Nestor yet.

He was waiting outside his apartment when Nestor came. It was a warm September night, just after dark, lots of people on the street, drunks streaming by. People were still in shorts and T-shirts. Lots of nice girls. Brooklyn Brewery had thrown some kind of concert near their headquarters earlier in the day, and Andrew could hear the music from here.

The car pulled up. It was black, nearly new, some kind of car service. Andrew didn't see a name. Nestor was in the back seat. He powered down the window and waved Andrew over. Two glum Hispanics sat in the front seat.

Nestor smiled, festive, maybe a little drunk already. 'Andrew. *¿Cómo estás?* How are you doing? Come on in. These guys are friends of mine. They're gonna drop us in Manhattan. Take us wherever we wanna go. All right?'

Andrew returned the smile. See? This was going to be a friendly chat about a topic of mutual interest. Maybe Nestor hoped for a piece of the action. Andrew might consider that. 'All right.'

They pulled out and drove south on city streets to the bridge.

'You want a drink?' Nestor said.

'Sure.'

Nestor pulled a bottle from the floor. He had two glasses all ready. The guys up front chattered on to themselves in Spanish. Nestor said something to them. The one in the passenger seat shrugged.

Nestor held up the bottle of clear liquid to Andrew. '*Aguardiente.* It's Colombian. Very good for the health.'

'Hit me,' Andrew said.

Nestor splashed two fingers' worth in each glass. '*Salud,*' he said, and he knocked his drink back.

Andrew did the same. The fire hit his belly immediately. Tears came to his eyes and he coughed the slightest bit. The car made the turn onto the bridge.

'Good?'

'Good.'

He said something again to the men in the front. The one in the passenger seat replied.

'OK,' Nestor said, 'now we talk.'

The man in front of Andrew turned all the way around. He had a gun in one hand. He pointed it at Andrew's head. In the other hand he had a pair of handcuffs.

'What?' Andrew said. 'What? You guys are kidding, right?' His heart thumped in his chest. No one had ever pointed a gun at him before.

'Take the handcuffs,' Nestor said. 'Put one on your right wrist, then attach the other one to the handgrip there above your head.' Andrew glanced at the handgrip. Out the window the bridge rolled by, all that empty space over the East River. Manhattan came closer, millions of lights glowing on towering buildings. The man up front poked Andrew in the forehead with the gun.

'Do it,' Nestor said. 'Before I lose my patience.'

Andrew did it. The metal of the cuff felt cold against his wrist. His right arm hung from the overhead handgrip, almost, but not quite, as if he were simply holding on.

'Give me your left hand.'

Nestor took the hand without waiting for Andrew to comply. He held Andrew's left wrist in a surprisingly strong grip. The man in the front still held the gun. He held it low now, still pointed at Andrew, but below window level. He laughed and said something to Nestor. Nestor said something back and the man in the driver's seat laughed without turning around.

Andrew was in a dream – a dream where he was unable to move or do anything. There was a buzzing sound in his ears.

'Nestor . . .'

'I'm going to tell you this once,' Nestor said calmly. Now he had pulled a pair of garden clippers from somewhere. They looked like they'd be good for clipping a rose bush, maybe something a little bigger than that. Trimming back vines, perhaps. They were like a big pair of scissors, and he caught Andrew's pinkie between the two blades of the open mouth. 'And only once. You are no longer necessary to the plan. You will no longer contact Dot. You will no longer be paid. If there is a problem with the computer, Dot will contact you and you will fix the problem free of charge. You will not call the police. Do you understand?'

'Nestor, I—'

'Do you understand?'

They were coming to the end of the bridge. The streetlight at the bottom was green. Traffic flowed smoothly along. It was Saturday night. Everything seemed to glow. There was excitement in the air.

'Nestor, don't do this.'

Nestor applied pressure to the clippers. 'Do you understand?'

'Yes. I understand.'

'Good.'

Then Nestor cut his finger off. It took less than a second, and for a moment Andrew didn't even realize what had happened. He thought

Nestor had cut his finger, he felt the sharp pain, then he saw the finger on the floor by Nestor's feet. Nestor held a white cloth to the hand and the cloth rapidly turned red. It looked black in the darkness of the car. Andrew stared at it, the blood spreading and spreading. Then he noticed his right hand was free. The guy up front had unlocked the cuff.

'Get out,' Nestor said.

A moment later – it seemed like an instant – Andrew stood in the street, near the sidewalk, holding the thick cloth to his bleeding hand. People walked by, glanced at him, and kept walking. There was a small grocery store, a bodega, there on the corner of the crowded street. There was an electronics store. A clothing store. Dozens of people were around and he was bleeding. Nobody even noticed. He wanted to say something, scream something. The car was still there and the window powered down. Nestor's face loomed in the window.

'Remember what I said.'

Something flew out, hit Andrew on the chest, and fell to the street. It rolled under a parked car, but Andrew caught a glimpse of it before it went. It was his pinkie.

The black car pulled away, the window gliding up as it went.

Now, months later, in the winter cold of an apartment that was unpainted, unheated, nearly unfurnished, and lit by one naked bulb, Andrew looked at the gun salesman.

'The twenty-five is no good,' he said. 'Too small. I need something bigger. And I need two of them.'

'What the fuck was the kid doing in Maryland, Sal?'

Block hunched in the dark office of his headquarters, the nerve center of his growing kingdom. In one hand, he squeezed a rubber stress ball, over and over again. It wasn't working. The more he squeezed, the more stressed he became. He stared across at Sal, his number two, who was standing in the doorway. Sal was getting beefy. He should start going light on the lasagna. And the wine. And the cheesecake.

Sal's voice, always calm, always soothing: 'Block, he went down there, he had a line on a Lamborghini. And so he got busted.'

'I know. You said that already. But we don't steal Lamborghinis, Sal. We steal Honda Accords and Toyota Camrys. You know why? Because that's what people drive. That's what people need parts for.'

Sal shrugged, said nothing.

'You're a rich man, Sal. You drive a Lamborghini? You ever been in a fucking Lamborghini?'

Sal's head gave a gentle shake. 'No, me? No.'

'You know anybody who drives a Lamborghini?'

'Not personally.'

'You know why? I'll tell you why. Because *nobody* drives a Lamborghini. One guy in Maryland drives a fucking Lamborghini, Sal. One guy in California. One guy in Long Island. One guy in Miami Beach. See what I mean? What was this kid planning to do with the fucking thing? Besides get busted, I mean?'

Sal the den mother raised his eyebrows and tilted his head to the side. He didn't speak. Sal tended not to answer rhetorical questions. He let a full minute pass.

'So whaddya wanna do, Block? About the kid?'

Block sighed. His shoulders slumped. 'How long has he been in?'

'Forty-eight hours.'

Block shook his head. 'Get him out. Whatever it costs. Send somebody down to pick him up and bring him back here. But I want to see him, Sal. I want him to come straight here, to this office, and I want to talk to him. I mean, before he takes a shower, before he takes a nap, before he eats a fucking Big Mac. OK?'

'Sure, Block. I'll take care of it.'

'I know you will.'

Sal shut the door, leaving Block alone. Going on ten years, Block had owned this office, and the working garage that sat below it. It was a small office, he barely fit inside of it, and he had never remodeled the place in any way. He had some vague notion that the cops would bust in here one day, and he wanted the place to look like he was a simple businessman, scraping out an honest living. Of course, no cop was going to believe that – he had ten cops on the payroll.

Block ran a hand through his thinning hair. All kinds of business-related bullshit had come across his desk today. Slow pays, a building in Jersey to think about buying, and this Puerto Rican car thief in jail down in Maryland. Desiree. And now more problems on the home front: Trish had called today from her Florida vacation. She wanted to take the kids out of the school they were in, and put them in another school. Trish always wanted to take the kids out of whatever school they were in, especially when she felt Block wasn't paying enough attention to the family. Halfway through their conversation, the real question came up. Why was he in New York while they were down in Florida? *Business, babe. That's what I do. I'm in New York so you can be down in Florida. So you can send the kids to any school you want. That's what I'm doing here – I'm providing.*

He was still providing right up until she slammed down the phone. He pictured the phone in the Florida condo they always rented. A real phone, the kind you could slam down. He pictured her fuming in the living room there, maybe knocking the phone off the table, with that deep blue ocean waiting right outside the glass doors.

Shit. What a waste.

He took the keys to the Lincoln out of his desk drawer and shrugged into his coat. He walked down the narrow paneled hall, waving through a doorway to Sal, who was at his own desk, murmuring into the phone, putting things in motion. Block walked down the steps to the street, the sight of Sal at work making him feel a little better. This was a good operation. Things could be a lot worse. And he was heading back out to Brooklyn. He was going to help Dick resolve this thing, whatever that took, and in doing so, he was going to put years of history to rest. He owed Dick that much, and he hated to have debts hanging over him. Within minutes, he was on the highway.

Fifteen years before, Dick had laid the foundation for Block's success. It was Dick, and Dick had never enjoyed the fruits of it. Instead he had run from it, and had left it all to Block.

'It's just one little job,' Block had said to Dick. 'One little job and I'm in. And if I'm in, that means you're in.' He gave Dick a wallop on the shoulder. He pictured Dick at that time, twenty years old, pumped body, slicked-back hair, a lady's man. A movie star.

'So what's the job?' Dick said.

'We need to get rid of a guy.'

'Get rid of? What's that supposed to mean?'

'What does it sound like?'

Block's cousin Macky had pull. Macky could get Block his own list. Loans, unpaid bets – people who owed. It was a list full of misses, deadbeats. Block could have the list – all he had to do was work it hard and kick a percentage of what he pulled in back upstairs. His very own list. This was a start. It could, and would, lead to bigger things. But he had to get in the door first, and there was a fee to enter. Macky needed somebody to disappear. Forever.

'Why don't we just bust the guy up a little?' Dick said. 'Tell him he should beat it to South America or Africa or some fucking place?'

They were sitting around Block's studio apartment in Astoria, drinking beer and taking shots of whiskey. The place was threadbare. The couch had been left behind by the previous tenant. The stuffing was coming out and it was all over the floor. The coffee table was a packing crate. That's what they did to you – they starved you for work and money. You want real money? Then do *this* for me. *This* was always something hard. *This* was always something you didn't want to do. Block didn't think the booze was going to cut the mustard, so he had bought some Dexies as a backup. Speed. It worked for the guys in the military – it would work for him and Dick.

Block shook his head. 'You know it doesn't work like that. This guy is a stone killer. You're not going to scare a guy like this. We hurt him, send him away, then next year he comes back and kills us both. Or Macky finds out we lied. Then . . .'

'Shit, Block. Is this what you really want?'

'Dick, this is what I really want.'

'All right, I'll help you get him there, but you're going to pull the trigger.'

Block handed Dick another shot of whiskey. 'Agreed,' he said, and they both knocked back their shots.

Only problem? When the time came, Block couldn't do it. He remembered how it was, in that warehouse, not two miles from where Dick lived now. Macky had given Block the keys to the warehouse. He had given Block a gun and a silencer. He had given Block the green light to dust the guy. 'Do this fucking guy and get rid of him,' Macky had said.

But nothing came as advertised. First the silencer didn't fit the gun. Then the guy – this hardened pro – turned out to be a wimp. He was probably forty-five, bald and thin. His clothes fit all wrong. He hadn't given Block and Dick any resistance at all – they had snatched him right off the street. They had him tied to a chair in the middle of this big empty warehouse, and the guy was crying, and if Block pulled the trigger in that echo chamber, it was going to make a noise louder than the fucking atomic bomb. People lived in this neighborhood.

So Block and Dick had dropped the Dexies. Now they were speeding along, drunk, wired, totally fucked up. Block started banging the gun over the guy's head. The guy was weeping now, fucking weeping. Blood streamed down his face.

'Look, man. I have a family, OK? I got two kids, an ex-wife. I pay child support. All right? I got people who need me.'

'Shut the fuck up! All right? Just shut the fuck up!'

Dick was off in the corner of this huge empty space, pacing back and forth. Block pointed the gun at the guy's head again. Just a little pressure, a twitch, and the guy was gone. They could get the fuck out of here, worry about the noise later.

'Don't do it, man,' the guy said. 'Don't fucking do this.' There was pleading in the guy's eyes. He looked like a fucking baby seal.

'Shit.'

Block stepped away. They had been here an hour with this guy. He couldn't do it. He couldn't fucking do it. He crouched down into a squat. He hugged himself. Then he started to cry. Twenty years old and crying. He was supposed to be a killer – that's what he was doing here, and he couldn't do it. He couldn't kill this man. Now he was crying. He was a baby, a fucking baby. His pulse thundered in his chest, racing now, racing. It felt like he was going to have a heart attack.

'Block, what the fuck are you doing?' Dick said. His eyes were wild, zooming.

'I don't know, man. I don't know.' He could hardly get the words out.

'Give me the gun.'

'No, I'm gonna do it.'

Dick put his hand out. 'Give me that fucking gun.' Block's hand seemed to move in slow motion as he passed the gun to Dick. He saw the anger in Dick's eyes. Dick hadn't wanted to be here. Now Dick was wired on speed and Dick was gonna do it, he was gonna do the thing Block couldn't do.

More slow mo . . .

Dick stepped to the guy and put the gun to his head.

'Don't do it,' the guy said. 'Don't fucking . . .'

Dick squeezed the trigger, once.

Nothing happened. He looked down at the gun, then back at Block.

'The safety's on.' He tinkered with the gun, slid the safety off. Then Dick stared at the gun for a full minute. He looked up at Block again. Block saw Dick's eyes go wide, and something dawned there. It seemed to happen slowly – just like a sunrise. Dick looked down at the guy. An exhalation came out of Dick's mouth, something between a grunt and a sigh. The guy was a bloody mess, he was crying, there was snot coming out of his nose. A stain was spreading on his pants. The guy had pissed himself. 'You know what?' Dick said, very quietly. 'We have to let this guy go.'

'Dick, the safety was on. That's all. Don't go cosmic on me here.'

'Block—'

'We can't let him go, Dick.'

But Dick was already squatting next to the guy. He lifted the guy's chin with the gun. 'Hey, man. Look at me.'

'Dick, we can't let him go. My cousin—'

'Don't worry about that. We can take care of that.'

'Dick—'

'Block, shut the fuck up, OK? I have a gun in my hand, and if I'm gonna use it on anybody, it'll be you.' Dick started to untie the guy's hands. He spoke to the guy. 'You understand what's happening here, right? We're gonna tell them we killed you. We're going to let you live, but you need to go away. Far away. You need to drop out of sight and never come back. They have to think you're dead. For your sake, and for our sakes. Because if they find you, they're going to kill you. And if I see you again, I'm going to kill you. Make no mistake about that.'

Block watched as Dick helped the guy out of the chair and over to the door. 'Run,' he said as the guy walked out of the warehouse. Block made no move to stop him. 'And don't stop running.'

'Great,' Block said, and it sounded like his voice came to him from the bottom of a well. 'What do we do now?'

'I have a plan,' Dick said.

Block laughed despite himself when he heard the plan. They went out cruising the late night streets. They found a stray dog – it was mangy, skinny, barely alive. They brought it back to the warehouse and killed it with a buck knife. 'Sorry, dog,' Dick said, just before Block plunged the knife in. Block couldn't kill the guy, but he could kill the dog. They got its blood all over the floor. Then they put its carcass in the trunk of the car, came back into the warehouse, and fired off two rounds in the empty space. They peeled rubber out of there and dumped the dog in a vacant lot in Queens.

That night, Block met his cousin for coffee at a diner. 'You made a mess in my warehouse,' Macky said. 'What's the matter with you?'

'Don't blame me. Your fucking silencer didn't fit. We made so much noise, I had to get lost in a hurry.'

Macky raised his hand, motioning Block to keep his voice down. He took a moment to think about that. 'OK, my fault. What'd you do with the package?'

'Put it in the river.'

'Good man. Let's talk about your list.'

Of course, Block had changed a lot since those days. If it happened now, it wouldn't go the same way. He was tougher now. But that didn't erase history. That didn't change the truth of his beginnings.

Now, in the car, Block glanced at the bright green highway sign that loomed ahead. 'Metropolitan Avenue,' it read. 'Next Exit.'

* * *

It was a rush job.

The day before, Dick had taken his time, scoped out hiding places, dark corners where he thought the body parts would sit undisturbed for weeks. Now he just zipped along, pulling the Lexus up to dumpsters on street corners, at construction sites, tossing limbs away like old newspapers. He had spent the afternoon lugging pieces of a dead woman – his woman – lugging her around the furthest reaches of Brooklyn and Queens, throwing a piece in an abandoned lot here, stashing a piece near a barbed-wire fence surrounding the airport there, burying some on the beach, in the shadow of the dismal housing projects of Coney Island.

It was a mess.

When he got back to the apartment, all he could do was stumble across the room and slump into his chair. He sat there for several minutes in the dark, not thinking about anything. Not a single thought crossed his mind. But gradually, he sensed that something was different. He sensed a presence in the big open space.

'Block?'

There was no reply. His eyes had adjusted to the dark, and he scanned the apartment. No. No one there. But there was a smell, thick in the air like sludge. He hadn't noticed it at first, but now he did, and he tasted copper pennies in his mouth. It led him to the bathroom doorway, and the smell was strongest there. He turned on the light.

There was a body in the tub.

At first, he couldn't make out who it was. Someone had run the water, and the water was dark red from all the blood. It was so dark it was almost black. He stared at it, getting closer and closer to the tub, moving on legs that didn't seem to belong to him. He wanted to run screaming from this place. But he had to see. He had to know. The handsaw Block had used to cut up Dot rested on the sink, and the floor was tacky with blood. That vague body, partially submerged, resolved into someone. He saw dark skin, and then he knew. Desiree, but somehow not Desiree.

God, he had mutilated her.

Dick stumbled backwards, his hand slapping the light switch, bringing on the blessed dark. But it was too late. He had seen her and the image stayed in his mind – a body in about a foot of water. He fled the bathroom, seeing nothing but that body. He found himself at the window, his forehead pressed against it, the glass cold where it touched his skin. Behind him, the heat was coming up from the radiator, the ancient pipes knocking.

It was a bright night, clear and cold. Lights twinkled in the distance.

The knocking of the pipes was loud, loud enough to mask any other sound. He turned and peered into the apartment. He couldn't bear the dark. Nestor – or something worse – could be hiding anywhere.

He reached for the halogen floor lamp that stood near the window. The lamp was strong enough that it usually brightened the whole place.

He turned the knob, going for bright, brighter, brightest.

Nestor watched the bathroom light go on in Miller's place. Good. Miller would see the gift Nestor left for him. But the bathroom was too far away from the window to make any kind of shot. Then the light went off again.

Miller's apartment was nothing but shadows now, and Miller a shadow among them. Nestor tore his gloves off and shrugged out of his long wool coat. The icy wind bit into him, even worse than before. He wore only a pair of slacks with a turtleneck sweater pulled over a T-shirt. He picked up the rifle, rested it against the three-foot-high wall that lined the perimeter of the roof, and waited. He could not be sure where Miller would appear. There were twelve panes of glass, two high and six wide. Each pane was eight feet tall and five feet wide, side to side, all the way across – sixteen feet high and thirty feet across in total. Of course, Miller would turn up somewhere near the bottom, but where along the bottom?

Nestor put the scope to his eye and moved the gun back and forth, looking for any sign of movement. He would get only one shot. He waited, but there was nothing. He raised his head away from the scope. Had Miller come in, seen the body, and then left again? Was it even Miller?

A light came on, right next to the windows. Miller was there, and the light became bright, almost as bright as daylight, as Nestor watched.

Nestor dropped his head and squinted into the scope.

Behind the grime of the window, Miller filled the crosshairs. The big man stood tall, unguarded, his hands pressed against the window. He was *right there*, as if Nestor could reach out and touch him. His chest was wide open. Nestor could blow a hole right through him, a sudden punch that would knock Miller off his feet and across the room, dead before he hit the ground, a wide-eyed look of surprise on his face that Nestor would pay money to see.

Nestor's finger caressed the trigger.

The wind bit deep, forcing him to steady the gun. Nestor's cheeks were numb. His hands were blocks of ice.

Miller in the circle.

Miller a dead man.

Nestor pulled the trigger.

The window shattered, exploding inward, spraying glass all over him.

The halogen lamp sizzled and burst into pieces, knocking out the light. Dick dropped to the floor. He lived through several long seconds of confusion. How had the window blown in? Was it the wind?

No, these were thick industrial windows. It was a gunshot. Someone had taken a shot at him through the window. He hadn't heard it, but he was sure it was a gunshot. Silenced? Yeah, probably silenced. He sprawled on the floor like a dead man. Seconds passed and he didn't move. Then a thought came – the shooter could be moving up on him right now, getting in position to take another crack.

Dick crawled along the floor, squirming through broken glass like a snake. He was in total darkness now, except for the light from the streetlamps outside. Cold air blew in through the ruined window, along with some whirling snow borne on the wind. All he could see were shadows in the apartment, and lights on in the building across the way. Was something moving on the roof there?

He crawled behind the easy chair, staying belly to the ground until he was safely away from the windows. He crouched in the gloom, staring alternately at the door and at the window. No movement. No noise but the wind. He crept deep into the apartment and waited. If Nestor came through the window, Dick would jump him in the dark. A slim chance, but all he had.

A loud banging came at the door.

'Dick? Dick, this is Block. Are you in there?'

Missed.

How had he missed? Fucking gun. It had been more than a year since he had fired it. OK, he should have fired some practice rounds, but he hadn't had time. When would he have had the time?

He broke the gun down with shaking hands, and placed it into its carry case. He left the roof, moving fast, staying calm. Miller wouldn't call the police – not with that ring of blood around his bathtub – but someone else might. Nestor descended through the stairwell of the building. He passed one person, a young woman, brown hair under a green wool hat, heavy winter coat, leather boots, carrying groceries up to her apartment. She barely glanced at him. No threat – no police, no CIA, no FBI, nothing. A normal person and a normal activity.

He hit the street and moved for the car. The car was parked on a side street within sight of the door to Miller's building. Nestor stashed the gun case in the trunk, then sat in the driver's seat, watching the building. He was in darkness here, away from the streetlights. He settled in to see what would develop.

Dick pushed Block back from the door.

'I need to talk to you right now,' he said. 'But we can't do it here.'

'Dick, what's wrong? What are you doing? Did Desiree show up? Did she clean the place?'

'No.'

'No?'

'Block, just trust me. Trust me just this once. We have to get out of here.'

They went outside into the cold night, and Dick walked fast, keeping Block moving away from the building. Dick wouldn't speak, not yet. He was drawn as if by a magnet to the Williamsburg Bridge. Block followed him. They climbed the piss-soaked steps, and walked out on the pedestrian ramp that led to a panoramic view of the city. The walkway was abandoned tonight. It was too cold. Dick gazed out at the lights, twinkling in the distance all the way up the East River. The Manhattan side looked festive, decked out in the holiday spirit. The Empire State Building was lit up green and red. In contrast, Brooklyn and Queens were dark and low slung, with a few lights blinking here and there in the wasteland. Far upriver, a helicopter moved from left to right across his field of vision. He followed its blinking lights until it was far out over Queens somewhere.

Block was talking. 'So you let the guy go?'

'I let him go.'

'And he's not going to call the cops?'

'I don't know what he's going to do.'

'You don't know?' Block grabbed Dick's arm. 'What do you mean, you don't know? If the cops come—'

'We got bigger problems than that.'

'Like?'

Dick didn't know how to say it, so he just said it. 'Block, Desiree is dead. I came home a little while ago and found her. She's in the bathtub. Somebody killed her. Nestor. Nestor must have killed her.'

Block turned and stared out at the lights far away. He didn't speak for a long time. Dick watched him to see what would happen. He half expected Block's granite façade to crumble, leaving nothing there on the walkway but a large pile of dust blowing away on the breeze. But nothing happened. Block just stood and stared. Time passed.

Finally, Block took a deep breath. When he turned back to Dick, his face had hardened. His eyes flashed anger as deep and black as a coal mine. 'OK,' he said. 'Killed her how?'

'I don't know. There's a lot of blood.'

Something to his right caught Dick's attention. He looked back down the walkway toward the Brooklyn side. A man walked slowly toward them. He was thin and wore a long winter coat. There was something about the way he walked. He was partially hidden by the shadows, but Dick could swear . . . Paranoid – the events of the past hour were playing tricks on his mind. Five thousand people a day walked across this bridge. Nestor would never dare an open confrontation with the two of them. He was the type who lurked in the shadows, took sudden potshots through windows.

The man was only about twenty yards away now, still in darkness.

253

He had his head down, obscured by the gloom. Block followed Dick's gaze.

The man looked up. His face was caught in the overhead lights. Their eyes locked. It was Nestor. He reached under his coat and came out with a large handgun. He took two steps forward, pointing the gun right at them.

There was nowhere to run. Block jumped in front. He reached into his own coat as he did so.

'Look out, Dick.'

White flame licked the end of Nestor's barrel.

Dick didn't hear the blast, but on the other side of Block's huge body, he could hear the instant of impact. It sounded like giant raindrops hitting the street. Block staggered backwards into Dick. They tumbled together onto the snow and ice. Block's head smashed into Dick's face.

They landed, Block on top, his weight driving the wind out of Dick. Dick didn't know if Block was shot. He didn't know anything. He blinked like crazy, the flashes of light from Nestor's gun imprinted on his eyes.

Block's bulk pinned Dick to the ground.

Then Block had his gun out. He fired and fired, the shots loud and echoing on the bridge and across the sky. Dick saw Nestor drop, falling backwards across the ice. Block kept firing, bullets flying everywhere. Nestor struggled to his feet and turned tail. He ran twenty yards, slipped on the ice and fell again. He got up and ran on. Block kept pulling the trigger long after his bullets were spent.

Dick squeezed out from under him and kneeled by his side. Block groaned in pain. His body writhed. His back arched.

'The fucker got me,' he rasped. His breath came in shrieks. 'What do you know about that?'

'Block, where does it hurt?'

Block grimaced, an attempt at a smile. 'Come on. Don't even bother.'

The bullets had hit him in the chest. There were ragged holes torn from the shirt he wore under his coat. Blood began to soak the outside of his coat.

'You're gonna be all right,' Dick said. He was lying. Block wasn't going to be all right at all. If that's what his coat was like, Dick couldn't imagine what was under his shirt. Dick peeled open the shirt and touched his chest.

Blood flowed out of Block's body. The shirt was saturated with it. 'Oh, fuck.'

Dick looked around. Nestor was long gone now. There was a streak of blood where he had fallen on the ice. No one was coming in either direction. The walkway was long and empty. They were alone. Cars flowed by beneath them.

In a dream, Dick reached into Block's coat and pulled out his cellphone. He dialed 911 and pressed SEND. A voice came on. Dick shouted into the telephone.

Man shot. Williamsburg Bridge pedestrian walkway.

Block blinked slowly. His lids seemed heavy and his eyes closed. 'Block! Block, don't go to sleep.'

Block's eyes rolled crazily. They settled on Dick.

'That was Nestor?'

'Yeah, Block. Nestor.' Dick was kneeling, cradling his head.

'Do me a favor.' Every word was a struggle for him. 'You get that guy. Put him in the ground.'

Dick looked up at the cold stars and the wisps of cloud blowing across the face of the moon. The wind was whipping. He gazed down and watched his friend struggle for breath. Darkness gathered all around Dick now and for a moment he thought it was a shadow from the other side, come to take him with Block. When he looked up, there was nothing except the howling wind, and white steam blowing from a large standpipe.

In the distance, the sirens started to close in.

The neon lights of the Ocean Breeze Motel flickered and hummed.

'Open Year Round!'

Hours had passed. Nestor sat slumped behind the wheel of his car, staring at the motel not fifty yards away. The office was closed. There were two cars in the parking lot. Nestor had looked at the cars closely when he cruised past. One, a Ford, had New Jersey license plates. The other, a Honda, was the one he was looking for. It was parked below a room on the second floor with its lights on behind drawn shades. Lydia was in that room – of that he had no doubt.

Nestor was in a lot of pain. He had taken two bullets. The first had hit his right shoulder, tearing apart the flesh there. He thought he was missing a chunk of bone as well. The second shot had ripped through the meat of his right forearm. His right arm, typically his gun arm, was useless. It hung limply at his side.

He had dressed the wounds as well as he could, wrapping the shoulder in bandages he had purchased at a convenience store, and tying off the arm below the elbow. He could no longer feel his right hand at all. He laughed when he thought of the teenage clerk who sold him the bandages and two bottles of Tylenol Extra Strength. The boy practically turned white at the sight of him.

'You want me to call somebody, sir?' the boy said.

Nestor shook his head. 'What you can do, if you'll be so kind,' he answered through clenched teeth, 'is open that bottle of Tylenol for me.'

Nestor swallowed twelve of the pills, one right after the other.

Now he felt a little better. There had been a period on the way out here when he had to pull the car over. He parked it on a quiet residential street. He felt a fever coming on, and he was no longer able to stay awake. It alarmed him a little, this sudden grogginess. But it was too powerful, and soon he slept. There were no dreams, and after some time, he awoke, still in the car, still parked in front of sleeping suburban homes, the engine still running, the heat pumping.

Now he was here. He was going to see Lydia. He was going to get her keys and her money. He was not going to play any games with her. If she resisted at all, he would shoot her at point-blank range, with his left hand.

Lydia was almost asleep.

The TV was on, and the two of them lay in separate beds, watching an old James Bond film, one with a young-looking Sean Connery in the lead role. For the first half hour, they had oohed and aahed over Sean in his tuxedo, Sean in his bathing suit, Sean in a striped sailor shirt and tight shorts. Over time, however, the fun faded and they lapsed into silence.

'Breeze,' Lydia had said, 'are you all right? Do you want to talk?'

'About what?'

'Well, your ex-boyfriend died yesterday. I thought that might be upsetting you.'

Breeze looked Lydia in the eye. 'Lydia, I'm sorry that Henry's dead. I tried to stop it from happening. But you should know that Henry was never very nice to me. He used to hurt me. And I don't think I was the only one. I think Henry hurt a lot of people. So in some way, I wonder if . . .'

'He got what was coming to him?' Lydia said.

'I wouldn't put it that way, but yeah.'

Now Breeze seemed to be asleep. She was wrapped in a blanket, but still dressed in jeans, T-shirt and sneakers. The movie was still on, but Lydia had long since lost track of the plot. A car chase, followed by explosions, followed by a poker game in a casino, followed by a clever female assassin trying to kill James Bond and winding up dead herself. Now there was a shootout between two large groups of people in some kind of subterranean chamber. Lydia wondered if this was even still the same movie – or if one James Bond flick had ended and another one had begun.

Lydia liked Breeze. That's what it came down to. Here was a girl who had been through a lot, was a runaway, had lived on the streets, and all these years later was still going strong, sometimes with a smile on her face. Breeze was cool. She had style. Lydia thought of that cigarette lighter Breeze carried around – the one that looked just like a gun. Every now and then she would fish this gun out from the pocket of her tight jeans, and light up. Sure, like a movie star.

Lydia put her hands behind her pillow, arched her back, and tried to focus on what sexy Sean was doing on the screen there.

Then the big front window came crashing in. It exploded, shattering into thousands of tiny pellets, most of which were blocked by the heavy curtain that hung down. But hundreds of the sharp pieces sprayed all over the floor. A torrent of cold air rushed into the room.

Lydia leaped from the bed. From the corner of her eye, she saw Breeze fly through the air like a startled cat. Breeze passed her and cowered by the table and chairs in the corner. The curtain ruffled and Nestor stepped through.

Lydia gasped at the sight of him. The color had drained from his face. His right arm hung slack at his side, tied with bandages. His right sleeve was empty – the coat merely hung over his right shoulder. His left arm was still working, though, and in his left hand he held a gun. His eyes were bright and aware, but she could see the pain in them. His face was lined with the pain.

He looked at Breeze. He spoke through clenched teeth. 'My, my, look who's here. The other young lovely.'

He raised the gun and pointed it at Breeze.

'You know?' he said. 'I don't think I need you for anything.'

Breeze moved with sudden speed. She dodged left and ducked just as Nestor fired. A crater erupted in the sheetrock wall behind her. She came up, hefting one of the dining chairs. She hurled it across the ten feet of space at him. It flew over the two beds and hit him in his gun arm, driving him backwards. He stumble stepped into the curtain and fell down.

That was Lydia's cue to leave.

Moving fast, she followed Breeze into the bathroom. Just before she did, she snatched the keys to the safe-deposit boxes off the table.

Smart girl, Lydia. Good girl. She was getting good at this game.

Breeze, screaming, a torrent of unintelligible syllables tumbling from her mouth, yanked open the bathroom window. She stepped onto the toilet seat and propelled herself headfirst out the window, catching for a second at the waist, then squirming free and diving to whatever fate lay below.

Lydia glanced out after her. There was some kind of sloping roof three feet below the window. It was covered in snow. Breeze had landed on the snow, turned around and was about to slide to the edge on her butt.

'Breeze!' Lydia screamed. 'Catch the keys!' She threw them out the window and in almost the same motion, put her foot on the toilet seat like she had seen Breeze do. She heard a click behind her. She turned her head and the gun was there. Its muzzle was a black hole not more than an inch from her face.

Nestor's tortured face hovered above the gun. 'If you say one word, if you even twitch, I promise I will kill you immediately.'

8
THE FALLING MAN

'That must have been Miller again,' Andrew said, looking at the call history on his phone. 'It's a blocked number, but so was the last one. That has to be him, calling from a payphone. I can't ignore him forever.'

Breeze shrugged. 'A million dollars says you can. A million dollars says you never have to speak to him again.' They were in a motel all the way out in Long Island now – Riverhead, the end of the highway. The room was small and threadbare. It was cold in there, and Breeze huddled under the blankets.

When she escaped from Nestor, she had run. She had run like never before, turning left, turning right, losing herself in a frozen suburban wasteland. She had crouched behind some bushes, shivering from the cold. Jeans, T-shirt and sneakers – in the first fifteen minutes, she thought she would die. But when she didn't die, when she was just cold and shivering, her skin purple, her teeth chattering, then she knew she would live. Eventually, after she thought an hour had passed, she crept out and walked. She found a coffee shop open, and a man there had lent her his cellphone.

Andrew picked her up and they drove here – so far away that Nestor couldn't possibly follow. That's what Andrew said, but Breeze wouldn't bet on it. Nestor could follow them anywhere. Now Breeze was trying to convince Andrew, gently, without pushing too hard, that the best plan was to leave. All right, so the whole Lydia thing hadn't worked out, and now she was back with Andrew. Times like these called for flexibility. Andrew was OK. She could do the Caribbean scene with Andrew.

'Listen, I like Lydia,' she said. 'She's like, I don't know, like a sister to me. But the plan, all along, was to get these keys.' She jingled the key ring. 'Now we have them. We win. It cost us a lot. It cost us Henry. It cost us Lydia. But we win.'

'No. We don't win. Not like that. I can't leave Lydia to be killed.'

'Andrew, Lydia is dead.'

'I don't know that. If I can save her, I will. But it doesn't matter if she's already dead. Nestor is going to pay. I can't let him get away with murder again. I can't have that on my conscience. And I can't live the rest of my life looking over my shoulder. I'm going to finish this now. I'm going to kill him.'

Was Andrew suicidal? He was crazy if he thought he was going to kill Nestor. Then again, Nestor was injured and obviously in pain. He was weakened – no longer all-powerful.

She stared at Andrew's anguished face, and yet another new plan started to form. She could feel her mind expand as the cells grew in her brain – it made her scalp itch. She saw how all of them – all the men – could go down at the same time. If she nudged things in the right direction, it just might happen.

'I don't want to lose you,' she said.

He wrapped his arms around her. 'You won't lose me.'

'OK,' she said. 'Do what you need to do. But don't expect me to go up there to the room with you. I can't face him. I just can't.'

He smiled and the smile looked like death itself. 'Don't worry. You'll never see Nestor or speak to him again. I promise you that.'

'Miller, we got your record,' the cop said.

He was a short cop, plainclothes, wearing a suit under a long wool coat. He had a bushy black mustache and he held a clipboard in his thick, stubby fingers. Somehow, he reminded Dick of a high-school gym teacher. They were standing in a hallway outside the antiseptic waiting room to the intensive care unit. Workers whisked by them, and the loved ones of various dying people milled around, both in the waiting room and the hallway. Some seemed tired, wiped out. Others seemed bored. It was eleven in the morning, and the place was alive with activity.

'Felony conviction for possession in California,' the cop went on. He raised an eyebrow at Dick. 'Intent to distribute. Two and a half years in, plus time off for good behavior. Now you're home, and your buddy – Kevin Blockovich, suspect in multiple felonies going back fifteen years, not a single arrest – gets shot on the Williamsburg Bridge in the middle of the night with you standing right there. And you expect me to believe you don't know who shot him?'

'I think you should believe whatever you want. You're going to do that anyway.'

The cop raised an index finger. He smiled beneath the mustache. 'OK, just answer one question. Why would somebody want to shoot him?'

'I don't know why. Why don't you ask him that?'

'I would, but he's in surgery having shrapnel removed from his chest.'

'Let me ask you a question,' Dick said.

'Shoot.'

'Am I under arrest?'

263

The cop scowled. 'Would you like to be? Because I'll tell you, Miller, I can arrange that.' But the question was enough to send the cop away.

Dick sat down in an empty plastic chair. An hour passed, then another. Then another. Dick was on his fifth cup of watery, tasteless coffee, and he was starting to get worried. He had slept three or four hours last night, slumped here in this shitty waiting room. He couldn't go back to the apartment – he couldn't face Desiree. Since then, he had tried to call the motel room three times, but couldn't get through. He had tried to call Andrew twice. No answer.

And Block was still in surgery. What the fuck was taking so long?

As he sat, he began to realize how tired he still was. His head began to bob, and while he knew it was bobbing, he was powerless to stop it. One moment he was thinking about how he should get himself another cup of coffee, and the next moment he was standing at the top of the walkway on the Williamsburg Bridge again. It was a cold, cold night and he was in the exact spot where Block had been shot, standing alone in only a T-shirt and shorts. But he wasn't alone. Dot was there, standing a little bit away, silent, watching him. He turned and faced her. She wore a red evening gown, diamonds around her neck. She smiled, that devil-may-care smile he remembered from the good times.

'Mr Miller?'

He looked up, the lights of the waiting room too harsh. A woman was there, dressed in white. Maybe she was an aide or a nurse or a doctor. Who could tell with these people?

'Yeah?'

'Mr Blockovich is awake and he wants to talk with you.'

'OK.'

Dick followed the woman through a double set of doors into the intensive care unit. Dick had never been in one before. It was a large open area with more than twenty beds. There was nowhere to sit down. Some of the beds were empty, but most were filled and surrounded by machinery. A few had curtains pulled around them. Dick glanced at the patients he could see – they already looked like corpses.

They came to Block's bed. The big man lay there, eyes open, his throat bandaged, his chest bandaged, a clear plastic tube running from under his armpit to a machine on his right side. The thing was creating some kind of suction that appeared to be sending air into Block's body through the tube. Block also had two separate IVs, one attached to each arm. Another tube ran out of his nose to an oxygen tank behind the bed. In back of all this, an EKG monitored his heartbeat.

An aide bustled about. 'He shouldn't try to speak,' she said. 'I told him that already.' Block made a face, a grimace at her, and gestured with his head toward the door, the rest of the unit, anywhere but here. She left.

Dick soaked in all the machinery. 'Jesus, Block.'

Block raised a hand. His throat worked. 'Save it. They tell me I'm gonna live.' He gestured at the machine and the tube that went under his arm. 'Took a bullet in the lung. They're blowing it back up.' His voice was little more than a deep croak, a frog in the marshes at night.

'Guy named Sal. At the garage. Call him. Tell him where I am.'

'OK.'

'That other thing we talked about. On the bridge. Remember?' He tried to say something else, but his voice was a rasp now, a coarse file being dragged across wood. He stopped, took a breath. 'In the ground.'

'I will. I promise.'

Block nodded.

A nurse was there. 'Mr Blockovich needs to sleep now.'

Dick went back to the waiting room and called Block's garage. He got the man Sal on the phone and told him what had happened. Sal spoke softly to him, expressing regret, telling Dick that he, Sal, would take care of everything. Dick hung up and tried Andrew again. The phone rang. Once. Twice.

'Hello?'

'Andrew.'

'Dick? Jesus fucking Christ, Dick. Where have you been?'

'What's the matter?'

'We have trouble. Big trouble.'

Nestor woke, in pain again.

The painkillers had worn off. It was dark, nearly black, in the room. He had drawn the curtains tightly. The door to the rest of the suite was closed and locked. The only light came from the crack under the door, and this was a weak light. The lights were out in the entire suite.

He had slept a long time. The clock on the bedside table said 4.15. It took him a moment to realize that meant the afternoon. All the same, despite the renewed pain, the sleep had done him good. He felt a bit refreshed, less groggy than before, and the answer to his problem had come to him in his sleep. He saw how it was the right answer, the one that came with the most pay-off for the least risk. Answers were like that – they often came in his sleep.

They were locked in here together, he and Lydia. When he threatened to shoot her at the motel, she had told him where the money was – in the trunk of her car. And it really was there, more than ninety-eight thousand dollars. She had thrown the deposit-box keys away to the girl, the girl he had just caught a glimpse of through the window, running across yards and alleys, moving fast, like a shadow. That was OK. The answer had come and he no longer needed the keys.

266

They had driven back here in the night, Lydia at the wheel of his car, he with the gun on her out of sight below the dashboard. Somehow, he had stayed alert during the drive. They had parked in the subterranean lot and rode the elevator to his suite, his gun in her back the whole time. He had tied her to a chair here in the bedroom, and then put the 'Do Not Disturb' sign on the front door. He had double-locked that door, then locked the door to the small veranda – in case they came rappelling like commandos down the side of the building. Then he locked himself and Lydia inside the bedroom. He placed two fully loaded guns here on the bed with him. All the weapons were in easy reach. If they broke in, if they came for him, he had to hope he would wake up in time, and with guns blasting.

But they hadn't come. Now, in the dark, the shape in the corner resolved itself into Lydia, still tied to the chair. Good. He took a moment to listen out beyond the door, through the rest of the suite. There was no sound. Very good.

They knew where he lived, of course, so they were somewhere nearby, probably just outside the building. Probably they were among the throngs gathering in the streets to watch the fabled ball drop and ring in the New Year tonight. Probably they would attempt to enter the suite at some point and rescue Lydia in a kind of final showdown. Well, that was fine. Because Nestor had a new plan.

In his sleep, Nestor discovered that the money he had now was enough – more than enough. The ninety-eight thousand, coupled with the thirty-five thousand from the cocaine deal, was a generous amount to begin a new life in a new location. Dot was dead, and New York was poisoned for him now. There was no sense in chasing the safe-deposit-box keys, and no way he could get on an airplane with Lydia in his current condition. There was also no reason to continue the silly, pointless struggle with Dick Miller and the others.

The new plan? Watch the ball drop with Lydia. It was good she was here – it was no fun watching the event by himself. Then take the money. Ride the elevator down to the parking garage, guns ready in case he encountered any trouble. Get in the car and drive north, crossing into Canada south of Montreal. Maybe in Montreal he could find a doctor, one who would treat him quietly. He would survive until then, and in Montreal, he would begin again. A new name, a new home, a new life.

And Lydia?

If they wanted her, they could have her. When they finally found a way in here, they would find Lydia waiting for them, still tied to the chair, her throat slit ear to ear.

Slowly, gingerly, Nestor pushed himself out of the bed. The pain moved in waves through his body. He went out into the suite, moving with some confidence in the semi-dark. The lights through the window were enough to see by. He poured himself a large glass of wine, downed it quickly, then poured another. He couldn't remember when he had eaten last, and the wine went straight to his head. He spilled a dozen Tylenol onto the counter and took them one by one, washing them down with the second glass of wine. Then he went back into the bedroom.

'Ready, Lydia?' he said. 'It's going to be an exciting evening.'

'I don't want to go back there,' Breeze said between great heaving gasps for breath. She sat bolt upright in the back seat, as if mega-doses of electricity poured through her body. Tears streamed down her cheeks and she held a lit cigarette in her jittery hand, stabilizing just enough to bring it to her mouth.

They cruised the highways in Andrew's car. For a moment, Dick didn't even know where they were – he had been so lost in thought. He looked for a road sign, an anchor to give him a sense of place. OK, Riverdale Avenue. Henry Hudson Parkway, in the Bronx, traveling south. Soon they would cross the Henry Hudson Bridge into Manhattan, and then they would see the George Washington Bridge against the sky up ahead on their right.

'He's the devil, man,' Breeze said. 'He's the fucking devil. Everywhere I go, it's like he's got a fucking radar beam on me. He calls me on the telephone. He shows up at the motel and comes crashing through the window in the middle of the night. How did he know we were there? How did he know that?'

'I don't know, babe,' Andrew said, putting on the man voice, hands gripping the steering wheel. 'I didn't tell him, that's for sure.' Andrew looked like he was going to pop – like his head was just going to pop right off his neck from the pressure building up inside his body.

Dick felt quiet, even somewhat in control. He hadn't smoked cigarettes in years, but he had cadged a butt off Breeze and now he sat in the passenger seat, smoking and watching the night flow by. His window was open a crack to let the smoke out, and cold air blew in, helping him keep his grip on reality. The Hudson River was on his right now, dark except for green and red lights way out on the water, boats probably, and the lights of New Jersey on the other side, a mile or more away.

'You told me this morning I wasn't going to have to go near him again.'

'Breeze, I said you wouldn't have to see him again. And you won't. But you do have to pull yourself together. We've all had our run-ins with Nestor, and me and Dick are keeping it together.'

'You didn't fuck him, Andrew. OK? You didn't have him inside of you. It's like he's part of me now. He's wired to me. It's fucking gross.'

It was possible, Dick realized, that Nestor had simply killed Lydia and dumped the body somewhere. The thought of that ripped Dick apart. It was also possible that Nestor was raping Lydia at this very moment. It was possible that he had finished raping her and was now torturing her. Anything was possible with this guy, this guy who seemed to take great relish in hurting people. Dick glanced at Andrew's left hand, the pinkie gone at the base.

Dick was going to kill Nestor tonight. What other choice was there? He was going to go up to his suite, he was going to walk in there, and he was going to kill the guy. He was going to wreck him. If Nestor wasn't there, he was going to use whatever means he could to track him down. Then he was going to go wherever Nestor was, and kill him there. If need be, Dick would spend the rest of his life tracking Nestor down and killing him. Revenge was a sucker move, but it was the only move he had left.

They passed Seventy-Ninth Street. Soon they would be in midtown. They had wasted hours driving around, talking about how to do it, building themselves up to it while Breeze slowly came apart at the seams. All the while, it had become clearer, so clear that Dick had known exactly what to do for the past two hours. Now they couldn't wait anymore. They were driving straight to Nestor's hotel, going up to his suite, and doing the job. Right now.

Dick had a fleeting thought that he should call his mother, but then decided against it. It was too much like a last goodbye. He didn't want to give that idea any room to make itself real.

Instead, he turned to face the back of the car. He felt he had more credibility with Breeze now than Andrew ever would. Andrew had gotten her into this thing. Andrew had gotten their friend killed. Andrew had pimped her to Nestor. Jesus. That was something Dick didn't like to think about. The world was a minefield right now, full of things Dick didn't want to think about. Like Desiree cut up and dead in his bathtub, lying in a pool of blood. Like the sight of Block shot full of holes on the bridge. Like Lydia in Nestor's hands right this minute.

Dick shook the thoughts away.

'Breeze, we got one last thing to do, OK? We do this thing, and then we're out of here. But we need your help.'

'What if you don't come back?'

'We're gonna come back, don't you worry. We're gonna come back with Lydia and we're all going to Nassau. Don't sweat it.'

'Lydia was like my mom. Like the mom I never had.' Breeze began to shake, holding back the tears.

Like her mom? Fa-uck. She just met Lydia yesterday.

'Breeze, there's no "was" about this. Lydia is still alive. He can't kill her. He needs her. He can't get at the money without her.' Dick looked at Andrew. 'Right? He can't get the money without Lydia?'

'Right,' Andrew said. He didn't sound terribly committed to the idea.

'Good answer, Andrew. Way to project confidence.'

Dick turned back to Breeze.

'Don't kid yourself,' she said, taking a savage toke on the cigarette. 'Lydia's dead, Dick. Nestor is the fucking devil and he killed her and ate her.'

Dick slapped her. He didn't plan it – his big hand darted out and made contact before he even realized what he was doing. He smacked her hard, leaving a sting on his palm and an instant red mark on the left side of her face. Her head swiveled with the easy force of it. He couldn't remember the last time he had hit a female – maybe when he was ten years old.

'That's fucking great. Hit a girl now.' Her bottom lip quivered. She was going to cry again, and ride this latest indignity for the public relations value, if she could.

But Dick wouldn't let her. He pointed a big index finger at her like a spike. 'Don't you ever say she's dead, you hear me? She's not dead. We're going in there, and we're gonna get her. And you're gonna stop your candy-ass fucking whining and help us with this. We need you. Lydia is alive. Lydia needs you. When we call you, we need you to pull this car up to the meeting point. That's all we need you to do, and you're going to do it. Understood?'

He had reached her. Somehow, he had reached deep into her mind and brought her back, brought her on board the team.

'Understood,' she said, her voice small.

Dick turned to Andrew. 'You got the extra gun?'

Andrew held it out to him, a .38, fully loaded. Dick put it in Breeze's small hand.

'You ever use one of these before?'

She looked down at it, uncertain. 'Once or twice.'

'If he comes here, you know what to do.'

Andrew pulled the car over to the curb. They were two blocks from the hotel.

Dick looked at Andrew. 'Ready?'

With one arm, Nestor dragged Lydia's chair across the carpet and into the living room. He employed his knee to help turn the chair so she was facing out the picture window toward the dazzling lights of Times Square. She could even look down and see the mad throngs of merrymakers. Soon, in just a few hours, they would drop the glittering ball and a new year would begin. Nestor didn't want Lydia to miss it. It would be the last spectacle she ever witnessed.

'Better?' he said.

'I have to use the bathroom.'

'You'll have to hold it.'

'I can't anymore. I've been sitting in this chair all day.'

Nestor shrugged. 'Then wet yourself. I won't mind.'

Despite everything, he was in high spirits. He felt relieved to know that he had a plan, one that seemed like it would work. Outside, in the cold air, among the teeming crowds, there was the glow of expectation. Inside here, in the suite, there was the glow of his buzz from the alcohol, and the glow that came knowing he would soon be away from here, living another life.

In the bedroom, in the bathroom, and behind the bar, his room phone began to ring. The telephone – he should just destroy it, throw it off the balcony, step on it, run it over with his car. All of the phones – these room phones, his cellphone, maybe every telephone in the world. Perhaps, in his new life, he would refuse to have a telephone at all. People who wanted to speak with him would have to come to his home.

He paced into the bedroom and answered the phone.

'Missed me,' the female voice said.

Nestor closed the door so Lydia would not hear the conversation. 'It would seem so. Perhaps another time, yes? I'd like to meet again.'

'Oh, that won't be possible. Brother, I'm not going to come anywhere near you again. But I was thinking we could make a trade. I have some keys and you have some money. Maybe we can swap them? At a distance, that is?'

Nestor smiled. The silly girl wanted to make a trade that would never happen. But Nestor was feeling good enough that he didn't mind playing along. Perhaps he could work out another meeting with this young thing. They had enjoyed quite a night together. 'That sounds interesting. I wonder what I would do with the keys at this point?'

'Maybe you and Lydia could run away together.'

'What makes you think she's still alive?'

'Call it a hunch,' the girl said.

'You're a very astute young lady. Why should I trust you?'

'Because I give you things.'

'Like?'

'Like information.'

'Hmm. Do you have any information for me at this moment?'

There was a pause on the line. 'Yes, I do. I thought I'd let you know there are some people coming up to see you. Right now. They're going to shoot first and ask questions later. Maybe that'll make you trust me.'

'My dear, how will they reach me? They can't get to this floor without a key. They can't gain entry to my suite without a key. Will they climb along the outside of the building like spiders?'

'They can get in,' she said.

'Yes?'

'I made a mold of your keys before I left your room that morning. They have copies of your keys. Good ones, I think.'

For a long moment, Nestor could not find his voice. He had survived this day – asleep, practically in a coma – by sheer luck. They could have come for him at any time, and they didn't. The girl had fooled him. She had made a fool of him. She had taken his photograph and he hadn't stopped her because of her flattery. Then she had stolen an imprint of his keys. If she had worked in the cocaine trade, he would have been dead long ago. He stared at the phone, trying to see into the mind that drove this treacherous bitch. If their paths ever crossed again, surely he would give her a very lengthy, generous and abundant hard time.

'I see,' he said. 'Well, I'll take that under advisement. Perhaps I'll speak with you again soon?'

'If you're still alive.'

The line went dead.

This is why people go skydiving.

Breeze sat alone in the car. It had terrified her to call him, to talk to him, to even think about him. Her antennae were extrasensitive, and the fact that anybody ever went near this guy was ample proof of that. He scared her from the first moment that she met him. It scared her that he was even still alive. If he were to return her call in the next few minutes, she simply would not answer.

But at the same time, she liked calling him. It amped up the electric tingle that seemed to race through her body at all times – it turned it into a powerful, thermonuclear thrumming. It excited her. It even turned her on. She had been with men who had better, sexier bodies. But there was something about him – the danger, *the evil* – that made her night with him different. No, she never wanted to see him again, at least not alive. But he fed her fantasy life in a way that no man ever had. Face it, Breeze had slept with the devil. It was every woman's fantasy, and she had done it. And through the miracle of modern technology, she could keep reliving it over the telephone.

The keys for the cash – it would never happen. Even if he agreed, it was way too dangerous for her to make the trade. What might happen is that poor Nestor, shot full of holes, might get the jump on the two able-bodied men about to bust in on him. With some luck, he might kill them both before dying himself. That would leave Breeze, and maybe Lydia, alive and with lots of money.

Breeze turned on the radio and searched the band, looking for a good song. There wasn't much left for her to do. Just sit here and wait, watch the crowds go by, and see if anybody came back alive.

They would come in through the front door. There was no other possible entry point for them. Further, he would hear the elevator come to his floor, and the elevator door slide open. It was a gift the girl had given him, truly a gift, this knowledge. Nestor was dimly aware that his opinion of the girl kept changing, and with the opinion, his mood. There was little he could do to control it.

He crouched behind the leather sofa. Just a few feet to his right,

Lydia sat facing in the other direction – out the window. He had debated killing her in these few moments before they came, and had decided that she was more valuable alive. Of course, seeing her dead, her brain blown apart, would give them an instant of shock, but then he could no longer use her as a bargaining chip, if that need arose. He had even debated the need to muzzle her again, but had decided against it. She couldn't warn them because she didn't know they were coming. Once they arrived, let her speak, let her beg, let her scream (the walls were comfortably thick in this building – his suite was so quiet, he might as well have no neighbors), let her whimper, let her say all manner of ridiculous and desperate things.

It would traumatize them to hold out hope for her, then witness her execution. So rather than gag her, he had blindfolded her instead. That way she couldn't see what he was doing and wouldn't know to warn them. He had left the bag with the money in it just on the other side of her as a final distraction. It sat there, the top open, more than one hundred and thirty thousand dollars in cash showing clearly. Perhaps one of them would waste a vital second gazing wistfully at the money – enough time to condemn that man to his death.

The guns they brought would be another matter. The sofa was good as a hiding place, and it afforded an excellent view of the door, but even a small-caliber weapon would punch holes right through it. After the opening volley, he would have to move from here. And if they brought powerful weapons, that could be an even bigger problem. Yes, the walls were thick, but the reports from a .357 Magnum would awaken even the dead.

Nestor's guns were silenced. Two 9 mm semiautos, one in his left hand and one on the floor to his left. With his right arm hanging limp, he would have no time or ability to reload. If he emptied one gun, he would simply need to pick up the other one and empty that too.

The last question? His aim. His left hand was not his shooting hand. Well, it wasn't far – less than ten yards certainly – from the sofa to the door. At that distance, with his arm steadied on the sofa, it would be hard to miss.

Somewhere deep in the building, the elevator hummed into life.

Nestor braced his left arm on top of the sofa, settling in, getting comfortable. There could be no mistakes. He pointed the gun at the door.

'Any moment now,' he said to Lydia. 'Any moment now and we will see.'

The elevator stopped at his floor. He heard the door slide open. There was the slightest possibility that it was the person across the hall who was arriving.

No, they were here. So quietly, so stealthily, a key turned in his lock.

He renewed his aim. His trigger finger twitched. His heart beat in his chest. Somewhere, waves pounded the empty shore then returned again to the ocean. Somewhere, the sun crested the horizon, heralding the first morning of the New Year. Somewhere, thousands of migrating birds rested after their long journey.

Without a sound, the doorknob turned and the door slipped open.

Dick turned the key in the lock. It worked. The key turned easily. He pushed the door open. Andrew, gun in hand, rushed in ahead of him. Dick followed, not a second behind.

Andrew would go left, Dick right. But something was wrong. Andrew burst in, still bent slightly, then grunted and stood straight up.

Dick sliced to the right. There was a bar here he could duck behind. He turned and saw Andrew thrash as another bullet tore through him, its exit ripping a crater in his back. Dick dove behind the bar, pressing himself against the floor.

He hadn't heard any shots.

The bar exploded around him, wood splintering, bottles smashing, glass flying, liquor pouring down all over him, all over the floor. He covered his face with his hands, protecting his eyes. When the shooting stopped, Dick looked back toward the door. Andrew lay on his back, eyes open and blinking slowly, mouth slack.

Shit. He knew we were coming. One down already.

Dick jumped into a crouch and peeked through a hole that had been blown through the bar. He scanned the room.

Big place. Sumptuous, with deep pile carpet, white or some light color, bound to get stained. The lights down low. A living-room area, with doors to the left and right. A huge bay window, sliding glass doors, looked out on the terrace. Even here, ten yards away, peeking from a crack in the bar, Dick had a view of Times Square. Nestor appeared, moving slowly as if in great pain. His hair was greased back. He wore pants with a matching vest and jacket. A suit. Why not? It was a special occasion, after all.

He moved to a chair and for the first time, Dick noticed what was in the chair. A person was there, facing out the window. Lydia, still alive! He knew it. He knew she was still alive.

Nestor positioned himself so that she sat between them, and he placed the barrel of his gun against her forehead.

'Come out, Dick, and let's talk like men.'

'Dick?' Lydia said. 'Dick, what's going on?'

Dick climbed out from behind the wrecked bar, his gun in a two-handed grip, trained on Nestor. Nestor's chest, shoulders and head showed just above Lydia. His right arm hung at his side. Dick had a clean shot – he could pierce Nestor's lungs from here. With a little luck, he could blow Nestor backwards and away from Lydia. But if he didn't, if he missed . . . she would die.

'Here's the murderer now,' Nestor said. 'Perhaps this will be interesting. Perhaps he will prove more of a challenge than his friends.'

'I'm here, Lydia. I'm here. Just stay cool.'

Dick held the gun on Nestor. Now was the time. Now he would see. He stepped closer.

'Dick,' Nestor said, 'I confess I am surprised you have come to meet me. Didn't you know your death awaited you here?'

'That's funny. I thought it was your death.'

'Dick, shoot him,' Lydia said. 'Just shoot him.'

Nestor smiled. 'He can't shoot me, darling. I have a gun to your head.'

'Shoot him, Dick. Shoot him! It doesn't matter. Just kill him.'

'Hush now, little one.'

Dick inched closer. Nestor was framed in the bay window, blazing neon lights behind him. He looked pale and sick, like much of the blood had run from him. He looked like a vampire at midday.

'Dick, I want you to know something. I've decided not to go to Nassau. I've decided that I don't need to be a millionaire. I can live well enough on the money in that bag there. Do you hear me, Dick? I don't need Lydia anymore. I can kill her if I like.'

'I'll blow your head off a second later,' Dick said.

'Yes, that's true. And that leaves us with an interesting problem. We can't stand here forever, but whatever we do, someone has to die. So I propose a bargain. You lay your gun down and I will let Lydia live. I don't really want to kill her – I don't like to hurt women. But you . . . I'll take great relish in killing you.'

'What about Dot?'

'What about her? I never hurt Dot. I placed her on a pedestal.'

'You lying sack of shit. You killed Dot.'

Nestor frowned. 'No. You did.'

They stared at each other. The night flashed in Dick's mind again.

Had he killed her? No conclusions. He never came to any conclusions. What did Nestor know about it? Was he there? Did he see it happen?

'What about it, Dick? Do we have an agreement? I'll count backwards from three. Three seconds, that's all. Then Lydia and I will both die.'

'Nestor . . .'

'Dick, shoot him! Just shoot him!'

'Three.'

Dick moved closer, so close he could almost touch them. He wouldn't miss from this distance, how could he miss? Would Nestor have time to pull the trigger? Dick couldn't take another death. Not now. Not Lydia.

'Two.'

'Dick!'

'Put it down! I'm gonna blow your fucking brains out!'

'One.'

Dick raised one hand off the gun. The gun was still pointed at Nestor, but one hand was in the air, fingers outstretched. 'All right. All right, you win. I'll do it. Just stop counting.'

Nestor smiled and took a deep breath. 'Thank you. I didn't want to die just then. Now place your weapon on the floor, and I will gladly release her. Then you and I can resolve our differences. Alone.'

Lydia's voice was almost a scream. 'Dick, don't do it. Don't trust him.'

Dick looked into Nestor's eyes. He couldn't tell what was in those eyes. Pain, certainly. Anger. Sincerity?

'I'll do it,' Nestor said. 'I'll let her go. Her life for yours.'

Dick had to make a decision. His life for Lydia's. If Nestor was speaking the truth, it was a fair trade. Maybe it was a way to make amends for . . . for everything. But why should he trust Nestor? The answer came to him in a flash: because if he wanted Lydia to live, he had no other choice. He opened his hand and let the gun drop to the floor. It made a dull thud when it hit the carpet.

Lydia's shoulders sagged. 'Oh, Dick, no.'

Nestor came around from behind her, his gun pointed at Dick now. Nestor kicked Dick's gun across the room. Instantly, Dick felt naked, defenseless.

'You're too tall, Miller. Get on your knees.'

'Just shoot me, you asshole.'

Nestor placed the gun to Dick's temple. Then he stepped back, as if thinking of something new. Without warning, he kicked Dick in the crotch. Dick sank to his knees and Nestor kicked him again. The kick came up from the ground and caught Dick on the chin. His mouth snapped shut with an audible click. The world went dark, then swam back into view. When it did, he was still on his knees, Nestor in front of him. Nestor had rung his bell, but he hadn't gone down.

Nestor brought the handgrip of the gun down like a hammer on top of Dick's head. The next thing Dick knew, he was lying on the carpet. He looked up and Nestor was there above him. He kicked Dick in the forehead.

'You fool. Now I'm going to kill you both.'

Andrew was alive.

The pain was intense, more than he had ever experienced. It was like the pain itself was now the entity, and Andrew was just a flea riding on the back of the pain. It had consumed him. It was everything.

But he wasn't dead yet. He was lying on his back, and it must seem to the others that he was dead, because now they ignored him. He looked around. His gun was . . . somewhere. He had lost it when the bullets hit. Miller was there, on his knees, Nestor's gun to his head.

Lydia was there, tied to a chair. The three of them took on a glow, like angels.

Near Lydia was a brown paper bag, which had fallen on its side and spilled out some money. That was the moneybag. OK. Further away, there was a door that led out onto some kind of balcony. Even further, there was a huge digital sign that towered over Times Square. On the sign, brown liquid poured into a cup with the Coca-Cola logo on the side.

Slowly, Andrew turned onto his stomach. The pain of doing that almost knocked him out. His vision went fuzzy, he went away for a little while, but then came back. When he did, he realized he was still wearing his glasses. Amazing. Get shot twice, maybe three times, lose your gun, hit the deck, and the glasses don't come off. He'd have to tell somebody about this. He pictured himself on a TV commercial . . .

'I was shot numerous times, and my glasses stayed on. I love my Calvins.'

Enough of this. He wasn't going to be in any TV commercial. He was dying. The pain was fading now and he was becoming numb. And cold. Soon he would pass out from loss of blood, and soon after that, he would be gone. And Miller – it looked like Miller was going to be dead soon too. And Lydia too, probably. That would leave only Breeze. Wasn't it just like Breeze to survive all this?

Andrew grunted. He had a plan. It came to him in a flash. There was one last thing he could do, if he could make it happen before all the blood drained out of him, or before Nestor spotted him and killed him with a quick bullet to the head. It would take everything he had left. But that didn't matter now. Nothing mattered except this one last thing.

Slowly, like a turtle half-crushed by a passing car, Andrew began to crawl toward the money.

*　　*　　*

Nestor aimed another kick.

This one caught Dick in the Adam's apple. Now Dick couldn't breathe. He gasped. He gurgled. His hands clutched at his throat.

Nestor was saying something. A speech. Even to Dick's frenzied mind, it sounded stilted, like he had prepared it beforehand. 'It's a shame I cannot stay here long enough to find and kill your family,' he said. 'I will have to satisfy myself with you, and with the lovely and talented Lydia.'

Nestor had him. Dick lay on the ground, his breath coming in harsh rasps.

'Isn't there a man among you?' Nestor said, and delivered another vicious kick. 'Is everyone here so easy to kill?'

Dick's face was squashed against the carpet. He had rug burns on his forearms. He was next to a sofa chair. He reached out with one hand and touched the chair a little, stroked it. It had a flower pattern. Nestor kicked him again, this time in the midsection. Dick barely felt it now.

'Hey!' someone shouted. It was more like a groan than a shout, but Dick heard it clearly, and so did Nestor. 'Hey, asshole!'

Dick squirmed around to see.

Andrew.

In all the confusion, Andrew had crawled out onto the balcony with the moneybag. He was lying there, just halfway out the sliding glass door. A smear of blood followed him along the floor, like the track left behind a snail. Now Dick could feel the icy wind blowing in through the open door.

'Look at all this money!' Andrew's voice was stronger now, almost joyous. He scooped the money into the air, double handfuls, and it flew away on the swirling wind. He knocked the brown paper bag over, and piles of money blew like leaves across the small terrace. Much of it was already in the air, already gone.

'Excuse me,' Nestor said, almost without emotion, almost to himself, but also to Dick and Lydia. 'I'll return in a moment.' He stalked toward Andrew, who kept right on throwing that money away.

Dick had to get up. He no longer knew where his gun was, but he had to get up. He could no longer see clearly, but he had to get up. This was his last chance. He pulled himself to his feet, using the flowery sofa chair. He stood on shaky legs. Visions danced in front of his eyes. Nestor had clobbered him, but not enough to put him under.

Dick watched as Nestor reached the balcony. Nestor tucked the gun into his jacket. Andrew lay back, panting, as one last great chunk of money blew away in a tiny tornado.

'Why?' Nestor said. 'Why did you do that?'

'So you,' Andrew said, 'can eat shit.'

Very slowly, Nestor put a foot on Andrew's neck and applied pressure. Andrew squirmed and grabbed at Nestor's leg. Nestor didn't say anything more. Instead, he increased the pressure on Andrew's neck. He pushed down hard, gripping the iron railing for leverage. Andrew didn't even try to stop him anymore. He just lay there shuddering, his arms at his sides. In a moment it was over.

Nestor took a deep breath and gazed up at the cold stars. Dollar bills still swirled on the night air.

'*Madre de Dios*,' he said.

Somewhere far away, Dick thought he could hear cheering. Yes, it was cheering. A tremendous roar had gone up from the crowd on the streets down below. Could it be midnight? No. It was too early. Maybe some of that money had reached the street.

Dick watched Nestor at the railing. No way was Nestor going to let him live. No way was he going to let Lydia live. And Dick owed this to Block. And he owed it to Desiree, and to Dot. And sure . . . why not? He owed it to Andrew and Henry. This guy had to be put down. Dick charged, releasing a groan of pain as he ran. He crossed the room, running low.

Through the doors and onto the balcony. A blast of wind, a burst of light and sky. Then Nestor.

Too late, Nestor heard him and turned around. Dick hit him hard, like in the football days. With his right hand, he grabbed down between Nestor's legs, found his balls and squeezed them. He was brutal with it.

Nestor howled. His face became a fright mask, a wide-open mouth, rows and rows of teeth, like a shark. His eyes glowed like monster eyes. With his left hand, Dick grabbed him by the collar. He hoisted Nestor up, crotch and collar, and he flipped him over the top of the balcony's steel railing. He heaved Nestor with all of his strength. Then he fell to his knees.

Nestor grabbed madly for the railing, his one good arm flapping like the wing of a great bird. It was no use. He was too far away to reach it. For an instant – less than a second – Nestor hung there in space. It reminded Dick of cartoons where the unlucky cat or bunny hangs in midair, realizes where he is, looks at the camera and then falls.

Nestor paused, twelve stories above the streets of Manhattan. Even with the certain knowledge that death had come, his eyes promised revenge.

Then he was gone.

Nestor fell through the air.

Two seconds. Three seconds. Worlds existed in those seconds.

Wind rushed past his ears. The wind was icy cold, but it was secondary to the feeling of speed. He was moving fast. His stomach dropped, as if he were riding a roller coaster. The lights of Times Square spun around him.

Four seconds. Five seconds.

An image came: himself, slogging through muck and gore and fire, the damned grabbing at him, the dark presence coming for him. The second death. No. It was a dream. Had to be a dream.

An image came: Miller, Lydia, lying on a Caribbean beach.

Six seconds.

The street rushed up at him. A car was there, a limousine.

A line of poetry: *To sleep, perchance to dream* . . .

No. No dreams.

Here came the car. Someone screamed.

No!

Nestor braced for impact.

Seconds passed, and then the screams came.

The moneybag was there with a small pile of cash that Andrew hadn't gotten to. Dick was on his knees, and somehow his hand had ended up in the bag. 'Every little bit counts,' he said to Andrew, who was lying nearby, eyes open and staring. There must have been fifteen or twenty hundred-dollar bills in Dick's hand. He clambered to his feet and stumbled back into the room.

'Dick?' Lydia said. 'Dick, is it you?'

'Jesus, Lydia. What a hell of a couple of days I've had.'

'You and me both, buster.'

He pulled the blindfold from her eyes. She saw him there for the first time, and they came together in a kiss. After a long moment, Dick pulled away.

'Hon, we gotta go. They're gonna be wondering about that guy, flying through the air like that.' He began to rip her bindings apart.

Dick grabbed his gun off the floor and he and Lydia rode the elevator down to the second floor. They got out and took the stairs to the lobby. Out on the street, a mob of people pushed and shoved.

Rubberneckers. Ambulance chasers. They hustled into the crowd, heads down, jostling this way and that. Dick's arms were pinned at his sides in the crush of humanity. Around the side of the building, squad cars were there, and ambulances with lights flashing. A girl's face swirled out of the mess. She stood in a fancy coat and dinner dress, weeping bitterly. A young man held her tightly.

Behind the police line was the remains of a limo. It was out in the middle of the street, where it must have been stopped in traffic. The entire roof was caved in, and covered with blood. The windows were smashed. An arm protruded from the top of it.

Here and there, people picked confetti from the sky. Dick looked closer. One-hundred-dollar bills.

They walked on. Three blocks in the cold. Drunk people bounced around. A teenager in a funny hat blew a horn at them, laughing.

Dick spotted the BMW at the curb, vapor coming out of the exhaust pipe. It was idling, waiting for them. He turned to Lydia, who was on his right arm.

'There's the car,' he was going to say.

But right then Lydia kissed him hard on the mouth, and he returned the favor.

Breeze pulled up in Andrew's car, nobody's car now.

Dick took the wheel, and for twenty seconds, they played musical chairs as Lydia climbed into the front passenger seat, Dick slid in behind the wheel and Breeze clambered into the back, right over the seats.

He pulled out into traffic.

'That was some kind of commotion back there,' Breeze said. 'Incredible. What happened?'

'Let's just say Nestor took a fall,' Lydia said.

'And Andrew? Where's Andrew?'

Dick looked back at Breeze. This was the part he hated. How to tell Breeze that Andrew was dead too? How to tell a person that in the course of just a couple of days, both of her friends had been murdered by the same man? Dick looked at the road again.

'What?' Breeze said.

From the corner of his eye, Dick saw Lydia turn to Breeze now. Maybe Lydia could do it. Maybe it was a woman's job.

'You're kidding, right? Don't even joke.'

Lydia hadn't said anything yet. The look was on her face. Shit.

'Take my hand,' Lydia said.

'Oh, fuck. No. Tell me no. Tell me no.' Her voice dissolved.

Dick drove on, headed downtown, listening to Breeze's quiet sobs. He checked her out in the rearview. She was back there, eyes closed, body shaking, hugging herself into a ball. She opened her eyes again, and they were red and rimmed with tears. Her cheeks glistened. He remembered her as he first met her, the day she had sprayed mace in his eyes. They made eye contact, and all at once Dick saw something there in the mirror. Breeze saw him see it.

Again he faced the traffic. They came to a red light. Around him, the yellow cabs flowed to a stop. He remembered another Breeze, somehow. What Breeze was this? A blonde-haired Breeze, very attractive, wearing a slinky green sequined dress. Moving through a crowd at a bar.

He watched as this other Breeze approached, winding her way through the Christmas partygoers. Jesus. A week ago. Dick's beer came. He reached to the bar, then turned back into the crowd. This slinky, sexy Breeze was passing at exactly that moment.

Oops. They bumped into each other.

Breeze's small hands moved like whispers over his hands. 'Oh, excuse me.' She kept going, barely even looking at him. But not before he noticed the teardrop tattoo at the corner of her left eye.

'Did anybody bump into you?' Block had said. 'That's how they do it sometimes.'

Now, Dick pulled the car over to the side. He cruised in next to a fireplug. A high-rise housing project loomed on the other side of a small park. No one was around. New Year's Eve and it was too cold to be out.

'Why are we stopping?' Lydia said.

Dick reached inside his jacket. The gun was there.

'Breeze?' He looked into the rearview again. There was Breeze, still there. If she hadn't seen it the first time, she really saw it now. The light, so to speak, had dawned. The tears were no longer flowing. What good were they?

'Yes?'

'Hand Lydia the keys to the safe-deposit boxes, will you?'

'Why would I want to do that?'

Lydia's face hovered on his right, concerned. 'Dick? What's going on?'

Dick whipped out the gun and swung it around to face the back. Too late. The Cool Breeze had already drawn her own. At close range it could do plenty of damage. And this was the closest possible range. Breeze sat directly behind Lydia, the muzzle of the gun placed against the back of Lydia's head.

'I will blow her fucking head off. You know I will.'

'Then I'll blow yours off.'

Breeze smiled. 'And go through life without your sweet baby.'

'Dick?' Lydia said.

Dick raised his left hand. 'Lyd, relax. It's gonna be OK.'

'No, it isn't,' Breeze said.

It could end this way, Dick realized. It came to him in a flash. Lydia dead, Breeze dead, both dead ladies here in the car with him on New Year's Eve. People in the nearby buildings would hear the gunshots.

The cops would come and find him sitting there, engine running, windows smashed out, blood and gore everywhere. Lydia dead. Their dreams of escape dashed. He couldn't stand to see Lydia die. If Breeze killed Lydia, and Dick killed Breeze, then the next step would be to eat the gun himself. What else was there?

'What does it look like?' Lydia said, still staring straight ahead.

'What does it look like?' Dick echoed. 'What does *what* look like?'

Breeze jabbed Lydia's head with the barrel of the gun. 'You shut up, bitch.'

'Her gun! What does her gun look like?'

Dick stared at it. It was an over-under two-shot, different from the gun he had given her earlier. Breeze had two guns? 'It looks like, uh...'

'Shit.'

Breeze squeezed the trigger.

ENDGAME – SEE YOU IN NASSAU

'A cigarette lighter.'

Dick had almost done it. He had almost blown Breeze's head apart. He had almost killed her in the instant when he saw Breeze shoot Lydia, in that instant when Breeze's finger depressed the trigger, and a spark, then a lick of blue came from the front of the gun, a lick of blue that strengthened and became the sort of yellow and orange flame that could get a nice fat cigar going. In that instant he could have shot her or he could have chosen to wait just one more second, and he chose to wait.

A cigarette lighter. Breeze was even crazier than he thought.

'I could have killed you,' he said. He still held the gun, the real gun, pointed at Breeze's head. She hardly seemed to notice.

She smiled and twirled her hair just a bit. 'It would have been fun trying to explain that to the cops.'

'You killed Dot.' It wasn't a question. Until he said it, he hadn't even been sure himself. But now that it was out there, sure, of course, it made perfect sense. A domino fell, then another, then an entire chain went down in a long blur. Not only had she drugged him, not only was she involved in Dot's murder, she was the one who had done it. All by herself. No one else even knew. And now they were all dead. He could imagine how Andrew would appreciate the way it all came together.

'You were the one,' Dick said.

Breeze shrugged. She smirked. She said nothing.

'Why did you do it?'

Breeze shook her head. 'You taping this conversation? You gonna call the cops now?' She paused, then lit a smoke with her gun. She inhaled deeply. 'No. You're not going to call the cops, are you? Nobody is. What would you say? That you just killed a man over a million dollars you stole? And because he shot your friend? Last time I checked, murder was still illegal, whatever your reason for it.'

Now Lydia had turned around and was staring at Breeze.

Dick held the gun pointed at the monster's head. He didn't understand the forces that had created this monster, but he did understand the force that would destroy it. A few ounces of pressure on the trigger would do the trick. Payback, and she richly deserved it. But that wasn't all, was it? The reasons went even deeper. As long as Breeze was still alive, he and Lydia would never be safe. She would be out there in the world, creeping, slithering, plotting and working her way back towards them. He would wake up in the dark of night, and there would be Breeze, standing over their bed. If he ever wanted to be free, he had to kill her now. It was his duty to Lydia, and to himself.

His grip tightened on the gun.

Do it. Do it now.

'You won't kill me,' Breeze said.

And she was right.

Dick couldn't do it. He could not kill a person in cold blood.

'Give me the gun,' Lydia said. 'I'll kill her.'

A short burst of laughter escaped from Breeze. It wasn't even a laugh of disdain. Dick couldn't be sure, but he would have said it was a laugh of warmth, of camaraderie, of high good humor.

'Lydia, I know you,' Breeze said. 'You know what I mean? I see you coming a mile away. You have trouble killing houseflies, am I right? You see a spider in the house and you can't stand harming it. You want somebody to shoo it outside with a magazine. And that's OK. It's good when people are that way.'

'Breeze, hand Lydia the keys,' Dick said. He said it no-nonsense now. He was done with Breeze. He just wanted her gone.

Breeze shrugged and did as she was told.

'Are those the keys?' Dick said.

Lydia shrugged. 'They look right.'

'Are they or not?'

'Yes, Dick. These are the keys.'

Dick turned back to Breeze. She already had her hand on the door lock.

'Get out.'

'Gladly.'

Breeze climbed out into the frigid night air. She stood in the empty street, and quickly scanned the barren blocks in either direction. The beast was back in the jungle. Eat or be eaten, that was the name of her game. She leaned over and smiled into the passenger side window. Dick only imagined the fangs suddenly growing in her mouth – they weren't really there. The plume of steam from her breath was bare inches from Lydia's face.

'See you in Nassau,' Breeze said.

Dick put the car in gear and pulled out into the night.

Acknowledgements

Once again, deep thanks to Noah Lukeman for being a great agent, and a great friend.

Thanks to Joy for her (nearly, but not quite) endless patience.

Special thanks to Brian Dunleavy for reading and commenting on early versions of the manuscript.

Thanks to Carolyn Chute for being a mentor and an inspiration. And for giving me a couch to drive.

Last, but certainly not least, thanks to Marion Donaldson for her insightful editing; copy-editor Yvonne Holland for her meticulous work on the text; and to Kate Burke, Lucy Ramsey and the whole hard-working group at Headline for doing such a great job with *The Takedown*. It's my privilege and pleasure to publish books with them.